Please Note

Any errors in this book, uninteresting content, boring blathering and nonsensical drivel is due solely to the editor. I apologize in advance :)

Enjoy!

More Completely Fabricated Reviews of
Christopher Kemper's
CLINGING TO ANONYMITY:

"Perfect punishment for the wayward adolescent."
—John Meyer, *Parole Officer News*

"You'll laugh and laugh and laugh…at the publisher's business sense."
—Stacy Stanley, *San Francisco Chronicle of Tedium*

"There is no book so bad that there is not something good in it!"
—Bachelor Sampson Carrasco

"When I met Mr. Kemper he claimed to be the world's most prolific creator of envy. That is certainly illusionary, but after reading his book I think you will agree that he's the world's most prolific creator of another four-lettered word."
—Cleat Joseph, *USA Tomorrow*

"Mr. Kemper presents a compelling argument for book burning."
—Kevin Malloy, *Justified Censorship*

"This would work better as a coloring book."
—Dane Ivers, *The New York Times Tables*

"Is the humor sold separately?"
— Sherlock Matlock, *The San Jose Thallium News*

"Mr. Kemper could quadruple the sales of his book, and the project would serve a higher purpose, if he printed his autobiofictionary on toilet paper and sold it in packs of four."
— Alan Yellowspan, *Chicago Quadbune*

"I haven't read it but it's the best book ever!"
— Mom

Also by Christopher Kemper

Fighting to Be a Lover

Why Do I Have To Do Everything?
   An Unabridged List of Complaints

What the Major League Record Book Would Look Like
   If I Had Decided to Go Pro

Several Anonymous Letters to Neighbors in NW Portland
   Who Don't Know How to Park

A Document That Has the Form and Function of a Resumé

A+Sexual: How to Improve Those Nights When There's
   No One Else Around

My Mom Died 17 Times When I Was in College and She is Still Alive!
   A Comprehensive Compilation of Excuses
   for Missed College Assignments and Exams

Coprophagy: Why You Should Attach a Salt Shaker
   to Your Dog's Collar

Why My Summer Vacation Was Better Than Yours
   (A Third Grade Composition)

How to Give Someone a Powerful Ear-rection:
   10 Easy Steps to Making People Smile

clinging *to* anonymity

BY CHRISTOPHER J. KEMPER

AN AUTOBIOFICTIONARY

Some Facts Have Been Changed to Protect
the Gruesome Truth

DINGO LINGO BOOKS™

BANKS ○ LONDON ○ NEW YORK ○ PARIS

Copyright © 2006 by Christopher J. Kemper

All Rights Reserved. No part of this book may be reproduced in any form or by any electronic or mechanical means, including information storage and retrieval systems, without permission in writing from the publisher, except by a reviewer who may quote brief passages in a review (but only if that review is favorable).

Originally published in three ring binder, June 2005

ISBN 0-615-13120-4

Special Thanks to Kelly Morgan

Edited by Sarah Cypher, The Threepenny Editor
www.threepennyeditor.com

Cover and Layout Design by Kristin Johnson, redbat design

Printed in the United States of America

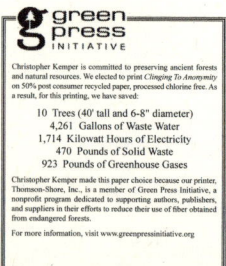

Christopher Kemper is committed to preserving ancient forests and natural resources. We elected to print *Clinging To Anonymity* on 50% post consumer recycled paper, processed chlorine free. As a result, for this printing, we have saved:

    10 Trees (40' tall and 6-8" diameter)
  4,261 Gallons of Waste Water
1,714 Kilowatt Hours of Electricity
   470 Pounds of Solid Waste
   923 Pounds of Greenhouse Gases

Christopher Kemper made this paper choice because our printer, Thomson-Shore, Inc., is a member of Green Press Initiative, a nonprofit program dedicated to supporting authors, publishers, and suppliers in their efforts to reduce their use of fiber obtained from endangered forests.

For more information, visit www.greenpressinitiative.org

For Nolan and Rosemary
Perfect parents

In creating these stories, I took the time to extensively interview every single word. "What are you doing to help this sentence?" I asked. Then I'd get more aggressive, threatening even. "I'm not sure I even need you in this sentence—what do you have to say to that?" During this slow, boring process, at times my frustration bubbled over and I capriciously fired a few promising words, deleting them from the page. When I settled back down, I'd realize that my literary downsizing was hasty and unwarranted, and I'd have to re-hire the words that I'd wrongly terminated. (I didn't actually re-hire the words, per se, but instead brought them back as independent contractors so I wouldn't have to provide them with health benefits). The point being, each word in the following pages has promised that it is capable of promoting clarity, humor and insight. If you find any of these words not performing up to snuff, please bring it to my attention. As we all know, words are cheap—so I won't hesitate to fire any underperforming words in favor of some new talent, even if I have to sneak some undocumented foreign words over the Mexican border. I care that much about entertainment. And despite any lazy or inapt words you may find in these pages, I guarantee you'll love this book! (Guarantee void where not prohibited).

Contents

Soul Shampoo 1
Altar Boy 17
Marathon 21
Battle Stations 45
A Cook Dies 49
It's Almost All Fun and Games 79
Clinging to Anonymity 83
The Emperor Reads a Book
    While Lounging in His New Clothes 109
My First Time 113
Some Assembly Required 117
Schooling the Olympics 125
A Dream Recounted 159
Kemperotic 165
Sasaquafish 169
The Cocky Before the Storm 191
It's Better to Give and Receive 197
You Say Peyronie's, I Say Peroni's 203
Atomic Defense 207
28 Minutes 237
C Eye A 267
Challenge Quest 271
Undermining Authority 303
Story Time 307
Rules of Engagement 317

Soul Shampoo

Even if my paternal grandparents were blind, they'd still take a camera on vacation. In this daydream of mine, my grandma and grandpa, endlessly selfless, would spend hours snapping photos on the off chance they might capture something interesting for the folks back home. Their photos would be random and blurry, many with unintentional, tilted horizons. There is an inherent conflict between photography and sightlessness, but my grandparents would persist, faithful that happenstance would deliver a picture that someone in their big Catholic family would appreciate. Upon returning from a trip, if asked, they'd sit patiently, handing over pictures one by one, exclaiming, "It really was the nicest place!"

A nondescript tree. A skewed picture showing half of an old house. Small, out-of-focus rocks on a sidewalk. Tangible items would represent small victories in the wake of numerous, uninspiring photos of blank sky. Blunders like forgetting to remove the lens cap and failing to monitor the location of thumbs wouldn't matter, such faux pas would be just as entertaining as the murky photo of a stranger's elbow. Love would compel me to study their photos with enthusiasm. "What a great picture! It should be in a museum!" My blind grandparents would beam with pride, thrilled to bring a grandchild joy. They lived to create happiness.

I'm happy to say my father's parents had excellent sight. It's not that I would've loved them any less if they were blind, but if they were I would have had a hard time stomaching their desecration of innocent rolls of film. Film gets less than a second to view the world, and each photo is forced to commit its single peek to memory. If I only got a millisecond during my entire life to open my eyes, and someone else got to choose the time and the place, I wouldn't entrust the decision to a blind person. Blind people with cameras sentence each frame of film to languish in the bottoms of dusty shoeboxes, forgotten in a closet, a random person's shoe emblazoned on its face. My grandparents wouldn't wish that on anything, purposely or by mistake. Their entire existence was undisputedly noble, selfless acts their trademark.

Blind to their modest means, they brought six kids into the world: my father and five daughters. None of their children were as prolific at populating the world with Catholics, but they each had at least two kids, counting twenty grandchildren in all. While I was growing up, all of our families lived within twenty-five miles of my grandparents' house, the only one they ever owned.

On Sundays, after mass, the entire clan would congregate at the Kemper Kastle, the name my grandparents had given to the cubbyhole where they spent their entire adult lives. A homemade oak sign hung by the front door to announce the moniker to the world, each letter carefully carved and stained dark to sharpen the contrast against the natural wood. The house bore no resemblance to the stately notion of a castle, though; and, fittingly, the "c" in castle was intentionally dethroned by a "K." If someone handed you a picture of the home you'd immediately deposit the photo in an old shoebox, if not the trash.

The small, well-kept assortment of aging wood and rusting nails contained three tiny bedrooms. The downstairs bedroom belonged to my grandparents, snugly adjacent to the only bathroom in the house.[1] Upstairs there were two more bedrooms, each the size of a modest walk-in closet. The stairwell leading up was so squat that dwarves would have to crouch to ascend. My youthful mind, oblivious to my grandparents' sacrifices and obstructed by my parents' selflessness, couldn't comprehend that my father had grown up sharing two tiny bedrooms with five sisters. A private bedroom was a birthright. The idea of six kids sharing such a speck of space seemed implausible, a concept so farfetched it didn't deserve any credence.

On the rare occasions that I wiggled up the stairs to where my father slept as a child—or, more likely, with five sisters, where he obtained blaring headaches—I imagined the two small bedrooms full of his sports equipment and childhood toys. Surely, at one time, there must have been a massive, six-bedroom wing attached to the small house that provided my dad and his sisters with spacious privacy. That part of the house, I figured, burned down after my father and his sisters had moved away. Instead of rebuilding, my grandparents probably donated the insurance money to charity. When I was old enough to realize the frightening truth, that my dad's collection of sporting equipment as a kid consisted of a pair of worn sneakers, I was in shock. Then I reflected on his parents, my grandma and grandpa, and imagined how much fun it must have been growing up there. It certainly was a castle in that respect.

Years of crowded conditions prepared the small house for the dozens of family members and friends who gathered there every Sunday. As my father steered the car into the driveway, my older brother, Karl, and older sister, Katrina, would help me out of the vehicle before it came to a complete stop, something older siblings have done since the advent of the Model-T.

"You're both going straight to hell," I'd inform them.

---

[1] My grandpa added on the indoor bathroom, with plumbing, when my dad was thirteen. Until then, going potty required a trip to the outhouse in the backyard.

After dusting off, I'd hit my younger brother, Kerry, to complete the natural downhill progression of bullying, and then run into the house to say hello to everyone. On my way to the front door I zipped past homemade birdhouses and intricate, decorative windmills my grandpa had built, amazing creations easy to ignore because they were part of my earliest memories of the place.

Once inside the Kastle, a swarm of aunts would shower me with questions about the day's church service. "Christopher, what was the sermon about today?"

"Jesus and love."

They'd laugh and giggle, thrilled by my feigned knowledge. Hugs were plentiful; praise handed out like Halloween candy. When the cackle died down, I was sent outside to get my ass kicked.

In addition to an older brother, I have six older, vile male cousins. As kids, the seven of them formed an informal pack of ferocious idiots. As I darted around the colorful rhododendrons in the front yard, I felt it my duty to tell them about their hideous flaws. I'd point out that they were dangerously stupidioactive, radiating dumbness throughout an innocent world, and then I'd call attention to their putrid aroma, varying physical deformities and their collective tendency toward pillowality, the excessive humping of pillows. Instead of facing their blatant personal deficiencies, they attacked the messenger. The sound of my solitary, bellowing laugh filled the front yard until I was captured. Then it was replaced by pleading.

Their wax-filled ears were deaf to requests for mercy. They administered inhumane thrashings, ignoring the lessons of love and forgiveness extolled by Jesus and recounted just an hour earlier during Sunday mass. I pontificated about the virtue of a "forgive and forget" lifestyle, but the Idiot Pack considered such sentiments heresy, firmly adhering to the concept of punish and remember. They enforced a strict penance policy that required a minimum of ten welts and one thunder wedgie per transgression.

After administering a whirlwind of punishing blows, they'd parole me on the condition that I wouldn't speak for the rest of the day. I never could live up to my end of the bargain; the severity of their whippings failed to overwhelm my powerful need to articulate the unsightly truth about their collective retardation. Despite the pain and their threats, something deep inside compelled me to verbalize their limitless shortcomings. It broke my heart that they couldn't comprehend my benevolent intent. I only pointed out defects that I was fairly certain could be remedied. I would never have declared that their ears were attached to their ass unless I was confident that a simple surgical procedure could correct the problem. I was only trying to help.

In the brief interim between my release and my mouth's subsequent parole violation, my cousins turned against one another, doing the only thing their minds could comprehend: fighting for no apparent reason. Primal creatures are only comfortable with primal relationships. If my only option in life other than brutish behavior was to park myself on the ground and drool out of the corners of my cavity and plaque-filled mouth, I'd probably spend my time beating up the innocent too. I took pride in knowing that my voice gave their lives purpose, uniting them to assail a common enemy half their size. I was their soul shampoo: they wetted me with their spit, smacked me around in the palm of their hands until my mouth foamed, rubbed me deep into the roots of my grandparents' lawn, rinsed me down with a garden hose and then repeated the process. When our Sunday visits came to an end and our respective families disbanded, members of the Idiot Pack walked away from my battered body uplifted, their souls inexplicably cleansed.

Persecution for truth-telling aligned me with Jesus and marked the holiest thing I accomplished each Sunday. The Bible doesn't document the times Jesus explained to certain individuals that they were, in fact, gigantic boogers, but I know he did.

Like me, he couldn't lie about such things.

By the time I turned eleven, Sunday visits to my grandparents had become far less violent affairs. Five of the Idiots had reached the age of emancipation, at least for purposes of attending church and visiting our grandparents. The missing Idiots were consumed by their own existence, typical for their age. (Years later, they all resumed regular Sunday visits. Once the wave of adolescence passed, we all did). But a reduction in Idiot Pack ranks didn't equate to tranquility. Karl and my cousin Tom, both a few years older than me, did their best to carry on the tradition, actively embracing the pleasures of gratuitous violence. They had both absorbed a few lumps of their own from older Pack members, usually while I was uprooting myself from the lawn and adjusting my jaw, but that experience had failed to impart empathy. The two were vicious. I never escaped a Sunday visit to Grandma's house without receiving a sharp kick to the shin or enduring the discomfort of involuntary sod consumption.

* * *

During seventh grade in my small hometown of Banks, Oregon, several of my friends christened chewing tobacco cool. Whenever I asked my buddies why they chewed tobacco, they'd offer the time tested explanation, "Everyone does it!"—a statement that left me and my pristine mouth feeling like a nobody.[2]

Karl and Tom worshipped the snuff. They practiced snapping chewing tobacco cans between their fingers for hours at a

---

[2] The belief that chewing tobacco was cool was a conclusion that was undoubtedly arrived at through independent thought and was in no way derived from the tobacco industry's carefully constructed advertising campaign aimed at kids. Local stores were flush with flashy "Skoal" signs and, with all the free t-shirt giveaways, I thought Copenhagen was an apparel maker, not a cancer precursor. My favorite ploy was an offer from Skoal. Anybody could send in, free of charge, for a Skoal wristband and written "tips" on how to hasten the development of a "cool chew can circle" on the back pocket of your denim jeans.

time. After wedging a can between the middle finger and the thumb on their right hand, they'd sit and snap their limp wrist to compact the chew inside the can, mimicking the farmers and loggers in town. Before developing an interest in this trick, neither had shown any sign of having an attention span, let alone one of more than 5-10 seconds. Their legendary inability to concentrate on any single activity had allowed me to escape extended beatings on several occasions. They'd start pounding me, usually with Socker Boppers, and then, as suddenly as they began, they'd stop. During the pause, for just a brief moment, they'd look at each other, bewildered, fists frozen in mid-swing. Then they'd look down at my bruised body, studious looks on their faces.

"Why are we beating him up?" one of them would ask.

The other would shrug. Then they'd ineloquently debate why I'd become the focus of their collective venom. When they failed to cobble together an explanation—understandable, since none existed—they'd walk away, too confused to continue, frustrated at being unable to remember why their clenched fists had been headed full speed into my gut. The simplistic idiocy of chewing tobacco cured their inability to focus, giving their infantile minds a mindless task that didn't require physical exertion. They snapped snuff cans for hours on end. The only thing capable of interrupting their rhythmic performance once they got it going was the need to spit out brown, gooey saliva, the waste product of a cancerous engine.

Despite constant encouragement from my friends—often disguised as harassment—I refused to chew tobacco. No matter how adamant my rebukes, my buddies wouldn't back down, their support for chewing tobacco unshakable, their denigration of healthy alternatives ferocious. Not once did any of them implore the completion of homework or advocate the benefits of a good night's sleep, but if there was an opportunity to get in trouble, they brought it to my attention immediately. And chewing tobacco was, by all adult accounts, a lure employed by the Devil to lead children down a path that led straight to the State Penitentiary.

My fear of God helped me resist the growing pressure to try chewing tobacco. I knew He'd kill me if I sinned, strike me dead for tarnishing my body with a sinful substance. During my middle school years, I staunchly refused chewing tobacco and all the other vices my friends advocated, fearful that if I gave in the Devil would pounce and, in no time, I'd be pointing a gun at a convenience store employee demanding free beef jerky.[3]

The same year that Tom and Karl began chewing tobacco they agreed to let me accompany them on a fishing trip to Grass Lake, a small, man-made lake stocked with sunfish and bass. The invitation was conditioned on my promise not to violate an imaginary ten-foot force field that surrounded them.

"The force field must be respected," Karl declared. "If you break it, you will be destroyed."

"Understand?" Tom added.

"Ummm...sure," I answered.

The three of us walked to the lake, a little over a mile from the sparse neighborhood where we lived, and fished all day. I had a great time and caught sunfish by the dozens. My bobber never spent an undisturbed minute on the surface of the water.

Catching fish in Grass Lake was about as difficult as realizing Karl and Tom were morons. After catching a couple dozen fish that day, I attempted to make the task more challenging. Before casting my line into the calm water, as the worm on my hook writhed in confusion, I yelled warnings to the fish.

"Do not, I repeat, do not try to eat the worm I'm about to toss in the water. It is a trick, you stupid fish. The worm is impaled on a hook, so if you try to eat the worm, you will be snagged and I

---

[3] By the time I reached high school my staunch resistance to vice met a diabolical end when my traitorous hands entered into a secret pact with a variety of vices, agreeing to assist them into my body with regularity. In middle school, I preached, "Repent!" By the middle of my freshman year, I added an option: "Repent...or share."

will reel you ashore, dragging you from your family and friends. Please wise up. You're embarrassing your species. I've caught over twenty-five of you today, employing the same simple ruse each time. Fool you once, shame on me. Fool you twice, shame on you. Fool you twenty-five times, you're insurmountably stupid, incapable of learning and you should do everyone a favor and go jump in a dry lake."

If anything, the warning inspired the sunfish to further flaunt their idiocy. They fought over the worm, oblivious that twenty-five of their schoolmates had disappeared under similar circumstances. Their actions verified that Idiot Packs can exist in aquatic environs. I knew that somewhere, under the surface, among the ravenous pack of idiots fighting to eat the worm, there was a small, intelligent, well-meaning sunfish, benevolently informing the others of their numerous shortcomings. He was trying to help them, to save them. *Don't eat that worm you irrepressible imbecile unless you want your bacteria-plagued scales and unsightly fins to be pulled from the water!* I empathized with the little fish, aware that his well-meaning honesty was greeted with condemnation instead of the appreciation it deserved. My bobber disappeared again, cutting short my empathy. Another idiotic sunfish with its gills attached to its ass struggled to get free.

While I fished, Karl and Tom chewed tobacco, spitting crap-brown saliva into the clear lake water like fertilizer sprinklers. I rejected their offers to join in.

"No thanks," I politely replied.

As the sun moved overhead, the two became increasingly determined, nearly insistent that I try some chewing tobacco. I responded by tacking an additional sentiment onto my polite rebuff.

"No thanks...you fucking losers."

The firmer my repudiations, the more they belittled. My decision to forgo chewing tobacco made me a "pussy" and a "chickenshit." These constant, unpleasant jibes were more than annoying; they were cause for concern. My mom had always assured me that names can never hurt you, but I'd recently discovered that she'd left out a very important clarifier, specifically that names can never *directly* hurt you. In real life, when an older brother calls a younger brother a "dumbass dummy," the actual name-calling is, in fact, painless, but the verbal assault inevitably sets in motion a perilous series of events that culminates with the younger brother incurring significant physical injuries.

For example, in response to a verbal assault, the younger brother might steal the older brother's Playboy and, after a thorough examination, he might leave the magazine in a conspicuous place, like the living room sofa, where Mom is sure to find it. After she finds the magazine, she interrogates the older brother while holding the contraband in one hand and a persuasive wooden spoon in the other. Eventually, the spineless older brother admits to owning the magazine and, as a result, the older brother is severely punished. Then the older brother, eyes red from a wooden-spoon spanking and facing two weeks without television, seeks out the younger brother and kicks his ass. And that hurts like hell.

On the walk home from Grass Lake, the name calling devolved. I threw first. Karl and Tom were twenty yards ahead of me on the skinny tree-lined path. I sent a dirt clod into the woods, purposely off to their left, a reminder of my growing resentment. Karl and Tom stopped and returned fire. Both of them could throw fairly hard, but their aim was miserable. Their projectiles tattered the trees and bushes around me despite their intent to crack open my head. Birds scattered while I held my ground, dancing slightly with my fishing pole to avoid the rocks and branches that, by chance, landed close by. Finally, harried by growing fear, I made an effort to halt the fray by lashing out with the most powerful tool in my arsenal. I threatened to tell Mom.

"I am going to tell Mom you guys were chewing tobacco."

"Bullshit. We were not," Karl shot back. A slather of brown goop oozed out of the corner of his mouth.

Their crackpot denials quickly became threats. Anger mounted. The volley of words ceased; the hail of dirt clods stopped. Frightened by the odd impasse, I turned around and walked down the path, back toward the lake, where I figured I'd wait things out. Within seconds of turning to walk away I heard the sound of two beasts rushing up from behind. I turned to look. Two sets of flaring nostrils were charging toward me at a full gallop.

I shouted, "The Zone, you're breaching the ten-foot Zone! Stay outta the…"

The Zone, apparently, was a rule of their convenience. My attempt at protest was silenced by a large wad of chewing tobacco. Apparently the duo had determined that their best defense against my threat to tell Mom was to make me an unwilling accomplice. Tom held my mouth open as Karl packed my throat like a musket barrel, doing everything but tamping the tobacco with a ramrod. Granules of chew cascaded down my throat, and I gagged.

By the time the attack ended, a half a can of Skoal was lodged in my esophagus. Amidst their evil laughter, I stumbled to my feet. To clear my throat, I inserted my right index finger deep into my mouth, triggering an explosion of black powder, expelling it from my body in a single, violent explosion. To placate Newton, after ejecting the tobacco, my head kicked back with equal force.

When I finally made it home that afternoon, I brushed my teeth for twenty minutes, pausing frequently to gag and spit, and then went directly to bed. My bedroom spun violently. I wanted to tell Mom what had happened but I doubted I'd be able to prove the assault beyond a reasonable doubt. Idiot Pack members are meticulous liars, a character trait common in prolific troublemakers, so winning a parental conviction would be difficult. I didn't like my odds against the denials of *two* practiced deceivers. If I snitched, the only thing certain was that Karl and Tom would seek retribution, and my gut couldn't handle another snuff attack. I lay in bed, fighting nausea, praying for revenge. Finally I drifted off into a deep sleep, dreaming of a world where the truth didn't hurt so much.

* * *

A few weeks after the tobacco incident, on a sun-splashed Sunday morning, I attended mass with my family. Tom and his family attended the same church service. Afterwards we all headed over to Grandma's. Tom and Karl were the only Idiots present. After the standard familial salutations, we went outside to play.

With the taste of tobacco still lingering in my memory, I wasted little time voicing my displeasure, my lips buzzing like a bee on the move. Karl and Tom scoffed when I informed them that they were "dickless," and, without checking the veracity of my assertion, they began chasing after me, swarming mad.

Like the wind I ran, already perspiring and battling fear on the warm, still day. I'm not fast, but I'm gnat quick, and I raced around the back of the house, weaving a path to stay out of their reach, bedeviling the pursuing Idiots. Despite their lumbering failure, they refused to give up the hunt. It quickly became clear that scurrying around the shrubbery near the front of the house wouldn't offer lasting protection, so I headed out back toward my grandfather's small apple orchard.

The green apples dangling from the limbs were famous for their crisp, juicy taste and were the only green things I willingly ate as a child. The sweet smell emanating from the ripe fruit often drew me out to the orchard, but now I ran there seeking safety. As I passed the first two trees in the orchard I felt a predatory breath on my neck and a pair of grasping fingers on my shirt. I took immediate evasive measures, dropping into a perfect baseball slide. The momentum of my pursuers carried them right by. As I slid to a stop, two fallen apples found their way into my hands. I instinctively closed my fingers around them. I popped up and headed in the other direction, carrying two potential weapons. The Idiots turned and followed.

Anytime I'm being chased, whether during a flag football game or by someone I've recently pelted with a water balloon, I imagine that I'm the one doing the chasing. In my mind, the people behind me are the ones fleeing; they just happen to be a world ahead of me. This day was different. Karl and Tom were so mad, their grunts so fierce, that my fear prevented any such mental escape. I was scared and running out of wind. Encouraged by fright, and with nothing to lose, I blindly threw the two apples behind me, one after the other, without breaking stride. I didn't aim or try to gauge my targets. The apples were guided only by the hand of God. And God's got great aim.

There were two distinct, solid thuds. Personally familiar with the sound of my grandfather's apples connecting with human flesh, I knew I'd scored a couple of direct hits. Their pain would be severe. Like an ancient knight discovering that the dragon is vulnerable, I was filled with jubilation. I didn't look back right away. I continued running, wanting to create a safe gap before turning to evaluate the damage. When I was about twenty yards away from the impact zone, I stopped to look. Karl rolled on the ground, whimpering and cupping his left eye with his hands. Tom hunched on one knee, vigorously rubbing his chin. Gazing upon my fallen foes, I felt exhilarated, fierce and dominant. David slaying Goliath suddenly seemed uninspired, paling in comparison to valiantly halting two giant foes with a couple of apples. I stood stoically, master of all.

I'm not a theologian but I am pretty certain in the biblical story Goliath didn't get back up. Karl, his eye already swollen, started toward me first. Tom, a deep, radiating red mark on his chin, followed close behind. I was no David. My comparison had been erroneous; apples to oranges, or, literally, apples to rocks. The difference was significant.

Fight or flight instincts took over, and since I never give the fight option any consideration, I ran for my life. Behind me, rage filled the air in stereo. Profoundly frightened by their screams, I headed for the front door in search of adult protection, a break with tradition. The hooves of my predators clapped close behind as I spun around the corner of the house. Luckily, the front porch was cluttered with adults, the lovely day inducing the cavalry to come out to greet me. I skidded to a stop in front of the porch, grinning the grin of certain salvation. Karl and Tom didn't break stride.

The two of them ripped the smirk from my face, rattling my teeth. I tumbled to the ground. They beat me wildly, throwing punches with urgency, aware that adults would soon arrive to stop the fray. Because their punches were unmeasured, most of the blows only grazed me. Before they could do any real damage, my mom rose from her perch on the porch to break things up. In a magical move that only moms can perform, she grabbed all three of us by the ear, using only her two hands. She pulled us to our feet, Karl and Tom in her right hand, I in her left. She marched us directly in front of the porch to face the jury.

"To be fair," I said, "if those two are going to have a jury of their peers, we're going need to find twelve people who've recently been whipped by a kid half their size."

The jury laughed tepidly. Mom didn't.

Sensing the jury warming to my cause, I continued. "Mom, you're the one who always tells me an apple a day keeps the doctor away. By the looks of them, seems the opposite is true."[4]

She gave my ear a good yank.

"I'm tired of you three fighting like cats and dogs," she said. My mind flashed to our family dog, Tootsie, who frequently curled up and slept with our cat, Snickers. Mom's blazing eyes bulged from their sockets, so I decided not to point out the problem with her analogy. She sensed I was considering another wisecrack.

---

[4] The problem with this saying is that the advice completely fails to inform the holder of the apple what they are supposed to do with it to avoid the doctor.

"Don't say another word," she snarled. She gave my ear another sharp pull.

Karl's eye was almost swollen shut. Tom continued rubbing his chin. I didn't expect a single acquittal. We stood there, awaiting judgment. Unlike Jesus and Barbaras, the populace wouldn't be given the opportunity to grant one of us clemency. I hoped the porch would erupt with chants of *"Free Chris, Free Chris!"* The support didn't materialize. All three of us were sunk.

As aunts and uncles debated our fates, my grandfather disappeared into the house. He emerged seconds later, his camera in hand.

"Line 'em up," he instructed. My mom stepped away while simultaneously pulling her hands together, yanking the three of us into a clump of guilt. I stood juxtaposed with the two Idiots, ready to accept my fate.

"Look up here," Grandpa insisted. The three of us acquiesced, turning our eyes from the ground to lens.

His finger fell and the shutter clicked. In an instant, the three of us were captured for eternity. The picture was sharp, clear, perfect. Karl grappling for sight, Tom squinting from pain, my smile stretching to reach two ears firmly attached to my head.

The ride home was quiet. No one spoke. We didn't stop at our local ice cream shop for our standard Sunday treat, the first nail of our contemporary crucifixion. There would be more punishment to come. Riding a wave of success, I didn't care. The pecking order hadn't changed, but in the coming months, the frequency and severity of the Idiots' pecking diminished. Soon, the quibbling between us died out almost completely, replaced by friendship, a situation hastened by my early growth spurt. Nothing brings peace faster than a formidable foe.

As our family car rolled through the beautiful farm country where I grew up, my fear parted, replaced by empowering, if temporary, courage. I could foresee a future free of Idiot domination, a vision that healed my wounds and lathered my soul.

End Note:

Everyone in my extended family referred to our grandparents' house as "Grandma's." It's not as if our grandma had furtively transferred title to the house into her name to prevent Grandpa from hobbling off with a hospice worker. Instead, the terminology sprouts from a special reverence for the maternal. This same reverence manifests in speeches and introductions, where females get first billing: Ladies and gentlemen. Then there's the common motto, Ladies first. The list goes on and on. All this and women still complain about unequal pay for the same work? Seems a bit greedy to me.

Altar Boy

My first Sunday as an altar boy, I was confronted with a major dilemma. Four dead flies were floating in the blood of Christ. I looked up at the altar, hoping for divine guidance. My hopes were greeted by an impatient glare from Father Murphy. *Okay,* I thought, *I'll let him deal with it.*

I carried the wine-filled chalice up to the altar and presented it.

"Their souls must be in heaven, right Father?" I whispered. Drowning in the blood of Christ seemed the holiest way to die short of crucifixion. Father looked into the chalice and grimaced.

The congregation was full of blank gazes that morning, as if most of the people had spent their Saturday night doing the same thing as the four flies—except the congregants had lived to repent. As I sat down, Father blessed the wine, raised the chalice high and then slowly lowered it down to take a big gulp. Later in the mass, when I returned to the altar to collect the chalice, only three lifeless flies remained.

Other than attending mass every Sunday, my altar boy training consisted of a two-hour course taught by Lyle Labonte, a kid who went to the private school operated by our parish. Lyle is a year older than me, so I listened to him. He strode around the front of the church demonstrating the chores an altar boy had to perform during the ceremony, fetching items for the priest, ringing a bell at certain times and, most importantly, always genuflecting when crossing in front of the altar.

My older brother, Karl, and cousin, Tom, attended the same training, but neither would let a younger kid tell them what to do, and they were far too cool to don an altar boy's black robe and surplice anyway. As Lyle taught, Karl and Tom played bloody knuckles.

A few weeks after my inaugural mass as an altar boy, Karl and Tom were scheduled for theirs. Each mass is attended to by a pair of altar boys, and the new kids were typically matched with experienced servers for their first few assignments. But since Karl and Tom were older, whoever made the server schedule must have figured the two could handle working their first mass together.

God, was that person wrong.

The service started, as usual, with the priest being led up the aisle by a pair of altar boys. As Karl and Tom sauntered by our pew, I looked at them and laughed, pretty certain they were going to embarrass the hell out of themselves. It didn't take long for them to deliver. As soon as they reached the altar, instead of sitting down in their assigned chairs, they stood next to the lectern like lost, strangely dressed tourists. Father looked down at them and pointed over to the chairs. The two shared a blank look and then walked over and sat down. This was going to be good.

For the next forty minutes, Karl and Tom wandered around the front of the church like they'd both had their cognition stolen. To keep mass moving forward, Father adopted the added duty of maestro, directing Karl and Tom around the altar with gestures and finger pointing. At one point, Karl got so carried away ringing a set of small bells that Father actually stopped a prayer mid-sentence and mouthed for all to see, "Stop with the bell." The only thing the dumb duo did right was genuflect each time they crossed in front of the altar.

Mom was mortified. Dad laughed softly along with my sister Katrina, my brother Kerry and me. When it was almost time for communion, my mom, hoping to salvage some respect, grabbed my shirt, pulled me past Dad and put her face next to mine.

"You go around to the side vestibule, call your brother over and tell him exactly what he needs to do for communion and the end of mass. Do it now."

I stepped out of the pew, kneeled briefly as I'd been taught, and walked out the back of the church. I rushed around to the side entrance and opened the door without making any sound. Karl and Tom were sitting across the altar, and I waved my hands to get their attention. Karl saw me and I motioned him over. He quickly got up and walked toward me, genuflecting as he passed in front of the altar.

"You're doing a great job," I whispered.

"Shut up. What do you want?"

"For you to stop embarrassing the family."

"Kiss my ass."

Salutations out of the way, I gave a forty-five second lecture on what Karl and Tom needed to do to prepare for communion and close out the mass. "And Karl," I concluded, "you are only supposed to genuflect the first time you pass in front of the altar, so make sure you and Tom don't do it anymore."

He nodded and started to walk back to his seat. I grabbed his surplice and pulled him back.

"Oh, and by the way. There were flies in the wine when I served a few weeks ago. After mass Father told me that we can't hand him the communion wine if it has anything in it. So if something is in the wine, like flies, you have to remove them before handing the wine to Father. Lyle told us to drink them out if necessary."

Karl returned to his seat, passing in front of the altar without kneeling. He leaned over to Tom, spoke for a minute, and then looked over at me. I gave both of them the thumbs up and then rushed out to rejoin my family.

"You get everything straightened away, Chris?" Mom asked.

"Yep. Sure did."

When it came time to prepare for communion, Karl and Tom walked across the front of the church to the small table holding the wine chalice and the communion hosts. They did not stop to genuflect. A few people in the congregation audibly reacted.

"That's the second time Karl didn't genuflect," Mom whispered. "What is going on?"

"I have no idea," I said.

Tom walked into the vestibule to fetch two golden patens, little plates shaped like ping-pong paddles that are used to prevent communion wafers from falling to the floor while they're being handed to congregants. As Tom disappeared from sight, Karl walked the bowl of communion hosts up to Father, and then returned to the small table to fetch the chalice of wine. As Karl walked the wine up the steps, he stared into the gold cup. When he arrived at the top step, he hesitated and then looked up at Father. Then back down into the chalice. Without warning, Karl took a quick drink of wine. He cringed at the taste. Father's mouth fell agape, and the congregation let out a gasp. Karl looked back down into the cup, then took another quick drink. Again he cringed. The congregation broke into a soft chatter.

My mom slumped down in the pew and buried her face in her hands.

After his second drink, Karl glanced one more time into the cup and then handed it to Father, who yanked it from his hands with a mixture of shock and disgust.

"What is he doing?" Mom pleaded to no one in particular, peeking through her fingers. She pulled her hands away and looked over at me. "I thought you were going to tell him what to do."

"Oh, I told him what to do, Mom," I answered with a wry grin. "I told him exactly what to do."

Marathon

"Do you ever get the feeling that you're being watched?"
Eight of us were sitting together for a night of Italian food and pitchers of beer at the Old Spaghetti Factory, a restaurant just off of Macadam Avenue in Portland. Scott, an old friend of mine, posed this question to the table. The question by itself was innocuous, even meaningless, but in context, it was part of a trend among my contemporaries toward overthrowing superficial banter as our conversational king. This coup was intended to inject our discussions with issues more mature than drinking and sex, two conversational themes that had capably sustained us for well over a decade. A revolutionary at heart, I understood their desire for change. A realist and student of history, I also knew that most revolutions turn out badly, particularly when they're premised on faulty ideals, and the idea that conversations about being watched should supplant discussions about getting laid was the worst one I'd ever heard.

This conversational uprising gained momentum about a year before I turned thirty. That was when I first noticed some of my friends attempting to engage in discussions that could be categorized as cultured. They were novices in the art of substantive conversation, so it was unsurprising that their early attempts were about as smooth as a teenage couple fumbling in the back seat of a car. Despite their struggles, they plunged ahead, determined to wax eloquent about being watched and dreams of being naked in public, the topical equivalents of a high school kid struggling to remove his girlfriend's bra.

I diagnosed this shift in conversational interests as a symptom of the debilitating disease I call modern adulthood. Attempting to halt the advance of adulthood is futile because the societal forces championing the disease are far too powerful and well-funded to defeat. But when the disease began to cripple my friends I vowed to do everything I could to reduce the rate at which the malignancy spread. By slowing adulthood's toxic effects, I hoped to extend my friends' fun-expectancy well into their forties. This singular aim emboldened me to challenge society's unrelenting insistence that we "grow up," and provided me with the courage to question America's fabricated timetable for getting a real job, a dog, a house and a spouse.

Just as Luke Skywalker had an innate ability to harness The Force, a gift that obligated him to battle the Empire, I too am blessed with an uncommon, almost mythical ability that compels me to lead the fight against adultism. After graduating from college, I learned that I could immerse myself in uniquely grown-up environments for long periods of time and come away unscathed, childish to the core. Like a person who eats only red meat and dairy products but still has a cholesterol count under 130, I can be exposed to adulthood without suffering personal maturation. Buffered by immunity, I've watched with despair as adulthood has toppled my friends with frightening efficiency. One friend after another, driven by self-actualization, imagined or real, or the acceleration of life, imagined or real, is fallen by the same societal force that manufactured a rationalization for the shoehorn.[1]

Though there is no scientific test to confirm the onset of

adulthood, initiating a conversation about 401(K) plans is a common symptom. Posing a philosophical question without first exhaling a plume of illicit smoke is another. In this vein, Scott's question about being watched was the diagnostic equivalent of listening to your great uncle recount his childhood in Atlantis; no further evidence was necessary to know he was losing it.

Like senility, the evidence of advancing adulthood can mount with disheartening rapidity, the flurry of symptoms growing increasingly severe, methodically ravaging the victim. Yet adulthood refuses to kill. It leaves that chore to less devious diseases like cancer and heart failure. Instead, adulthood toys with its victims, unleashing its fiercest weapons, monotony and responsibility, to cruelly and slowly sap life. It ruthlessly weakens some victims to the point that they willingly commit to monogamy in the presence of family and friends. Now that's one dastardly ailment.[2]

Scott's question hung over the table for several moments without a response. Everyone seemed to be giving the question earnest consideration. Hoping to block any momentum that the topic might pick up, I sprang to action.

"Scott, do you ever get the feeling that you've asked a table full of friends a ridiculously stupid question?" I stared him in the eyes, my tone clearly identifying me as a loyal supporter of superficial banter.

A smattering of chuckles sprinkled the table. Unfortunately, before I could begin recounting a story about inebriation and French kissing two different girls in a single night, the question about being watched gained traction. One by one, everyone at the table came to the same conclusion; yes, at one time or another they had sensed that they were being watched. I didn't

---

[1] The act of using a shoehorn to force your foot into a tight fitting, inflexible shoe is no different than raising a white flag or crying uncle.

[2] As with many males, I considered marriage a silly proposition until I found someone confused enough to marry me.

participate. I sat quietly, waiting for an opportunity to share a fabricated story about the time I was super close to participating in a threesome, but how at the last minute both the girls remembered they had to go to a modeling shoot. When the conversation waned, I cued my story. Before I could pounce, though, my girlfriend at the time, Tierra, revived the topic.

"How about you, Chris?" she asked. "Have you ever felt like you were being watched?"

"Me?" I shrugged, emphasizing my lack of interest. "Not that I can think of. I once was really close to participating in a ménage a four though."[3]

Tierra sighed at my childish reply. "No really," she urged, "have you ever felt like you were being watched?"

"Do I ever feel like I'm being watched?" I paused for dramatic effect. "Sure I've felt that way, that is if you count the unseen societal forces constantly hovering over me, commanding me, *'Fall in step, join the crowd, you must, you must!'* And to that, I say, 'No thanks! Buzz off!' I do not, and will not, consult with society when making decisions, no matter how fiercely life stares me down. But if the question is limited to whether I've ever felt that I was being watched by an actual person or creature, then no, I have never felt like that, and that pisses me off. Why aren't people watching me? I *should* be watched, I *deserve* to be watched. I don't care if it's overt or surreptitious, but people *should...* watch... me... all... the... time!"

My answer sparked a new conversation, a probing review of all the reasons people shouldn't watch me. The group made remarkably persuasive arguments. Under cross-examination, though, they conceded that under certain circumstances that people should stare at me, possibly even gawk. If I were, for example, on fire from head to toe and running down a crowded street, or if I had straws protruding from each nostril, then, yes, they agreed, people should watch.

---

[3] If you are going to lie, lie outrageously.

"But that's not the point," insisted one of my friends. "Have you ever felt like you were *just being watched,* by someone or something, just sensed it, could *feel* that you were being observed?"

He was too late. I was standing on my chair with two straws sticking out of my nose. The guests at nearby tables were watching. My actions were clearly making them uncomfortable, but they were watching. After ten seconds of being watched, I sat back down.

"I'd like to amend my original answer," I said, reopening the issue. "I *have* felt like I was being watched, rather recently I might add."

As the evening moved forward, the table continued to engage in conversations that didn't revolve around sex or getting drunk. With every word, I felt youth slipping away. I juggled salt shakers, stuck a spoon to the tip of my nose, I even grabbed a nearly full pitcher of beer and drank the entire thing in one smooth motion, *the* skill I developed in college. Nothing I did could derail the semi-cultured conversation. My antics, deployed to save my friends from a perilous fate, were dropped into the evening like anchors attempting to secure a fading past. Each attempt failed, and life's waters continued to rise, forcing superficial banter to scramble for high ground.

Part of the reason I cling to childhood is the hope that others will join in, but mostly I do it because I prefer the lifestyle. In my childhood home, my mom, a fiercely passionate first-grade teacher, hung a poster entitled *Everything I Need to Know I Learned in Kindergarten.*[4] The tenets listed on the poster provide a guide to a well-lived life: *treat others with respect, share, don't hit people, say you're sorry, play fair, clean up your own mess, live a balanced life, take naps.*[5] It's a pretty convincing piece of propaganda, a well-

---

[4] Out of respect I never pointed out to Mom how this proclamation made her first-grade teaching job irrelevant.

[5] Unless I slept through some crazy shit that went on during kindergarten naptime, I think that there are a few vital life lessons that the traditional kindergarten curriculum does not cover.

scripted blueprint for elusive world peace. Kindergarteners don't wage war—adults do, and they do it for reasons that any kindergartner can tell you are patently absurd. In a way, then, I'm a peacenik battling adulthood in an effort to disarm it of its well-documented immorality, and as long as I live, I will continue to fight the good fight.

That night at the Old Spaghetti Factory, the battle wasn't going well, but my mobile phone rang loudly enough to stop conversation at the table for a few moments. As usual, the screeching ring seemed to frighten the lining of my pocket, causing the material to recoil and shrink wrap around my phone like a Venus flytrap closing on an unsuspecting insect. With each successive ring my phone seemed to scream louder, as if panicked. I fought to free it. My frustration grew. Several restaurant patrons shot me looks of scorn, understandably annoyed. I was being watched, and I didn't like it. After the fourth ring, my pocket finally went limp with shock. I retrieved my phone, flipped it opened and answered the call.

The call was from my older brother, Karl. He complained about how long it took for me to answer my phone, and then reminded me that he was running the Portland Marathon in the morning. A close mutual friend, John Meyer, was also running. I had a vague memory that the two were participating in the event, but I'd forgotten when the race was taking place.

"Well, good luck with the race," I told Karl. "Need any tips?"

"Actually, I do. I need to know where I should park my car. I'm not really all that familiar with the downtown area."

I gave Karl the parking information he wanted, wished him luck again and then bid him good bye. As soon as I hung up, Tierra asked me who had called.

"Karl. He's running the Portland Marathon tomorrow. So is John."

"They're really going to do that! Wow!"

I had yet to conquer the natural aversion a male has to a girlfriend expressing significant interest in the activities of other males, so I reflexively lashed back.

"It can't be all that hard."

This comment attracted the attention of the entire table. A few more pitchers of beer were ordered to foster discussion. My friends grilled me about my offhanded assertion that running a marathon wasn't an overly difficult task. Since my initial statement contained very little wiggle room, I was forced to defend a contention that I didn't believe. My attempts to play the comment down failed, and the table continued its attack. The pressure mounted. Soon the discussion reached the pivotal point, the moment in which I had to make a tough decision: concede my mistake or embrace my stupid statement and go on the offensive.

"Chris, claiming a marathon isn't very hard is fucking childish!" Tierra laughed. "How old are you anyway? Four?"

Her good-hearted taunt made my decision easy. If the claim was childish, I was going to stand by it. Over the next ten minutes I became increasingly entrenched in a dim-witted position. I compared running a marathon to a stroll on a moving sidewalk and claimed that it took all the effort of an extended yawn.

"Then why don't *you* do it?" Tierra grinned.

"What's the point?" I snarled.

"To prove your point," she shot back.

I didn't dare argue with her circular, infantile logic. That would be like turning my back on family.

"I'm in!" I exclaimed. This was the type of childish stunt that could possibly slow the progression of adulthood, an act of juvenility so fantastic it might be able to stem the flow of convention washing over my friends. I'd do it for them! Fears of fading youth scattered. I felt born again.[6]

The start of the race was only ten hours away. I called Karl

---

[6] Sadly, adherents to conventional wisdom fail to understand that there is no new wisdom in convention, or much entertainment for that matter.

and told him that I was going to run with him. He laughed, but I reminded him that for the last couple months I'd been running three or four times a week, 4-5 miles at a go. That was the positive. When I hung up, I acknowledged the fact that I was moderately intoxicated and had never run more than seven miles. But I was sure I would finish, or die trying. Like Luke Skywalker, I was willing to risk everything for the cause.

As our meal wound down and I polished off my final beer, I formulated a plan. I lifted my strategy off the back of a shampoo bottle: I'd run 4-5 miles, something I could do, then repeat. And repeat. And repeat. And repeat. And, one last time, repeat.

* * *

In 490 B.C. about 30,000 Persians sailed into Marathon, a small Grecian coastal town about twenty-four and a half miles northeast of Athens. The Persians hadn't bothered to inform the Athenians that they were coming. Nonetheless, Marathon's Chamber of Commerce embraced their arrival, thrilled to see such a large group of visitors sailing into their port. Marathon was holding a big rugby tournament that weekend and the Persian squad, adorned in fancy, armor-clad uniforms, would help fill out the tournament bracket. The legion of Persian fans that had accompanied the team would be a boon to the Marathon economy. *What a wonderful surprise!* the local businessmen thought.

The welcoming mood soon soured, mainly because the Persians began killing everyone in town. Distressed, the Marathon Chamber of Commerce voted to kick the Persians out of the tournament and refused to give them any of the souvenir rugby t-shirts. The Persians, upset about the vote, killed the members of the Chamber and took the t-shirts anyway.

Meanwhile, approximately 10,000 Greeks, mostly Athenians,

sat high on a hill above Marathon, watching the carnage unfold. They'd come to watch the rugby tournament and, like modern day soccer hooligans, the Greeks were drunk and belligerent. Still, most of them were coherent enough to recognize that the Persians weren't playing by the rules. The rules of rugby were a bit unsettled at the time but none of the variations allowed wanton killing of opposing players.

"They don't seem to understand the rules," one of the Greek men muttered.

"You cannot use an opponent's head as a ball!" another yelled down.

After a few hours of watching the Persians massacre the Marathonians, the Greeks began to suspect the Persians didn't even care about the rules.

One of the Greek men ran down the hill and addressed a group of the unruly visitors.

"It's all fun and games until someone loses a torso," he screamed.

The Persians quickly killed the Greek. Before he died, the man motioned over to where his torso lay and condescendingly boasted, "See!"

After watching the Persians kill their countryman, several of the Greeks felt the need to confront the Persians and explain to them the importance of following the rules. A spirited debate ensued. In a close vote, the Greeks opted to engage the Persians rather than returning home to Athens.

"There sure are a lot of Persians down there," observed one of the Greeks. "It's going to be difficult explaining the rules to such a big group."

"You know who's really good at explaining the rules of rugby?" replied another. "The Spartans!"

The city of Sparta was over 100 miles away. Because communications at the time weren't all that modern, getting a message to the Spartans presented a bit of a problem. It was decided that someone would have to travel to Sparta, and fast.

"Hey Pheidippides," one of the elder Greeks yelled, motioning to a young, lanky man dressed only in a loincloth, "I need to talk to you."

The spry Pheidippides hustled over. When he got close to the old man, Pheidippides stopped and stood at attention. "What can I do for you, sir?"

"I don't really know you well enough to ask a huge favor," said the old man. "But the people who know me well would never agree to do it for me, so I need your help."

Pheidippides stared at the old man, perplexed. The elder continued.

"Won't you be good chap and run over to Sparta and tell the whole city to come over here and help us explain the rules of rugby to these crazed Persians."

"Sure, but can I borrow a horse?" Pheidippides asked.

"Silly Pheidippides," the old man laughed, "where is the lasting legend in that? Now run along."

So Pheidippides ran. To Sparta. And then back. He made the round trip in less than two days.[7] Despite the Athenians' plea for aid, the Spartans didn't race over to Marathon to help because they were in the midst of one of their annual pagan festivals.

"Sorry," the Spartans said, "but for the next week or so, we are religiously obligated to have wild sex orgies and drink excessively. Maybe we can make it over there once we recover, in about ten days or so."[8]

As it turned out, the Spartans' well-reasoned delay didn't matter. Before Pheidippides made it back to Marathon with the news, the anxious Greeks, tired of watching the carnage, charged down the hill to deal with the unruly visitors. On the plains of Marathon, a mighty clash raged. The Athenians fought fiercely, steadfast in their view that killing opposing rugby players was un-

---

[7] Imagine if this guy had proper footwear.

[8] You can be sure Spartans didn't spend time talking to their friends about being watched. Instead, with such uninhibited festivals, they spent time productively, telling friends, "Dude, watch this!"

sportsmanlike. The Persians fervently disagreed, opposing any rule that would hinder their right to kill everyone in sight.⁹

When Pheidippides arrived back in Marathon, he gawked at the gory battle in the valley. The old Greek who'd sent him to Sparta spotted Pheidippides and called him over.

"Hey Pheidippides, are the Spartans coming?" he asked.

"Not for a while, they're drinking and having sex."

"Sex and drinking? Those damn Spartans are never going to grow up," the old man grumbled. "They need to get their priorities straight. Do they know they're missing out on one hell of a bloody fight here?"

"I'd be happy to run back and tell them," Pheidippides replied. "I'll even stay there all week in order to explain to the Spartans just how childish they're being."

"No, we need you here. Good effort running to Sparta for us. You've earned a five-minute break. When that's done, put on some armor and go assist our boys down in the valley."

Minutes later, one of the older Greek men strapped armor on Pheidippides, placed a large hammer in his hand and pushed him down the hill, instructing him to club sense into the Persians. By the end of the day, about 6,000 Persians had decided they'd rather die than play by the rules. The rest of the Persian gang got back on their boats and left town, setting sail in search of a rugby tournament with less stringent regulations, one where the spectators wouldn't interfere with their style of play.

As the Persians sailed off, the old Greek man summoned the weary Pheidippides.

"Pheidippides, I need you to deliver a very important message to the head politician in Athens."

"That's over 24 miles away," Pheidippides pointed out. "I've run over 200 miles in the last seventy-two hours and then spent all day fighting the Persians. I'm a bit tired. Can I use a horse

---

⁹ According to historians, this was the most vicious fight over a sporting rule until the American League adopted the designated hitter in 1973.

this time?"

"When I was your age," the old man responded, shaking his head, "we called that a day's work. Now run along."

Despite his crushing exhaustion, Pheidippides was flattered by the responsibility. Fate had cast him into the eye of a historic event. The sealed envelope entrusted to him by the old man undoubtedly contained vital news—news proclaiming the victory over the pesky Persians. It also probably contained a warning to the city of Athens that the remnants of the Persian team might sail there in search of a fight. On a grander scale, Pheidippides knew this victory would nurture the tender roots of Greek civilization, thereby allowing the sapling of Western culture to blossom and spread.[10]

Rejuvenated, Pheidippides clutched the envelope and took off for Athens at a blazing pace. About three hours later, fatigued near death, he hobbled into the city and delivered the message to the top Athenian councilman.

"It's very important," Pheidippides gasped.

"Thank you, Pheidippides," the politician praised, "you have served your people well."

"Read the note," Pheidippides urged. His breath was short. Pride was the only thing filling his lungs.

The councilman opened the sealed envelope and removed the note with a sense of drama. He peered at the document for quite some time. Finally, he looked into Pheidippides' proud eyes.

"Apparently my wife wants me to pick up a loaf of bread, some butter and a pound of rice on the way home from work," the politician said. "Thanks for delivering this *important* news."

Stunned, Pheidippides collapsed and died. The politician promptly freaked, shocked that his little joke had killed the

---

[10] Historians hypothesize that a Persian victory at Marathon would have collapsed the developing Greek juggernaut. Over the next three centuries the Greek Empire established a blueprint for Western civilization and spread the seeds of pseudo-democratic thought throughout the Western world. They also made curiosity cool. Hundreds of years later the Greeks, tired of power and its associated hassles, handed the cultural torch to Rome.

spunky runner. The message Pheidippides had delivered had indeed contained vital information about the Persians. The politician, afraid that the body of a young, heroic figure lying on the floor of his office would end his career, called an intern into the room for assistance. The young woman entered the office and gasped at the sight of the dead hero. Seizing the opportunity, the politician coerced the dazed girl into having sex with him on his desk. The politician then sent the intern away. After she left, he dragged Pheidippides' body into a utility closet.[11] Shortly after hiding the body, the politician held a press conference. He informed the populace that the Persians had been defeated at Marathon. He also warned of the continuing Persian threat, and then closed his speech by telling the people that he had been forced to kill Pheidippides when he caught him trying to force sex on his intern. Over the coming weeks, the Athenians, with help from the bloated Spartans and a few other Greek tribes, completely trounced the remnants of the Persian team.

Several centuries after Pheidippides sprinted to fame in Southern Greece, the Romans created the world's most renowned athletic event, the Olympic Games. The marathon, a foot race that covered approximately 24.5 miles, was one of the original events, respectfully included in the Games to commemorate a man who died as a result of a moderately funny joke. At the 1908 Olympic Games in London, the marathon distance was altered, extended to 26 miles in order to cover the ground from Windsor Castle to White City stadium, a change adopted to assuage the King of England's whim. London organizers, apparently unaware that the very idea of royalty is absurd, added an extra 385 yards so that the finish line for the race would be directly in front of the royal box. For the next sixteen years, the International Olympic Committee debated the "real" marathon distance. The issue wasn't resolved until the 1924 Paris Games, when the Committee

---

[11] This is how the political term "skeleton in his closet" originated.

announced that 26.2 miles would be the official race distance. It remains so today.

* * *

The Rockport shoe company launched an advertising campaign in the 1980s that featured a man running the New York marathon while wearing a pair of Rockport dress shoes. *The shoes are that comfortable!* the company promised. During the commercial, filmed during an actual N.Y. marathon, the Rockport running man effortlessly trots past other competitors. As he passes, the other runners laugh and point at his shoes in cheerful amazement, as if to say, "How neat! The man passing us is wearing dress shoes."

The Rockport commercials marked my first exposure to the marathon. Prior to the commercials, running had never interested me. When I learned a man could run breezily for miles and miles while wearing dress shoes, I turned my back on the idea. *Can't be much of a challenge,* I thought.

I also knew enough about myself to realize that, for me, marathons would be violent affairs. If a man trotted past me while wearing dress shoes in *any* race, I'd have a decidedly different reaction than the people in the commercial. The moment the Rockport man tried to pass me, his race day would be done. I don't deal well with condescension—at least not the receiving end—and running by someone while wearing dress shoes is mockingly cruel, like winning a swimming race in a cement Speedo. If such a display is part of a self-deprecating act or a joke, that's fine, but if someone actually tries to beat me in a physical event while wearing ridiculously inappropriate equipment, I'm going to lash out. I've often pictured the Rockport man trying to pass me during a race, and my imagination has never left him alive.

On the morning of the 1998 Portland Marathon, I woke up

at 5:00 with a mild hangover. I threw on my running gear and engulfed a banana, hoping the oddity of fruit entering my digestive tract might shock my body numb. I made my way out to my car and drove toward downtown Portland as the sun peeked over the eastern skyline. Its shine made my eyes water. Until that moment I'd only accepted the sunrise as a metaphor, a concept, possibly a Native American myth. I'd seen the sun set countless times, but until then, I'd never witnessed it rise. I thought it just as plausible that the sun started the day like a light bulb, flashing to life when someone very important flipped a switch. Watching that orange globe arching upward like a waking eyelid, I understood, for the first time, why Hemingway's *The Sun Also Rises* doesn't contain a question mark in the title. The sun actually does rise, at least it did on this day, offering a beautiful and educational start to the morning.

At 6:10 I entered the lobby of the downtown Hilton, race headquarters for the Portland Marathon. Hordes of people dressed in running gear flocked into the building and headed downstairs to the hotel basement. I followed the crowd down and soon encountered a row of temporary booths, each with a sign describing its function: Pre-registered Runners. Information. Day of Race Registration.

"Where's the booth to fill out a last will and testament?" I asked a fellow runner. I smiled. He answered with a solemn look that had a serious vibe, and rudely moved along. If he'd been wearing Rockports, I'd have kicked his ass.

I went over to the Day of Race Registration booth and filled out a registration form, my gateway to 26.2 miles of leisurely fun. After entering all the required information, I handed the form to an energetic lady working behind the booth.

"First marathon?" she asked, looking over the form.

"And first sunrise," I shared.

She looked at me and laughed, certain I was kidding.

"I'm always interested to hear what motivates a person to do their first marathon. What was it for you?" she asked.

Motivation had no hand in my decision. Hard-headedness, maybe. Poor debate skills, probably. A mouth that allows words to escape without even a cursory review of content, absolutely. Still, I searched for some sliver of traditional motivation to share with the lady.

"Life expectancy?" I offered meekly.

Again she laughed, as if I were joking. While she laughed, I gave my answer some thought. Reviewing my comment, I realized it had been dead-on. Life expectancy is motivation's primary ingredient. Without it, motivation would cease to exist.

After I paid the entry fee, the kind registration lady handed me a race number and some safety pins.

"Pin this to my shirt?" I asked.

"Yes. To the front. Before doing that you need to write your medical information on the back side—such as emergency contact person, blood type, and the like. If something goes wrong during the race, the medical response people know to check the back of your number for information."

"Seems a bit serious."

"Well, marathons are serious business," she quipped.

I grabbed a pen and set my race number on the table, back side up, in plain view of the lady. I penned in my information.

Emergency Contact: Me
Contact Information: On the ground next to you
Blood type: Red
Allergies: Cauliflower, Tyrants, Rejection
Health Insurance: Karma and Luck

When I finished writing, I looked up at the lady. She'd been watching.

"Marathons aren't *that* serious," I said through a smile. As I walked away, she called out "Good luck," in a tone that struck me as overly concerned.

Outside in the starting area, I found a surprising cross-section of body types. I'd expected nearly all the participants to resemble the marathon runners in the Rockport commercial: scrawny, wiry people with the odd look of someone who regularly rides a unicycle. There certainly were some oddballs bouncing around, but the great majority of runners stretching and warming up looked like husbands and housewives, college students and mechanics. Even more surprising, the slightly rotund outnumbered the rail thin. Recreational runners, identified by older gear and nervous facial expressions, had at least a five to one advantage over serious runners.[12] The scene injected me with a dose of confidence, a sense of belonging.

I couldn't find Karl and John right away so I mimicked some of the other competitors and began stretching, something I never do except when trying to touch something just out of reach. Within minutes, the façade of stretching became unbearable, so I moved on to practicing my sprinter's start—getting down in a four-point stance, butt high in the air, then springing up and forward in a quick blur of energy. Over and over I practiced.

"What are you doing?" a man in his mid-fifties asked.

"Key to a good race is a good start. Just want to make sure I get out of the blocks strong."

He shot me a quizzical look but I gave no indication that I was screwing around.

"The marathon is about preparation, proper nutrition and pacing," he said. "You know that, right?" His voice was both hopeful and frightened.

"Boy, are you in for a long day," I replied condescendingly. I got down into a sprinter's stance and practiced one more start.[13]

---

[12] These numbers mirrored the Persian to Greek ratio at Marathon, a fact that thankfully turned out to be coincidental.

[13] The thought had occurred to me to go to the very front of the starting field and purposefully false start, firing out of my sprinter's stance a few seconds early, leaving all the other runners at the starting line waiting for the gun. In the 1996 Olympics, Linford Christie, the reigning Olympic champion at 100 meters, false started twice in the finals and was disqualified. I didn't how many times a person had to false start to get disqualified from a marathon (had it ever been an issue?), but if the other runners had looked more intimidating, I would have chickened out and false started over and over until officials pulled me out of the event.

About ten minutes before race time, Tierra showed up to wish me luck.

"Have you seen John and Karl?" I asked.

"They're back over by those trees," she said, pointing. "By the way," she added, "I wrote you a very important message and I'd like you to carry it all the way to the finish line." She handed me a carefully folded, miniature envelope. "Please don't read it until you cross the finish. Just put it in the little pocket you have in your shorts and let the anticipation carry you all the way." She grinned and gave me a quick kiss.

"Thanks," I answered, intrigued. I tucked the note into the small pocket inside my waistband. "I've got to go find those guys." I pecked her on the cheek. "See you at the finish."

When I found Karl and John, they were discussing pacing—the minutes per mile rate that they wanted to maintain over the course of the race. Only vaguely familiar with the concept, I listened intently, trying to keep up. The discussion had some pre-race significance, I learned, because runners had to line up for the race in areas that corresponded to their estimated pace. The section closest to the starting line was reserved for runners expecting to average a pace of seven minutes a mile or better. The section farthest from the start was for runners who expected to average over fourteen minutes per mile. This was the first marathon for all three of us, so we weren't really sure where we should start. After a short, unenthusiastic debate, we agreed to line up in the nine minute per mile section, mostly because that group contained the highest number of girls our age.

A large digital clock arched over the starting line and it counted down to the start of the race. Each tick augmented the tension. My nervous energy was increasingly anxious to convert to kinetic. Thirty seconds before the start of the race, people spontaneously began wishing everyone around them good luck, clapping, shaking hands, slapping high fives. A communal mood washed over the runners. Karl, John and I joined in, the three of us a portrait of congeniality. Five seconds before the start, an elderly lady in impressive shape patted my back.

"Good luck. Go get 'em!"

I turned over my right shoulder, looked her square in the eye and responded in a calm, serious voice. "I'm going to crush you." The lady shrank back into the crowd as the horn sounded to start the race, and we were off.

Why I said this to the lady, I don't know. Karl and John both hit me in disgust, but I could see, as the crowd shuffled forward, that they both were smiling, entertained by the sight a young man trash-talking a senior citizen. With four thousand people packed into the starting area, space limitations muted the enthusiastic surge of runners. We moved slowly, bumping and tripping along, but the pent up energy didn't lead to anarchy. The runners around us were kind and patient during the two minutes it took us just to get up to the starting line. My only discomfort came from knowing a chagrined old lady shuffled along directly behind me. Every time I thought of what I'd said to her, I released a muffled laugh, a sound eerily identical to the noise made when good karma abandons the body.

The first six miles went smoothly, the pace easy, and the density of the runners along the race route thinned. As the cluster of runners broke up, Karl, John and I settled in behind a stringy, tall girl in her mid-thirties. For the next ten miles, we panted lightly at her heels. Not in a lustful, luring way, mind you; our grunts resulted from the natural operation of our bodily exhaust systems. Yet despite the innocuous nature of our stalking, about thirty yards before we reached the 17 mile marker, the girl, without warning, issued a powerful, makeshift restraining order. She crapped her pants. Loudly.

The brown liquid raced down her legs. The smell zoomed to meet our nostrils. The three of us immediately slowed our pace and fell back.

"She could have just told us she had a boyfriend," I whispered to Karl and John.

As we fell back, the girl pushed on, extra baggage and all. She didn't break stride or act as if anything had happened. I can understand accidentally shitting your pants after running 17 miles, a body protesting the strain, but proceeding as if nothing had happened struck me as extremely strange. Was this part of her social arsenal? I imagined what her co-workers must deal with. *I'm not going to ask her to collate those copies. You know how she reacts when you ask her to do petty jobs!* I analyzed the girl from a safe distance and the only rational explanation that came to mind was a concept offered by Stephen King in his story, *The Long Walk.*

I read the story years earlier and the details had blurred, but like most of King's work, the title could have just as well been *Something Creepy Kills Everyone.* In general, *The Long Walk* is a story about a hundred men who enter into a competition that requires them to walk for as long as they can. The winner of the event is the last person walking. The 99 losers, those who either stopped walking or failed to maintain an established minimum pace, were killed as soon as they were eliminated. Despite the high probability of death, the race drew eager competitors because the winner of the event received pretty much anything he wanted. For a brief moment, watching the turd-girl trudge forward with unnatural determination, I feared I'd been transported into a Stephen King story. *Get beaten in this marathon by a girl that craps her pants,* I thought, *and you will be forced to read every Harlequin book ever published, and some of the ones that Harlequin rejected.* Facing that, I'd rather be killed by something creepy.

The turd-girl, still ahead of us, arrived at a bank of portable toilets. She stopped cold—though warm in some areas. Those waiting in line kindly let her cut ahead of them, something I didn't understand. If I were in line, I would have protested her request to go to the front of the queue. "Excuse me miss," I would have said, "you'll have to get in line. All of us *still* have to go."

We moved past the porta-potties and left the girl behind. Moments later we encountered the only significant hill along the entire route, the on-ramp to the St. John's Bridge. The hill is relatively short, but it's steep. As always, gravity brought its "A" game. We struggled up the hill toward the 18 mile marker, our controlled breathing turning into huffs and puffs. This was the first time I considered quitting. If I was certain Stephen King wouldn't appear out of the brush with a box of lazily written romance novellas, I probably would have given up. My legs had been holding up moderately well, but the hill sapped their resolve. By the time we reached the crest of the hill, the three of us looked at each other with concern.

"We'll make it," Karl said sternly. And that was that.

From mile 18 to 23, Karl methodically increased the pace. John and I struggled to keep up, our strides noticeably labored.

"Well look at that," John gasped a few minutes after we had passed mile marker 23.

"What?" Karl asked.

"That street sign." John pointed to a traditional green street sign standing on the corner of the approaching cross street. *Meyer St.*, it read. Meyer is John's last name.

"We are not stopping to steal it," I huffed.

"I don't plan on stealing it," John assured. "I'm going to lean on it. The race organizers must have known this is where I was going to stop and rest and they placed the sign here to remind me. I'll see you guys at the finish."

He stopped at the sign as if he'd hit a force field. He grinned and waved. Karl and I continued on. Karl striding comfortably, me struggling to keep up.

At the next aid station, in addition to the food and drinks handed out by the enthusiastic volunteers, a man offered runners a flat wooden stick, the kind a dentist uses, with a clump of Vaseline perched on the end.

"Vaseline! Who needs Vaseline?" he yelled.

"Who'd have thought we'd ever see a man offering strangers

Vaseline in public?" I asked Karl. I grabbed one of the sticks from the man, the chafing in my crotch screaming for attention.

"And who'd have thought you'd accept?" Karl replied.

I removed the Vaseline with my right hand and threw the stick on the ground. Without breaking my strained stride, I rubbed the lubricant all over my crotch, essentially the same act that ended Pee Wee Herman's career.

Just before mile 25, both my hamstrings began cramping. My legs stiffened. Karl instructed me to squeeze the cramping muscles to increase blood flow to the area. He also suggested that I take deeper, longer breaths to better oxygenate my blood. Our pace slowed. I worked to keep going, alternating attention from one hamstring to the other, squeezing the back of my legs, all the while trying to continue forward motion.

People began to pass us, but Karl wouldn't leave me, even when a pair of ladies in their fifties jogged by.

"Didn't train enough," one of the ladies said to her running companion.

I don't think she intended me to hear the remark. Never have truer words been spoken, but still, bitterness seeped in, filling me with renewed determination. I squeezed my hamstrings even harder, breathed even deeper. Within a couple minutes we were able to return to our previous pace. I drew on every last store of energy to move even faster, intent on catching the lady who'd commented on my lack of training. As we picked up speed we quickly reeled them in. As we passed, I casually looked over at the women and did my best to veil my agony.

"Actually ma'am," I said. "I didn't train at all."

At mile marker 26, I spit on the pavement, cursing the King of England for insisting on adding another 385 yards. As we closed in on the finish line, the crowd lining the street thickened. When we rounded the last corner, the people were stacked three and four deep along both sides of the road. I couldn't help but feel I was being watched. Less than fifty yards from the finish, I leaned over to thank my brother.

"Thanks so much. I couldn't have run it this slowly without you." Even in gratitude, brothers are required to insert a slight.

We crossed the line nearly shoulder to shoulder, Karl ahead by a fraction. Somehow the official race results listed that I had crossed the line first, by a full second, a point of contention for my brother to this day.[14]

Volunteers swarmed us as soon as we crossed the finish, offering water, congratulations and shiny, space-age looking blankets. I gulped a bottle of water and reached into my pocket and pulled out the note from Tierra. Several times during the race, in need of inspiration, I'd considered retrieving the letter and reading it. But as instructed, I'd held off. I unfolded the paper slowly, with an air of drama. The message was short, simple. Two small words surrounded by doodled happy faces.

"Don't die." I giggled, happy to be alive, basking in success.

A young boy appeared and interrupted my mental celebration. He was wearing a volunteer t-shirt and was eager to help.

"Sir," he said as he tugged at my shirt. "Sir, do you want another blanket?" He extended a glittering silver blanket toward me.

"Did you call me sir?" I asked in wonderment. I'd never been referred to in such a manner.

"Yes. My parents say I'm supposed to call adults 'sir.'"

I fell to my knees dramatically. After surviving 26.2 miles, I'd been felled by a child, a three-letter word his sword. *Sir!* The word echoed in my head. The boy had also referred to me as an adult, twisting the verbal blade. I rolled on the ground in anguish, dying a death far worse than the one endured by Pheidippides, the death adulthood brings, an affliction that callously keeps you alive.

"Sir! Sir!" the boy exclaimed, "Are you okay? Sir!"

---

[14] Our official times, 3:46:49 and 3:46:50. Maybe next time, brother.

clinging *to* anonymity

Battle Stations

By the corner of N.W. 18th and Pettygrove, I was concerned. My stomach had been bothering me for the last mile, but suddenly the mild annoyance had escalated into the red zone. The waves of a rollicking sea swashed in my belly. I held my breath and clenched my buttocks, hard, as if a group of aliens had tied me to a gurney as they discussed various probing options. But the sea rollicked harder.

Forty minutes earlier, nothing had been amiss. After eating a leftover chicken salad sandwich, I'd pulled on my running shoes, grabbed my iPod and headed out the door for a five mile run. It was Sunday afternoon, a perfect spring day.

The strain of nature's call was causing beads of sweat to populate my forehead. Still, I wasn't concerned. Home was only five blocks away, up on 23rd. I figured the pressure would soon subside and I'd be in the clear. But for the moment I was at a dead stop, in the middle of a residential neighborhood, unable to move, fighting a battle in which surrender wasn't an option.

I'd faced similar situations while exercising, but my previous gastrointestinal episodes had lasted no more than a minute before subsiding, at least temporarily. This time my runner's watch counted more than five minutes before any respite. When it arrived, I managed only three steps before I had to stop again. The nominal advance reminded me of World War I, when opposing armies, hunkered in their trenches, fought all day to capture a few yards of territory. This was serious.

Over the next twenty minutes I inched my way to the corner of 23rd and Quimby Street. I could see my front door, a mere thirty yards up the sidewalk to my left. During the agonizing, five-block journey I'd just survived, any time a pedestrian walked by I fidgeted with my iPod, took my pulse, acted as if I was stretching—anything to conceal the battle raging within. It took another ten minutes to advance fifteen yards. The steps leading up to my porch were only a couple feet away. At that point a stalemate ensued. Five minutes passed without me gaining a centimeter. Every bit of strength and focus was consumed with quelling my internal opponent.

I was stationed directly in the middle of the sidewalk, frozen like an uncomfortable statue. Seven people walked by over the next ten minutes—including two couples. They all stepped around me like I was a rude traffic cone. Too embarrassed to look up, I never saw their faces, and remember them now only as Nike, Nike, Adidas, no-brand, no-brand, boots and flip-flop. I finally attempted to take a step, but the slightest twitch of my hip nearly caused me to lose it. My leg snapped back reflexively and I clenched my butt cheeks so hard my back arched. About a half a block away a young family strolled down the sidewalk toward me. The couple was in their early thirties. Mom pushed a stroller. Dad held hands with his young son, lending balance to new legs.

They advanced slowly. I cringed at the thought of forcing them to steer the stroller around me. I had a decision to make, and not much time to make it. I looked up at my front door, and back at the approaching family. Thirty yards and closing. Twenty-five. I looked up at my door, then swiveled my head back again. The little boy, now walking independently, stumbled a bit. He grabbed his father's pants to right himself. Twenty yards. I decided to make a break. I slowly removed the key to the front door from my back pocket, and then in preparation, clenched my backside, hard, like taking a deep breath before a deep snorkeling dive. All I needed to do was cover thirty feet of ground. I could do it.

The gamble backfired, immediately. Before my foot landed to complete my first stride, the levy broke, filling the lining of my running shorts. By the end of my second step, the elastic in the lining gave way and the sludge spilled down my legs. I remained on task, never hesitating. Three strides from the front porch, another explosion, like I'd stepped on a land-mine. I never looked over at the family, but my sudden, panicked movement left no doubt that they'd witnessed the entire event.

I hustled up the steps and battled to unlock the front door. After getting inside, I went directly to the shower and got in without taking off my clothes. The cool water soaked my shorts and shirt, both destined for the trash. When I was thoroughly drenched, I removed my battle worn gear and washed out the filth. Even trash shouldn't be that dirty.

Standing in the shower with only my shoes on, I knew I'd look back and laugh someday. But I also knew that I'd always feel horrible about the debilitating impact the event must have had on that young toddler's potty training progress. I feared that after witnessing something so traumatic, the toddler might grow up to become the type who regularly defecates in public. Then I thought about the girl I encountered on my first marathon, and I wondered what she had seen as a child. It must have been dreadful.

A Cook Dies

"I'm sorry Chris. I am pretty sure he's dead."

Katie's tone was sorrowful, similar to the one an emergency room doctor uses to deliver bad news. She grasped my left hand and caressed my palm. The sincerity in her voice affected me more than her words. She seemed to have a mutant gland near her epiglottis that secreted generous amounts of tenderness onto every syllable. Even so, I couldn't pinpoint the feeling mushrooming within me, but it wasn't the emotional convulsions that typically accompany news of death.

As I stared into Katie's sullen eyes my mind scrambled to understand my mild reaction to her announcement. I'd met death before, and unless it was befalling someone in the process of mugging my mother, it proved invariably gloomy. Yet in the wake of Katie's words, I stood unaffected, as if immunized against death's devastation.

This was not the death I knew. This death had apparently enrolled in a comprehensive etiquette course, reforming its ways to become a compassionate, downright cordial death. *Hi! Death here. Sorry about all the senseless violence. That's in the past, I'm reformed!*

Here's a coupon for half-priced ice cream. Take care! Or maybe death was washed up as a villain, its emotional wallop finally giving way to the ravages of time. Regardless, Katie's message didn't extract tears. It made me giggle.[1]

* * *

On my deathbed, surrounded by loved ones, my labored wheezing going silent as I slip from this world to the next, I plan to use my last breath to eke out a final lament: *I should have spent more time at the office.*

While others work diligently, even desperately, to leave their mark, I am content to wait until the very end to establish my indelible greatness. By delaying my celebrity until the last possible moment, I've freed up a lifetime to focus on leisure.

After I die, some people will still proclaim, "No one on their deathbed has ever said 'I should have spent more time at the office.'"

"On the contrary!" the enlightened will correct. "There was one man. Hailed from Oregon, I believe. A fascinating, strapping gent. Made his money speculating on goat cheese futures. On his deathbed, he said exactly that!" My legend will grow. I'll become the benchmark for anyone striving to carve their own path. Pioneers in every field will hang charms around their necks that bear my likeness, same as travelers do with St. Christopher medals.

Though society continuously attempts to undercut my blueprint for prominence, soliciting me to strive for greatness without delay, coercing me with unbridled access to a variety of consumer goods, I stand firm. I ignore the blathering pleas urging me to tap my potential. Like the virgin awaiting marriage to

---

[1] Death is no laughing matter—it regularly appears in horror films for a reason—but I couldn't help myself.

copulate, I staunchly refrain. "Stop pressuring me!" I say. "I am not going to achieve greatness until death!"

But I am different from the committed virgin in more ways than my active attempt to have sex before marriage. The virgin's stance is centered on delayed gratification, a concept I wholly distrust since there is no guarantee I'll be around when the gratification arrives. My strategy is based on delayed greatness, a liberating concept that allows me to focus on gratification and avoid all the headaches that accompany greatness: heightened expectations, responsibility, unreasonable demands on my time, stress, a badgering media, paparazzi. I don't want these burdens. Postmortem greatness is my goal, an eternity of basking in peaceful celebrity six feet underground, where I'm safe from stubbing my famous toe and alerting fans to the reality of my fine-tuned mediocrity.

I struck upon the concept of delayed greatness while studying history at Stanford. History is rife with people who have lived impressive, fascinating lives. I relished learning the details of their daunting failures and glorious successes. But in the process I discovered a universal truth about historical figures: the masses don't remember them for their wonderful intricacies or their array of accomplishments. Rather, they become household names as a result of a single utterance or phrase. Few people know what John F. Kennedy actually did or believed in, but almost everyone knows he said, "Ask not what your country can do for you but what you can do for your country."

Kennedy's actual contributions and failures, and those of other historical figures, may percolate in the subconscious and enjoy indirect appreciation, but few people can attribute specific accomplishments to specific people. To have lasting historic appeal with the populace, all that's truly required is a single catchphrase or snappy slogan. Historical fame is a simple matter of Marketing 101—it's The Best a Man Can Get, Intel Inside and, yes Al Michaels, I do believe in miracles, particularly the miraculous possibility that I can achieve lasting fame without toil or risk.

Most historical figures obtained greatness by enduring unimaginable pain and grief, battling to overcome monumental obstacles to achieve an honorable goal. Some have gone so far as to die in order to secure name recognition. All these people could've forgone the hassle if they'd done a better job of marketing their famous taglines. For example, as the British placed a noose around his neck, Nathan Hale, a brave revolutionary patriot, said, "I only regret that I have but one life to give for my country." No one remembers Hale for his courageous exploits or for swinging from the gallows; it's the catchy statement he delivered right before dying that etched his name into history. If he'd marketed his cards right, Hale could've kept the fame *and* his neck—and probably made a bundle on the lecture circuit.

Patrick Henry, another famed patriot, stoked the flames of revolution at the 2nd Virginia Convention in 1775 by exclaiming, "Give me liberty or give me death," a statement that is singularly responsible for giving his name everlasting life. The fact that he continuously risked his neck standing up to British tyranny is lost on most people, a detail that his public relations team should have pointed out. And John Paul Jones, a U.S. naval pioneer whose adventures are largely forgotten, cemented his fame by declaring that he'd "not yet begun to fight"—and being of Scottish descent, all this meant was that he hadn't finished getting drunk.

Each of these famous figures could have stayed home and coined their famous phrases from a comfortable rocking chair on their front porch. A Manhattan marketing firm could've done the rest. Their hindsight is my insight.

Admittedly, my catchphrase to fame doesn't have the inspiring ring of these other historic quotes, but those men had the contextual advantage of war and revolution, fantastic fodder for memorable comments. Should I find myself in a sweeping historical movement, I will abort my *more-time-in-the-office* quote in favor of a rousing inspirational line. If I ever find myself facing death at the hands of the enemy, I'll take the opportunity to correct Benjamin Franklin's famous fallacy, "Nothing in life is certain except death and taxes."[2] To remedy his mistake for posterity, right before dying I'll proclaim, "Nothing in life is certain except death and comeuppance!" I'll then die famously, certain my executioners face imminent peril because, if nothing else, I've learned that comeuppance is not only certain, but often timely as well.[3]

Whatever my final words, in the end, when the doctor informs me of my malfunctioning heart, or immediately before the noose goes taut around my neck, I will not cry or worry. I will not beg or plead. Instead I'll utter words that will captivate imaginations and galvanize future generations. Then, as I pass into uncertainty, I'll let out a relaxed, contented giggle as greatness and I are introduced for the first time.

* * *

Death made a horrible first impression on me. I'd heard rumors of its heartlessness from a young age, but death exceeded its reputation. We were introduced through a fiendish attack on goodness, death's preferential prey. The Grim Reaper fancies the benevolent because they're too busy bettering the lives of others to see him coming.

Death did not send advance notice of its intention to trespass my life. There were no gunmen. No onrushing torrent of water. No airplane engine going silent in flight. Just me and my soccer uniform.

There's a moment in every boy's life when he is forced to become a man, or at least to attempt to. Ceremonies exist that

---

[2] Come on Ben, get a good accountant.

[3] On occasion, just for me, comeuppance has even displayed a willingness to launch pre-emptive attacks.

attempt to artificially pinpoint this moment—Catholic confirmation, Jewish bar mitzvahs, Native American vision quests—but these events are wholly symbolic. The actual journey from boy to adult occurs only when circumstances require. History has developed a core set of situations capable of triggering this metamorphosis: the government hands you a weapon and tells you that your country needs you to fight. Holding a firstborn. Leaving home to live on your own. Explaining to a younger sibling that he will never see his father again.

Three days earlier my father had been admitted to the hospital with what turned out to be a mild heart attack. When Carol, a family friend, picked me up for soccer practice, my younger brother, Kerry, had to come along because our mom had abruptly left for the hospital. Dad was being held for observation because he had endured previous heart troubles—a triple bypass six years earlier—but no real concern had hung over our home. If any anxiety existed, Mom disguised it well, convincing her children that the hospital stay was nothing more than a temporary inconvenience. The previous day, during a visit to the hospital, Dad's mood was jovial. Impressive looking medical machinery filled his room. Doctors roamed the halls. He was safe and well looked after. It was only a matter of time before he'd be discharged and return home to fill our lives with laughs and cheer.

When Carol later pulled me out of soccer practice and delivered the news, I grabbed Kerry by the hand and led him away toward a grove of trees. An accelerating maturity ran through me. I couldn't control my tears, but next to my trembling brother, I felt incredibly old. When we reached the grove, I sat Kerry down on a small bench and struggled to explain something I scarcely understood. He began to cry.

As I fought to contemplate the news, my subconscious took action. It is incredible how efficiently and fully a person can close an emotional valve for personal protection. Within hours of learning of my father's death, I'd choked off pain's lifeline.

The tears ceased, sadness retreated. It took no thought or conscious action, it just happened. Like the body's natural response to physical injury, my subconscious shut down certain emotional functions to save the whole. My ability to feel emotions—from pain to love—completely collapsed, leaving me with an emotional engine that didn't work. Though I was unaware this was occurring, I appreciated the result. In spite of all the grieving and sadness surrounding me in the days to come, I felt pretty good.

This odd, blissful existence lasted for nearly fifteen years. A couple aunts passed away, some distant relatives died. I cared for these people, but they weren't an integral part of my life. I reacted to each death, and for that matter, any emotional moment, with vague, fleeting curiosity, the type experienced when reading a newspaper article about a tragic event in a far off land. A friend crying about the loss of their grandmother touched me as deeply as a story decrying the inability of pandas to successfully mate in captivity. I couldn't differentiate the two.

* * *

Fifteen years later, it was death that returned to reclaim the comforting numbness that it had bestowed. When my dad passed away, my paternal grandfather filled the void. And when he died nearly fifteen years after my father, the dam in my subconscious crumbled. Pent up emotions gushed.

As I stood at the church lectern attempting to adequately eulogize my grandfather, looking out at the family and friends who provide meaning to my existence, I began to cry. For the first time since the day my father died, corralled pain spilled forth. My written notes, blurred by my streaming tears, were rendered useless. Seizing the opportunity, humiliation swooped in.

There exists a wide variety of ineloquence in the world, and incoherent blubbering is the worst. My gulps for air outnumbered intelligible words. As my emotions spun out of control,

I began spraying tears like a sprinkler. I hid behind the lectern, embarrassed, bridled by the distinct sense that my performance was making the attendees wish that they, too, were dead.

When the service ended I headed straight for the exit, but a determined horde of family and friends blocked the way. I braced for abuse, half-expecting the crowd to shackle me to a tree and stone my life away. Instead of condemnation, my relatives and family, quite inexplicably, showered praise. "Beautiful!" "Amazing!" "Heartwarming!"

I found the unjustified praise amusing, no different from hearing a young mother exalt her newborn for pooping his pants. *Oh you did so good, making messy in your pantsies.* I felt like a diapered baby—I'd just crapped out a eulogy and was now the recipient of unjustified cooing. But as funeral goers continued to approach and offer misguided commendations, embarrassment became courage. With each word, each teardrop, I had the urge to herd everyone back into the church. If they were prepared to praise crap, I could deliver it in spades.

I'm capable of extracting pride out of the oddest circumstances, yet their exaltations failed to augment my ego. The reality of my performance wouldn't allow it. Standing outside our country church, mourning the loss of my grandfather, I realized that it was the display of heartfelt emotion that'd delivered me from embarrassment. The words were of nominal importance.

Few moments in life are powerful enough to initiate a life-altering transition. The day of my grandpa's funeral was a wake-up call, alerting me to feelings I'd unwittingly repressed. From the day my father died, I'd subconsciously employed joviality like porcupine quills, a protective coat of jest to prevent the recurrence of deep despair. As the dark clouds above the church opened, scattering people toward their cars with a deluge of rain, I took off on a different journey. As others sought protection from the elements, I embarked on a crusade to remove a layer of protection that had hindered my life for too long. This fresh path soon led to a new perception, and eventually evolved into a new understanding, a new life, one where I was able to distinguish between fertility-challenged pandas and human heartache.

Right after the funeral I began the arduous process of coexisting with my emotions. I spent the following weeks and months dusting off feelings I had last used during Reagan's first term. In the early stages of my emotional rehabilitation, the biggest challenge was trying to calibrate the proper balance between expressing emotions and controlling them. During this experimental period, I often floundered. A few months after my grandfather died, during a blind date, I told a girl that I loved her before appetizers arrived. Later that same night, I wept in her presence while listening to a Lionel Richie song. But I got better.[4]

When I met Katie, my grandpa had been dead for almost three years. By then I'd worked out most of my emotional kinks. I took great pride in my progress. I no longer feared emotional pain, I dealt with it. I didn't shun love, I embraced it. I no longer cried when I heard a Lionel Richie song, I threw the radio across the room. That's what made my reaction to Katie's announcement frightening. I didn't feel sad or sentimental. No hint of emotional turbulence. In the face of death I felt nothing. I feared I was having a relapse, joviality quills sprouting anew to guard against feelings that I no longer thought I feared.

Standing next to Katie, her death announcement hanging in the air, I searched for an answer. Then, in a flash, a revelation delivered relief. I was not suffering a relapse. I wasn't laughing for protection, or because I couldn't deal with death. Instead, I realized Katie's mutant gland, the one so full of tenderness, also secreted generous amounts of stupidity. I didn't respond to the news with compassion or sadness because her comment, though innocent, was absurdly dim-witted.

* * *

---

[4] The six girls who I have subsequently dated dispute this assertion.

I met Katie toward the end of a long night in a Melbourne bar. I'd traveled to Australia to play baseball for the Williamstown Wolves, a small club team located just outside Melbourne proper. Baseball isn't a top tier sport in Australia, or a second tier one for that matter, but the chance to travel Down Under to play professional baseball was too enticing to pass up.[5]

Prior to traveling to Australia, I was trapped behind a lovely mahogany desk in a plush corporate office in Santa Clara, California. When the opportunity to go to Australia was presented by an old acquaintance, I ran the numbers—twice—and calculated that leaving my corporate lawyer gig for the sunny skies of Melbourne would require me to take a 99.3% pay cut. I wrestled with this financial fact for nearly thirty seconds before my desire for freedom pinned my checkbook to the mat. Minutes later, I walked into my boss's office, gave notice and returned to my computer to book a flight to Melbourne. When the time came to leave, I missed my flight on three consecutive days, a cycle of ineptness driven by excessive celebration and mind-splitting headaches. Then, with the help of a couple close friends who didn't want to face murderous hangover number four, I finally boarded a plane to Australia.

I'd been in Melbourne for a couple weeks when my hosts, James and Cameron, brought me to a local bar to witness a celebration being held by the members of an Aussie rules football club. The fact that the players were merely celebrating the completion of a Thursday afternoon practice didn't dilute their commitment to the task. The group, clad in matching, soiled rugby shirts, filled the bar with a continuous, pulsating roar. Countless pints of Victoria Bitter were consumed. The players chugged their drinks aggressively, gulping down beer as if exacting some sort of vengeance.

---

[5] "Professional" is used here in the most basic sense of the word, meaning the receipt of compensation, no matter how nominal, in return for services rendered. I was paid three cold beers per game—four if I played well.

Soon after we walked into the bar James led me to a table surrounded by rugby shirts. We pulled up some chairs and James attended to introductions. When the players learned that I'd never seen an Aussie rules football game, they described the brutality of the sport with great joy.

"No tougher game exists!" a meaty member of the team insisted.

"Well...in Australia," I added.

Another player put down his beer. "What do you mean by that?"

"Aussie rules is the toughest sport played in Australia, that's all I mean."

Faces around the table contorted. Their looks of dismay reminded me of my brother Kerry's expression when he unwrapped the Easy Bake Oven I'd given him for his birthday. Unlike Kerry, these guys weren't secretly thrilled inside.

"What do you mean 'in Australia?'" another player demanded. Before I could reply, he continued. "Unless you have a game in the States that I haven't heard of, one played with sledgehammers and alligators, then you Americans don't have a sport nearly as tough as Aussie rules football!"

"What about American football?" I asked matter-of-factly.

Dozens of eyes, reddened by alcohol, peered at me in disbelief.

"American footballers wear pads and helmets!" one brute reminded me.

"The way American footballers tackle is an acceptable means of greeting friends in Australia," another screamed.

In the eye of a drunken storm, I took a deep breath and calmly explained my viewpoint. "American players are so big, strong and fast that they have to wear pads to prevent death on impact. You guys should be thankful you're small, weak and slow. Helmets and pads are expensive."

My analysis didn't curry favor. Before I could amend or retract it, three of the players grabbed me and pulled me toward the large open area in the center of the bar. In typical belated fashion, while being dragged across the floor, I remembered that inciting ire typically ends poorly for me.

When the players hauled me to a stop they informed me that I was going to get a first-hand glimpse at the brutality of Aussie football. Despite my clear, unmistakable objections, I was told I'd be participating in a makeshift "bounce-up," the method used to restart an Aussie football game after a dead ball. It is similar to a hockey face-off, where two men (or in this case, one man and me) stand face to face with an umpire (or, in this case, a drunken brute) who drops the ball between them. When the ball is dropped, a fight for possession ensues.

One of the brutes gave vague instructions as to what I could expect. An even bigger brute stepped up to participate in the bounce-up. I looked directly at him, trying to display a quiet confidence. He glared back, mouth bubbling with adrenaline, his disposition fueled by intense inebriation. In a show of ridiculous overkill, while one of his mates ran out to their car to get a ball, he gnashed his teeth. Tables in the vicinity were cleared away to protect them from splatters of American blood. Curious bar patrons joined the team members who had encircled us. As the crowd chatter escalated, I gazed at the guy who would soon be responsible for my death.

He spat on the floor with vigor. "You're about to know what it is to be a man," he warned.

If I was going to die, I wanted it to be quick. "Oh, apparently you haven't spoken to your sister," I said. "She taught me all about that last night. Is your whole family into teaching?" The crowd let out a loud shriek. The brute shook his head disbelievingly, maybe disappointed that he was going to spend the next twenty years in an Australian prison for beating the life out of a wiseass American.

His teammate returned with an oblong football in his hand. "Let's get this thing going!" he shouted.

"By the way," I yelled. I waited for a relative hush to come to the crowd, then continued. "I wish I would have spent more time at the office."

The ball dropped, my opponent charged and I closed my eyes. My back slammed hard onto the bar floor. The brute, quickly on top of me, threw a few forearm shivers to my chest before bouncing up to retrieve the ball. He scooped up the football and quickly returned to tower over my prone body.

"You guys should wear pads," I advised.

"Your turn to buy a round," he said. He smiled and held out his hand to help me up.

I dusted myself off and headed to the bar.

That's when I saw her. Graceful. Adorable. Dispensing beer with purpose. A perfect, playful smile adorning her face. Her astonishing beauty, by itself, could serve as a company's entire employee-retention program. *I don't care about the dreadful working conditions—as long as she works here, I'm staying!* Her name, Megan, was printed on the homemade button pinned to her simple blouse. I was in love.

"What can I get you," she asked.

"Three children and a life together," I replied.

"Let's start with a drink order."

"I'd like ten beers."

"American, are you?" Megan asked.

Her reply revealed one of the primary reasons I adore Australian girls: the American anti-accent is enough to gain their sincere interest.

"Well yes, I'm from America," I responded, capitalizing on the novelty.

"And you need ten beers?" she asked. "Thirsty I take it?"

"I just have a bit of a dry throat, that's all."

She smiled. I wanted to marry her. What would we name our children? Could the novelty of an anti-accent sustain her interest for fifty or sixty years? I'd never experienced love at first sight. I liked it.

I frantically searched for something else to say, preferring a clever quip, but I was willing to settle for a sound, any sound, to prolong the interaction. She placed two large serving trays on the bar and began filling pint glasses with Victoria Bitter. As the frosty mugs filled, the thick condensation on the glasses faded. I watched Megan closely and prayed for divinity to place interesting words in my mouth. Like the first runner of a relay, my anti-accent had gotten things started. Now the conversational baton had been passed to my brain, and it was off to a stumbling start.

"Twenty dollars," Megan requested cheerily, awakening me from a trance of nervous pining.

"Can I use that towel?" I asked, pointing to the first thing behind the bar that caught my eye.

She turned gracefully, grabbed the towel and tossed it to me.

"Can I please get a glass of water, too?" I asked.

She snatched an empty pint glass from under the counter, packed it with ice and filled it with water.

"Thanks so much!" I said in my best I-want-to-share-the-rest-of-my-life-with-you voice. I handed her a red Australian twenty dollar bill, along with a five dollar note for a tip. As she turned to put the money in the register, I grabbed the glass of water and poured most of it onto the bar. Then I splashed the rest on my shirt.

"Shit!" I squealed in my best I-have-fairly-decent-earning-potential tone.

The water spread slowly along the bar top. Just before it trickled over the edge and onto the floor, I contained it with the towel. Then I went to work on eradicating the rest of the liquid mess. After cleaning up the spill, I dabbed my shirt. As I dried off, I looked up at Megan and flashed a look of embarrassment.

Suspicion pulled her eyebrows upward. She glowed with distrust. The American novelty was fading.

"I should have known this was going to happen," I lamented. "The second I asked for the towel, I knew something was amiss. You see, I get premonitions all the time. Unfortunately the premonitions are never crystal clear, but rather come to me as vague hints. I asked for the towel because I sensed that I'd need it; but I wasn't certain why I'd need it. Then, sure enough, I spilled the water."

"That's the worst line I've ever heard," Megan responded.

"Don't believe me?" I asked firmly. I placed my hand to my forehead as if deep in thought and waited a brief moment. "Hand me a phonebook," I demanded as I dropped my hand to my side. "I need to call a restaurant to make a dinner reservation for two. I don't quite know why I need the reservations, but by the end of the night I think we'll both know." I grinned hopefully.

Megan rolled her eyes, but in a way that suggested she found my pathetic attempt to woo her a tad appealing—or in a way that said, *I could really use the extra tip money, so I'll play along and act mildly interested until I bilk this American for every dollar he has.*

Encouraged, I left another five dollar Aussie note on the counter, increasing the tip to an amount I gauged was just short of a bribe. I picked up one of the trays of beer and returned to the table. After dropping off the first tray, I went back for the second. At the bar, before grabbing the second tray of beer, I left another five dollar bill on the counter. If I had to bribe, I would.

"Thanks for keeping an eye on my beer for me," I yelled over to Megan, who wasn't paying any attention.

Over the next couple hours, I visited the bar several times, buying beer, stealing glances.

Around three in the morning, one of the other bartenders yelled, "Last call," Australian code for "Panic!" Patrons flocked to the bar. I knew Megan would be penned in for a while, so I searched out James and Cameron, both of whom had relocated to a different table by the front door. They were sitting with four girls I'd never met before.

James struggled with the introductions. "I'd like you to meet..." he started. He paused and glanced around the table, the universal mayday call for forgotten names. After an uncomfortable silence, one of the girls caught on.

"I'm Katie," she offered sheepishly. "Are you the American these guys have been talking about?"

"I'm an American. Whether or not I'm the American these guys were talking about, I'm not sure."

"Are you living with them?" Katie asked.

"Yes."

"Then you must be the American they were talking about." She sounded proud to have solved the mystery.

"How do you know there aren't other Americans living with them?" I asked, wanting her to earn the satisfaction.

Katie looked at James quizzically. "Are there?" she asked.

James shook his head, indicating that I was the only American sleeping on his couch, and the look of satisfaction returned to Katie's face. The other girls introduced themselves quickly, their names now residing in the inaccessible part of my mind that houses the Pythagorean Theorem and silverware etiquette.

At any other moment in my life I would've been taken aback by Katie's perfect features, her soothing voice. But my throbbing fascination with Megan dampened my reaction. I made small talk with the table, frequently glancing over at the bar. It took about fifteen minutes for the last-call crowd to dissipate. When Megan emerged from behind the fading curtain of people, I excused myself from the table. I stood up, emboldened by beer, ready to solidify my future with Megan. Katie interrupted my departure.

"Chris," she said, "I'd love to go out some time, learn a little more about America. I want to travel there sometime soon."

I barely comprehended what she said. My mind was busy mulling a future as a married man.

"Sure, that would be fun," I offered without giving much thought to it.

Katie grabbed a pen from her purse, scribbled her number on a napkin and handed it to me. I shoved the napkin in my pocket, said goodbye, and began to walk toward the bar.

"Call me tomorrow and we'll work it out," Katie added as I

departed, her vocal cadence typical of Australian females, the last syllable spoken three octaves higher than the rest.

I walked to the bar with heightened confidence. I had the phone number of one stunning girl in my pocket and was walking toward the girl of my dreams. The moment marked the most self-assured instant in my life. I felt desirable and invincible. I slowed my gait, taking a brief moment to enjoy a private coronation. I was King of the World. The memories of long, maddening droughts with the opposite sex were summarily dismissed. Energized by my monarchial might, I sauntered on, confident I'd sweep Megan off her feet.

"Well Megan, how'd your night go?" I asked as I arrived at the bar.

"Fine. And yours?"

"Great! I'm Chris by the way." I extended my hand and she shook it softly. "I have to get going pretty soon, my friends are ready to leave." I motioned with my head back toward the table where Cameron and James were sitting. "Is there any chance I could get your phone number?"

"Sure," she responded without blinking. "Would you like me to write it on the same napkin that that other girl used, or would it be more convenient if I wrote in on a separate slip of paper?"

She didn't speak the words cruelly or cross. Her tone actually had a hint of disappointment. She turned away and returned to work, cleaning up behind the bar.

My kingly confidence crashed to the ground, dethroned by the unthinking acceptance of a napkin with a girl's name and phone number scrawled on it. My short reign had been guillotined.

Unwilling to abrogate the throne without a fight, I protested. "Wait a minute! You've got me all wrong. Get to know me and you'll see I'm not like that. Not at all!"

Megan turned to look at me. "Sorry, but I'm not interested in some American playboy."

A quandary. The girl of my dreams was accusing me of being

exactly what I'd always wanted to be, but she coupled the flattering accusation with rejection. Part of me wanted to accept Megan's words as gospel, to walk away from the bar and move forward with my life, not as a king, but as a Casanova. But a single glance at her, and the rigid reality that I could never be a playboy, resolved the issue.

Desperate to change her mind, I resorted to my standard pick up line. "Please! Please!" I begged.

She rolled her eyes.

"How about giving me part of your phone number—say four or five digits," I pleaded, "and I'll just dial every possible combination until I get it right. That will show my dedication!"

She smiled briefly, not harshly, and again returned to work. I shrank back into my shell and sulked away like a distraught tortoise.

Fate, clearly, is not infallible. During the next ten days I gave fate several chances to make amends, to redress its gaffe. I returned to the bar four separate times, hoping to repair the damage. Megan was never there when I stopped by. Not once.

* * *

After almost two weeks of frustration trying to track down Megan, I figured it was possible fate actually *did* know what it was doing. Maybe fate had orchestrated the entire Megan debacle in order to set the stage for sweet redemption. This is a common gimmick fate uses; it frustrates people by dangling enticing opportunities just out of reach, but then, eventually, it guides us to an even better end. Hopeful, I picked up the phone and dialed Katie's number.

Katie's dad answered the phone. He was busy with a call on the other line but promised to have Katie ring me right back. The conversation was brief but the man sounded overanxious, almost desperate, like a father concerned about his daughter's dating prospects. "She *will* call you back shortly!" he insisted.

Katie possessed a stunning beauty, the singular trait that assures male pursuit, so I couldn't imagine that she had any shortage of suitors, debatable intentions aside. The hint of salesmanship in her father's voice raised an alarm, suggesting that some lurking secret overshadowed Katie's physical appeal. Possibly he just wanted to get her married off so he could finally convert her bedroom into a reading den, but it was just as plausible that Katie commonly sacrificed puppies to appease her cult leader. In spite of my concern, justified or not, I knew I had to go out with Katie at least once. I owed fate the opportunity. Plus, debatable intentions being what they are, Katie was hot.

Ten minutes later the phone rang. I figured it was Katie calling back—possibly under threat from her father—so I patiently waited until after the third ring to grab the receiver, my way of playing hard to get.

"Hello, this is Chris," I answered.

"Hi there!" Katie exclaimed with refreshing energy.

After several minutes of awkward conversation, we agreed to meet later that day in Melbourne to walk around town and grab some dinner. We were both reliant on public transit so we decided to meet at the Flinders Street Station, a major downtown train stop. I'd been in Australia less than a month and wasn't really comfortable with the train schedules and proper transfer points, so I decided to depart early to allow for mishaps.

My trip downtown went smoothly. I made the proper train connection and arrived at Flinders Street nearly an hour early. I used the time to explore the station, stopping occasionally to enjoy the bustle of the ever-changing crowd. Fifteen minutes before I was scheduled to meet Katie, I made my way to the main entrance of the station, the area we'd agreed to meet. Outside the entrance there were about a dozen guys, none older than twenty, who were milling about on the cement steps. They were heavily inebriated and playfully roused pedestrians. The scene resembled an Aussie rules football club celebrating the completion of a Thursday night practice, sans matching rugby shirts.

One of the drunken boys was louder and more animated than the others, stumbling around shirtless to the amusement of his companions. He appeared to be a native Pacific Islander and he spouted gibberish at anyone who came near. His tone was friendly, but his haphazard horseplay was dangerous. The Islander bounded about wildly, as if a drunken puppeteer was controlling his body. His drooping eyelids foreshadowed the end of his bountiful energy and the pending arrival of a deep slumber.

Triggered by an impetus only the Islander could perceive, he started running up and down the stairs that lead from the station to the street, covering two or three steps at a time. Up and down he ran, maneuvering uneasily but with great passion. His friends cheered. Caught up in the clamor, I joined the howls of encouragement. The sound of my American anti-accent stopped the Islander in his wobbly tracks, as if my voice were a lasso. He came to an uneasy halt and took an extended moment to gather his balance. When he regained some control, he shakily turned and faced me. I flashed a nervous smile.

"You're doing great!" I yelled.

Playing to the continuing chants from his friends, the Islander jumped in place deliriously, occasionally pointing up in my direction. The audience yelled louder, encouraging him to do…something. The drunken kid dropped his right hand to the ground and ducked his head as if preparing to charge. The crowd's hollering came to a crescendo. I felt as if I should've been wearing a tight-fitting sequined outfit and waving a blood-red cape. Tension was high.

Suddenly, like a possessed bull, the Islander exploded up the stairs in my direction, arms flailing madly, eyes on the ground. I held my position, more confused than fearless. The closer he came, the more he veered off course. Like a seasoned bullfighter, I stepped to the side as he barreled forward. When the Islander got to the top step, his feet continued searching for stairs that were no longer there. His body careened forward, past me.

I tracked his course, curious as to where momentum would deposit his body. His stumble turned into a collapse just as Katie emerged from inside the station. She let out a startled yip as the drunk kid fell past her—his mission, and likely his day, coming to a climactic end on the tiled station floor.

I ran up to Katie. "Are you all right?" I asked, more out of courtesy than concern.

"Yes," she said softly without conviction. "What was that all about?"

"That's my brother," I replied, motioning to the drunk. "I hope you don't mind, I invited him to join us tonight."

"That's your brother?" Katie asked. "Really?"

I flashed a mischievous smile.

"That's really your brother?" she asked again.

This time I gave her a quizzical look, waiting for her to break into a laugh or give some other coy confirmation that she was being facetious. But her face continued to question me, waiting for an answer.

"That's not my brother," I assured. "I was kidding."

She looked at me with odd bewilderment. "Oh...you were kidding."

Though she couldn't register blatant sarcasm, Katie looked like a Vogue cover. She was dressed in a flowery summer dress that stopped mid-thigh. The material happily relaxed on her subtle curves. I grabbed her hand and led her away, anxious to see if we could forge a connection.

We headed toward the Melbourne Casino. Located along the Yarra River that slices through downtown, the casino area is filled with trendy restaurants and an active nightlife. Katie floated down the sidewalk with breathtaking grace. I'd never before appreciated a girl's grace independent of her appearance, but with Katie I did. She walked perfectly, casually. I stopped to fiddle with my shoelace just to watch her slow down, come to a stop and turn back toward me. Her countless physical attributes demanded attention, but my admiration honed on her elegance. Grace, I discovered, is magnetic.

Unfortunately, grace can't prevent a conversation from lagging. Katie greeted my attempts at humor with perplexity. Unrehearsed jokes and off the cuff quips gasped their final breath right before they entered her ears. Tangential comments were completely off limits, which left a straight and claustrophobically narrow lane for discussion. Bouts of silence dominated our walk.

"Where would you like to eat?" I asked as we neared the restaurant district, thankful for a straightforward subject.

"Doesn't matter to me," Katie answered.

Unfamiliar with the area or its restaurants, I pointed to the first place I saw.

"The Fox Grill looks good," I offered, pointing toward a restaurant just down the street.

"No," Katie quickly replied, "let's try something else."

Katie's quick reply supported a general theory I'd been postulating for years: every woman, tracing back to Eve, is genetically predisposed to manipulate men. I'm not necessarily talking about devious manipulation. The majority of girls use subtle methods to achieve premeditated goals. Thousands of years of genetic mutations and societal shifts have varied the specific manipulation tactics used by the opposite sex, but similarities in the foundational approach remain. Analogously, dietary differences populate the planet but everyone still puts food down the same hole. Setting aside the differences in the details, it is scientifically unassailable that all women, at some level, are compelled to try and guide men to the *right* answer, even if that answer is wrong, or exorbitantly expensive.

Katie's courteous rejection of my Fox Grill suggestion indicated that she had the mild manipulation gene, the one in which the female attempts to fool the male into thinking that he's a vital component in the decision making process. This approach allows the girl to get her way while allowing the male to think he's not being controlled. In theory, this keeps everyone happy, particularly the girl.

The gentle form of manipulation starts with the female feigning indifference about plans, such as which restaurant or movie she'd like to go to. "Anything but Mexican food is fine with me," she might say. Or, "I'll go to any movie as long as we get popcorn!"

Katie executed stage one of the manipulation by telling me that she didn't care where we ate. Like most heterosexual males, I responded to Katie's indecision by suggesting a random course of action.

"How about that one?" I asked, pointing to an eatery a half block past the Fox Grill.

"Is that even a restaurant?" Katie asked.

This is how the subtle form of female manipulation unfolds. Girls, for some mystifying reason, commonly refuse to inform males what they truly want, preferring that the male continues guessing until he chances upon the right answer. And make no mistake, the girl has a right answer in mind. From the moment Katie and I made plans to meet, I suspect she knew exactly where she wanted to dine. As it turns out, the Fox Grill and the other eatery I suggested weren't in her confidential plans. This cycle of suggestion and rejection would continue until I came across the answer Katie was looking for.

After Katie turned down two more of my suggestions, I pointed to a restaurant named Roxie's. "How about that one?" I suggested.

"Perfect!" Katie replied, thankful that I'd finally named the restaurant that she had her heart set on.

The magnificent aspect of mild manipulation is that it gives the man the thinly veiled impression that he has something to do with a decision. In truth, the male's only role is to rattle off suggestions or, more accurately, guesses. This process works for movie selections, hiking destinations, vacations—about any decision a couple might face. Females who lack patience often employ a more aggressive tactic to accelerate the process. After the male makes one or two failed guesses, an impatient girl will simply provide the right answer in the form of a question. "What do you think of Roxie's?" they might ask. This avoids a lengthy guessing ordeal, but it deprives the male of the perception that his opinion matters. I prefer girls who wait until I guess the right answer, and Katie's patience reinvigorated my effort to find conversational common ground.

From the moment we were seated at Roxie's, however, silence enveloped the table. Silence isn't conducive to eye contact, so my gaze roamed the restaurant, searching for a topic to discuss. I shared my fascination with the restaurant's potted shrubberies and lauded the shine of the floor, but the comments didn't spark any lasting dialogue. Katie would nod, shrug, and the silence would resume.

Was I really this inept at talking to girls? My paranoia grew with each passing moment, and it led to boredom-induced hallucinations. Satan appeared over the table with a movie camera, filming my dating calamity. Images of the unfolding disaster were pumped via satellite to several large televisions lining the deepest chasms of hell. Millions of damned souls, forced to stare at my discomfort, wailed in horror. Pangs of agony from the netherworld echoed in my head. Unlike the damned, I muffled my pain. I sat stoically in the air-conditioned coolness, absorbing the sweltering silence.

After I finished my meal, and while waiting for Katie to finish hers, I broke another long bout of silence with a random personal fact. "I got seventeen rabies shots when I was five years old, a shot a day for seventeen days, several of them right in my butt."

Katie scrunched her face but didn't otherwise respond. The information lacked context, but its sheer randomness deserved an opinion or inquiry.

"Are you having a good time?" I asked.

"Definitely!" she said, covering her food-filled mouth.

Were we sitting at the same table? Another stretch of silence followed. I used the time to assess the situation. In the process of pondering the best way to bridge our conversational gap, I unearthed a social constant: when you no longer care whether your words impress, there is always plenty to say. I resurrected my rabies story, interesting or not.

"Well, I got the rabies shots after playing with a litter of kittens."

Katie showed no detectable interest, but I continued, detailing the unsubstantiated rumors that the kittens had rabies and how, by playing with the tiny creatures, I'd fallen under suspicion as well.

"So," I continued, "a couple days after playing with the kittens, despite an astounding lack of evidence, I was convicted and sentenced to seventeen rabies shots. Can you believe that?"

Katie didn't seem to care, and I didn't care that she didn't. Tired of the uncomfortable silence, I continued.

"The needles they used were as long as my arm and as thick as my finger! For seventeen straight days, a nurse—who had a huge nose with a couple of warts on it, like a witch—plunged that massive syringe into me! And you know what the nurse told me? Guess. Just guess!"

"I have no idea," Katie answered.

"Better safe than sorry. That's what she said every time she plunged the needle into me. Can you believe that? I've been afraid of safety ever since."

Katie remained indifferent, distant.

"How you doing?" I asked.

"Great!" she assured. Her reply didn't really matter. I was going to continue with the story even if she would've broken into tears.

"The one thing that helped me persevere through the rabies ordeal," I continued, "was the joy I reaped from the hyena-like howls emanating from my brother, Karl, and sister, Katrina, as they received their shots. Every one of their cries of pain filled me with pride. You see, it was my false testimony that got them convicted. When I found out that I had to get seventeen shots for petting kittens in the park, I told my parents that Karl and Katrina had touched them, too. In truth, they were playing Frisbee with some friends and never had come within ten feet of those kittens. I framed them with nothing more than a point of my finger and a lie. Each time that needle penetrated my skin, the pain was eased by knowing that they were next."

"What color were the kittens?" Katie asked.

"Black."

"I like kittens," she added.

When dinner ended, Satan and his camera crew slinked away to the relative comfort of hell. I paid the bill and Katie and I walked out into the warm night.

"Thanks for dinner," Katie said sincerely.

"You're welcome."

"Do you still want to go to the Rialto Towers?" she asked.

"Sure. I'm up for it," I said.

During our phone call we'd discussed going to the Towers. The two matching skyscrapers are the tallest buildings in Melbourne. James had told me that the observation deck at the top of one of the towers provided a 360-degree view of the city, and he suggested the vista would help me get a feel for Melbourne. Katie had lived in the area all her life, but she had never been to the Towers' observation deck. She was eager to go.

During the walk, Katie and I continued to struggle to make a connection. By the time we arrived at the Towers I'd abandoned any hope of kindling a conversation. Once inside, I briskly walked to the elevator and pushed the call button, anxious to get moving.

I've always loved elevators. They're filled with drama and surprise, especially in tall buildings where the chance for multiple stops during a single journey is statistically enhanced. An invigorating anticipation mounts in me during the short time between an elevator stopping and its doors sliding open. *Who will be on the other side? Who is getting on? Who is getting off?* Every stop is like a Christmas present, the doors mechanically unveiling the gift.

My elevator wish-list never varies. All I want is a smiling person. That's it. My needs and wants aren't great. If the person happens to be female, young and attractive, that's gravy. Sometimes you get what you dream of; other times the elevator delivers something you don't remotely want, like the rude, gruff person who gets on at floor nine. He's the type of gift that most people want to return. He smells like smoke and complains about discrimination against the nicotine-addicted. If luck is on your side, this person will get off the elevator before you do, something I consider a re-gift *(Sorry floor fourteen, he's yours now!)*. Fittingly, while Katie and I rode up to the observation deck, the elevator didn't stop a single time. Our date was Christmas without gifts—Katie was beautifully decorated but something significant was missing.

The view from the observation deck was stunning. Daylight was fading and the city's lights were blinking to life. As we made our way around the circular viewing platform, I fired questions at Katie, sincerely interested in the city where she grew up.

"What is that building?" I asked.

Katie scrunched her face, unable to provide an answer.

I pointed down to the glimmering casino area. "Is that the area where we ate dinner?"

"Maybe," Katie answered. "Sure is a beautiful view."

"Sure is. What direction is your house?"

"I'm all turned around," Katie answered. "I really can't tell."

She knew less about the city than I did—and I hardly knew anything. During our circumnavigation of the observation deck, she was unable to identify a single building or landmark. It didn't seem to bother her, but I grew impatient.

"Is that the Melbourne Cricket Grounds?" I offered, placing the answer in her mouth just like an impatient female.

"I think it is, but I am not sure."

I considered placing a hand on the front of her dress and asking, "Is this your breast?" Concerned how Katie might react to uninvited groping, I opted for a different easy question.

"Is that a park down there?" I asked, pointing at a vast area of greenery sliced up by serpentine trails.

"Yes!" Katie answered excitedly, her eyes lighting up. "That is a big park!"

I gave a congratulatory headshake. Katie, encouraged by her success, continued.

"We took a field trip there when I was young. Captain Cook's house is there. He was a famous explorer who discovered Australia. He liked it here so much that he stayed, and he had his entire house brought to Australia from England. They rebuilt his house in that park!"

"So they tore down his house back in England and shipped it here?"

"Brick by brick. They re-built it just the same as it was before—and it's right down there."

"Captain Cook is quite famous," I offered. "I'd love to meet him. We should go down and knock on his door to say hello."

I smiled softly. Katie moved her eyes to meet mine. She grasped my left hand, the one I should have placed on her breast.

"I'm sorry Chris," she said. "I am pretty sure he's dead."

The trip down the elevator was quick, present-less. When we exited the Towers, I turned toward Flinders Street Station, ready to catch the train home.

The short walk to the train station went quickly, quietly. Within minutes of arriving at the station, Katie's train pulled in. We said brief goodbyes and hugged. I watched her stroll off. She was exquisite. Watching her walk away made me long for adolescence, a time when intellectual connections and emotional chemistry scarcely matter, a period of life when strategically placed friction is enough to sustain a relationship. Age and maturation clutter up the simple dating puzzle, adding an assortment of complicated, non-anatomical pieces.

Once Katie made it safely onto her train, I walked over to my boarding area to wait. Captain Cook sailed across my mind and I laughed out loud. I thought of Megan. I cursed fate, but realized I had no realistic alternative; if left to my own devices, I'd certainly muck things up far worse. I have plenty of other things to concentrate on anyway, like future greatness. The world is full of office spaces of all shapes and sizes, and I have to be careful to avoid all of them so that when death arrives to claim me, I'll be able to make my final lament sincere and meaningful. Powerful enough to secure an eternity of greatness.[6]

End Notes:
1. When ideas and thoughts attempt to cross my mind, they commonly run out of provisions somewhere near the halfway point, right about the peak of my cranium. There they sit idle, stranded. Eventually, in a desperate attempt to stay alive, my ideas and thoughts devour each other, much like the Donner Party. This may be a good thing, a fortunate genetic mutation that prevents most of my awful ideas from escaping. On the night I went out with Katie, Captain Cook was able to voyage across my entire mind, a testament to his navigational skill, even if he is dead.

2. Silverware Etiquette: the army of silverware that accompanies a formal meal is mind-boggling, particularly when you realize that billions of people in the world are capable of eating an entire meal with a pair of sticks. For me, any place-setting that includes three or more forks is a prelude to embarrassment—as is any meal where I'm only supplied chopsticks. To avoid the humiliation of using my salad fork to eat the entree and the dinner fork to flick ice cubes, I've adopted an approach for fancy, silverware-laden meals whereby I don't use any of the forks. I use the little spoon for salad, and the knife and the soup spoon to get the main course and dessert to my mouth. When people ask what I'm doing, I tell the table I had a very bad fork experience as a child and insist on leaving it at that. This makes me oddly intriguing as opposed to terribly inelegant.

---

[6] Like I'm going to settle for fifteen minutes of fame. Please.

3. I've written an extensive discourse on the relationship between manipulative genetics and sexuality, entitled, "Yes You Will, No I Won't." If you are interested in the details of the theory, there are two Xeroxed copies in print. In sum, the theory explains why lesbian relationships are less common than one would expect given the soft, supple nature of women and the hairy, disgusting nature of men. Women are, unquestionably, more desirable than men. Despite this fact, about 90% of women prefer a male for a mate. It makes no sense on paper, but that is where the manipulation gene steps in. Women want to have their way about most things, and men don't care about most things—like what restaurant to patronize. This hard truth makes males and females very compatible and explains how women overcome their natural aversion to the male physical appearance and our abominable behavior. Conversely, lesbian relationships are only possible when one or both partners have a weakened or absent manipulative gene, because two regular manipulative genes—like two positive charges—violently repel each other, resulting in catfights. Luckily for men, most women have a fully-operational manipulation gene that drives them away from the unmatched loveliness of the female form and into our arms. Gay men have an advanced, anti-manipulation gene, a genetic variation that allows them to hear the constant buzz of female manipulation, and it resonates in their ears like high-pitched whistles. The torturous sound is powerful enough to drive them away from the superior female form. The only way for gay men to dampen the high-pitched whistling sound of manipulation is through inordinate cleanliness and matching attire, which explains why homosexuals are so orderly and clean. Note: mainstream science has not yet adopted manipulation gene theory.

It's Almost All Fun and Games

I'd been wearing the blue shorts and long-sleeved gold top for over an hour and still had fifteen minutes to wait before my mom and I would leave for soccer practice. I always dressed for practices and games hours ahead of time.

I lay on the couch in the family room, weighed down by images of the amazing soccer feats I'd perform at practice. The phone rang, disrupting my imaginary athletic achievement. Three fierce rings filled our home before someone upstairs answered the call. I faintly heard Mom talking on the phone in the kitchen. A moment later, she screamed down the stairs for my older brother Karl.

"Karl we have to go to the hospital. Right now!"

I got up and jogged toward the stairs, arriving at the stairwell just in time to see Karl and Mom rushing out the door. Mom hesitated when she sensed my presence and looked down at me. I stared back, confused, wondering who was going to drive me to practice.

"Call Corey for a ride," she said. "And take Kerry with you."

Corey was a soccer teammate and my best friend. I called his house and caught him just as he and his mom were walking out the door.

"Corey. Hey, it's Chris. I need a ride to practice."

"No problem. We'll come by and get you."

"Why does your girlfriend pass me love notes in class?" I laughed. Then I hung up.

Twenty minutes later Corey and his mom, Carol, pulled into our driveway. I rushed out to greet them, pulling my younger brother with me. I hurried Kerry into the backseat and jumped in behind him. We sat motionless in the driveway for several seconds. The car idled as Carol studied me through the rearview mirror. Finally she eased the gray Buick Skylark into reverse, inching it back into the road.

"Where's your mom?" she asked.

"I think the hospital called. She had to go in."

Carol's expression turned noticeably nervous. Until that moment I hadn't felt an inkling of concern. My innocence, coupled with a belief that Dad was indestructible, allowed me to ignore Mom's unplanned, swift departure. Now, fear invaded.

Not a word was spoken during the rest of the drive. When we arrived at practice, I quietly asked Carol to call the hospital to check on things, speaking softly so Kerry couldn't hear. Since HAM radio was the only mobile communications available to civilians at the time, Carol had to go find a payphone. Corey and I got out of the car. Carol quickly departed and Kerry, still sitting in the backseat, stared at me blankly as they pulled away.

I joined in the ongoing soccer scrimmage, floating around the field as if in a time warp. My body moved adequately on muscle memory, but my mind was somewhere else. I glanced toward the parking lot every few seconds, watching for Carol's car. I can't recall how long the wait lasted but I remember her easing the Skylark into the parking lot. I rushed off the soccer field. My teammates played on.

"Carol, is my dad okay?" I was out of breath.

"No," Carol answered. Tears ran down her cheeks.

"Is he alive," I asked.

"I am so sorry Chris, I can't say yes to that question."

Even though I couldn't fully appreciate the importance of the moment, tears flowed. I felt like a helpless plumber, the tears so violent that they pooled in my ears. For the first time in my life I cried tears that sprang from something other than a fistfight with a brother or losing a game. I was fourteen years old, my world was collapsing and my eight year old brother stood staring at me, frightened pale.

"You have to tell Kerry," Carol whispered while hugging me.

Without thought, I grabbed his hand and led him away into an uncertain future.

clinging to anonymity

Clinging to Anonymity

For a while my father drove an Opel Kadett. The car looked like a toy that had been soaked in growth hormone. People often gathered around the vehicle to gawk.

"Forget Hot Wheels, I'm asking Santa for one of those!" was what most kids said.

"Look, someone took a giant crap in this parking space," was the typical adult response.

The Opel Automotive Company is a car manufacturer, not a toy maker. Its assembly facility is located in Europe, likely hidden away in a remote village that's off the electrical grid. Building cars by candlelight must be difficult, the faint illumination and shadowy production line undermining quality. I'm sure Opel's workers strive for excellence, but it's difficult to get the alignment right, the paint properly applied, the upholstery snug and the brakes operational when you can't really see what you're doing. The first Opel I ever saw was my dad's Kadett. I was standing in our kitchen, looking out toward the driveway. I stood and gawked, wishing Dad would've opted for a Hot Wheels car.

In the early 1970s, in an effort to expand into the North

American market, Opel management shipped ten introductory vehicles to the United States. A rich Boston architect embroiled in a nasty divorce bought one of the cars, the Opel Kadett that would one day be ours. After buying the Opel, he contacted his divorce attorney.

"I really want to get closure on this divorce," the architect explained. "So tell that bitch I'll throw in a brand new European car. That should do it."

"A brand new imported car?" his attorney asked. "Are you sure you want to add that to the settlement offer?"

"Absolutely!" the husband exclaimed, laughing devilishly. "But she needs to sign the papers today."

The Opel was a cruel joke, the husband's way of taking one last jab at his wife, a woman who had the gall to catch him sleeping with the nanny—twice. The other nine introductory Opels never sold, primarily because Opel's marketing department insisted on pawning the vehicles as legitimate transportation, an assertion even consumer-mad Americans wouldn't fall for. The nine unsold Opels sat idle in a New Jersey sales lot for over two years, collecting jeers from passersby. When it became clear that no one would buy the cars, the nine remaining Opels were shipped to Newfoundland, where they were sunk in the North Atlantic as part of a jetty expansion project, unceremoniously buried in the same ocean they'd traversed two years earlier, dreaming the American dream. Not every immigrant story ends happily.

Opel might have succeeded in America if its management would have seized on the insight of the Boston architect. If the company would've marketed their cars as practical jokes, their foray into the U.S., powered by a catchy advertising campaign, could've been wildly profitable. The Opel commercial might open with compassionate parents helping their son pack for college. The father pulls a set of car keys from his pocket and dangles them in front of the boy. The budding collegiate grabs the keys, glowing with excitement. His eyes begin to water. He hugs his mom and then embraces his dad. Glimmering tears are visible in all three. The boy bolts out the front door, thrill on his young face. As he emerges into the daylight, running toward the driveway, he sees a brand new Opel. The boy slows, stops, pauses, then doubles over with laughter. When he recovers, he turns back toward the front door. His parents are standing there, laughing along with him. The son flashes a grin that says, *Aw- shucks-you-got-me*. Friends and siblings appear from the shrubbery, sharing in the amusement of the staged gag. When the laughing subsides, a few of the friends fill the Opel with candy, transforming the car into a makeshift piñata. Someone fetches a sledgehammer from the garage and the real fun begins. The screen fades to black. A tagline appears: *"Opel: Laugh with Us!"*

The Boston architect's soon-to-be ex-wife didn't find the Opel amusing—life is about perspective that way. When she discovered the Opel in her driveway, she didn't flash a knowing, *aw-shucks-you-got-me* grin. She screamed.

"That damn sonofabitch!"

After exercising her lungs, the ex-wife unleashed her wrath on the car. First she grabbed a shovel from her gardening shed and beat in the windows. After clearing the shards of glass from the driver's seat, she hopped in and repeatedly drove the Opel into a large birch tree in her yard, smashing the grille, ignoring the whiplash. When she grew tired of ramming the car into the tree, the ex-wife got out of the Opel and retrieved a set of tire chains from the trunk. She used one of the chains to repeatedly strike the sides and back of the vehicle. After she finished defacing the car, she drove it into the Berkshires and abandoned the Opel on a lonely mountain road, leaving the keys in the ignition.[1] Some desperate soul found the Opel and coaxed it to life. From there the car migrated west, incurring additional bumps and bruises

---

[1] The architect's ex-wife collected car insurance on the "stolen" Opel and used the money to hire a private investigator. The P.I. located marital assets that the husband had been hiding. The husband was ordered to cough up an additional $300,000 in the divorce and he spent 90 days in the pokey for providing the court with fraudulent financial information. The ex-wife laughed. The husband cried. Life is about perspective that way.

along the way. Finally the Opel found its way to our home, a Mecca for cars seeking refuge from the local junkyard.

Our family history is littered with vehicles that should've come equipped with a flagpole attached to the back bumper, on which to hoist a white flag of surrender. The appearance of our cars already shouted *I give up*, but the flag would've removed all doubt. By conceding defeat, other drivers might've been sympathetic rather than derisive, replacing obscene gestures with a compassionate lowering of their eyes. The white flag could even have been enough to move some people to deliver a heartfelt prayer on our behalf.

Dear God, please send someone to steal that car so that poor family doesn't have to suffer the indignity of being seen in it for even one more day. Have mercy. Amen.

Like all our previous cars, the Opel implied that we were indigent. We were, in fact, solidly middle class. My dad simply had an odd collectibles fetish; instead of *Buy American* he strived to *Buy Bankrupt*. If a car manufacturer teetered on collapse, Dad felt compelled to own one of their vehicles. "They don't make 'em like this anymore," he'd remind us every time we complained about the cars he brought home. He seemed oblivious to the many reasons why.

Dad was the only member of the family to embrace the Opel. It was tiny and ugly, a rare combination in the late 70s, an era when big and hideous dominated America's roads. The Kadett, however, proved that being unique doesn't necessarily correlate to a compliment; owning the Opel was like being the one child a year who has an extreme allergic reaction to the chicken pox vaccine—not really what you want to be known for.

Its diminutive size and poor craftsmanship made the car incredibly dangerous. A moderate sneeze could shimmy its frame. My younger brother, Kerry, once dented one of the Kadett's door panels by tossing a Nerf basketball into it from a few feet away. The headlights must have seemed bright compared to the candles in the Opel factory, but on our American highways, they were as effective as strapping a couple of coal miners with hard-hat-mounted headlamps to the hood. It was as if Opel's engineers had commingled the schematics of a car and a trash compactor, yielding a mobile machine hungry to treat occupants to a painful, metal-mangled death. Place an alluring piece of cheese on the dash and it would have been a perfect human-trap.

Dad tried to put a positive spin on the car's lightweight frame and miniature size, lauding the Opel's gas efficiency. Initially I felt this praise was downright disingenuous. Our gas needs were inherently limited; Dad worked six miles from home and our family rarely took long trips. Yet the Kadett's fuel-efficiency soon proved to be far more important than even Dad had claimed. Soon after he acquired the Opel—or found it abandoned on a lonely country road—it became apparent that the engine didn't always take orders from the ignition key. Turn the key on and the engine might respond, but it probably wouldn't. If the car was already running, turning the key to the off position rarely had an effect. Sometimes the car would spontaneously start with no key at all. You just never knew. As a result, we became accustomed to leaving the engine running all the time, even while we shopped or went to church. Dad continued to brag that the Opel got 38 m.p.g. on the highway and 28 m.p.g. in town, but he conveniently ignored the 0 m.p.g. the car achieved while idling in our garage and various parking lots.

When our family went out to a movie, we would all wiggle out of the tiny Opel and head in to catch the show, hopeful the engine wouldn't die while we were gone. Every film became a drama. *Would the Opel still be running when we returned? Would the park brake hold? Would the car (please) explode?* We never worried about theft. Despite a running engine and unlocked doors, thieves wouldn't touch it. No one steals headaches, and the Opel, at a glance, was a migraine. Still, my father focused on the positives—right after making them up—and always insisted the family refer to the Opel as the new car.

"Go get in the car Chris, we need to leave soon," Dad

would say.

"Dad, can we please take the *old* Subaru?"

"Nope, we are taking the Opel. I didn't buy a new car to let it sit idle in the driveway."

"The only thing it does well is idle in the driveway, so why don't we leave it right there in its comfort zone? Can we please take the Subaru?"

"Go get in the car Chris," he'd repeat. And I would.

The Opel dogged our family for about a year and a half. One day it stopped running and refused to sputter back to life. My father tried every tool in his mechanic's bag; duct tape, staples, Elmer's Glue, expletives. The harder he tried to nurse the car back to reliability, the more it deteriorated, typical for all of my father's automotive patients. Our garage resembled a vehicular emergency room, a place where cars regularly flat-lined despite Dad's best efforts. His love of the underdog blinded him to what the rest of us clearly understood; he was a hospice worker for dying autos, nursing decrepit vehicles that the rest of society had shunned. The Opel languished in our garage for several days, comatose and engine-dead, our dad consoling it every night with R-rated encouragement.

In a last desperate act, Dad threw a handful of pepper on the engine block, a "trick his dad had taught him." The Opel didn't respond. Dad nearly wept. The rest of the family quietly rejoiced, certain that any replacement with three working wheels would constitute an upgrade. Because the other nine North American Opels were resting and rusting safely at the bottom of the North Atlantic, there was reason for optimism.

To our surprise, Dad took the unprecedented step of having the Opel towed to a repair shop. Involving a mechanic amounted to sacrilege, a direct assault on Dad's policy of fix it yourself or stoically surrender. The day after the tow truck removed the Opel from our garage, a mechanic called our house. My father asked what it would take to get the Opel running again. The mechanic replied, "NASA." Ding dong, the Opel's dead.

A few days after the Opel died, my father picked me up from our local park where I'd spent the late summer afternoon playing baseball with some friends. The recreational area was full of activity and the parking lot was packed. I was too absorbed in the game to realize my father had arrived to gather me. He walked out near the third baseline and caught my attention. While I grabbed my jacket from the dugout, he clowned with a few of my friends. We said our goodbyes and headed toward the parking lot, my eyes scanning the area for our wretched Subaru hatchback, the family's sole remaining car. I didn't see it anywhere.

"I got a new car today, Chris," Dad announced.

I scoffed at his use of the word *new,* aware that his assertion meant, at best, that the old piece of crap he'd purchased had a new fender or a fresh set of spark plugs. Still, I looked hopefully out at the parking lot. The expansive lot brimmed with possibility, loaded with shiny trucks and sleek sports cars. The possibilities dwindled as I methodically eliminated the cars that I recognized, those owned by neighbors and acquaintances. In a small town, you know nearly everyone and their vehicle.

Then I saw it, a car I'd never seen before. It was a beautiful white Cadillac.[2] The Cadillac was a bit gaudy and tired-looking, at least five years old, something dad conceivably might buy. The vehicle wouldn't stimulate pride, but it wouldn't burden our family with embarrassment. For the first time in my young life it appeared that we had a car that would allow me to sit up straight in the backseat. For years I'd twisted down onto the floorboard of our family cars, humiliated by the four-wheeled lemons my parents drove. Mom warned that I was tempting scoliosis, but I embraced the risk. For me, the decision between a deformed backbone and social ridicule was easy—I was prepared to drag my hunched body to the grave. The Cadillac wouldn't be anybody's first choice, but given our family's car history, it was far from my last.

---

[2] "Beautiful" in the sense you wouldn't impulsively throw rocks at it when it came into view.

I ran toward the Cadillac, awed by its dent-free exterior. When Dad caught up I could barely contain my excitement.

"Do you have to push start it?" I asked.

"I don't think so."

"Do the brakes work?"

"I bet they do," he grinned.

"Dad, you are the best!" I threw my arms around his waist.

"Hell of a car ain't it son." He patted my head.

"The greatest," I whispered back, emotions hampering my speech.

"Too bad it's not ours."

I didn't move. I hoped that he'd say he was kidding, or for him to offer a meaningless technicality—*The bank owns it*, or *I have three days to return it to the dealer without penalty*. His silence broke my heart. The car was not ours. Some parents help their kids develop skills and character traits; mine seemed intent on aiding the crippling curvature of my spine.

I loosened my hug. Dad slipped away, walking farther into the parking lot. I followed, close on his heals. He circled several cars, taunting. He'd stop in front of a decent van or a modest sedan, fiddle with his keys long enough for me to salivate, and then move on.

"Nope, that's not it either. Darn it, which one of these cars did I buy?"

I began humming loudly in his shadow, purposefully lowering my hum every time my father neared a semi-attractive vehicle I didn't recognize. When he arrived at the target of my desire, I'd go silent. I was playing a game of musical cars that I prayed would end happily. It didn't.

My hopes and dreams were smashed by a car so rancid that nightmares couldn't conjure it. The moment I spotted its army-green paint, I knew it was ours, a car only my father could love. Grotesque and gigantic, it looked as if someone had reclaimed the nine Opels from the bottom of the North Atlantic and welded them together to create a double-hulled attack vehicle. The result was more tank than car. The absence of a gun turret made the monstrous machine look naked.

My father walked toward the hunk of steel. I hummed hopefully, louder and louder, desperate for our game of musical cars to continue. Dad stopped right by the driver's door. I began screaming, pleading for help, even for an Opel. Dad slipped the key into the lock. The moment took on a game show quality. Tension oozed. *Would the lock open? Would the Kemper family take home this "new" car?* My dad turned his hand, the lock popped up and we'd won an even bigger headache.

"Please Dad, tell me you are not serious. You did not buy this...thing."

"If you want a ride home, get in."

"In this? This thing is ours? Did you trade in the Opel or did this car swallow it?"

He didn't answer. He grasped the driver's door with both hands, heaved it open and climbed in. My protest ended with the start of the engine. Too tired to walk the four miles home, I scrambled around to the passenger side, battled the massive door open and hopped in the front seat. As we drove off, Dad began to whistle a Sinatra song, his subtle way of informing me the radio didn't work. The ride was rough, the giant shocks unwilling to respond to anything less violent than a mortar impact. Every bump and pothole bounced us around. My heart ached with despair.

With every passing sign post, the reality of ownership grew like a tumor. By the time we were halfway home, my eyes were damp with tears. Less than a week earlier a tow truck had hauled the Opel away, creating a window of optimism that a decent car would take its place. Instead, Dad found a car that would make Stephen King scream. Within a week, my friends dubbed our new car *The Thing*. Within a month, everybody in town knew it by that name. Eventually my family and I adopted the moniker as well, thankful that the community had selected a relatively friendly name out of a sea of exceedingly less flattering options.

The Thing was a twenty-six footer, and that's no fish tale. The American Motors Company, effectively defunct by the time Dad purchased The Thing, manufactured the car in 1969. They built it to fill the small transportation niche that exists between the station wagon and a full-sized charter bus, designing the car to comfortably accommodate a family of fourteen. Branded the "Ambassador," the car did nothing diplomatically. We never signaled when changing lanes—the signals were broken—we'd just slide over and watch other cars scatter, their drivers too frightened to honk. As an added bonus, The Thing met all the federal parameters of a certified nuclear bomb shelter. Our entire family slept easier knowing that The Thing sat in the garage, its trunk loaded with jugs of water and canned goods, just in case the Soviets got frisky.

Dad always manned The Thing's helm; Mom was a tad too short to reach the pedals. Even with the front bucket seat in the full forward position, Dad still needed to extend his right arm to reach the steering wheel. He never wore a formal uniform when driving The Thing, though the car's military aesthetic would have allowed it.

Shortly after The Thing arrived in our driveway Kerry brought home a makeshift phone that he'd made in kindergarten, two empty tin cans connected by a string. The device quickly became The Thing's communication system. The string spanned thirteen feet, just enough to reach from the driver's compartment to the opposite corner in the back seat. When Dad needed navigational information, he demanded reconnaissance reports from his crew.

"Is it raining out the back?" he'd shout into one of the tin cans.

"An absolute downpour, some hail mixed in," I'd respond from my hunched position, desperate to remain concealed from the eyes of the world.

"Well, it's blue skies up here. You should be out of the rain in a couple of minutes. Since the front wheels are operating in good weather, I am going to speed up a little."

Speed was something The Thing did not possess. On its best day it was able to accelerate from zero to 57 m.p.h. in 39 seconds. We never got it to sixty. AMC manufactured The Thing as a muscle car, but in the years between its manufacture and our possession, those muscles had atrophied. The Thing limped, struggled and backfired, but it never sped. On days it maintained forward progress, we claimed victory.

Getting The Thing into motion required a concerted effort. Every kid in the car—and, with friends, there were often eight or more—was required to rock back and forth to initiate movement. Defeating inertia is a formidable task for a car that couldn't fit through the Panama Canal. And once The Thing started moving, the physics of acceleration reared its Newtonian head. Even with an engine the size of an Opel, The Thing couldn't muster the force required to accelerate its hefty mass. Hills, and the gravity they wrought, were avoided whenever possible. Flat roads provided some relief, but only when the air was still. The Thing, aerodynamically modeled after a parachute, battled to defeat even the slightest headwind. If the headwind was stiff, Dad was forced to tack The Thing back and forth like a sailboat to maintain momentum.

Poor mobility was only the start of The Thing's problems. Turn on the headlights and it took at least three minutes for the bulbs to flicker to life. When they did light up, they didn't illuminate the roadway. Instead, the right lamp peered off to the side, spotlighting the road shoulder. The left lamp looked skyward, examining the heavens. When we drove The Thing at night, we looked like a pack of paranoid hillbilly poachers, searching for elk on the side of the road while simultaneously monitoring the sky for government helicopters we knew watched our every move.

Despite appearances, we weren't a hunting family. We all thought wild creatures ought to roam peacefully around the countryside where we lived. But The Thing didn't share our peaceful convictions. Any time a critter crossed the road in front of us—be it a raccoon, opossum, squirrel, cat, dog, skunk, deer, or chicken—The Thing attacked. At first we blamed the high number of roadkills on The Thing's poor braking performance. It took between 7 and 13 seconds for the massive frame to come to a halt; fantastic for an aircraft carrier, abysmal for a car. It soon became apparent, however, that when an animal crossed the road in front of us, The Thing chose to ignore the application of the brakes altogether, refusing to slow down until it tasted blood on its grille. Its bloodlust bothered all of us, but we didn't have the courage to confront The Thing, worried it might turn on us next.

The windshield wipers were worse than the braking system. After being turned on, the vacuum-operated wipers took days to swing into action, a glitch that made successful implementation dependent on a reliable three-day weather forecast.

To its credit, The Thing did have noteworthy safety advantages over the Opel, and every other passenger car. The steel hood was so expansive that in the event of a head-on collision we'd have plenty of time to exit the car and walk to safety before the wave of impact reached the passenger compartment.

"Damn, looks like we hit a tractor trailer," Dad might explain. "You know the drill. Everyone out of the car. Let's all meet up at that McDonald's by the off-ramp that we just passed. Order me some fries and a chocolate shake. I'll go talk to the other driver. We have at least two minutes before the force of the collision reaches us, so take your time and watch your step."

The Thing also made it easy for me to hide from a gaping public. Its roomy bowels made slouching downright comfortable. With the right collection of blankets and pillows, The Thing's backseat made for an adequate guest room. The vehicle's size also ended family feuds that used to erupt at the drive-in movie theatre. The car's elongated frame provided a multitude of viewing options, with the occupants in the front and back having premium seats to different movie screens.

A month after Dad acquired The Thing, our family took a weekend trip to Vancouver, B.C. When we tried to cross into Canada, the border patrol impounded the car for over two hours. The ordeal started when two Canadian border guards saw me hiding on the floorboard, surreptitiously using the tin can phone to communicate with my father. Apparently my secretive manner, together with the fearsome appearance of our family assault vehicle, caused the guards some concern. When we pulled up to the border gate, the guards approached our car, eyeing us, as if we represented the first wave of U.S. ground troops dispatched to formally annex the Great White North. They immediately segregated us from the mainstream traffic, directing Dad to pull off to a side area for inspection. When the guards discovered enough food and water in the trunk to feed an army, we were instructed to relocate to yet another cordoned off area and were forced to exit the car. Once we evacuated The Thing three guards did a meticulous search of the interior. One of the guards actually placed his hand on his gun before slowly opening the glove compartment hatch, a seemingly silly precaution until you consider the compartment was large enough to conceal an entire Navy SEAL advance team. As he slowly lowered the glove compartment door, I grew excited by the prospect that my parents led double lives, like a pair of CIA operatives engaged in international shenanigans. The guard stepped back as he released the compartment door, letting it fall open, but no infantrymen flooded out, confirming that my folks were nothing more daring than a school teacher and a C.P.A. After a round of half-hearted apologies, the border guards cleared us and our smoke-spewing monster to enter Canada. Within a week of returning to the States, newspapers around the world reported that a giant hole had formed in the ozone over the North Pole. For that, on behalf of my family and The Thing's ozone-depleting engine, I belatedly apologize.

The Thing stayed with us for nine eternal months. During that time, tow trucks stopped stalking my father, something they had done from the moment he earned his learner's permit. When you ride around in mechanical calamities, tow trucks swarm like buzzards, waiting for the car to keel so they can swoop in and make some money. And with my father's cars, there was money to be made. Local towing operators had memorized his AAA membership number. Every Christmas we received a card from Ed Strauss, owner of Tuff's Towing, thanking Dad for making their season bright. The year we owned The Thing, we didn't receive a Christmas card from Mr. Strauss, or from any other tow operator. The massive vehicle had presented the towing industry several opportunities to cash in, coughing to a stop on numerous occasions, but the vehicle was too big for traditional tow trucks to handle. Not many vehicles are capable of hauling away a year's worth of United States steel production.

The first time The Thing broke down, my father suggested it was just "taking a break," as if the car had joined some automotive union that had a contractual right to a fifteen minute rest every hundred miles. When fifteen minutes turned into an hour, and The Thing still refused to return to work, Dad walked to a pay phone and called Tuff's. When he asked what it would take to get The Thing towed to a mechanic, Mr. Strauss replied, "NASA."

Somehow Dad managed to get The Thing running again, but the car protested all the way home, belching smoke and unleashing frighteningly loud backfires. All this—the stalling, the restarting, the smoke and blasts—became commonplace. The Thing danced with death but constantly cheated it; that is until our highly anticipated family summer vacation to the Inn at the Seventh Mountain, a vacation resort in Central Oregon.

The final autopsy suggested suicide. The engine imploded, melting the pistons into a heap of disfigured metal. The Thing, wanting a fresh start and aware that its metal organs would be donated to a recycling center, blew a gasket. Its disjointed headlamps eyed reincarnation. The Thing wanted a new life, a chance to make a positive difference, to be reborn as a million little blender blades so it could make milkshakes and smoothies all day.

The Thing died in June. Its passing was untimely only because it died at an inopportune time. In the shadow of Mt. Hood, on our way to a rare, weeklong family vacation, The Thing wheezed to a stop. The trip gauge told us we'd traveled exactly 118.3 miles from home. Our view of majestic Mt. Hood informed us that we were two mountains shy of our destination.

"Too bad there isn't an Inn at the Fifth Mountain," I joked as The Thing oozed odor and smoke, "because this is right about where the parking lot would be."

My comment aside, we were all sure that The Thing would eventually come through. It had proven temperamental but dependable. It regularly threw fits, but after a short break, it always returned to the road, the persistent warrior. Like a pioneer getting ready to tackle a daunting mountain pass, The Thing just needed a chance to catch its breath for the remaining challenge. Following its lead, we all took a moment to stretch and recharge, nary a doubt that Dad would have the engine churning, or at least sputtering, in no time.

* * *

The entire family was looking forward to our vacation at the Inn at the Seventh Mountain. For five straight summers, a non-stop schedule of sports and extracurricular activities had foiled a long family vacation. The trip to the Inn was a special treat. A full month before we were scheduled to depart, our house filled with excited talk of swimming, rafting and hiking. Several family friends had been to the popular resort and they had all raved about its amenities and sunshine. I couldn't wait to join the Inn crowd.

Because The Thing had the trunk space of a cargo plane, my siblings and I were allowed to bring nearly anything we wanted. If it wasn't nailed down and we could conceivably use it during the vacation, into the trunk it went. I brought my entire collection of Star Wars action figures and several paper bags full of green, plastic army men. It rarely rained at the Seventh Mountain resort, and almost never in the summer, but if rain clouds opened fire, I was prepared to fight back with an array of toy warriors. My sister Katrina brought a box of old clothes and another of unwanted toys, "just in case we pass a Goodwill Store." We could have brought our entire house if we had access to a crane large enough to set it down atop The Thing, on the spot where the gun turret belonged.

Since the incident at the Canadian border, The Thing had become somewhat of a homebody, never venturing outside a fifteen mile radius of our house. The lack of long distance training didn't dent our collective confidence in its ability. Give it water every fifty miles to cool its overheated attitude and we were certain it could get us to the moon. Leading up to our trip to the Inn, The Thing had performed its limited duties admirably.

Our faith in the car didn't stop us from pining for a different one. The moment we merged onto the two-lane highway leading out of town, rolling toward the Seventh Mountain, I pressed my face against the back window, as did Kerry, Katrina and my older brother Karl. We all stared at the luxury cars roaring up the road from behind; the ones with treads on the tires and front bumpers. Oh, what the four of us wouldn't have given for a car that didn't spout smoke like an antiquated train; a car with four seatbelts in the back seat, not three, so we didn't have to play seatbelt roulette.[3]

Twenty miles into our trip a family zoomed by in a Mercedes sedan. As they passed, the man in the passenger's seat mockingly motioned to my father to sound the air horn, forming a

---

[3] When my three siblings and I were riding in the back of The Thing, we rotated seatbelts every 15 minutes, methodically alternating seatbelt protection. When it was Kerry's turn to go unsecured, I'd use the opportunity to scream, "Oh my God, we're gonna crash!" He cried every single time.

right angle with his elbow and moving his arm up and down, the universal signal kids use to encourage truckers to toot their horn. The two kids in the back of the Mercedes found it incredibly funny and they joined in, making the same signal, laughing heartily. My dad honked the horn and waved back, well aware of the ridicule but incapable of a vengeful response. Shame and embarrassment melted me to the floorboard.[4]

The Thing performed wonderfully for the first hundred miles of the trip, clopping along like a horse and buggy. Our 4-50 air conditioning delivered plenty of cool air.[5] Dad spiced up the drive by barking orders like the captain of a disabled aircraft carrier, intent on keeping his ship afloat.

"Roll up the left rear window an inch and a half!" he ordered, his method to improve gas mileage.

He told Mom, "Honey, engage and disengage the cigarette lighter every ten seconds for the next 2 miles!" the apparent solution to a hydraulic steering problem.

"Karl, how do you expect the car to maintain an acceptable engine temperature with you reading *that* book?"

Cars with "character," my dad's favorite synonym for shitty, require unconventional tactics to keep 'em running, and he employed plenty. Dad had a metaphysical connection with The Thing, always pushing the right buttons to prod it onward. Strangely, when Karl agreed to read a different book, the engine temperature dropped below the critical range. Dad's orders, bizarre as they were, always seemed to produce positive results. I'd never trust The Thing as a getaway car—that's begging for jail time— but with Dad at the helm, I knew it'd keep moving…eventually.

---

[4] There was one derisive event that actually made me laugh. Our family was riding in The Thing and a trucker in an 18-wheeler passed us. As he went by, the trucker signaled to my dad to pull the air horn. Coming from a trucker, that's funny as hell. We all signaled right back and the trucker responded by giving his horn three long pulls.

[5] As Dad explained, four windows rolled down while going fifty miles an hour.

As he drove, my siblings and I released our pent-up anticipation. We rocketed around, burning with excitement as The Thing crept down the road like a tank commissioned back when the air force consisted of rocks and catapults. I wrestled and played with my brothers and sister, three of us loosely confined by seatbelts, the fourth secured by headlocks and half-Nelsons. As the miles passed, our delirium faded and we settled into counting cars and taking in the sights. Capitalizing on the relative calm, Mom triggered our curiosity by pointing out a guardrail with a fresh, gaping hole. The torn ends of the metal barrier bent away from the road, indicating that somebody had had an awfully bad day. We sped past.

"What do you kids think caused that?" Mom asked.

For the next half hour we discussed the issue with passion. The lack of information spawned speculation. The imagined death toll soon rocketed to 73 souls. All told, fifty-six cars had plunged through the opening, including one driven by our Aunt Pam. We'd miss her sorely and everyone agreed that she'd done an admirable job veiling her substantial wealth, living in a trailer and dressing like a homeless lady. We respected her for saving her money; respected her more for bequeathing it to us. After a few seconds of mourning, we spent fifteen minutes discussing how we'd spend our unexpected windfall. That's what Aunt Pam would've wanted.

As we finished spending our deceased aunt's well-hidden wealth, Mom, eager to keep our energy in check, pointed out a road sign.

"See that," she said. "Safety Corridor, Next Fifteen Miles. Sorry, you are all going to have to sit still. No talking, no hitting. State law requires it."

Fifteen miles down the road, Mom's short-sighted ploy backfired spectacularly when we passed another road sign:

Now Leaving Safety Corridor!

The sign literally had an exclamation point, egging travelers to toss inhibitions out the window. Mom said nothing, but we all saw it. Karl reacted first, triggering a fight with Katrina by delivering a wet Willy. As they tangled, I unhooked my seatbelt, dropped my drawers and used my underwear-covered butt to pin Kerry's head to the seat.

"Chris you get your pants back on right now!" Mom yelled.

"But we're out of the safety corridor!"

"Pants back on right now!" she demanded.

I pulled my pants back up and promptly pinned Kerry's head down again, this time with my denim-covered backside. As Kerry squirmed underneath, fearlessly tempting flatulence, a car of young adults passed. One of the passengers in the backseat held up a full can of beer and flashed a broad smile. He popped the beer open and took a swig. I respected him for respecting the law. He had responsibly waited to start drinking, or to restart, until his vehicle was squarely outside the safety corridor. I too had responsibly waited, controlling my desire to squash my little brother's head until we'd exited the safety zone. Instead of the praise I deserved, I was chastised, a glaring example of my mom's ability to overlook good behavior.

A hundred and thirteen miles into the trip, we pulled off at a rest stop to relieve bulging bladders and building tension. My siblings and I, trapped in the back seat for over two hours, were a pot of water on the brink of boiling. We weren't the only ones at risk of bubbling over. The Thing also showed the strain of the trip. Puffs of white smoke seeped from under the hood and, inexplicably, from the trunk. Our parents weren't concerned, or they hid it very well, and within ten minutes we piled back into the car and drove off. Five miles down the road, The Thing decided to take its own, permanent vacation.

Moments after leaving the rest stop, the whiffs of smoke turned into a dark, billowing plume. Dad tried to sweet-talk The Thing into continuing on to the next exit, but the motor froze up and shut off, forcing us to pull off into a small turnout on the right side of the two-lane, undivided highway. The Thing rolled to a stop, stranding us on the eastern side of Mt. Hood, the sun half hidden by its peak.

Up the road about thirty yards on the other side of the highway there was a small fruit stand. A rickety looking cottage sat behind the stand, about twenty yards off the roadway. Leaning against the fruit stand was a handmade plywood sign, painted red and green.

Marge's World Famous Jam

Dad picked up the tin can phone to address the crew. "Everyone stay calm. There are plenty of lifeboats. Stay where you are until further notice." After the announcement, he promptly abandoned ship. He jumped from the car and headed up the road to meet Marge.

"Mom," I asked, "do you really think that jam is world famous?"

"If Marge says it is, I suppose it must be."

"Well then, I'm world famous too."

A debate followed. Karl claimed he too was world famous while adamantly denying that I was famous outside the Northern Hemisphere. Negotiations continued, threats were made, Kerry's head was pinned to the seat by various butts. In the end, reasoned minds prevailed. When Dad returned from Marge's jam stand, he stepped into a shitty car full of world famous people. He told us that Marge had let him use her world famous phone to call a tow truck.

"The towing folks said it would be almost an hour to get someone out here," he explained as he slipped behind the wheel. "I really don't think we will need it, but I asked them to send a truck just in case." With that, he popped the hood, got out of the car again, and went to work.

"Why don't we all get out of the car," Mom suggested. "You can each get something out of the trunk to play with. Just stay close to the car and away from the road."

"I think you should make an exception for Karl on the 'stay away from the road rule,'" I suggested.

"Be safe," she implored, ignoring my comment.

"But the safety corridor is behind us," I reminded.

"See this hand?" she asked rhetorically. "We are now in *my* safety corridor and this hand will be used on anyone I find in violation."

The four of us exited through the right, rear door and walked around to the trunk. The enormous cavern resembled a Toys "R" Us store. I grabbed a model Millennium Falcon, one of three that I'd brought, and walked around to the front of The Thing to check on Dad. He was peering into the Ambassador's innards, mumbling words ambassadors shouldn't speak.

"Can you fix it?"

"As easy as riding a bike," he said.

I had never seen Dad on bicycle. "Can you ride a bike?" I asked. He was too focused on the smoking engine to respond.

Over the next forty minutes, playing on a swath of grass between the road and the adjacent forest, I lost the Millennium Falcon I was playing with by throwing it into the trees with the confidence that comes from having two nearly identical toys at my disposal. Karl lost a baseball and Katrina lost our brother Kerry, but only for five minutes. We were having the time of our lives.

After aborting my search for the lost Millennium Falcon, I emerged from the woods to find Dad still examining The Thing's engine, his clothes now covered with grease. Mom stood by his side, a single smudge of car-blood on her khaki shorts, another small smear on her blouse. It was then that Dad answered the proverbial question, "If a father yells 'shit' near the woods, does his son hear it?" Yes. He most certainly does.

Sensing his clear frustration, and being world famous, I moved in to help, saddened by a pair of troubling revelations: first, The Thing seemed to be dead, placing our vacation plans in doubt. Second, my dad had lived his entire life without ever learning how to ride a bike.

"What are you doing?" I asked him as I approached.

"Clinging to anonymity son, just clinging to anonymity." He sighed deeply.

Mom let out a laugh.

"Can I help?" I continued, uncertain what he meant but eager to assist.

"Chris, you help me cling to anonymity more than your brothers and sister combined. But let's keep that our little secret."

Mom laughed louder. Pride overwhelmed me. I was Dad's best helper, better than my siblings combined, and I planned to tell them the first chance I got, secret be damned. On top of that, I was world famous. What a day. I headed back out to play.

When the tow truck arrived, Dad yelled for us to return to the car. As I stepped out of the woods I saw the tow truck driver talking into his radio, shaking his head. The entire family assembled at the front of The Thing for an update, its once deadly grille now lifeless.

"What's going on?" Karl asked.

"Apparently they need to send out a bigger truck," Dad answered.

After setting down his radio, the tow truck driver walked over to us.

"I'm going to need your AAA card, sir." Dad dug through his wallet, removed the card and handed it to the driver.

"Kemper, huh. That name sounds familiar. You folks from the Banks area by any chance?"

"Yep," Dad responded.

From that moment, the tow truck driver treated us like royalty. Dad's history of clunkers, car trouble and tow trucks had finally paid off. Within the towing industry, our family name commanded reverence.

"Well Mr. Kemper, we will get a bigger truck out here as soon as possible," promised the driver. "Instead of you and your family waiting out here, I'll drive you to Deschutes River State Park. It's just down the road a bit, a good place to wait. I'll have the other tow truck driver bring your vehicle to the park. We can figure out our next move then."

"That sounds good," Dad replied awkwardly. He was not comfortable being catered to. I enjoyed watching him receive the admiration he deserved.

Our entire family squeezed into the tow truck like trained clowns, our experience with the Opel coming in handy. We drove off, leaving The Thing to dream of its reincarnation. When we arrived at the state park, a beautiful oasis on the bank of the rushing Deschutes River, just short of where it converges with the mighty Columbia, we didn't wait, we played.

A couple hours after being dropped off at the park, a different, larger tow truck pulled into the parking lot. The Thing was strapped to its sizeable flatbed. We all gathered around and listened to the driver as he talked to Dad. The tone was pessimistic. In all likelihood, The Thing would have to be decommissioned.

We climbed up onto the flatbed and unpacked the trunk, no small task. My parents removed all their personal possessions from the glove compartment. The scene had all the makings of a goodbye.

Once the trunk was unloaded, my father searched out the park ranger. The campground was full, but the friendly ranger, sympathetic to our plight, allowed us to set up our two large tents in a makeshift campsite overlooking the river. We gathered some river rocks, made a fire pit and settled in.

Later that evening the first tow truck driver, by then known to us as Dave, returned to the park to deliver the official death notice. The Thing was done. We would never see it again. The car would be junked, an event that would wreak havoc on the worldwide market for recycled steel.

Before leaving the park, Dave offered to drive a rental car out to us on Thursday, his day off. Dad humbly accepted the offer, meaning that we would stay at the park for at least a few more days. We filled the time with hiking, fishing and river play. We had enough fun to make the Inn crowd envious.

On Thursday, as promised, Dave showed up with a rental car. It was a large Ford station wagon with less than 10,000 miles on the odometer. It was the newest old car I'd ever dreamed of riding in. Since we'd been having such fun, we decided to stay and camp through the weekend. Each day I spent an hour or so sitting in the back seat of that Ford, perfect posture, spine straight. It was magical. Life's little detours are fertile ground for memorable experiences. I'll never forget that trip.

A rental car, by definition, has to be returned. On Monday the Ford went back to the rental agency. That same day, Dad started his search for our next headache, sifting through the balance sheets of various auto manufacturers, looking for one in financial peril. He ended up buying an old Datsun, a rickety, small car that resembled the Opel. The purchase apparently set off alarm bells at Datsun's headquarters in Japan. Company management, fearing any association with our family, promptly changed the company name to Nissan. We were all sure that our dad's purchase of the Datsun was directly responsible for the change, making him world famous.

* * *

During a family dinner a few years ago we spent nearly an hour reminiscing about the cars that littered our past. The Thing stood preeminent. "Penny wise, 14,281 pounds foolish," I opined. I also spent a good deal of time bitching about my battered back, still plaguing me after all these years.

"I could've been 6'2"" I groused. "I lost at least four inches by having to crouch and huddle in the backseat of all those crappy cars during my prime growth years."

"Oh, please," Mom answered.

"That's just the beginning," I continued. "Because of The Thing, I'm fearful of large, cavernous places, like churches and lecture halls. It's like I'm the opposite of a claustrophobe."

"You don't seem to have a problem with taverns in large buildings," Mom pointed out. "And Christopher," she added, "your father drove junkers so we could afford to live in a nice house and buy you kids enough toys and sporting goods to supply a small country. He always dreamed of owning a Mercedes, a dream he never realized before he died."

"Well, we shared the same dream," I smiled. "I wanted him to own a Mercedes too. He was pretty selfish not to buy one."

Mom scowled, dismayed by my comment. "How is that selfish?" she demanded. "He did it for you, for all of us."

"Well, he could have gotten a night job. Then I could have had three Millennium Falcons *and* a Mercedes!"

My mom and siblings stared at me, and not because of my startling good looks.

"I'm kidding. You know I am." I looked directly at Mom. "The only dumb thing Dad likely ever did was to allow us to drive him into anonymity, pun intended."

"That's what he wanted." She stated it matter-of-factly. She looked passed me, and smiled simply. "If you have kids, you should do the same."

"I'll do whatever a Mercedes will allow," I said, and clutched my back like an old man.[6]

End Notes:

1. My dad enjoyed his beer, but I don't think I ever saw him drunk. Still, the cars he bought suggested that he only went car shopping after polishing off a fifth of tequila. I imagine the day after buying a car he'd wake up with a blazing headache, look out the window at the driveway and think, "Good God, what have I done?" From personal

---

[6] The way things are going for me financially, if I do have children, they will have a great car, which is important because we'll be living out of it.

experience, I know you can beer-goggle anything. I once lived in an apartment that resembled a prison cell for an entire year because I viewed the space and signed the rental agreement while piss drunk. I woke up on the kitchen floor the next morning wondering who had snuck in during the night and decorated my new apartment in a crack-house motif.

2. Our family always wondered what would happen if someone actually did steal one of our family's cars. If the person were caught, we weren't sure whether the guy would be treated as a criminal, or if the judge would let the thief go, ruling that taking one of our cars made him nothing more than an "unaffiliated" sanitation worker.

3. By the time my dad and I arrived home from the park that first day with The Thing, my tears had pooled on the passenger floorboard, forming a small reservoir of sadness between my feet. That night I dreamed that my tears eventually formed a sizeable swimming pool on the enormous floorboard. In the dream, neighbors flocked to our house on hot days to cool off in my pool—for a price. I towered above them in the passenger seat, my makeshift lifeguard stand, protecting them as they beat the heat. My sister, Katrina, sold concessions out of the glove compartment. A sturdy rope hanging from the rearview mirror was used by kids to swing into the deep end. In the dream, I put the money raised from the venture aside until I had earned enough to buy our family a new car—and not my father's type of new.

4. If reincarnation indeed exists, I want to come back as a lion. These majestic creatures sleep about 20 hours a day and, when called upon by nature, can have sex up to 50 times in a single 24 hour period. The females in the pride do most of the hunting and everyone refers to you as King of the Jungle. I'm sure that the line for lions at the reincarnation clearing house is long, but it'd be worth the wait. You could probably return to earth almost immediately after dying if you were willing to return as an ant or a North Korean, but where's the fun in that?*

* This is not a condemnation of North Koreans who, like most humans, are certainly kind and loving people if placed in a decent environment. At this point in time though, I'd rather come back as The Thing than live the oppressive existence of a North Korean citizen.

The Emperor Reads a Hilarious Book While Lounging in His New Clothes*

,
 ;   !

                    ?
           .   ;
                              .”
"
       .
         "   .”

---
* Humor so profound only the comically blessed can see it.

clinging to anonymity

!
.

:   "   "

.

?

&   (
).

.   !
       !!!
.

"

"

?
>   %
     $
  (   )

The Emperor Reads a Hilarious Book...

/ {
} "
."

.

@
!

.

.
,
?

?
" ."

" !"

" ?"
" !"

clinging to anonymity

!

(
—).

?!?**

** If you can see the punctuation, but not the words, this indicates that you are on the *verge* of being comically blessed. As the final step to reaching comical fluency, all you need to do is divest all your assets and send the proceeds to the author of this book.

My First Time

In the summer of 1986 the baseball team I played on traveled to North Carolina to participate in a national Babe Ruth tournament. To make the trip financially feasible, the local residents of Durham hosted players in their homes and fed us during the entire five-day event. I stayed with the Parker family, along with three of my teammates.

On our second night in Carolina, after a tournament-sponsored barbecue featuring spit-roasted pigs, the Parker family drove us back to their home. A light rain was beginning to fall. Back at their house they made popcorn—the real kind, popped with hot oil and slathered in real butter—and we all gathered in the living room to watch the local news. A young weatherman in a tidy suit stood in front of a map of the Eastern Seaboard. A storm system off the coast had him excited, and he speculated that it could develop into a hurricane. The baseball tournament was in jeopardy. We watched and listened with great interest.

The background map showed the borders of the East Coast states, but none of the states were identified. As the weatherman spoke about the potential ferocity of the storm, a nifty graphic depicted the worst-case scenario, showing how the weather system could evolve into a monster storm and slam into the coast.

"This could happen," the weatherman warned.

"Don't worry too much, boys," Mr. Parker said. "The system is swinging south of us." He walked to the television and pointed to North Carolina on the weather map.

"Shouldn't be a problem," Mrs. Parker added.

"Sure looks like it's going to be a problem for that state south of here," I laughed. "What is that? Georgia? They're going to get hammered."

"Uh, Chris, that's not Georgia," Mrs. Parker said, holding back a laugh.

"That's the dumbest comment in the history of the planet," said Tim, one of my teammates.

"Well, if that's not Georgia, then what is it, smart guy?"

"What state do you think is south of *North* Carolina?" another teammate, Dean, mocked.

"Georgia," I said. "That's Georgia."

"Umm...just to the *south* there, on the coast," Mr. Parker laughed. "In these parts we call that South Carolina."

I sat silent for several seconds. "Okay. Okay. That was stupid," I finally laughed. "But, Tim, that is not the dumbest thing ever said."

"What's dumber?" Dean challenged.

"Yeah," Mr. Parker grinned. "I'd like to hear a stupider comment."

"Okay," I said. "I heard there was this minor leaguer from Mississippi—big farm-fed white guy. He was playing in some league in Iowa, in the Mariners' farm system I think, and he married some girl from Des Moines because he got her pregnant. She wasn't as farm-fed as the guy, but she was just as white. Anyway, they're in the delivery room and the girl gives birth to a little boy and, get this, the kid is black as night. The minor leaguer is beside himself and he stumbles out of the room, cussing. A nurse follows and catches up to the guy and convinces him to sit down so he doesn't hyperventilate.

"'Deep breaths,' the nurse instructed. 'Take deep breaths.'"

Once the guy settles down, his eyes start to water.

"It's going to be all right," the nurse tells him.

"'My marriage is over,' blubbered the ballplayer. 'If I would've known this could happen I'd have never slept with that black girl when I's back in Mississippi this past off-season, I swear.'"

The room erupted in laughter.

"You're right," Dean said when the laugher died. "That is dumber."

"Okay," Tim agreed. "Your comment was the second dumbest ever."

Everyone in the room concurred, nodding their heads.

"Thank you," I said. "Thank you very much." I grabbed a big handful of popcorn out of the bowl on the coffee table and shoved it in my mouth.

The story about the minor league baseball player was something I'd fabricated for moments when I needed to divert attention from my inanity. That day in the Parker family's living room was the first time I ever told the story. I've told it 3,492 times since.

Some Assembly Required

I opened the coffee shop door just as two very elderly ladies were on their way out. I stepped back and held the door so they could exit.

"What a gentlemen," one of the ladies said.

"You were raised right," mumbled the other. "Your mom must be so proud."

You don't fucking know me, I thought. "Have a nice day," I said.

"What a nice boy," commented the first one, and they shuffled away.

Their assessment was mostly correct. I am a nice boy. But up until the unexpected demise of my VW Bug, I was saddled with a troubling dark side, one that I was able to conceal from the world because I only unleashed it on inanimate objects. If a printer refused to operate properly, I'd put on my work boots and kick the shit out of it and then toss the battered components in the trash. This behavior happened more often than I like to admit, but it drove me crazy that some engineers didn't take the time to design things properly. Even more aggravating are the manufacturers that refuse to fully assemble their products. They casually sidestep this major shortcoming by inconspicuously noting on the product packaging, *Some Assembly Required*. Translation: We, the manufacturer, decided to perform only the easy steps.

But nothing riled me more than poorly constructed cars, and I've owned more than a few. I once had a Datsun coupe with such severe engineering flaws that I had to use a crowbar to replace a stubborn headlight, and it twice forced me to employ a hacksaw to change its windshield wiper blades. In general, if a car gave me trouble, I gave it right back. Rational thought went out the window — unless, of course, the window wouldn't roll down, in which case I'd break the fucking thing with a tire iron.

The most troublesome car I ever owned was a 1969 VW Bug, a blue slug of a car with a white, vinyl interior. The Bug was a hand-me-down from my brother, Karl. The vehicle had treated him with respect, but it hated me. On the first day I drove it, the right rear blinker gave out, and things got progressively worse from there. If I hadn't needed it for transportation I would have happily traded it for a Beta VCR that required some assembly.

I drove the Bug during one of the worst years of my life. My brother gave it to me just after I graduated from Stanford with degrees in political science and economics. Ever curious, after finishing college I decided to explore the possibility of becoming a doctor. I soon discovered that prospective medical school students needed a bunch of science prerequisites, the type of courses I'd eschewed during college in favor of courses that taught me words like eschew. So if I wanted to be a doctor I first had to go back to college and learn some science — unless I wanted to undertake the type of medical training that relies on chanting and the use of severed chicken heads. Because I prefer my chicken on a sandwich instead of in my medicine cabinet, I moved back home and enrolled in a local community college. My course load consisted of the science courses that medical schools require — chemistry, biology, biochemistry and physics. To pay for school I had to get a job. The combination of a full course load and full-time employment was incredibly taxing.

In addition to working and going to school, I suffered the indignity of being a college graduate who lived with his mother. To make things even worse, a week after I moved home, I got a DUI—admittedly well-deserved. The judge took away my license for an entire year, which really made driving a hassle. I was forced to heed the speed limit and obey every stop sign, rules of the road that I'd always considered to be nothing more than charming proposals.

Inconspicuous driving was difficult behind the wheel of a loud, smoky Bug. A constant whine blasted from the tiny engine, which was housed just behind the backseat. The engine drone was a steady reminder of the car's addiction to motor oil. Soon the Bug's need for a daily dose became prohibitively expensive and I couldn't afford to feed its habit. As a result, smoke often seeped inside the car, creating a haze that nearly justified the purchase of a gasmask. Also, a very small man with a corncob pipe seemed to have taken up residence in the tailpipe, and kept blowing his smoke rings out the back. The electrical system worked intermittently and the car refused to go in reverse, except when I wanted to go forward. I think the tires enjoyed going flat, especially when I was running late. Because the driver's seat was stuck in a partially reclined position, when I drove I felt like an astronaut inching toward the moon. I cursed at the Bug daily, first while kicking the fender to assert my superiority and, minutes later, while begging it to start.

The entire year consisted of careful driving, menial jobs, challenging academics and virtually no sleep. The days trudged by. When I completed my last exam, a three-hour physics final, I didn't really care how I'd performed, I was just happy to be done. I handed the exam to my professor and scrambled out the door, eager to move on with my life. In two short days I would be on a plane headed for Massachusetts to start my summer job at Winadu, a sports camp for boys. I'd worked there the previous summer and liked being around the kids. Because it was my second year on the job the camp director was paying me pretty well.

By the end of camp I'd have my license back and enough money to buy a decent car. When I got into the Bug to head home from campus after my physics exam, I knew it was the last time I'd ever have to drive it. Hallelujah.

I punched the key into the ignition and the Bug started up without a problem. But by the time I reached the highway the car was backfiring and spitting smoke. The scent of melting plastic and burning rubber flooded the interior. At first I laughed. Soon the laugh became maniacal. Before long my year of frustration started to inflate into a bulging balloon, and each backfire gave it a little pinprick. After a particularly loud bang from the engine, I screamed, "You worthless piece of shit! I absolutely fucking hate you and every inch of your fucking fuck shit fuck." Then I burst. I slammed the dash, and it felt good, so I did it over and over. I spit on the passenger seat, and then hit the dash again.

I turned up the stereo to compete with the increasingly loud engine whine. Dre was rapping that it was Nuthin' But a 'G' Thang, a song that tramples on the English language as fiercely as the Bug humiliated motorized transportation. I sang along, modifying the lyrics. "Yo Bug, you ain't nuthin' but a piece of shit thang, baaaaaaby," I screamed. "I'm loc'ed out because you making me craaaaazay!" I kept on yelling, and the insults mounted right up to the hook. "Bug you're like shit and like shat and like crap and uh," I screamed over and over. A mountain of stress and hard work was in my rearview mirror and I did nothing to control my elation, or my spite. The car, to me, was the oppressor, and I held nothing back. "You're going to the junk heap you piece of crap — if it will have you! I can't wait to put you out of *my* misery!" I hit the dash again, then the ceiling. I smacked the rearview mirror and it snapped off its stem. Without pausing, I hit the dashboard again. "Take that! Fuck!"

When I turned off Highway 26 onto Banks Road, a hilly strip of skinny pavement that connects the highway with the town of Banks, and my home, the Bug was struggling hard, more than it ever had before. The engine sounded woeful and the light, acrid smoke in the passenger compartment thickened.

"Whatsa matter, you piece of shit?" I yelled. "Can't take a little criticism? Three more miles is all I need out of you. That's it. Then we're through, you crap shit car."

Toward the bottom of the second tall hill I jammed down the accelerator to build momentum for the incline to come. The Bug coughed, as if gagging on its own exhaust. The frame shuddered. Then the engine died.

"We're only two miles from home!" I screamed. "Fucking quitter! Fine! I don't mind walking and leaving your wretched crapass stupid shit ass here!" I pumped the accelerator, trying to coax two more miles out of the car. The Bug didn't respond.

I coasted high enough onto the next hill to make it to Aerts Road, a gravel lane off to the left that runs adjacent to a golf course. As I coasted to a stop, the Bug began belching smoke. I yanked up the parking brake, grabbed my backpack and jumped out of the car.

"Fuck you, you piece of shit," I hissed as I slammed the door. The Bug gave one last wheeze, and I stormed off.

I'd only traveled about twenty feet when I realized that I'd forgotten to grab my wallet out of the glove box. It didn't contain any money or ID—I had neither—but I still felt naked without it. I started to head back. As soon as I turned I saw a small flame shoot out of one of the air vents in the trunk's hatch. I stepped forward slowly, uncertain if my eyes were playing tricks. Another flame flashed, and I leapt into action. I hustled over and sprung open the trunk, protecting my face with my right hand as the engine came into view. Little specks of flame danced on the engine block. I started shoveling gravel and dirt into the trunk to extinguish the flame, but the bits of fire were multiplying. The blaze grew and spread. I worked even harder, shoveling and spitting, trying to rescue a car that I hated. Somewhere deep inside I realized the Bug had been a loyal friend, and that it really hadn't done anything wrong. The car was old, and it had over twenty years of loyal service to its credit. Looking back, I suspect if an artist were to represent that year of my life, using a beach as a canvas, the sand would show only one pair of tire prints.

"I'm sorry, Buggy!" I yelled as the fire spread.

The flames jumped into the backseat and erupted. As the fire expanded I was forced to back off. A group of golfers had gathered along a chain link fence that separated the course from the road. "Get away," one of them yelled. "There ain't no saving her!"

He was right. A strange sadness hit. A blaring siren pierced the peaceful valley, beckoning volunteer firefighters to the small firehouse in town. Ten minutes later the fire trucks arrived. By then the Bug was wrapped in flames. Fire was shooting ten feet high out all four windows. The tires had exploded. The frame was charred. I knew I had hurt its feelings, but I never expected the Bug to take it so hard.

The firefighters, most of them townsfolk I'd known for years, attacked the flame with two hoses and used a third to soak a wheat field on the other side of the road. They were serious and professional, but each found opportunity to flash me at least one mocking, good-natured grin. The fire was out within minutes. The smoldering metal carcass was barely recognizable.

One of the firefighters gave me a ride home, and I explained to my mom what had happened. Next I called a local wrecking yard. The owner agreed to pick up the Bug, free of charge, but he needed me to meet him at the car with the title. We decided to rendezvous at Aerts Road at 10:00 the next morning.

The following day a friend drove me to the Bug around 9:30 so I could have some time to say goodbye before she was towed away. I brought along a crescent wrench and some duct tape. There's an adage among Bug owners: the cars are so simple that any mechanical problem can be fixed with tape and a wrench (my father believed this applied to any car). Although the Bug was beyond repair I wanted to mend the most severe wounds, as a mortician would. I carefully wrapped duct tape around the blackened wheels and the driver's seat. I moved around to the trunk and clanged the melted motor block with the crescent wrench, giving the engine attention that was long overdue. I felt horrible, like I'd berated the poor thing to death. "Sorry buddy," I whispered over and over.

The man from the wrecking yard arrived and loaded the Bug onto a flatbed truck.

"Take good care of what's left of her," I said as I handed over the title. "She deserves it."

Watching the truck pull away, I felt guilty. The Bug's blackened shell was irrefutable evidence that nothing good came from my violent tirades against defenseless, inanimate objects. I've always disliked politicians because they insist on justifying their agenda rather than basing their agenda on what is justified, but I realized that I hadn't been acting much better. I'd been justifying my outbursts instead of embracing rational behavior. As the tow truck disappeared from sight I made a commitment to stop unleashing my frustration on innocent cars and gadgets. Although I somewhat enjoyed bashing things to smithereens, the catharsis never lasted.

Ever since the Bug incident I've refrained from assaulting malfunctioning fax machines and jammed staplers. Instead, I now treat inanimate things as if they have feelings. The radio doesn't strive for horrible reception—it's saddened by its failure, much like a normal person who fails at work. So now when I'm faced with a faulty product or a deficient contraption, I take a different tack. I carefully dismantle the item and delicately pack the pieces in a box. I take the box to the post office and send it off to the manufacturer. In the package I include a note that reads: Enclosed is the defective item you sold me. Please send me a replacement that works (and to do that you might need to call one of your competitors). To recognize the item, some assembly may be required.

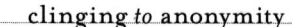

Schooling the Olympics

During the three-year stint I served in law school, the professors used the Socratic teaching method, an instructional technique that educates through active classroom discussion. Professors generated student participation by posing thought-provoking questions aimed at sparking debate. The technique is common in American law schools, and it has its advantages. Students are an active cog in the wheel of learning, refining their critical thinking skills while avoiding an unexciting lecture. But like everything in this world other than free government cheese, there is a downside.

Students are students for a reason; they lack a working knowledge of the relevant subject matter. Handing the instructional reigns to a group of uninformed novices is a leap of faith, a wild gamble that embraces the dubious notion that *even-a-blind-squirrel-finds-a-nut-once-in-a-while*. The sentiment has its charm, but in reality the sight-impaired squirrel never finds a nut. It either starves, or it staggers into the road and meets a violent, flattening death.[1]

---

[1] Blind squirrels have it tough. First, being four-legged creatures, they have a hell of a time holding on to their white guide canes. Second, their seeing-eye dogs tend to eat them.

To keep the students from unintentionally sabotaging their own education, the Socratic teaching method allows professors enough of a leash to guide students back on track, away from the four-lane highway. Still, material scholastic progress doesn't occur unless a student happens upon a piece of applicable knowledge, a nut of insight to be shared with the class. During the hunt for a valid point, eager law students often wander right past a coherent thought and stumble into nonsensical drivel, an intellectual wrong turn that culminates with the student shoving his foot into his mouth. If you think kids say the darndest things, check out a first-year law school class. The delicious humor is a product not of childish innocence, but of the desperate desire to sound intelligent, or to just sound.

In my first year of law school, during a criminal law class, our professor asked the following hypothetical question: *During a bank heist a robber pulls a gun and shoots at a security guard. The bullet misses the guard and hits the bank robber's friend, a member of the bank robbing crew. When the shooter realizes what has happened, he drops his gun and rushes to his friend's side, yelling, "I give up!" His friend later dies in the hospital due to injuries from the gunshot. Should the distraught bank robber be charged with murder?*

The question is crafted to focus attention on the perpetrator's intent, a critical element of criminal law theory. When determining appropriate justice, prosecutors ask first and foremost, *"Dude, what were you thinking?"* A continuum of intent, from premeditated action to honest accident, generally correlates to sentencing outcomes that range from the gas chamber to a slap on the wrist.

In the bank robbing example the shooter didn't intend to kill his friend, but he did intend to shoot the security guard. So is this murder? An excusable accident? Something in between? The only right answer, or more accurately, the only definitive one, is issued by a jury of the defendant's peers, a consortium of twelve citizens each incapable of concocting an excuse sufficient to escape their civic duty. As with all Socratic scenarios, the bank robbery hypothetical consisted of a conglomeration of "facts" manufactured by the professor to create an arguable issue. The question is meant to foster learning by forcing students to probe the inexact science of weighing actual outcomes against a person's intent. Despite the deliberate uncertainty built into the question, many students in the class acted as if they knew *the* answer.

In response to the professor's question, one of the several overzealous students in the class shouted out, "I saw a special on television where some people staged a fake bank robbery to test the accuracy of eyewitness accounts and they discovered that a lot of eyewitness accounts are inaccurate!"

Though our kindly professor had endured countless other nonsensical responses during the semester, she winced at the non-answer. "That's interesting information," she said diplomatically, "but let's revisit that idea later in the semester when we cover evidentiary issues. Anyone else?"

Another ambitious student gave it a try.

"I had a friend who *was* a security guard *at* a bank and he told me that as part of their training they were taught to scrutinize people wearing hats because 72% of bank robbers wear some type of hat!"

The professor reacted with a noticeable slump. The anecdotes exposed a gaping hole in the Socratic method: it may be true that there are no dumb questions, but law students have an ample supply of dumb answers.

Like the professor, I knew these answers were moronic. But I hadn't done the assigned reading—primarily because my only interest in criminal law was how to commit minor crimes and not get caught—so I had nothing of value to add. Still, I wanted to do my part to keep the discussion moving, so I raised my hand.

"Chris, you have something to add?" the professor asked hopefully.

"I totally agree with that bank robber and hat thing!" I asserted. "Because I once wore a hat into a bank and the security guard couldn't stop looking at me. The guard was female though, so...." I shrugged shyly, suggestively. The professor cringed.

I'd just exposed the second biggest flaw in the Socratic teaching approach. For every pointless answer, there's a student, like me, willing to support it. I attended class almost exclusively to capitalize on these opportunities to cultivate absurdity, purposely fertilizing the vines of senselessness until they wrapped around the entire class, choking intelligence, lowering the grading curve. I doubted I could outwit my classmates even if I applied myself, so instead of studying, I tried to drag the competition down to my level.

"Anyone else?" the professor begged. "Anyone?"

Eventually, through the use of leading questions and transparent hints, the professor dragged the class into a productive discussion. Along the way she was forced to navigate a minefield of perplexing remarks, some which were so stratospherically idiotic that the bank robber, had he been in the room, probably would've turned the gun on himself.

"Can we really blame the shooter for the fact that his partner wasn't wearing body armor?" one student asked the class. "Who robs a bank without body armor?"

"I don't think people should rob banks!" another student declared.

Before the professor could intervene and redirect the discussion, the class was transported to the seventh circle of educational futility by a *What-if-er*. What-if-ers are students who interject complex factual twists into a professor's original hypothetical question, thinking, I suppose, that if they can't provide an answer, they can gain some attention—any attention—by modifying the question. The ludicrous scenarios that What-if-ers concoct are so implausible, so bizarre, that they freeze up the academic pistons, halting all progress.

"What if," the student began, "a man is driving by the bank at the same time the robbery is taking place, and what if this man has an epileptic seizure, loses control of his car and smashes through the bank wall? And what if his car, after slamming through the wall, strikes the bank robber at the exact same time the bullet strikes him? If this happened, we wouldn't know the precise cause of death—car impact or bullet—so nobody could be charged with murder! If you tried to charge the driver with murder or manslaughter, he'd invoke, as his defense, the alternate and wholly viable theory that the man was killed by the bullet, not the car. If you charged the shooter with murder, he'd proclaim that his bank robbing friend was killed by the car, not the bullet. You'd never get a conviction! Reasonable doubt!"

The What-if-er sat back in his chair. He settled into a pose that suggested he'd just verbalized genius. A smile covered his face, emblazoned there by imagined cleverness.

The What-if-ers are a small but vocal academic contingent, universally allergic to common sense. They're bright individuals outside the classroom, but once inside, sitting in front of the professor and surrounded by classmates, they devolve into fools, their neurons short-circuited by a powerful yearning for recognition, for attention, for respect. The scenarios they devise are so muddied by improbable circumstances that it's impossible to extract anything of educational value—unless pitying someone for trying too hard is instructive.

I personally experimented with a what-if comment as a kid, but unlike other vices, I only tried it once.[2] It happened on the first day of the summer after fifth grade. My brother, Karl, got up before me and ate the last bowl of Captain Crunch cereal. This forced me to eat a bowl of Special K, which is decidedly unspecial. Launching the summer with a cereal that wasn't coated in sugar put me in a sour mood. After three miserable bites, I shoved the bowl aside, incensed by the blandness. I went to the garage, grabbed a nearly full bag of peat moss and dragged it to Karl's bedroom. I dumped the entire contents at the foot of

---

[2] For the record, when I tried a what-if statement, I didn't inhale. I blurted it out in one, long exhalation.

his bed, a subtle reminder that Captain Crunch was *my* favorite cereal. When Mom discovered what I'd done, she flipped. She pelted me with a verbal barrage that boiled down to, *"Son, what where you thinking?"*

The crime wasn't premeditated, so I hadn't prepared a rational, exculpatory explanation. Determined to retain a roof over my head, I made up a *what-if* scenario on the spot, hoping the diversion would cause enough confusion to create reasonable doubt.

"Mom," I started sincerely, "what if a fire broke out in the middle of Karl's room, a fire he started while playing with a book of matches that you had told him not to touch, and he, being a fierce coward, fled for his life at the first sign of smoke? And what if, upon seeing the smoke surging from the room, I bravely ran in with this bag of peat moss and, being a quick thinker because I come from the same gene pool that produced your enormous intellect, I poured the peat moss on the fire, smothering it and saving the house?"

My three weeks of double-chores and no desserts made for an excellent educational experience. I also got a severe spanking, and haven't touched a *what-if* comment since.

Unlike Mom, law professors don't spank students, at least not to correct behavior.[3] Without the threat of corporeal punishment, What-if-ers let their mouths run ridiculous under the law school's roof, hopeful the professor—or anyone—might construe one of their obscure scenarios as sage. With rare exceptions, however, What-if-ers come across as intellectually oblivious, the academic equivalent of a blind squirrel tap dancing on a well-traveled interstate.

"What if the bank robbers are aliens—would the law of their home planet or the law of earth apply?"

---

[3] Some professors will, however, spank consenting students late at night in the privacy of their homes, or so I've heard. Unlike a spanking meant to punish, the type of spankings professors give can have enormous upside, improving grades and reference letters alike.

"What if the bank robbery shooting was all an elaborate act, the blood and everything was fake, and it was just part of the bank robber's escape plan?"

"What if the bank robber actually intended to shoot his bank robbing friend because it turns out the shooter was *really* in cahoots with the security guard all along and the so-called *accidental* shooting was part of a devious plan between the shooter and the security guard?"

I have no strong opinion about epileptic drivers, alien bank robbers, Hollywood escape plans or secret bank robbing alliances, but I could never pass up a chance to dumb down the classroom. As a law student, I seized every opening to perpetuate classroom foolishness. I raised my hand to interrupt the storm of what-if comments.

"Yes, Chris, you have something else to add?" the professor asked.

"Well, I have an uncle who told me that he's seen aliens in his cornfield. He also is prone to epileptic seizures, especially while driving. But I don't recall him ever crashing his car into a bank, so if a car actually did crash into this hypothetical bank at the same time as the fictitious robbery, it probably wasn't my uncle driving."

"Anyone else?" the professor begged. "Anyone at all want to touch on the shooter's intennnnnnnnnnnnnnn...?"

"Intent!" cried one student. "Of course, we need to look at the shooter's intent! The crux of the bank robbery scenario is whether a prosecutor, under applicable law, could *transfer the intent* of the shooter—his intent to shoot the security guard—onto the act of shooting his bank robbing partner."

"Exactly!" the professor cried, relieved. "Transferred intent is exactly the issue."

A What-if-er, desperate for praise—and apparently unwilling to secure it by accepting a late night spanking from the professor— jumped in.

"What if the robber who got shot died at the hospital as a result of a medical care mistake? For example, a doctor gave him the wrong drugs and it was the drugs that killed him before the injuries from the gunshot did?"

"A great point!" replied the professor. "Next week we will talk about how the law deals with such intervening acts, but let's get back to intent. There's still a lot of ground to cover there."

Successful *what-if* comments are extremely rare, but they do happen. It's these uncommon successes that provide What-if-ers with the courage to megaphone their hogwash in pursuit of an intelligent nut. Driven by the same dynamic that compels lottery ticket buyers, What-if-ers blindly press forward, ignoring the odds. *There's a chance, admittedly remote, that if I say something, anything, it will make sense! Look, that person just won! You can't win praise if you don't speak in class, and I'm willing to gamble every cent of self-respect that I'm about to get lucky!*

At hearing the professor's praise for a fellow What-if-er, other What-if-ers sat up, tantalized. One of their own had just hit the jackpot. I decided to derail what was starting to amount to academic progress. I raised my hand.

"Chris...something to add?" the professor asked hesitantly.

"What kind of gun did the bank robber use?"

"How is that relevant?" the professor asked.

"I know a guy who is thinking of buying a gun and since the bank robber was aiming at one person and hit another, whatever type gun he was using doesn't sound too good."

"Anyone else?" the professor pleaded. "Anyone?"

* * *

The summer after my second year of law school I traveled to Atlanta to watch the 1996 Summer Olympics. The airport was abuzz when I stepped off the plane and into Atlanta's Hartsfield International Airport. The previous day a small bomb had detonated in Centennial Park, the central gathering place for thousands of sports fans converging on Georgia for the Games.[4] The perpetrator hadn't been identified. Theories abounded throughout the airport. The raging, animated debates about who was responsible for the attack gave birth to a roaring chatter.

A number of passionate opinions pierced the decibel haze. One predominant view linked the incident to the Oklahoma City bombing. Others pointed to a connection with the 1993 World Trade Center attack. Pro-life extremists earned peripheral mention, placing them a respectable third in the poll of potential villains. Because Coca-Cola is based in Atlanta and the company was the primary sponsor of Centennial Park, a smattering of sentiment suggested Pepsi was behind the explosion. As the rest of the world debated which diabolical organization, disturbed individual, or devious soft drink maker carried out the attack, I contemplated the legal implications of a Turkish man who died in the park right after the bombing.

After deplaning, I collected my duffle bag at baggage claim and stopped at an airport bar, curious about the large crowd inside. Every chair was taken. Several more people crowded along the walls. Nearly everyone had a beer but hardly anyone was drinking, their eyes glued to the bar's multiple television sets. To better gauge the fuss I set down my duffle and squeezed deeper into the bar until I had a clear view of a screen. The volume blared from hidden speakers. On the television three well-groomed people sat behind a standard news desk.

I leaned over to an older man standing next to me. "What's going on?" I asked.

"Some lawyers are going to discuss the likely criminal charges against the bomber." The man motioned toward the television set.

"They caught the guy?" I asked.

---

[4] The park was dubbed "Centennial" because the 1996 games in Atlanta marked the 100th anniversary of the modern Olympic Games. The Games were resurrected in 1896 in Athens after a long hibernation.

"Nope," the old man replied without altering his gaze from the glowing box. "This is all hypothetical, what might happen if he's brought in alive."

"You think they'll bring the bomber—or bombers—in alive?"

"If they do, I'd like to kill 'em myself," he said. A man next to him nodded agreement and added, "And I'd help you." Emotions in Atlanta, and the country, were understandably frayed.

Forty-eight hours had passed since the bombing. The networks, unable to subsist on repeated speculation about the culprit's identity, had expanded news coverage to include tangential story angles in order to exploit the public's thirst for information.

I, too, wanted information, and the news segment that was starting had a legal slant that heightened my interest. I'd recently completed my second year of law school which, at some level, made me part of America's legal community. With a substantial chunk of legal education under my belt I was confident that I'd understand the segment far more than those around me. I fixated on the television, puffed up with an imagined air of superiority. I figured that when the news segment ended, depending on my altruistic vibe, I'd either field questions from the people in the bar or give a short speech further illuminating the relevant legal concepts. From the looks on their faces, people in the bar sincerely wanted to understand the issues. Who was I to deny them their wish?

The man sitting in the middle of the news desk was a longtime network newscaster who only seemed to handle marginal news stories, like interviewing the lady who designed JonBenet Ramsey's costumes. When I started watching, he was in the process of summarizing the basic facts of the bombing: an explosive device had detonated in Centennial Park, the authorities hadn't identified a suspect (though there was no shortage of accusations flying around the airport), and a local woman had died from shrapnel-inflicted injuries. The newsman then introduced his guests. The female on his right, a middle-aged, graying woman with a sullen, bitter appearance, had been a prosecutor in Georgia for over twenty-five years. The fellow to the newsman's left was noticeably younger, a slick gentleman sporting a three-piece suit and impeccably groomed hair. He was introduced as a renowned criminal defense attorney from New York. The newscaster didn't introduce me, so the people in the bar had no idea that a budding legal superstar lurked in their midst.

"So," the newscaster started, turning to the former prosecutor, "if the bomber *is* caught *alive,* what can we expect from the legal system?"

"The defendant, or defendants, will face a first degree murder charge for the death of the female bystander. And I fully expect the State of Georgia to pursue the death penalty."

"I agree," the defense attorney quickly conceded.

Their conclusion wasn't difficult. If you detonate a bomb in a crowded place and someone dies, a charge of murder is hard to dodge. Do it in Atlanta, during the Olympics nonetheless, and the fine folks of Georgia will roll out a red carpet leading directly to a high-voltage chair. A current of electricity was already pulsing in the crowded bar, as if the waters of revenge had been chummed and scores of blood-thirsty electrons had assembled, ready for action.

"What possible defenses could the bomber raise?"

"On these facts," offered the prosecutor, "other than *I didn't do it,* I'd say an insanity plea is the only realistic route."

"That's probably true," the defense attorney added, "but let's not forget that whoever is charged with this heinous crime is innocent until proven guilty. The State must prove, beyond a reasonable doubt, mind you, that the defendant committed the crime." He sat back with a smile of satisfaction, emblazoned there by the television camera.

I understand all this, I thought. I scanned the room. Everyone else appeared perplexed.

Try as he might, the newscaster couldn't seem to find a point of contention between the former prosecutor and the defense attorney. Without an arguable issue, the segment stalled. The moderator grew noticeably anxious. If the segment didn't improve, and fast, the network would probably roll out a red carpet leading the newscaster to an interview with Kato Kaelin's step-cousin.

"What other criminal implications are there?" the newscaster begged. "Either of you...anything?" An uncomfortable moment passed. "Anything?" he repeated.

Luckily for the newscaster, attorneys get paid by the hour. The two guests happily grappled to find a debatable issue, something to prolong their television exposure, and to increase the length of their stay. For a couple minutes, they babbled nonsensically, searching for a nugget of insight. Then, when all seemed nearly lost, the defense attorney mentioned the Turk, a man who represented, in terms of billable hours, a winning lottery ticket.

"Prosecutors will likely come after the bomber with a murder charge for the death of the Turkish man who was in Centennial Park at the time of the explosion," the slick man said, "because prosecutors *always* overreach when charging defendants."

I wasn't aware that the bombing had caused a second death. By the looks of the patrons in the bar, I wasn't alone. Attention intensified throughout the room. Everyone sat quiet, salivating for an explanation. The newscaster, now smiling, scribbled madly on his notepad, likely drawing a firm line through *Tomorrow, catch early flight to Omaha to cover story on rock shaped like Jesus.*

The defense attorney, smiling broadly, explained to the citizens of America that after the explosion a Turkish cameraman, working for a (the?) Turkish television station, had sprinted toward the scene, his camera in hand, determined to film the aftermath. It's likely that the Turk didn't know the cause of the blast, whether it was a bomb or part of the Olympic celebration. Witness accounts, as the defense attorney explained, had the Turk determinedly rushing through the crowd toward the area of the blast. During his rush to capture the chaos on film, he suffered a heart attack. He died later at a local hospital—and not as a result of being given the wrong medicine by doctors.

The former prosecutor promptly weighed in, insisting that the Turk was a victim of the bombing. She asserted that a sufficient connection existed between the Turk's heart attack and the explosion, and that this nexus supported a separate charge of murder for the Turk's death. The criminal defense attorney ardently debated her conclusion, asserting that the connection between the Turk's death and the bombing was too tenuous to sustain a murder indictment. The issue distilled down to whether the Turk was a heart attack waiting to happen or a healthy man whose strong heart was sent into cardiac arrest by the explosion and subsequent ruckus. It was a classic Socratic hypothetical; a question with no right answer. The case would be difficult for a jury to decide, but it was a perfect scenario for a lawyer. Legal ambiguity requires argument and debate, and argument and debate requires long, drawn-out cases. And long, drawn-out cases deliver a plethora of billable hours. In effect, ambiguity is a lawyer's ATM, so for a hungry attorney, getting a case like the Turk's death is the equivalent of a legal jackpot.[5]

As the news segment progressed, I felt increasingly bad for the Turk. His death was being discussed as if he were a case study instead of a human being. The confluence of facts surrounding his demise reminded me of the intellectually stimulating scenarios created by law school professors to promote learning—the type of circumstances rarely delivered by real life. No matter the instructive potential, it seemed wrong to reduce the Turk's life to a legal hypothetical. I thought of his family, his last moments, the broader effect that his death would have on the Olympics, an event created to unite people, not shatter lives. The attorneys continued to coldly dissect his passing, pressing forward with their pointless discussion to increase their cam-

---

[5] Unlike most lawyers, when I think of billable hours, instead of relishing the money to be made, I cringe at the work involved.

era time. Practically speaking, the bomber, if caught, would be charged with murdering the female bystander. The culprit would undoubtedly be convicted for that crime and would be sentenced to death. So essentially the Turk's death, as it related to the culprit, didn't really matter. If the State of Georgia passed a law mandating that any person sentenced to capital punishment had to be killed once for each victim, a process that would require a series of electrocutions and resuscitations, then sure, let's debate the Turk. But barring that, the Turk was, sadly, dead. The bomber was a disturbed person who, if apprehended, would face a clear charge of murder for the death of the female victim. Case closed.

By the end of the segment I'd become so troubled by the discussion about the Turk that I opted not to field questions from the crowd and refused to give a brief lecture on the technical aspects of criminal law. Instead, like a law professor tending the flock, I monitored the ongoing discussions. Patrons ranted about the Turk, pounding the table, stridently sharing their views as if divinity had provided each of them with *the* answer. As debate raged, the pride and distinction I'd felt as a result of my law student status faded. For the last two years I'd paid a hefty sum to the University of Oregon School of Law to get the exact experience that these barflies were getting for free. The Constitution aside, they had no right to carry on like this. I was the one who had enrolled in law school, the one who'd leveraged my financial future, the one who'd industriously doodled during class. These people had no right to discuss these matters without paying me an ungodly hourly sum.

I grabbed my heavy duffle bag and made my way out to the MARTA stop to catch a train into Atlanta. A volunteer standing near the train platform directed me into the next available railcar. I pushed into the train along with dozens of other tourists, most of them clad in red, white and blue. After we were packed in tight, more people squeezed onto the train. The conditions were cramped and suffocating. Passenger complaints, made to no one in particular, were constant. I found myself pressed against the sweaty flesh of two beautiful girls who appeared to be from Brazil, their bright yellow and green soccer jerseys attractively set off by their brown skin. In almost any other situation, pressing up against the Brazilian duo would have fulfilled a fantasy, but I was ready to get off the train before we even left.

As the train pulled away from the station, several passengers struggled to lift their luggage up onto their heads in order to create some breathing room. I joined in, hefting my duffle up. For the next twenty minutes, I wrestled my bag with Olympic intensity. When we arrived at the downtown stop near Centennial Park, most of the riders exited, leaving me to travel on to the Buckhead neighborhood in relative comfort.

Robbie, a friend from college who lived in Buckhead with his lovely wife, Alice, had encouraged me to come to Atlanta for the Games. He promised to provide me room and board in return for a thank you card. After exiting the train at Buckhead I followed the directions that Robbie had given me, wandering down Peach Street until I came to the proper crossroad. I turned off and walked just under a half-block to his house. A spare key was hidden, as promised, under a green porcelain frog in the small flower garden to the right of the front porch (it's probably still there if you want to rob the place). Immediately after entering the house I tossed down my duffle bag, glad to be rid of my unwieldy companion, and hastily washed up. Within ten minutes I headed back to the MARTA stop, excited to get to Centennial Park, not wanting to waste a single Olympic moment.

When I stepped off the train in downtown Atlanta, I found myself besieged by rampant commercialism. The area looked like the bomb that exploded the day before had been packed with corporate advertisements. *This explosion brought to you by United Airlines!* The main square resembled a refugee camp for corporate logos, placards and slogans, especially the ubiquitous Coke ads. Corporations had unabashedly painted these Olympics green. Any structure capable of hosting a sign or a flag carried a banner of capitalism, each encouraging visitors to give shopping their Olympic best.

Strict security measures had been implemented as a result of the bombing. Armed officers patrolled the perimeter of Centennial Park. Days earlier, I learned, the primary security force at the park consisted of unarmed private guards hired to work the Games. The newly deployed—and armed—uniformed police officers and national guardsmen conducted intense searches of everyone entering the gates, complete with pat downs. Those carrying a backpack, camera, video equipment and similar tourist gear experienced especially long waits as authorities closely examined all extraneous possessions. For efficiency, authorities had set up expedited lines for people without bags or packages. The bomb's *Boom!* had, in effect, provided folks with no material possessions, like me, a rare advantage at an event that catered to consumers.

Once I made it through the security lines, capitalism trumpeted its survival. A bank of mobile ATMs welcomed folks into the park and guarded the area against empty pockets. I love the convenience of the ATM, but when I inserted my bankcard to withdraw a portion of my paltry savings, I received a dour reminder about the evils of monopolistic pricing.

"There is an $8.00 convenience fee per transaction," the screen explained. "Hit the *Enter* key to accept." No ambiguity there.

The fee seemed ill-named. As scores of visitors begrudgingly pressed *Enter*, sounds of anguish, not convenience, reverberated. I hesitated, sickened by the cost, imagining all the things I could buy if the I didn't have to be *convenienced*: three pairs of new socks, a 12-pack of good beer, four loads of laundry, lunch. From behind me a forced cough erupted, the international signal for *I'm waiting patiently...for now*. A glance back confirmed a menacing line was forming. In a moment of panic, feeling pressured to make a decision, I pressed *Enter*. As the button compressed, I released a morbid groan, and just like that I'd effectuated the single biggest waste of money in my entire life. Since I could only afford to be convenienced once, I withdrew my entire Olympic nest egg, $160.

With money in my pocket and thirst in my throat, I searched for a place to buy a drink. I soon spotted a soda and pretzel vendor just a few yards from the mobile ATMs. I headed over. When I got close enough to read the price board hanging on the back of the booth, I blinked—over and over.

Olympic Commemorative Cans of Coke, Only $4.50

I flickered my eyelids again, but the price didn't change. The only other beverage option was a sixteen ounce bottle of water, for *only* $4.00. I glared at the vendor.

"A can of Coke for *only* $4.50?"

The vendor smirked. "It's a *commemorative* can."

"You can't be serious!"

"Hey, it's *only* $4.50."

"Well, before I steal a can of soda from you I'm *only* going to shoot you four and a half times."

The vendor flashed a devious little grin. He was selling cans of Coke for $4.50, a job that certainly required him to be steeled against far worse harassment than I could contrive.

"Do these cans contain the original Coke recipe, the one with dashes of cocaine?" I asked. "Because maybe then I could justify dropping $4.50 for a snort."

"I don't think so."

"No cocaine, no new experience for me, no deal."

"Fine," replied the vendor.

"I'll take my business elsewhere," I threatened.

"If you plan on spending less than $4.50 for a Coke, you'll have to take your business out of Centennial Park," he said calmly.

I wanted to walk away but the cans of commemorative Coke were stashed in finely crushed ice, glistening with the promise of refreshment, enticing my parched throat.

"Okay," I started again, "I'll give you a dollar if I can hold one of the cans on my forehead for thirty seconds."

The vendor shifted his eyes shadily. "For a buck I'll let you hold it for fifteen seconds. That's the best I can do."

"No deal!" I shot back. "How about fifty-cents for a handful of ice?"

"Nope."

"A quarter if you let me look at the cans for another thirty seconds."

"Please leave."

And I did.

For the next seven hours I wandered around, licking the salty sweat from my arms in an attempt to satisfy my thirst. When my legs gave out, I lugged my dehydrated body back to the MARTA stop and returned to Buckhead. Robbie and Alice had arrived home from work, and Alice fed me, filled me with water and gave me an ice cold, non-commemorative can of Coke, free of charge. After lapping it all I up I fell fast asleep.

The next morning, well rested, I high-jumped out of bed, Olympic fever brewing in my veins. By the time I'd showered and made my way downstairs, Robbie and Alice had left for work to their respective law firms. A note on the kitchen table directed me to the cupboards that held cereal and bagels. After inhaling two bowls of Cheerios and a toasted egg bagel, I forced down an entire gallon of cold water, my only defense against Olympic-priced beverages.

I walked to the train station, stopping at a newsstand along the way to buy a paper. The front page headline, in bold, oversized print, announced that authorities had identified a bombing suspect. The suspect hadn't been arrested or charged, and the evidence was still being assessed, but the tone of the article suggested it was just a matter of time before the man under scrutiny would be on death row. The suspect was a local man named Richard Jewell, a security guard who had been working in Centennial Park the night of the bombing. According to the story, Mr. Jewell had discovered an unattended, suspicious looking backpack prior to the explosion. Adhering to instructions from his employer, instead of searching the bag he reported his find to authorities. The backpack turned out to contain the bomb. Before the police arrived to inspect it, the device detonated. Despite fulfilling his basic duties, Mr. Jewell had made two critical mistakes. First, he was employed as a security guard. Second, he was pretty fucking fat.

As it turns out, for most Americans, and certainly for all the journalists and law enforcement officers working the Olympic bombing case, the phrase, *The fat security guard did it,* rolls off the tongue as breezily as *Have a nice day* or *Please drive carefully.* From what I could extract from the newspaper story, authorities obtained a search warrant for Mr. Jewell's apartment and pickup truck based solely on circumstantial evidence, likely explaining to the judge, "Well, Your Honor, the suspect is fat. He is a security guard. He owns a pickup truck, *with* fog lights mind you, *and*, get this, he was in the vicinity of the crime when it occurred!"

This compelling evidence was enough for the judge to issue the warrant. Soon thereafter, FBI agents combed Mr. Jewell's living quarters and his truck. As they searched, Pepsi's management undoubtedly chuckled, *We have our Lee Harvey Oswald!* Though the search failed to turn up any evidence that linked Mr. Jewell to the crime, many in the media, citing anonymous law enforcement sources, reported that the case against him was a slam dunk.

After I scanned the article on Richard Jewell, I spent the rest of the MARTA ride listening to the other passengers put him on trial. The only tangible evidence was a photograph of Mr. Jewell dressed in a security guard uniform, the seams of the light blue, employer-issued shirt strained by his portly frame. His hillbilly pickup truck was in the background. The photo was powerful enough to unify the passengers' minds: *He's guilty!*

"Oh, he did it, no doubt!" a black man seated across from me stated, assuring everyone within earshot that prejudice, like the pursuit of happiness, is now available to all Americans.

The other passengers quietly agreed, shaking their heads affirmatively. Months later, after Jewell was cleared of any wrongdoing by every level of law enforcement involved in the case, the FBI and most Americans were left scratching their heads, thinking, *So there must have been another fat security guard in Centennial Park that night!*[6]

Despite a prevailing eagerness to convict someone, anyone, my two years of legal education allowed me to reserve judgment, exemplifying my deeper understanding of the justice system. As people on the bus jumped to conclusions, I kept an open mind. Maybe Mr. Jewell was innocent. His picture in the paper suggested that the rotund security guard likely had committed several crimes, many of them probably serious, but he didn't appear to be the type to carry out a bombing. And, to me, Jewell just didn't look smart enough to build an operable explosive device.

It is difficult for any criminal system to mete out justice when burdened with ingrained prejudice—like a distrust of fat security guards. The existence of such prejudice hamstrings the sacred paradigm that people are innocent until proven guilty, a glaring flaw in the justice system exposed by Mr. Jewell's legal travails. This same systemic flaw is why the makers of the famed board game *Clue* can't add a character named *Fat Security Guard* to the game's original stable of suspects. Adding a *Fat Security Guard* character to the game would be like adding *Ku Klux Klan Man* or *Central American Dictator*; the inclusion of such obvious villains makes a fair review of the evidence impossible. Place *Fat Security Guard* in a line-up with Professor Plum and Colonel Mustard and the evidence won't matter. The guilty finger, as if guided by prejudicial gravity, will settle on the chubby guy every time. At the beginning of each new round, *Clue* participants would

---

[6] Don't feel too bad for Mr. Jewell—he brought a lawsuit against NBC for character defamation and they eventually paid him $500,000, 14 lifetimes of security guard pay even when adjusted for inflation. On that note I'd like to offer my name to any media outlet to muddy as they see fit, no restrictions, for the low, low price of $25,000. I was Darth Vader's lover? Sure, why not.

take one look at a picture of *Fat Security Guard* and quickly agree, "Okay, we can dispense with the who-done-it issue. We all know the fatty rent-a-cop is responsible." An implication by anyone that Miss Scarlet or Mr. Green committed the crime would bring immediate rebuke.

"Did you miss that part about there being a Fat Security Guard in the vicinity?"

"Read my lips: Se-cur-i-teeeeee Guard! Faaaaaat! Duh!"

As the MARTA train drew close to downtown Atlanta, I considered addressing the other riders. They needed to know that while most criminals might, in fact, be fat security guards, society shouldn't rubberstamp a conviction against Mr. Jewell. For the good of the system, and to protect innocent people from incarceration, society had to at least allow for the possibility that the perpetrator was a disheveled looking black man or a kaffiyeh-wearing Arab. Not wanting to invite ridicule though, I kept quiet.[7]

When the train arrived at Olympic Village I debarked and headed directly to the basketball arena. The previous day I'd overheard some people in Centennial Park talking about a brisk scalping business that had taken root on the road adjacent to the west side of the basketball pavilion. Committed to seeing an event, any event, I arrived at Scalper's Square—as the area had been dubbed—full of hope and ready to spend upwards of $30 for a ticket, any ticket.

Before entering the scalping fray I took a few moments to measure the established transactional etiquette, watching buyers and sellers interact. What I saw was an economist's dream, a perfectly fluid marketplace, supply and demand interacting unimpeded. The scalpers auctioned and finagled, constantly adjust-

---

[7] I don't believe in racial profiling, but I do believe in common-sense profiling. If law enforcement finds a burning cross in someone's yard, they should investigate white suspects first. If I find a dead bird on the front porch, my first instinct is to question the cat, not the dog. If I'm at the gym and smell a fart, I immediately suspect the guy doing sit-ups, not the dainty girl stretching her neck.

ing prices, fighting for every dollar. Buyers haggled and bitched. But the scalpers were seasoned salesmen and they leveraged the novelty of the Olympics for every penny. Like the athletes representing the United States, these scalpers were America's best, and they were doing the country proud.

After spending several minutes watching, I joined the fray, walking right into the heart of the Square. For over an hour I circulated and listened, waiting for a scalper to offer a ticket in my price range. A ticket to a basketball game between Angola and China sold for $230. A ticket for the morning session of men's gymnastics fetched $280. The swimming events commanded at least $250 a seat. When I heard a scalper announce that he had a single ticket for an early round table tennis match, I thought I heard opportunity knocking.

"How much," I asked.

"$150," the scalper answered, straight faced.

"No, really. How much?"

"You heard me, $150," he shot back. "Asians love this stuff. The match starts in about an hour. I'll sell it for at least $150, you watch."

"It's fucking ping pong for Christ's sake! I'll give you $30. That's a gift, from me to you."

The man walked away as if I didn't exist. I followed, taunting.

"I could sell a ticket to a nose-picking contest before you could sell that ticket for more than $30! Now my bid is $20, and that's only because I have an Olympic-sized heart."

Just as I finished my rant I found myself in the eye of a bidding hurricane—and not for tickets to my proposed nose-picking event. Three Asian gentlemen converged on the scalper with the ping pong ticket. Each of the three men bid frantically on the single ticket, as if their next heartbeat depended on watching two men play a resounding game of table tennis. In the midst of this perfect scalping storm, the ticket price soared. As the bids climbed, I joined in, the only participant having the wherewithal to hold firm to my original offer.

"180," one of the Asian men said in broken English.
"190," another answered.
"200," offered the third.
"I'll pay you 30!" I yelled.
The bidding stalled, odd looks were delivered.
$210 came, then $220 and $230.
"30 is my final offer!"
$250. $270. $290. The price continued to rise, but I held firm.

"$30 damnit! 30! Fuck! 30, 30, 30." I stuck my fingers in my ears. "30, 30, 30."

The ticket, for a *ping pong match*, sold for $310. After the sale, the scalper, properly thrilled, found fit to overlook my unconventional bidding technique. He patted me on the back and leaned in to offer some free advice.

"If you really want to see an event and you don't have much cash, then check out the bicycle road race on Wednesday morning. You can see it for nothin'. Stand pretty much anywhere along the race route, goes all over Atlanta. But you ain't gonna get no ticket for no thirty bucks to nothin'."

He whispered the words like the information was a gigantic scalper secret, as if hearing the word "free" would knock the hordes of ticket seekers back to reality, a place where offering $30 for a ticket to a ping pong match is foolishly extravagant rather than hopelessly cheap. I thanked him for the tip and left Scalper's Square, disappointed that I wouldn't be seeing an Olympic event in an official venue, but thrilled with my exposure to a real, living, breathing microeconomic marketplace. The Square had taught me more about free-market activity and laissez faire economics in two hours than Adam Smith and Stanford's Economic Department had imparted on me in five years.[8]

Since the free Olympic road race wasn't scheduled until

---

[8] This is in no way a condemnation of Stanford or its unmatched Economics Department. The comment serves only to condemn my alarm clock for its failure to apply itself during my undergraduate years.

Wednesday, I wandered back toward Centennial Park to search for other free things to fill my time and, with any luck, my stomach. As I walked toward the Park, I passed a large Christian group singing hymns *(for free!)* and handing out informational brochures *(again, free!)*. There were countless such groups at the Olympics, all assuring that Jesus Christ loved everyone, and that he also had a burning desire to save me, especially if I made a small donation *(not free)*.

As I passed by the group, a very young girl dressed in a flowery summer dress approached. She gently reached out her hand and offered a brochure.

"Jesus will save you," she said. I stopped and engaged.

"When will Jesus save me? And from what?"

She hesitated, her pre-adolescent mind not programmed by parents or parishioners to respond to such an inquiry.

"I think it's in the pamphlet," she finally answered, before adding, "He *will* save you!"

I looked skyward and made a loud, specific request. "How about saving me from $5 cans of soda?"

The girl giggled.

"Thanks for the brochure," I said. "I look forward to being saved."

There is a jolt of goodness that hits the soul when you cross paths with a little kid earnestly trying to be good. Although I didn't feel saved, I felt rejuvenated. As I walked away, a skip joined my step and I absentmindedly hastened my pace. Within minutes, just as the young girl had promised, I encountered salvation.

Budweiser Beer School!
Free of Charge!

The sign, strung between two trees, glistened in the sun like an angel. Jesus was speaking my language, and he was using exclamation points for emphasis. I was saved!

Beer School is a marvel of modern corporate marketing. It's

a large mobile classroom constructed by joining two large tractor trailers together to form an educational forum dedicated to all things Budweiser. Its existence is a testament to Budweiser's passionate commitment to higher learning: admission is open to everyone, poor and rich, old and 21, lawyers and security guards, fat or slim, without preference or prejudice. Like utopian Justice, Beer School is blind. No matter your color or creed, if you're interested in consuming alcohol, Budweiser is eager to teach you exactly why you should.

Unlike the lengthy application process favored by accredited universities, Beer School's entrance requirements are short and simple. No personal essays. No agonizing tests. No letters of recommendation. Just hand your state authorized ID to the pretty girl in the Beer School booth, sign a waiver, and you're in.

"Congratulations!" the Budweiser girl exclaimed as I scribbled my name on the standard waiver form. "You've been accepted to our 1:30 class! Classes last 45 minutes. Please come prepared—thirsty!—and tell your friends. We have eight classes a day. The first class starts at 10:30 in the morning. We're here throughout the Olympics."

"Every day?"

"Yes, every day!"

"Do I have to fail the class to attend again or do you guys let graduates come back and sit in whenever they want."

"You can take the class as many times as you care to!"

Thank you Jesus! His trick of turning water into wine never really impressed me—give me a few months and some grapes, I can do that—but free Budweiser, now that's the kind of thing that could really reinvigorate Christianity.

At the appointed hour I showed up at Beer School's door and walked into the brightly lit and meticulously clean makeshift classroom, anxious to learn. The room had that *brand-new-conjoined-tractor-trailers-turned-into-a-classroom* smell. The four rows of stadium seating were bisected by a center aisle. Each side row contained five seats, giving Beer School the capacity to educate forty students at a time. Out of scholarly habit I headed straight for the back row. I took a seat in the middle of the row on the left side. The rest of my classmates, the *Class of 1:30 p.m.,* shuffled in and took their chairs. When everyone was seated, a real life Budweiser Beermaster stepped to the front of the room.

"Welcome!" he said cheerily.

A detailed model of Budweiser's beer making process adorned the wall behind the Beermaster, complete with miniature brewing vats and a beechwood aging holding tank. Forsaking Socrates' teaching methods, the instructor lectured. He spoke passionately about the history of beer. He explained the importance of the unique yeast strain Budweiser has used since 1937. He harped about the company's commitment to quality ingredients.

At several points during his presentation, the Beermaster referred to the wall model to explain the purpose of each vat and tube. When he finished walking the class through the entire brewing process, the Beermaster instructed his assistants, who were dressed in ridiculous elf-like costumes, to distribute samples of various Budweiser beers. The elves delivered the samples one 12 oz. bottle at a time, giving each row a single bottle to share. In each row, the student nearest the center aisle received the bottle, poured a small amount into a paper "testing cup," and then passed the bottle down the row so that each student could take a small amount for sampling. This process was repeated six times with six different Budweiser brews.

Because my classmates and I wanted to create the appearance that we'd come for the vaunted education, not the free beer, each sample bottle arrived at the end of the row still half full. As the Beermaster described the various traits of each sample, my fellow students paid close attention, frequently nodding their heads to illustrate growing enlightenment, acting as if Beer School were the first step toward a new career, a new life. Each sample was sniffed, swirled and sipped while the Beermaster explained why some beers emit a hoppy scent, others a fruity fragrance. After he finished up his comments on the last beer sample, a Budweiser winter brew I'd never heard of, the Beermaster wrapped up.

"Thanks for coming to Beer School. But we couldn't call ourselves a legitimate educational institution if we didn't give our students a little test."

I reflexively sunk down in my chair. I *was* there for the free beer. I hadn't paid close attention to the presentation and, as the Beermaster eyed the class, I worried that a substandard test score might bar me from participating in future Beer School sessions.

"Can anyone tell me the difference between a lager and an ale?" the Beermaster asked.

Only two students raised their hand. The rest of the class hung their heads in shame.

"Yes, you," the Beermaster said, pointing to a girl in her mid-thirties dressed in a swarm of stars and stripes.

"Ales are made with yeast that float to the top during the fermenting process, or top-fermenting yeast, and the yeast used to make lagers are larger, so these yeast sink to the bottom of the fermenting vat during the process."

"Very impressive!" the Beermaster congratulated. "You've won a prize."

I sat up in my chair reflexively. *A prize?* The Beermaster pulled an official Beermaster hat from behind the lectern, just like the one he was wearing, and he tossed it to the lady. Unlike the boring commemorative certificates other schools traditionally present to the valedictorian, or the mundane job offers awarded to college graduates, the Beermaster hat was a reward worth the toil, discipline and effort. I was inspired.

After leaving Beer School I located a convenience store and bought a small notepad and pen. I promptly returned to the sign-up booth and re-enrolled for another Beer School session, prepared to learn. Employing knowledge from my first Beer School class, I craftily selected the last seat in my row, the position where the sample bottles arrived half-full for the drinking. When the Beermaster started his presentation, instead of thinking solely about liquid refreshment, I found my mind concentrating on solid information. I was seated in the first row, paying close attention, taking notes. For the first time in countless semesters, I was motivated to learn. When another student talked or laughed during the presentation, I shot them a stern look, letting them know that they were infringing on my learning experience.[9]

My second class at Beer School was led by a different Beermaster, a man shorter and stouter than my first instructor. I hung on his words, transfixed by the brewing process, visions of a Beermaster hat dancing in my head. The Beermaster took us through a very similar presentation, but this time, as the brewing process was described, I scribbled diagrams in my notepad. I listened as he discussed each sample, sniffing the beer and sipping it slowly, happily draining every precious drop of the free liquid from each sample bottle. As the lesson came to a close, the Beermaster posed a question to the class. This time I confidently raised my hand to answer.

"Yes, you," the Beermaster said as he pointed toward me.

"Well, Budweiser uses rice as its source of carbohydrate during the brewing process," I answered. "And, as you pointed out during your presentation, it is interesting to note that Budweiser is the largest single purchaser of rice in America."

"Exactly!" he replied, his tone informing the rest of the class that he was sincerely impressed. To the envy of all, he handed me a Beermaster hat. I strolled out of class, slightly buzzed and fully brilliant.

I returned to Beer School seven more times over the next

---

[9] Every time I chastised a fellow Beer School student with my eyes, I felt like I'd been possessed by one of my law school classmates, the ones who often turned around and looked scornfully in my direction during class. Each time I spun around to stare down a rowdy Beer School participant, I honestly expected to see me sitting at the point of disruption, paper airplane in hand.

three days, driven by an insatiable thirst for knowledge. Each time, as soon as the doors opened, I scrambled in to secure a spot at the end of a row in order to maximize my sampling experience. As Beer School's most devoted student, I pelted the Beermaster with questions and hypothetical situations for my own edification, and as a gift to my classmates.

"What if Budweiser used potatoes as the source of carbohydrate instead of rice, or maybe diced pineapples or corn, how would that affect the flavor of Bud Light? And, instead of beechwood aging, what if Budweiser used birch wood, or maybe balsa wood?"

I was particularly mesmerized by the magical world of yeast, the world's true Beermasters, tiny organisms capable of ingesting sugar and excreting alcohol.

"Like modern-day athletes, could we feed the yeast steroids in order to increase their efficiency and productivity?" I asked. "How about yeast hookers? Would the yeast respond to a bunch of yeast tramps, a little sexual incentive, or are yeast asexual?"

The Beermasters, likely threatened by my advancing knowledge, became noticeably agitated every time I chimed in with a question. I persisted, though, foraging for information. As the facts piled up in my head, my questions became increasingly advanced, so much so that on several occasions the Beermasters couldn't provide an answer.

"That's an odd question," the Beermaster responded with a heavy sigh. "I have no idea if cows have yeast lining their digestive tract, and, if they do, I don't know whether a cow's yeast, if they have any, would be able to produce beer in the event the cow somehow ingested the right ingredients in the right order at the right time intervals. But that really doesn't have anything to do with what I'm here to talk about today. I can assure everyone here that Budweiser is not going to shift its brewing process from vats to cows. Let's move on."

Concerns about job security have a strange impact on people, so I didn't take offense to the Beermasters' increasingly snide responses to the questions I posed. When not in class, I kept my notepad close, studying every chance I got.

My last visit to Beer School was the Wednesday *Class of 3:15*. I'd attended two classes earlier in the day—after watching the free Olympic road bike race—and I had already sampled the equivalent of eight beers. Since I hadn't been getting much sleep, the alcohol had an amplified impact. Right after the 3:15 class started, I fell asleep. My head plopped down on the table and I drifted off, right there in the front row. While the Beermaster instructed, I slept, dreaming of genetically engineered cows capable of carrying out the entire brewing process in their four stomachs: one stomach for brewing, one for beechwood aging, one for heat pasteurization (or cold-filtering, depending on the season), and the final stomach serving as a storage tank for the finished product. I'd feed the cows hops, barley, water and rice, wait a day or two, then suckle my private label microbrew right from their udders.

A tap on the shoulder ended my dream. Two uniformed police officers hovered over me.

"Sir, you need to come with us," the taller officer said in a deep voice. He had a hint of a Southern accent.

"Now?" I asked.

"Yes, now."

"Did I miss the sampling?"

"It doesn't matter. Time to go."

I stood up, wobbled, and walked wearily toward the door. I'd been expelled from Beer School, sent packing because of my devotion to sampling. The Class of 3:15 looked on quietly.

The officers backed away from their threat of handcuffing me and let me walk freely. When I arrived at the Beer School door I stopped and looked back at my classmates. The scene had a sense of finality. This was, no doubt, my last Beer School class, and as Beer School's most storied student, I felt I had to make a dramatic exit. I considered a Nixon-like victory wave, but the shorter policeman, sensing I was preparing a theatrical gesture, gently grabbed my arms and pulled them behind my back, forcing me to settle for a verbal goodbye.

"You all look so sad. Please tell me that the government didn't reinstate prohibition while I was sleeping." I quickly made a frightened face, then added, "Please! Oh, please!"

My classmates broke out in laughter. Even the Beermaster and policemen chuckled. I walked out, satisfied, positive I had tapped Beer School for every ounce of educational insight it had to offer.

Once outside, the two policemen fired questions at me. Surprisingly, they determined I wasn't a risk to the public or myself. The interrogation soon turned into a comfortable conversation.

"You sure you are okay, that you don't need anything?" one of the officers asked.

"I could probably use around-the-clock parental guidance. And if you could give me directions to the nearest hotel with an *On-the-Lam* special, that would be helpful. Other than that, I'm fine."

Both officers laughed heartily, emboldening me to push my luck.

"Or how about just a can of Coke? It'd wake me up a bit."

In the spirit of Southern hospitality, my two newest friends escorted me to a nearby convenience store, the same one where I'd bought my pen and notepad for class. The officers were kind enough to buy me a Coke, a non-commemorative can, but a Coke nonetheless. We shook hands, shared goodbyes and parted ways.

After downing my Coke I headed to the MARTA stop. I needed to return to Robbie's house in Buckhead and regroup. As the train pulled away from Centennial Park, I reflected on my Beer School accomplishments. The friends I'd made, the good times, achieving a command of the curriculum. It had been far more than Olympic-sized fun. For the first time in my long and varied academic career, I'd applied myself, paying attention, studying diligently, slurping up sample cups full of knowledge.

In three weeks time I'd be back at law school for the start of my third and final year. Prior to enrolling in Beer School, I'd dreaded going back. Law school meant a reunion with classmates who'd had an entire summer to think up annoying questions. They'd buy textbooks, show up early for class and sit in the front row, take notes, drink coffee to stay awake and concoct silly *what-if* questions involving Willie Wonka and a Class-Action Factory. I'd make fun of their exasperating antics and pity their future clients—*Ladies and gentlemen of the jury, can you really rule out the possibility that my client was framed by epileptic aliens?* But now, at least, I understood the reason behind their irritating buffoonery. The explanation was as obvious as the Beermaster hat resting proudly on my head: they cared.

End Notes:

1. In almost every legal matter—or any argument—there exist two parties: one seeking to clarify, the other seeking to confuse. The party that wants to clarify has the facts in their corner. For the confuser, facts are their death knell. This is particularly true in criminal trials. One party, almost always the defendant, tries to cloak facts with innuendo and tangents. Confusing the situation is always more challenging—this is the reason why good defense attorneys can charge so much—but the smart money backs the clarifier every time.

2. Prior to the paying the ATM convenience fee at the Olympics, my previous biggest waste of money was paying a NYC street vendor $6 for a 12 oz. bottle of water on a muggy July day. In my defense, the price of the water wasn't posted. I gave the vendor a $10 and he gave me a bottle of water and four singles. Dazed by the absurdity of the cost, I started to walk away. Before I was out of earshot, a lady approached the vendor and asked, "How much for a water?" I stopped to watch. The vendor looked at me, then back at the lady, before sheepishly mumbling, "$6?" "Fuck you you fucking bag of shit," the lady yelled. "How much is the fucking water?" The vendor, clearly suscep-

tible to haggling, replied, "$2?" Oh, the wonderful bluntness of New Yorkers. What really bothered me about the episode was that I wasn't even wearing my *I'm an Out-of-Town Yokel* t-shirt. I still don't know how the vendor identified me as a tourist and detected my country roots through my shroud of sophistication.

3. The media suggested that the case against Mr. Jewell was a slam dunk. It makes no sense that the phrase *slam dunk* is used by Americans to suggest certainty. In a nation where most people can't touch a regulation basketball rim without the aid of a trampoline, this inference is grossly misleading. The phrase should be used to refer to things that almost certainly aren't going to occur. When asked by my boss, "Will that memo be done by the end of the day?" I confidently and truthfully respond, "It's a slam dunk!" The next morning, when my boss asks why the memo isn't done, I turn the tables and tell him what a boob he is for thinking I could dunk a basketball in the first place.

4. If the makers of *Clue* ever wanted to add Fat Security Guard as a suspect, they could compensate by adding a new element to the game, one that required players to name the fast food item eaten by Fat Security Guard right before the murder. Fat Security Guard did it with the candlestick, in the library right after eating Kentucky Fried Chicken. Makers of *Clue*, that one is yours, royalty free.

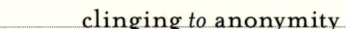

A Dream Recounted

"Evolution, you're a lazy fucker." The ill-mannered comment drifted through the heavens.

I was raised to believe God doesn't use coarse language, but unlike my mouth, my ears don't lie. The comment lacked all of the thundering panache one would expect from God. Instead of an outraged admonition, God's foul comment reeked of whimpering frustration. It was mildly surprising to discover God swears; it was downright shocking to find out He's not good at it.

I looked forward to sharing this revelation with my mom. When I was a kid she always greeted my use of "uneducated language" with severe reprimands, employing an array of torturous methods to exorcise my wicked tongue. After administering her punishment, she always asked, "Do you know what God thinks of language like that?"

Mom asked the question with thundering panache, but she never indicated whether she knew the answer. Maybe she thought it was self-evident, or else the question was rhetorical, but there was also a chance that Mom thought I was a selfish mystic oracle who refused to share my knowledge. She continued to ask, I suspect, because she hoped I'd eventually relent and tell her what I knew. In any event, now I *did* know. When I swore, God raised His fist in Heaven and cheered, "That's it kid, tell it like it is!" I grinned wide. Decades of harbored guilt, the cumulative result of being scolded by authority figures every time I swore, dissipated. For the first time in years I felt I might escape eternal damnation.

Evolution has a reputation for being exceedingly lazy, as every soul from Hell to Heaven will attest. Despite God's comment being spot on, Evolution threw his hands in the air.

"I am not lazy," he insisted. "I'm methodical!"

Evolution's attempt to put a positive spin on his lethargy failed to convert anyone. The angelic audience responded with eye rolls and a shrill release of deep, mocking sighs. Evolution pressed on. "God, you're the one in charge around here. If you'd do your job, provide me with some semblance of a long-term plan, then I could get some work done. I go millennia without updated strategic information. Eons ago you spent six days creating this earthly headache. Then on the seventh day you rested. The Bible, however, omits the fact that you also rested on day eight, day nine, and every day since. If you ever get around to telling me what you want done, I'll do it. Until then, keep your holier-than-thou attitude to yourself." [1]

Tension wrought the heavens. Throughout the universe, thunderous storm clouds materialized. God's spat with Lucifer had started the same way.[2]

I held my breath along with apprehensive angels, my gaze

---

[1] I wish God could've built the world in, say, three days and then rested on the fourth. Then we'd have only a three day work week between each Sabbath—and we could still insist on a Saturday. A three day work week! That's almost reasonable enough for me to consider finding full-time employment.

[2] When I say that Lucifer v. God started in similar fashion, I'm referring to the tension and storm clouds. The reasons for the disputes were quite different. The confrontation with Lucifer sprang from an embezzlement scandal.

shifting between the cloud-covered floor and meteors hurtling through the space-time continuum. The saints grew silent, uptight. The Three Wise Men hyperventilated.[3]

Time yielded to the celestial trepidation and stopped in its tracks. Teetering on the brink of a heavenly war, every ear perked, awaiting God's response. God hesitated, something He rarely does. When His response came, it reverberated with magnificent force, a proclamation that shook my bones.

"You goddamned insolent ass! You're on thin ice, Evolution—in fact, you know what? Effective immediately you are officially being placed on unpaid leave and your health benefits are hereby suspended."

Tension thickened into a fog of unease, so dense it was hard to breathe. Then, quite unexpectedly, came a scattering of muted chuckles. Soon, countless angelic bellies quivered with uncontrolled laughter. One of the angels leaned over and whispered, "Can you believe God had the audacity to mention benefits? Our benefits stink! They've been dwindling for centuries! The inadequacy of our medical and dental coverage is just appalling. God claims it's because of budget restrictions, but somehow He finds the resources to continue expanding His empire to other galaxies. Power hungry, I tell you! Wing repair, birth control, medicinal marijuana—none are covered. And don't get me going on the lack of life insurance options."

I nodded appreciatively.

God and Evolution, literally the oldest of friends, were nose to nose, glaring. Under God's unrelenting stare, Evolution began to shrink, his physical form deteriorating further with each

---

[3] It's unclear whether their hyperventilating was attributable to the tense dialogue between God and Evolution. The Wise Men are prone to hyperventilation. Antagonistic angels have been known to induce panic attacks in the three by updating them on the monetary value of the gold, frankincense and myrrh they presented to Jesus at his birth. The Wise Men had horribly miscalculated the true value of their gifts and, as a result, their descendants are still wallowing in debt, gnawing on boiled bark for sustenance.

passing asteroid. Tremendously overmatched, Evolution, quite smartly, blinked. He bowed his head in surrender, genuflecting at God's feet, hoping to avoid banishment.

God sternly studied Evolution's huddled mass for a tense moment. Then He exploded into uproarious laughter. Evolution joined in and began to roll on the ground in unabashed frivolity. His trembling hadn't been fear, but suppressed laughter.

God reveled in the absurdity of having earlier used His own name in vain.[4] The All Mighty, I realized, enjoys harmless sin as much as I do. The Ten Commandments might be etched in stone—except in U.S. courthouses where displaying the Commandments is expressly forbidden—but God overlooks trivial violations, even participates in them from time to time.

It'd been several millennia since the pair had engaged in a ruse of this magnitude. Lackluster as ever, and still chuckling, Evolution slinked back to his office. Once there he lumped down in a plush, dinosaur-leather chair, propped up his feet and reclined, certain God would never remove him from the simplest job in the universe—doing literally nothing. Or close to it.

On the rare occasion Evolution makes it into the office he runs through his lengthy to-do list like a chicken with its legs cut off. Most days, from morning to night, Evolution snoozes on his front porch swing, ignoring earthly pleas for urgently needed biological updating. Urgency, however, is not Evolution's strong suit, as your average brachiosaurus would attest. Worse, God refuses to prod Evolution forward, displaying a brazen lack of the managerial oversight you'd expect from someone who doesn't have boss and is guaranteed a tomorrow.

I felt a bit cheated. I wanted to see God and Evolution brawl. As a child I'd read the glorious horrors promised in Revelations, every word delightfully frightful. Maybe God couldn't live up to the hype.

---

[4] The only thing God enjoys more than this ironic delight is pretending to worship another god.

I also felt disappointment. Evolution's unmatched job security means life on earth will continue to meander. I won't evolve into a man who can jump buildings like Superman, and therefore I'll never have my own pay-per-view special.[5] Unlike Evolution, God has earned the right to take things slow. He made man out of mud, yet when I shower I don't dissolve and flow down the drain. That's impressive, and it gives God substantial laurels on which to rest. In contrast, Evolution has been and continues to be magnificently unproductive. His priority project—Turn Ape to Man—is in shambles. Granted, there have been some aesthetic improvements. I thank Evolution for swimsuit models while cursing the swimsuits that they needlessly wear. Get past the superficial, though, and what you find is troubling. Humans intentionally kill each other by the millions. Apes don't. If things proceed as they are, I fear God will abandon hope for man and turn the world over to a more humanitarian species, like dogs or dolphins, and send humans to extinction's warehouse to lament with the dinosaurs.

Beads of sweat dotted my hairline and formed puddles of anxiety near my temples. Evolution's slothfulness was going to drive man into extinction. The thought of human eradication took me to the brink of hyperventilation.

Nearby an angel softly uttered "$4.3 trillion." I looked over just in time to catch a glimpse of the three hyperventilating Wise Men collapse like dominos. Mr. Gold went down first, slamming into the other two. (Mr. Gold always falls first, his financial gaffe the worst of the three). A mob of snickering angels surrounded the tangled trio. I wandered over to take a closer look. As I neared, I started to laugh, too. Under their robes, they were wearing matching lacy underwear sets.

---

[5] With my current skill set, the only way I can imagine making money from a television special starring me is a "pay-*or*-view" format in which the television-watching public was required, through governmental decree, to watch my annual variety show unless they paid a $24.95 fee.

I stood over Mr. Gold.

"Stupid bastard," I snickered, playfully shaking my head.

The comment set off another wave of laughter. I reached my hand out to help him up.

"We all make mistakes," I said. "Don't worry about it."

Mr. Gold grasped my waiting hand and I pulled him to his feet. I helped brush off his gown and then slipped him five bucks. "Get something to eat," I told him. "And stop caring so much. It's just money."

He nodded knowingly. "You're right." We then helped up his two eternal companions, and the three hustled away.

At that moment, down on earth, a man refrained from killing another man.

"One good deed leads to another," Evolution intervened, "and I'm not in the business of good deeds."

"What business *are* you in?" I asked, but Evolution was already snoring.

I looked around for God. I had some questions I wanted answered, about Earth, humans and our future. But He was already gone, off tending to one of the other three billion planets that have life.

Then I woke up.[6]

---

[6] I pray that God fires Evolution and replaces him with whoever He currently has in charge of creating my dreams. Then the world would resemble a Dr. Seuss landscape and I'd be king of pretty much everything.

KEMPEROTIC[1]

Like everything other than religious fundamentalists, the English language has evolved. Over the years definitions have been tweaked, spellings slightly altered, pronunciations tinkered with. Some words have been lost, and new ones have been added. Shakespeare made up over 500 words to aid his stories, unprecedented literary leeway that gave him an unfair advantage. Because of this, I have no reservations about creating words to fill the gaping holes in my vocabulary, and it's also why I consider Shakespeare an overrated blybian.[2]

Dumb people have also been allowed to add to the lexicon—people like Sir John Harrington and Sir Thomas Crapper. Though plumbing lore is unclear on which one of these fine English gents invented the toilet, both felt compelled to attach their name to the contraption. If I had invented a depository for urine and feces I wouldn't have let my name anywhere near it. Instead I would have named it after someone who had wronged

---

[1] Kemperotic (kĕm-pər-ŏ-tĭk): An insightful, funny, wonderful vignette.

[2] Blybian (blī-bē-ən): A person who mistakenly believes he writes better than I do.

me, like Alan Schroeder. *"Honey, I'll be out in a minute. I'm on the Alan."* That's music to my ears. John and Crapper missed a golden opportunity.

The French Minister of Defense during World War II, André Maginot, made an even graver naming gaffe. The French, rightfully leery of the crazy German with the miniature mustache, built a defensive line along its border with Germany. The Maginot Line, as André proudly dubbed it, included concrete fortifications and various obstacles (like drive-in movie theatres that showed boring, over-dramatic French movies capable of repulsing anyone). Maginot assured the French populace that his namesake wall was impenetrable, and that it could repel any German assault. We'll never know if he was right, though, because those cheating Germans avoided the Maginot Line, waltzing into France via Belgium, laughing (and shooting) every step of the way.

Arrogantly lending your name to a project that turns out to be a total failure isn't the worst sort of naming blunder, though. For confirmation, just ask any descendant of Mr. Giovanni Pedophile, a well-meaning and harmless sixteenth century children's advocate from Italy.

After something has a name, it needs a spelling, and it seems that the creators of the English language decided to tackle this task by adopting more exceptions than rules. It's as if early English linguists simply decided to hold a gigantic, all-comers spelling bee to establish the proper spelling of every single word. Since no official spellings existed, it was nearly impossible to get eliminated. There were virtually no wrong answers. Mr. Webster of dictionary fame probably moderated the event. He'd give a contestant a word and regardless of what the participant blurted out, Mr. Webster would nod in agreement and record the result. When the village idiot spelled knife with a K, no one questioned it. And when a shy contestant with a horrible stutter spelled b-o-o-k-k-e-e-p-e-r, Mr. Webster accepted it as gospel.

I imagine the contest lasted for several months and the only contestants who were ever eliminated either slept through their turn or tried to insert numbers.

"Concentrate. C-O-N-C-E-N-T-R-8. Concentrate."

"Sorry, sir," Mr. Webster would say. "The rules are clear. No numbers allowed. You're out."

The consequences of creating a language in this manner have rippled forward into the present day, bridling us with a language that's saturated with confusing, contradictory rules. On the bright side, we can be thankful that Mary Poppins didn't participate in the inaugural spelling bee. (Supercalifragilisticexpeialidocious? Any responsible nanny would have found a way to spell that in nine letters or less.) But still I get frustrated every time I get stuck trying to spell words like acquiesce or phonics.

As with all whimsical annoyances, what is often a source of headache can also be a springboard to childish entertainment. For example, I always enjoy it when a rental car customer service agent asks me how to spell my last name.

"I didn't get that, sir. Does your last name start with a T or K?"

"Oh, I'm sorry. It's a K, as in knife," I respond. "Then an E as in extraterrestrial. M as in mnemonic. A P as in pneumonia or psychology, you choose. And another E. Then an R as in any word that starts with R." This usually gets a small laugh, or they hang up. If the agent stays on the line, I ask a favor.

"And I have a special request."

"What's that, sir."

"Please make sure that the local map you provide indicates the location of every barpital in the area."[3]

Denhet.[4]

---

[3] Barpital (bâr-pĭ-tl): A bar within walking distance of a hospital or, better yet, a bar with an ER on site.

[4] Denhet (pronunciation key unavailable since the word was just invented): The end.

clinging *to* anonymity

Sasaquafish

I started fishing in the summer of 1977 with a rusty rod and reel. The pole originally belonged to my cousin Ron. He used it to buy my silence.

Ron is the son of my Uncle Denny and Aunt Sharon, though the two downplay the relationship. Our family used to stop by their house on late Sunday afternoons, or on a whim, to use their pool or just to visit. Every time we pulled into their driveway, my mom reminded us about the connection between death and Ron's blue mini-motorbike.

"That motorbike is deathly dangerous," Mom ranted. "None of you are allowed to even touch it."

"Listen to your mother," my father would say.

"You can't ride it either, Nolan," Mom would tell my father.

"Listen to your wife," I'd tell Dad.

"Shut the hell up, son," Dad would chuckle.

"I want each of you to promise not to ride that bike," Mom would demand, looking at my father for support.

My younger brother, Kerry, was still too young to leave Mom's side so he was exempt from replying. My brother, Karl, and sister, Katrina, always answered promptly, both swearing that they had no intention of riding the motorbike; wouldn't even think of it.

"Chris," Mom warned in a threatening voice, "you promise me, too!"

"Sheesh Mom, I didn't even know Ron owned a motorbike," I responded on one occasion. "It doesn't matter anyway. I have no interest in those things."

"It's the same motorbike I grounded you for riding last summer."

"Oh, *that* motorbike."

As soon as we entered their home, Mom would seek Ron out to cover all her bases, making him promise that he wouldn't let any of her children ride his deathtrap.

"You won't let them near it, will you Ron?"

"Not a chance," he'd reply.

"If you do, I will kill you," she promised with scary sincerity.

Ron trembled. "I promise I'll *never* let any of them ride it."

The day I acquired the fishing pole, Ron let me ride his motorbike.

Ron was already out on the far end of their property when we arrived that day, riding his deathly dangerous blue mini-motorbike around a small dirt track he'd built. The course included a couple of small jumps and a nifty S turn. When I learned Ron was riding out on his track I told Mom that I had a moral obligation to go out and warn him about his impending demise.

"You come right back," she muttered before returning to her conversation with Aunt Sharon. Rarely did Mom let her maternal watcheye slip, but when engrossed in an adult conversation, she was prone to giving unwitting approval to rob a bank.

I'm going to rob a bank, Mom.

Okay. You come right back.

Karl and Katrina followed me out to the track, as did Ron's younger sister, Brenda. We all watched Ron zip around the dirt loop. He completed several laps, looking over at us frequently to confirm that we were duly impressed. Then Ron stopped to brag.

"Pretty cool, huh."

"It's okay," I shrugged.

"You know you want to ride," he mocked. "Sorry, but you guys aren't allowed."

"I don't want to ride!" I yelled. Ron pulled away, spraying dirt at me.

He stopped again after a few more laps, took off his helmet and flipped his long hair back, all in all pretty suave for a raging dork. He sat on the bike, the motor still running.

"How does it work?" I asked. "I didn't really listen last summer when you explained it."

Ron gave a fifteen second rundown on the operational basics.

"Twist back on this handle to give it gas. This here's the brake. You shift by clicking down on this here lever with your foot."

Shift? I was nine years old and had no idea what that meant. With the enticing rev of the engine ringing in my ears, I didn't really care. I just wanted to ride. I knew I'd be severely punished if I got caught, and being a troublemaker afraid of getting in trouble, that scared me a bit. But the idea of the wind rushing through my hair and the glory of taming an adult machine got the better of me.

"Come on!" I insisted. I stepped up next to the motorbike. "Let me ride!"

"You better not," Karl warned from just behind me.

"You promised Mom you wouldn't," Katrina added from her perch on top of a nearby cedar fence, like a nagging guardian angel.

What had I really promised my parents? I reflected back on my fabricated memory, doing my best to recall the exchange with my parents about the mini-bike. Best I could remember, Mom had promised unlimited candy to anyone who could tame the motorized monster, and Dad had declared that real men make their own choices and laugh in the face of danger. It seemed out of character for them to entice me into taking unjustifiable risks—Mom dangling candy, Dad taunting—but I didn't want to disappoint them.

Ron put his helmet back on and rode a few more laps around the track. I watched intently as the motorbike spit dirt around every turn. My hands filled with the sweat of anticipation, as if salivating at the opportunity to grab the handlebars. By the time Ron stopped again, my mind was made up.

"You need to let me ride!" I insisted. "I can do it. It seems easy enough."

"Okay," Ron answered without hesitation, "your funeral."

His lack of responsibility was appalling. *Damn you Ron*, I thought, *you're old enough to know better.* He could have easily used his physical advantage to stop me, but he didn't even spend the energy to try and talk me out of it. Shameful.

Karl, Katrina and Brenda followed Ron's irresponsible example.

"Go ahead then," Karl encouraged. "I can't wait to see you fall."

"I wonder if I can crash bad enough to make my face as ugly as yours?" I shot back.

"Well," Katrina jumped in, "I don't think you can get any uglier, and you don't have much of a future, so where's the harm?"

"You know he's going to crash, Ron," Brenda added. "So make sure he wears a helmet."

Further compelled by their doubt, I hopped onto the worn seat, the fake black leather torn in several places, tan foam poking through. Ron held the mini-bike steady as I mounted. My toes hung down just far enough to trace little paths in the dust. Ron placed the helmet on my head and I snapped the strap tight. A moment later, I twisted back on the handle's thingamajig and took off. As I accelerated, I glanced down at the foot peg on the right side, hoping to figure out the shift mechanism, curious as to its function. By the time I looked up, I was staring danger in the face. I did not laugh. I shook, uncontrollably, frozen in a blizzard of fright. Before I could cry out in dread the bike disappeared from under me and I was flying over the handlebars. Once clear of the mini-bike, I howled out a girlish, bloodcurdling scream. For a brief moment, suspended in air, a bird's eye view of the track, I caught sight of a bumper sticker stuck to the side of Uncle Denny's tool shed.

I'd Rather Be Fishing

So would I! The sticker had a cartoon picture of an old man in overalls, smiling a happy smile, fishing rod in one hand and a string of fish in the other. It was the last thing I saw before the lights went out.

The impact smarted. My eyes squeezed closed, afraid of seeing the pain. I bounced awkwardly, twice, before sliding to a stop. Dizzy and afraid, I kept my eyes sealed, lacking the courage to examine the physical damage. Blood discovered various exit points on my body; scraped knees, abrasions on each elbow, drips of blood from my nose. Tears leaked onto my cheeks. The invigorating feeling of manhood, rushing through my veins just moments earlier, had hastily retreated, the start of a lengthy hibernation. Ten more seconds passed and still I couldn't bring myself to open my eyes and look at the carnage. Blood continued to evacuate. The motorbike's engine hissed and whined.

"I don't see any serious damage," Ron yelled above the screech of the motor.

I was comforted by his comment, wrongly believing he'd been referring to me. I pressed open my eyelids and blinked the world back into focus just in time to see Ron hit the engine kill-switch and pull the mini-bike upright. Brenda and my siblings stood by him. They were all examining the bike.

"Looks fine to me, too," Karl said. Katrina and Brenda

shook their heads in agreement. Ron turned the bike around and rolled it toward the tool shed. Karl, Katrina and Brenda escorted him like a pack of security guards.

"Are you okay, Chris?" Katrina called out as they walked away.

"Fine, thanks. Don't worry about me." And they didn't, at least not yet.

I took a moment to assess my injuries. Aside from minor bleeding, I discovered an expanding bruise on my left shoulder. A swipe of my tongue detected a tiny chip on one of my bottom front teeth. My confidence was nowhere to be found, having scurried for safety like a frightened rat the moment the minibike started to move under me, not a bad decision given that I wasn't able to negotiate even one turn. I hadn't even managed to veer. When the track turned, I froze and continued straight, plowing the motorbike into a small dirt bank. If the track had been perfectly linear and infinitely long, I would've been fine. But Ron lacked the engineering and design foresight to accommodate my riding abilities.

As with all such predicaments, as soon as my head cleared I began the unpleasant task of parceling blame. Informing others that they're responsible for my failures is as uncomfortable as answering phone calls from creditors, but I do it because it's important for my friends and family to understand that they are holding me back. My siblings and cousins were wrong to persuade me to ride the motorbike; that much was clear. I mulled their individual culpability, doing my best to deliberate fairly before announcing my findings. As I pondered the proper allocation of fault, the four perpetrators returned to the scene of their poor judgment. I dusted myself off and stood up, prepared to lecture them on the importance of responsible behavior. Before I could get started, Ron initiated damage control.

"No one can tell our parents about this. *No one* talks," he pleaded. "If our parents find out, we'll all get in trouble, me most of all. My dad will take my motorbike away."

His words almost toppled me back to the ground. The magnitude of his blunder seemed lost on the rest, but not on me. Though he spoke with impressive calm, his words made it clear that he was petrified. He'd acknowledged that *he had the most to lose out of any of us,* the negotiation equivalent of pleading for your life. I shifted into dealmaker mode.

"What's it worth to you?" I asked.

"What do you mean?"

"What's it worth to you for me to keep my mouth shut?"

"You'd get in trouble, too."

"Yeah, but not as much as you—and I don't have a motorbike to lose!" I barked back.

"I don't think you have the guts to tell!" Ron snarled.

Whether I had the guts was irrelevant. It's unlikely that I'd voluntarily implicate myself in a misdeed to prove a point. I just wanted a deal, some compensation for my pain and suffering. I decided not to posture, worried if I pushed my luck that I might walk away without anything except some scrapes and bruises. I made a quick settlement offer.[1]

"Okay, you give me that fishing pole," I said, motioning to a pole resting against the nearby shed, "and I'll tell my parents I got these cuts diving into a bush to catch a Nerf football." The lie was solid. While at Uncle Denny's we often played catch with the football, running elaborate pass patterns that took us through and over the backyard hedges. The activity was violent enough to account for my bruises and welts.

"Fine," Ron agreed, "but if you tell..."

I could've kicked myself. Ron's unhesitating agreement made it clear that I'd aimed too low, demanded too little. There was more bounty in the bargain if I would've played it right. I should

---

[1] When both parties in a negotiation have either something to hide or lots to lose, you have the optimal environment for a quick settlement. This truth explains why no friendships on earth are forged faster than the ones between two kids on their way to the principal's office to explain why they were fighting on the playground.

have asked Ron what he thought was a fair deal and then counter-offered. I was upset at myself and wanted to reopen negotiations. Given my nominal leverage though, and anxious to secure something of value, I nodded, sealing the deal.

As part of the transaction, Ron agreed to take responsibility for concocting an explanation for the minor damage to his motorbike. There was no way he could hide the small dent on the fender from the trained eye of his dad, a whiz at refurbishing cars and all things mechanical. Before we all walked back to the house, Ron spread dirt on his clothes and elbows. Once there, Ron did an admirable job of convincing our parents that he had taken a spill on the motorbike.

"See," my mom said, "that thing is so dangerous. That's why I won't let you kids ride."

"Thanks for that, Mom," I said.

The outpouring of parental sympathy for Ron was so overwhelming and sincere that I almost admitted I had crashed the bike. But I resisted the limelight, not wanting to risk my new—and first—fishing pole. When concern over Ron's fall faded, I shared the news about the fishing pole with my parents.

"Mom! Dad! Ron gave me his fishing pole."

"His new one?" asked Uncle Denny.

"Yes!" I squealed.

"No I didn't," Ron corrected. "I gave him the old one."

"The old one?" I asked, confused.

"I thought you threw that away months ago," said Denny.

"Nope," Ron said. "I leaned it on the shed a few months back and forgot all about it."

I'd been had. The reward I'd wrested from Ron with my laborious conniving was not cool or valuable; it was a piece of unwanted garbage. Life truly wasn't fair. Minutes removed from being the proud owner of a new fishing pole, I now plummeted into disappointment. No matter, I thought. Any bum can catch fish with fancy equipment. With my vast innate gifts, I'd find a way to succeed even against menacing odds. Hank Aaron could've hit home runs with a toothpick. Einstein unlocked physics without a computer. The great ones find a way. Catching fish with my decrepit pole might be a challenge, but I had no doubt that I could.

In the years to come I roamed the banks of Grass Lake, a manmade body of water near my home, my trusty fishing pole in tow. The owner of the lake, Dr. Grass, had constructed it to be his private water skiing playground. He stocked its waters with sunfish and bass to keep aquatic vegetation in check. I used my tattered fishing pole to reel in these fish at a furious pace, displaying the crafty confidence of a grizzly pouncing on an unsuspecting salmon. After my first few outings to Grass Lake, each wildly successful, I adopted a special fishing persona. The practice was not without precedent. When I played basketball in the driveway, I became Dr. J or Larry Bird (Magic Johnson passed the ball too much for my liking). Pull on a baseball glove and I become Ozzie Smith; with each swing of the bat, George Brett. I didn't know any famous fishermen—that would be like knowing a famous shoe salesman—so unable to borrow a fishing persona, I created one. After much deliberation, I settled on a combination of two iconic figures—Aquaman, appropriately enough, and Sasquatch, the large, hairy ape-man that roams the Pacific Northwest.

Aquaman's inclusion requires no explanation. He's kick-ass cool and he rules over all things aquatic. My selection of Sasquatch had everything to do with timing. On the day before I decided to create a fishing persona, while watching television, I saw a clip of the famous Patterson Film, the grainy, jittery film clip of Sasquatch sauntering through the forest. The cameraman was some hoaxer named Patterson and his staged film gag made Sasquatch a household name. What really impressed me about Sasquatch was the way he maintained a calm demeanor as he sauntered away from the camera, looking back into the lens with a cool, *I-just-fucking-dare-you* look.

The next day, Sasquafish was born.

During long summer days, when I needed a break from my beloved sports fantasies, I grabbed my decrepit fishing pole and transformed from regular kid into Sasaquafish, a virtual fishing machine. I lured fish like Aquaman then hooked 'em with the ferocity of a big ape. After each catch I'd stealthily move to a new spot and cast again. While I fished, Dr. Grass vigilantly searched the lake shores for fish poachers, a camera in hand to record evidence. I kept on the move to avoid capture and, like my Sasquathian brother, I proved elusive. Dr. Grass rarely spotted me, and when he did I strode out of sight quickly, confidently, never allowing him to catch a clear glimpse. Though Dr. Grass took several pictures of me, coming so close at times that I could hear the camera's shutter click, my stealth thwarted his pursuit, leaving him nothing more than a photographic blur. I heard a rumor that he showed the shadowy pictures to local authorities, insisting that a beast stalked the shores of his lake. Apparently the police were skeptical and dismissive, and they refused to open an investigation. Seeking support for his cause, Dr. Grass attempted to raise a posse of townfolk to help him hunt the creature down, a campaign that made Sasaquafish a legend in the area. *Some ancient creature is lurking around Grass Lake,* locals warned out-of-towners. *Beware!*

At the Grass's dinner table each night, I suspect the good doctor awed his family with tales of Sasaquafish, stories of a phantom creature sweeping down on their lakeshore from God knows where, luring fish like a Pied Piper, and then slipping away like a ghost. In their wildest dreams the Grass family never could have fathomed that the mythical creature was really just the alter-ego of the little shit living a mile up the road.

Unlike shooting hoops in the driveway or hitting wiffle balls off a tee in the backyard, a day of fishing required planning. On the days Sasaquafish decided to go to Grass Lake, I got up early in order to collect night crawlers that overstayed their welcome. Next I'd inventory my tackle box to make certain I had the glue and duct tape necessary to keep my pole in one piece. After making a couple of peanut butter sandwiches, I'd close my eyes for the transformation. I'd shiver and shake as my veins filled with fishing prowess. When I finally opened my eyes, I was no longer an MVP shortstop or international soccer star, but the one, the only, the mighty Sasaquafish.

"Mom, Sasaquafish is going to the lake today. Would you like me to bring you home some fish?"

"I'd like for you to stop referring to yourself in the third person."

"Suit yourself. Sasaquafish will leave quietly." And off I'd go.

Walking the winding trail through the woods that led from our house to Grass Lake took about twenty-five minutes. Once there, Sasaquafish would hunker into a spot on the bank, affix a wiggling worm to the hook, adjust the bobber to the proper position, liberally apply duct tape to the weathered pole, and let rip a cast. Ten minutes rarely passed without hooking a good fight.[2]

* * *

"Give a man a fish and he will eat for a day, teach him to fish and he will eat for a lifetime."

We are reminded of the ancient importance of fishing. In many parts of the world, it is a survival skill. In America, though, the grocery store has replaced the lakeshore and riverbank as the primary food source. This luxury has allowed fishing to evolve into a recreational undertaking, a beacon of leisure that allows folks to connect with nature without the unsavory neediness of basic survival.

---

[2] I almost always released the fish I caught, but I did bring a couple of bass home from Grass Lake once. "You kill it, you eat it!" my mom commanded as I showed off my catch. Then she taught me how to "clean" a fish, a lesson that left two lasting impressions: 1) Bringing fish home is more trouble than any glory you get out of it, and 2) it's not wise to entrust another species to "clean" you.

Hunting has undergone a similar transformation, but the advent of the gun has derailed a smooth transition. I lack experience packing bloodlust into the forest but I can imagine it's not overly difficult to outfox a deer with a rifle. Instead of man versus beast, modern hunting is beast versus bullet, a poor match-up for any species. Hunting with a bow and arrow seems fair and honorable. Killing something with a gun is unsportsmanlike, like sneaking up behind a deaf invalid and hitting him over the head with a crowbar.

Unlike gun-toting hunters, recreational fishermen utilize equipment that maintains a level playing field. This egalitarian notion is one I embrace, a concept I champion in all areas of life except in the rare circumstance where I hold the natural advantage. So when some of my law school buddies invited me to Montana for a week of fly fishing, I made sure to bring along a wealth of compassion. I'd fight the fair fight, confident I could outwit any creature with a pair of gills. But a week later, as I boarded the plane for my return flight to Oregon, I vowed to return to Big Sky country to fish its rivers again. And next time I planned to bring a gun.

* * *

"It's 64 and sunny in Billings," announced the pilot over the plane's PA system. His words were muffled by the scream of the small plane's engines and its whirling propellers. The pleasant weather didn't prevent the obligatory bumpy ride over the Rocky Mountains. The plane bounced uncomfortably as we passed over the Continental Divide;[3] a turbulence tax assessed by the mountain range for the magnificent aerial view. The stewardess came by my seat and collected the four empty beer bottles that

---

[3] I've never liked the term "Continental Divide" because it's so...divisive. I suggest we recast this grand mountain range as the Continental Seam.

I'd stuffed into the seat pocket. The beers were free, compliments of the airline, their way of saying, *Yeah, a 21- passenger prop plane. They don't make 'em anymore. We're all nervous. Drink up.*

During the flight, we flew over Bozeman, the nearest town to the cabin where my friends and I were going to spend the week fly fishing. I hadn't fished for years, but I was sure I hadn't lost my touch. As the plane passed over, I looked out the tiny window at a winding river below, the place Sasaquafish would be reborn. Countless trout waited in the river, shaking with fright, drinking beers to calm their nerves. I imagined one of the elder trout lecturing a large school of young fish: *Yeah, Sasaquafish is coming. They don't make 'em like him anymore. We're all nervous. Drink up.*

When the wheels touched down on the runway it marked the end of the flight and the start of Sasaquafish's Second Coming. I'd been lured to Montana by my friends with assurances of huge steaks and cold beer, surefire bait. I strolled into the terminal confident that the innate fishing talent I'd displayed as a child lurked within, anxious to resurface. Fishing in Grass Lake with worm-bait couldn't be all that different from fly fishing rivers. Get me in close proximity to fish-filled water, hand me a fishing pole and watch Sasaquafish emerge, rusty but invincible.

My four buddies were waiting in the airport bar when I arrived, sharing drinks. I walked up to the table just as Dan and Beaver, the two guys who'd arranged the trip, were explaining to John and Slasher the details of our itinerary.

"Sasaquafish is here!" I trumpeted, interrupting the discussion. "I'm surprised I haven't caught a few fish already."

"Sasaqua-what?" Dan bellowed, mockingly.

"Sasaquafish!" I repeated. "For the rest of the week, each of you will call me by my angling moniker, Sasaquafish. Feel free to follow me around and take notes. You may learn something. You'll definitely be awed. Now say it with me... Sas-aqua-fish."

"Fuck you," John muttered.

"That's close," I offered encouragingly. "We'll work on it."

"Jesus!" Dan added, flabbergasted. "You've never been fly

fishing before. It's harder than you think. The casting technique alone takes years to master."

As Dan spoke, the others moaned and shook their heads. They all doubted.

"I've cast a regular fishing pole before," I informed, "and fly fishing can't be all that different."

"Casting a fly fishing pole is completely different," Beaver argued. "Completely!"

"I've also cast countless aspersions," I pointed out. "So that should help."

No response. Their faces oozed disbelief. I would prove them wrong. But words don't convert the skeptical, so I refrained from trying to make my case, withholding the lengthy, remarkable tale of my former fishing feats. They'd be enlightened soon enough. Before the week was through they'd worship at the Sasaquafish altar. It was just a matter of time.

Beaver—not his given name—was the only one of the group who lived in Montana. He had done most of the organizing and would act as our guide for the week, his battered Ford Bronco our covered wagon.[4] After pulling out of the airport's small parking area, Beaver steered us through the town of Billings, heading, he explained, for I-90 and Bozeman. On our way to the interstate, on the outskirts of Billings, we passed the Montana State Women's Prison.

"Let's stop in for a conjugal visit," I suggested.

"With who?" Slasher shrieked.

"Anyone who's willing," I offered.

"I don't think it works that way," Beaver said.

"Can't hurt to go in and find out. We can at least see if it's an option. Maybe you *can* just go in and sign up, like a community service volunteer program. Just tell the penitentiary staff that you're willing and able and the guards go in and ask around to

---

[4] This comparison overstates the speed, reliability, comfort and maneuverability of the Bronco.

see if any of the inmates are interested. If any of the prisoners *do* have that certain hankering, game on. We should stop. It's my civic duty, as a citizen and a lawyer, to do what I can to help rehabilitate the incarcerated."

"I don't think *that* would help anyone," John shot back.

"It might help me," I said.

No one seemed interested in my well-being. We continued driving, past the prison gates, disappointing confined, lustful women, giving them yet more free time to think up new crimes to commit as soon as the parole board set them free. And like that, in the exhaust of Beaver's beaten Bronco, a chance to lower Montana's criminal recidivism rates was lost.

The drive to Bozeman was intermittently beautiful and desolate. The landscape begged for John Wayne to ride over the westerly ridge, pause just long enough to doff his cowboy hat, then gallop off to save a small town from some ruffians. Wildlife abounded; bison, deer and elk roamed the open spaces unimpeded. The landscape didn't need any beauty sleep. It could stay awake for a few thousand years and still pull off an incredible cover shoot for National Geographic.

On the way to Bozeman, Beaver stopped at several historical markers so we could all read about how America conquered this wonderful wilderness. One of the markers recounted how a band of Native Americans pulled off a crafty, successful escape from Union troops. I couldn't help but feel a small sense of satisfaction, the kind experienced when hearing about a paraplegic spitting venom into the eyes of a would-be attacker who's charging at him with a crowbar. Peering beyond that historical marker at the unscathed beauty of this wild place, I wondered whether America, great land that it is, wouldn't have turned out even better if the white man had been placed on reservations, confining our lust for concrete, and the natives were left to tend the fruited plains. Together, the historical information and beautiful surroundings convinced me that my friends had been right not to stop at the Women's State Prison. Enough people had already been royally fucked in these parts.

Once in Bozeman we drove straight to Beaver's favorite fly shop, River's Edge Outfitters. Ed, the proprietor, helped me select equipment for the week. As I searched for the perfect fly fishing vest, Beaver told Ed that we were headed over to Big Timber, a small area outside town. Ed brightened at the information and proudly launched into a monologue about the movie *Horse Whisperer*, which had been filmed in and around Big Timber a few years earlier.

"Beautiful location for a movie...or anything," Ed said.

"I'm a bit of a Fish Whisperer," I offered.

"Really?"

"Yep. Never fly fished before but I've conquered other forms of fishing, so I figured I'd give this a try."

"Well that area of the river is prime fishing territory," Ed assured. "Fish are going crazy right now, gobbling up caddis flies. Novice or not, it'd be impossible not to catch a fish up there if you have half a dick."

Having, anatomically, at least half a dick, I left River's Edge Outfitters geared for conquering. A handmade sign welcomed us to Big Timber, but the town lacked any other trace of human life. Elk and deer seemed to be the only residents, and they'd done a great job decorating. The landscape was resplendent.

Our cabin was located a few miles past the welcome sign. Once we settled into the homey log structure, I grabbed a beer and sat on the porch, facing the rippling river at the bottom of a slightly sloping grass meadow, about a hundred yards away. *Poor trout,* I thought, forever the caring vanquisher. They'd undoubtedly heard of Sasaquafish. They surely felt the presence of fishing greatness. I don't know if fish sleep, but regardless, the trout in the river below wouldn't enjoy a slumber this night. They'd stay up all evening, hunkered down in their Alamo, calculating the depressing odds of survival. On the other hand, I knew I'd sleep well, slumbering on a pillow of confidence, certain that during the night I'd transform from a *moy*[5] into a virtual fishing machine; Sasaquafish, ruthless dominator of all things finned.

In the early, crisp morning, while eating a breakfast of eggs and bacon, I ridiculed Dan for offering casting lessons, dismissing him as if he were a child inviting Van Gogh to a painting seminar. After filling my stomach and arming my fishing vest with an array of artificial, hand-tied caddis flies, I pulled on my waders and left behind my inferiors. I lumbered purposefully toward the river. Sasaquafish was giving a lesson on natural selection and every trout in the region was invited.

The concept of natural selection has matured to the point that it's made significant inroads into the hearts and minds of the general population. But given enough time, even the most scrutinized scientific theories tend to untangle a bit. Exceptions are discovered—or the entire theory is wholly disproved. It used to be widely believed that the world was flat (it's not), that the sun revolved around the earth (it doesn't), and that homo sapiens couldn't survive without a brain (just consider the driver who cut me off on Highway 26 last week). In short, we live in an ever-changing world, a place where nothing scientific is certain, a planet full of surprises, both pleasant and cataclysmic, where you can't move a mountain, but if you wait long enough, tectonic plates will do it for you. For thousands of years nature has sensibly favored the strong, the skilled, the brilliant, carefully adhering to the concept of natural selection. But during the five days I spent in the Montana wilderness, chaos ruled—up was down, left was right, natural selection was discarded and my fishing pole and I couldn't catch a damn thing. From the moment the great Sasaquafish left the porch on that first morning, the sun glimmering on my waders, until I packed my bags five days later, a large gathering of meek trout were afforded a taste of how it would feel to inherit the earth.

---

[5] Moy: half man, half boy, a transition stage I seem stuck in.

For five sunny, beautiful days my fishing skills betrayed me. As I tossed my line in the water over and over again to no effect, my friends reeled in trout with regularity. Each time one of them pulled a trout from the river, they'd carefully remove the hook, release the fish back into the water and then remind me, through a variety of mocking jibes, that I fished with the futility of someone trying to sweep a dirt floor clean.

"Hey Sasaquafish, I caught another!" they'd yell. Their voices echoed through the skinny valley. "It's a brown trout, speckled, about thirteen pounds. I'll send you a copy of the pictures when they get developed."

"I caught one too," I'd yell back. "Five feet or so in length, about 323 pounds...oh, sorry, it's just John's mom."

Sasaquafish was constantly mocked, razzed and belittled. My harsh retorts masked my sincere disappointment and burning frustration. During lulls in the harassment, my friends took turns patiently explaining how to cast, how to manage the line after it hit the water, and several other fly fishing tactics. In return, I showed them my middle finger and taught them how to drink beer with an irritated scowl.

Trout were about the only thing I couldn't catch. I snagged my jacket, my waders, the thick shrubbery populating the river bank. I hooked trees, my hat, a fence. Each cast brought a new, unintended victim. My right ear seemed downright magnetized, attracting my hook on four separate occasions. To its credit, each time I snared it, my ear put up a hell of a good fight.

I took some solace from that fact we were fishing in a mandatory catch and release area. At the end of each day, no one had a single fish to show for their effort. My friends pretended to derive joy from the pointless exercise of catching fish and letting them go, snapping pictures to capture fish that they couldn't keep. To me, that's no different from taking a girl on a date and delivering her home without a kiss goodnight. That's just not Sasaquafish's style.

I tried to blame the lack of success on a dearth of fish, an excuse that became increasingly implausible with every trout my friends landed. Truth be had, between untangling my line and tending to each involuntary ear piercing, I saw hundreds of fish jumping in the crystal clear water, swimming circles around my inability. I tried a variety of techniques to turn the tide—drinking while sitting, drinking while standing, drinking slowly, drinking quickly, urinating in the river, on the bank. And still I caught nothing.[6]

After skunking me for the first three days, the trout, in a classy show of sportsmanship, sent in their second and third stringers in order to level the playing field. Ancient trout that could barely jump or move were sent out from behind their protective rocks to join the trouncing. The scene resembled an old-timer's game, an opportunity for those with wheezing gills to taste their former glory. These frail fish would slowly approach my fly, examine it as it floated past, and move on. My presentation of the bait couldn't even fool the river's octogenarian set.

On day five, the trout cleared the bench, sending in nearsighted fish, handicapped fish, fish that had lost fins and tails, fish with ruptured gills, a few with only half a dick. Some of the trout I faced on that last day in Montana appeared to need swimming lessons. A few blind trout banged into my legs. Still, not a single strike tensed my line. Being dominated by the first-string trout humbled Sasaquafish. Being toyed with by second and third stringers filleted the ego. When the biologically battered fish joined the fun, I lost control, all too cognizant that I was in jeopardy of being the first person ever nominated for the Trout Fishing Hall of Fame by the trout themselves.

As the sun set on the last day of our trip, I began smacking the water with my pole, attempting to false-hook a gill or a fin, anything to catch a fish. During the tirade I slipped and fell into the water. My waders began to fill. Drowning was a distinct

---

[6] Every time I urinated I examined my penis and asked myself, "That's at least half a dick. Isn't it? Isn't it?"

possibility. I fought toward the shore, flailing my arms, screaming. Eventually I managed to crawl my way to the riverbank. My friends, having heard the commotion, were assembled on the shore as I struggled out of the water like a half-drunk, frustrated man emerging from his illusion. Their laughter dominated the air and I yearned to return to my youth, to the motorbike and the birth of Sasaquafish, a time when fiascos were collectively covered up rather than ridiculed.

As I rose to my feet I pressed cold river water from my waders and melodramatically tossed my pole on the ground in disgust. Then I made a beeline for the cabin. My attempt to storm off was halted by a sharp yank on the back of my head. During my tantrum, the fly on my line had somehow hooked into my scalp. I squealed like a pig as the hook dug in. The laughs around me grew louder, salting the wound. To release the tension on the line, I slowly walked back toward the water. After a few awkward attempts to remove the hook on my own, Dan stepped forward to help.

"Bite your lip," he suggested.

Before I could bite down, Dan ripped the hook out. My eyes watered. I closed my eyelids tight, fighting the tears. Without warning, while my eyes were still closed, I got a firm push from behind. I tumbled into the water.

"Catch and release is mandatory in these parts," Slasher laughed. "Back you go."

That was the final humiliation. I picked up my pole and threw it down, again, and marched away in the direction of the cabin. As I retreated from the river and its dastardly fish, I felt like Custer, another brave soul who'd come to these parts with visions of glory only to be embarrassed at the hands of the natives. At least I'd be leaving with my scalp still attached.

John, who had disappeared a few minutes earlier, came bouncing toward me from the direction of the cabin, his new video camera rolling.

"Hey Sasaquafish," he yelled, "smile for the camera!"

"Fuck you."

"That's close," John offered encouragingly. "We'll work on it. Now smile for the camera."

Sasaquafish ignored the request and sauntered past the video camera, a frown furrowing his face, ready for a long, hot shower. When the roar of laughter emanating from the riverbank subsided, Sasaquafish looked back, displaying a calm, collected demeanor. Before disappearing into the cabin, Sasaquafish slowed, looked directly into the lens, flashed a *I-just-fucking-dare-you* grimace and raised his middle finger. Sasaquafish then casually turned away a final time, walking out of mythology and into a three day drinking binge.

That was the last verified Sasaquafish sighting, and the only time he was ever caught on video. Sasaquafish has not been seen or heard from since. The legend, now nearly forgotten, lives on in the rivers of Montana and, from time to time, is recounted with great reverence around the dinner table at the Grass household. If Sasaquafish ever surfaces again, I expect he will be spotted in Big Sky Country, roaming the riverbanks around Big Timber, drinking beer with abandon and recklessly firing an assault rifle into the peaceful, pure water.

clinging *to* anonymity

The Cocky Before the Storm

A fisherman lounges on the bank of a winding river, his eyes dreamily studying a sky burning blue. A few cotton ball clouds mar the otherwise unblemished sky, the white puffs dotting the world's roof in perfect asymmetry. Inches from the man's feet, a rush of untainted water swirls around in eddy currents. On the other side of the stream, the water ripples and rushes with purpose. Glittering droplets decorate the man's waders like sequins. A fishing pole rests loyally on his right side; on his left, a small, red Coleman cooler.

The man sits up and stretches his arms to the sky as if attempting to pluck a cloud, and then reaches into his cooler and pulls out a big foil package. He tears away the covering and a glorious sandwich emerges like a butterfly breaking free from its cocoon. The majestic sandwich demands admiration. The fisherman gazes at it lustfully; almost too lustfully.

Enraptured with his lunch, the man fails to detect the grizzly bear that lumbers out of the high grass on the opposite bank several yards downstream. While the man locks his jaws onto the sandwich, the bear strides into the water with surprising finesse. It strolls upriver, but doesn't notice the fisherman. The man soon notices the bear though, and he starts to tremble uncontrollably.

The bear is consumed by its search for fish and continues to mill about in the water. Despite its legs being half submerged, the grizzly is so huge it has a bird's eye view of the river. But it must be unhappy with this already impressive vantage, because it increases its range of reconnaissance by standing up on its hind legs. A moment after rising, the bear slowly lowers itself back down, eyes transfixed on a specific spot in the stream. *Splash!* The bear slaps its right paw into the water and yanks out a large, wriggling salmon.

The grizzly's technique is masterful, as if it had studied under Sasaquafish for years. It pins its prey on a nearby rock and prepares to feast. But now, at last, it catches sight of the frightened fisherman. The man starts vibrating as if someone has inserted a jackhammer into his posterior. The bear reacts with intrigue, but it doesn't leap to action; it shifts its eyes from the man to the squirming salmon, then back. Both salmon and man bulge with panic. Neither one displays anything resembling courage or composure.

As my television flickers, disrupting the unfolding drama, I shift positions on my cushy couch, literally stirred by the cowardice unfolding onscreen. The fish has reason to be frightened—it's already in the bear's clutches—but I'm perturbed by the man's lack of valor. He is a good forty yards from the bear and has the advantage of a human brain. Instead of seizing the opportunity to be a predator, he whimpers like prey. Removed enough from the drama for calm reflection, I wonder how I'd react in a similar predicament. Fear, I decide, would not be a concern. No shaking or trembling for me, just calculated cunning. The situation would, however, present some tactical dilemmas. Would it be better to begin my assault on the bear with a jab to its jaw, or a swift kick to its ribs? Which of my versatile fighting moves should I use for the kill blow? Would it make more sense to purchase a freezer to store all that bear meat or would it be more economical to lease a large refrigeration unit? Is bear best served barbequed or broiled...and the choice of wine; red or white—or beer? Burdened by this conglomeration of annoyances, I decide that killing a bear with my hands would be more trouble than it's worth. If I were in the fisherman's waders, I'd walk away and avoid the hassle.

Before I can analyze the slew of decorative problems associated with owning a bearskin rug, honesty arrives to ruin my illusion. Like a heckler revealing the tricks of a street magician—*The card is in his left sleeve! Pull up your left sleeve, hotshot!*—honesty obliterates my visions of bravery and stoicism. To its credit, honesty doesn't shout or heckle. It speaks clearly, concisely and, most troubling, truthfully. The moment it arrives, visions of courage vanish from my imagination, replaced by the unsettling images of the night I watched *The Wizard of Oz*. I slept with the light on, fearful that the cowardly lion was going to get me. *Holy crap!* I thought. *The cowardly lion is hiding in my closet, right behind my jacket! It's going to maul me to death!*

Honesty, a ruthless interrogator, compelled a personal confession. If I encountered a grizzly in the wild, I'd die *before* any physical altercation. As soon as the bear started to charge, I'd shake, tremble, cry, soil my pants and then my heart would stop. That's what happens to people who swat at mosquitoes as if they're being attacked by vampires. When honesty finished revealing my true nature, I bowed my head in prayer: *God, if I have to die at the claws of one of your wild creatures, I humbly request you send a predatory squirrel to carry out the gruesome task. Amen.*

Death by squirrel is something I could handle. Squirrels are playful creatures that don't evoke fear. They approach people slowly, quizzically, fuzzy tail standing straight, whiskers wiggling. Unlike a bear, the presence of a squirrel doesn't raise alarm. It calms. If God sent a squirrel assassin to take me out, the last thing I'd expect as it approached is imminent death. I'd reach out my hand in peace. Talk to the squirrel in my best baby-talk voice. Then, as I offer a warm smile, the squirrel would spit an acorn into my temple with deadly accuracy, catching me off guard. I'd die almost instantly, well before fear could deploy its humiliating rituals.

Conversely, if forced to face down a bear, I'd not only beg and plead, I'd bribe. I'd offer directions to my older brother's home, disclose the hiding place for his spare house key and give specific instructions on how to operate his antiquated microwave. *You could move in, run him and his family out, live there in comfort, Jacuzzi every night. Just...spare...me.* In the event the bribe failed, I'd die of fear the moment the bear moved toward me, passing into the netherworld long before the beast could swipe its paw or sink its fangs into my body. Days later a park ranger would discover my stiff, pristine body. When interviewed by the local paper, the ranger would use the opportunity to warn hikers that playing dead to thwart a bear attack can be taken too far. The newspaper article chronicling my death would speculate why my last act was to scrawl my brother's address into the dirt. *He must have really loved his older brother, a last goodbye,* the reporter would write. Through the cloud of speculation, my brother, Karl, would realize the traitorous truth, seeing my last act for what it was: an attempt to save my own skin at his expense.

I returned my attention to the television screen. The bear was still weighing its menu options, alternating its gaze from fisherman to fish. Then, suddenly, the bear drops the large salmon, and *Splash!* It bounds up the stream toward the man, determined, voracious, predatory.

The fisherman jumps to his feet with surprising swiftness. Inexplicably, before scampering away, he rewraps his sandwich and places it in his Coleman as softly as you'd set a tiara on a princess. The peculiar decision costs him valuable time. When he finally turns to run up the riverbank, the bear is a mere twenty yards behind him.

The man's scrambling feet dislodge loose dirt and rocks on the slope. He quickly glances over his shoulder to gauge his chances. The scene flashes to a shot of the bear's fierce, slobbering jaws. The fisherman scurries to the top of the bank and then sprints down a short path leading to a beat-up Dodge pickup.

As he approaches the vehicle, he looks back again. To his surprise, the bear is no longer in pursuit. Instead, it is sitting cross-legged by the cooler, eating the masterpiece sandwich, grinning like Yogi.

The fisherman clenches his fists and sputters some unintelligible curse. Defying logic, he runs down the hill to confront the bear, fists up. The bear spots the charging man, calmly sets down what's left of the sandwich and grabs a pair of boxing gloves from its kangaroo-like pouch, revealing to the audience that it is, apparently, a rare marsupial grizzly. After deftly slipping on the gloves, the bear stands on its hind legs and tauntingly swirls its paws around like a boxer preparing to attack. As soon as the man is in range, the beast pummels him with a series of perfectly executed jabs. Then, with one powerful right hook, the bear knocks the fisherman stupid. The man wobbles, stumbles, takes a last lustful look at the sandwich and falls to the ground, face down in the dirt. The bear plucks the boxing gloves from its paws and slips them back into its pouch. After dusting off his fur, the bear picks up the remainder of the sandwich and shoves it in its mouth.

While consuming the remnants of the sandwich, the bear rummages through the man's pockets, takes his keys and wallet and then scurries toward the truck, running like a man. When the beast arrives at the Dodge, it rips off the driver's-side door and slides its furry bottom smoothly into the cab. The bear fires up the engine, revs it a couple times and drives off. As the vehicle barrels down the road, kicking up a cloud of dust, the bear looks into the camera and exclaims, "I gotta get another one of those sandwiches."

A tagline appears on the screen:

Barry's Sub-Shop
Now Serving Fresh Smoked Salmon Sandwiches

The entire segment was an advertisement for a local sandwich shop, a place I'd seen but never visited. I was sold. Next chance I got I was going to Barry's. Anyone capable of training a bear to walk, talk and drive like that is going to get my business no matter what they're selling.

I turned off the television and headed to bed. The next morning I was catching a Horizon Air flight to Billings, Montana, the start of a week-long fly fishing vacation. I had never fly fished, but I'd seen *A River Runs Through It*—twice—so I had a pretty good idea of what it entailed, and what it takes to bed Jennifer Anniston…and Angelina Jolie. Ever since my law school buddies had scheduled the trip I'd been itching to toss a line in the water. On the riverbank I'd transform once again into Sasaquafish as my twenty-pound test whisked peacefully through the air, destined for success. I couldn't wait to show off my skills, and to hear their praise. The commercial ratcheted my booming anticipation. It also awakened me to the wildly untapped potential of the animal kingdom. With proper training, could wild trout learn to iron? Could bison baby-sit? I couldn't wait to find out.

End Notes:

1. I've always loved the juxtaposition of a lazy swirl of eddy currents nestled against hurried rapids. It's a great metaphor for several things. It could be used in a commercial to promote a company—*rushing by the competition*—or as personal inspiration—*which part of the river do you want to be in?* Every time I come across a river, I invariably find myself standing on the bank near the eddy currents, staring over at the rushing water. I look over hopefully, longingly—then look down and see my reflection in the eddy current and decide I'm happy just where I am.

2. I wish I possessed the necessary restraint—and courage—to avoid swatting wildly at mosquitoes because I believe these bugs might know the secret of life. I think they yearn to tell us, flying up to our ears every chance they get, buzzing with excitement, aching to share their knowledge. Somewhat ironically, we humans slap them away, unwilling to listen. There's a parable in there somewhere. Or an allegory. Or fable. I just wish I could refrain from slapping at the mosquito long enough to hear what it has to say. Then I'd kill it. There's a parable in there, too.

It's Better to Give and Receive

"Never try to buy a candy thermometer on Christmas Eve," Mom warned.

I was sitting at the kitchen table with my brothers and sister, nibbling on Christmas cookies that our mom had made the day before. Her tone caught us all by surprise. It reminded me of the passion in her voice years earlier when she warned us to avoid drugs.

"Okay, Mom." I answered. "I'll avoid candy thermometers at all costs, on *every* day of the year."

My siblings laughed, but the mocking reply didn't seem to register. She went on to explain her advice. "The candy thermometer I've had for years stopped working yesterday and I went to three stores to get a replacement and couldn't find one."

"That's awful," my brother Kerry said with exaggerated concern. We all laughed again, but Mom kept working away, stirring a large vat of some candy concoction that she was cooking up on the stove.

All parents tend to give their kids obvious advice on occasion—don't crash your car, avoid people who carry guns, pay your bills. Our parents did, too, but Mom tossed enough quirky gems into the usual mix that we always listened. And from time to time she'd reward our attention with obscure, unsolicited guidance, telling us not to put eggs in our beer and promising that we could subsist on construction paper if we ever found ourselves in the midst of a famine. "The red paper tastes the best," she said.

As my siblings playfully pondered the value of the thermometer advice, I changed the subject. "By the way Mom, there are some presents for me under the tree and the tags on 'em say that they're from Santa. I'm 32 years old. How dumb do you think I am?"

Mom added some more sugar to one of the bowls by the stove and stirred the contents. "I don't think you want me to answer that. And if you don't like presents from Santa I can take them back," she threatened.

"Take them back to who?" I asked.

"Just back. You needn't worry to whom."

"Well I love gifts from Santa," I promised. And I do.

I spent most of the day with my family and then headed home to Portland for the night. The next day I'd return to Banks to celebrate Christmas Day, but I still had some shopping to do downtown. I drove to Pioneer Place Mall and joined a slew of other procrastinators for last minute gift buying. The large crowd was formidable but I forged ahead, buying scores of gifts on instinct, and my instinct was to buy more gifts for me than for anyone else. *I really have been good this year,* I thought.

Typically I wrap presents with the care of a toddler playing with crayons at daycare. I employ large strips of duct tape and concern myself only with concealment. But this year I had a plan, and it required carefully wrapped gifts, so I paid some ladies at the mall to wrap everything, including the six presents I'd purchased for me. Their gift-wrapping skill was impressive. Each present looked divine, covered with opulent ribbons and bows. At my request the ladies even filled out the gift tags, and at my direction they wrote Santa's name as the giver.

The next day when I arrived at my mom's house I brought the presents in and scattered them under the tree, mingling them with heaps of other gifts. Then I joined my family in the kitchen for our traditional, informal Christmas breakfast. After we finished eating and clearing away the dishes we moved into the living room to open presents.

"Here, Karl," I said, handing a present to my brother. "This one is from me."

He tore away the wrapping to reveal a small, portable refrigerator. "Thanks, I can use this," he said.

"No need to thank me," I insisted. "Just sign the enclosed thank you card and drop it in the mail."

"What?" Karl asked.

I got the attention of everyone in the room. "Just so you all know, this year, to make it easy on you, I've enclosed a thank you card with each gift. The card is already filled out and comes with a stamped, pre-addressed envelope. Just sign the card, put it in the envelope and drop it in the mail. Got it?"

In each of the cards I'd written similar messages. *"Dear Chris,"* I wrote. *"Without doubt, you have given me the best present. I don't even like the others—I wish I had a million family members like you, then I'd get a million perfect presents. Actually, I wish I could be you, just for one day even. Now that would be the ultimate present. You are the best. I love you. God, I really, really admire and envy you. Great gift, greater man. Thanks."*

Karl read the thank you card, shrugged and then threw it into the fireplace. "Thanks for the fridge," he said. My other family members followed his lead, each glancing at my flowery thank you message before tossing the card into the fire where their social etiquette literally went up in flames.

Kerry handed out most of the gifts, grabbing presents from under the tree and delivering them to the identified recipient. As he worked, the pile of presents at my feet continued to grow.

"Here's *another* one for Chris," Kerry kept saying. I scrambled to keep up.

"Look what Santa got me!" I exclaimed. "A new car stereo, and a gift certificate to have it installed."

My mom looked at my step-dad, Mike. "That was from Santa?" she asked.

"Yep!" I said.

I ripped open another gift. "And look," I screamed, "Santa got me...a Bose Stereo for my room! Holy crap!"

My mom was perplexed. She was Santa, and Santa was starting to think she was losing her mind. The Bose Stereo got my siblings' attention. Santa always made sure that the cumulative value of gifts for each Kemper kid was approximately equal. Karl, who was out of gifts to open, looked at his pile of presents with a bit of dejection, and Kerry and my sister Katrina couldn't believe that Santa hadn't brought them anything more substantial than some boring shoes.

I tore open another present. "New snowboard boots! And a season lift ticket to Mt. Hood Meadows! Are you kidding me? Santa kicks ass!"

My siblings shook their heads in disbelief. Mom, after some reflection, interrupted. "I know I didn't buy that. Actually, I didn't buy any of that."

"Of course you didn't. These are from Santa. And I still have three more!"

Next I opened a new ski jacket, and then some new Kenneth Cole shoes. By this time, my entire family was chagrined.

"What is going on?" Katrina lamented.

"Still one more to go!" I bragged. I pulled away the packaging. "What can this be?" I asked. I waited a moment. My family stared. "Oh good birth of Jesus! It's a candy thermometer! Oh thank you, thank you Santa. I've been wanting one of these! But, in the spirit of Christmas—and since Santa's already given me a car stereo, a home stereo, snowboard boots, a season lift ticket, a new jacket and new shoes—well, Mom, this is for you. From Santa, to me, to you. I love you. I love you all!"

"Sometimes I wish I wasn't required to love you," Mom whined.

My siblings bombarded me with wadded up balls of discarded gift wrapping and a series of uncomplimentary taunts. But their attempt to deflate my joy failed because Santa had finally given me almost everything I deserved.

End Note:

My brother Karl is a horrible gift-giver. His heart in always in the right place—at least since adolescence—but he can't select a decent present to save his life. I used to think he selected gifts by running around a second-hand store with a shopping cart, blindly ramming it into the aisle dividers. Whatever fell in, he bought. Simple as that. Statistically speaking though, this random approach should have resulted in a few cool presents, even at a discount store, but that never happened. After several years passed without a single cool present to his credit, the oddity of his gift-giving led me to formulate a new theory. I sincerely believe Karl uses presents as a way to expand his knowledge base. When giving a gift, instead of saying, "I was hoping you would like that," Karl might instead be thinking, "I was hoping you can tell me what that is."

You Say Peyronie's, I Say Peroni's

My mom's maternal grandparents were married in Italy and then immigrated to America in two steps. First my great-grandfather took the long boat trip to America, leaving his young bride with only a kiss, a bun in the oven and the promise that he'd send for her as soon as he had the money. He returned to Italy two years later to see his wife and daughter, and to explain that he still didn't have enough money to bring the family to America. Before he returned to the States he managed to get my great-grandmother pregnant again. Another two years passed before my great-grandfather could afford to send for his family. When my great-grandmother got the word—and the dough—she packed up the kids, boarded a boat (carriage class, which ain't good) and eventually ended up at Ellis Island. A train brought them across the country to Oregon, the place my great-grandfather had settled.

Three years and a new daughter later my great-grandmother was deported by the Federal Government. She had suffered a nervous breakdown, and back then that was decidedly un-American. Apparently in those times the feds retained the right to send the huddled masses packing if they displayed any sort of mental health deficiency. A few years after my great-grandmother was sent back to Italy—my great-grandfather opted to stay in America—the government abandoned this reprehensible deportation program because, as I understand it, the mayor of Los Angeles complained that getting rid of the delusional prevented his city from maintaining a stable population base.

The story of my great-grandmother's immigration travails explains why millions of United States citizens consider themselves Italian-Americans or Irish-Americans, African-Americans or Arab-Americans. It's not necessarily that these people have any deep longing for ancestral lands, but rather they adopt these hyphenated nationalities out of respect for the sacrifices made by their family members who came to America, and as a tribute to those who made it and were sent back.

My mom doesn't refer to herself as an Italian-American, but she has a connection with the country that can only be forged by someone with a significant amount of Italian blood. For this reason we celebrated her 60th birthday by taking her to a small Italian restaurant in Northwest Portland called Piazza Italia. The restaurant closely mimics the bustle and informality of an Italian eatèry—good wine flows freely, the wait staff speaks Italian and the owner, a short, portly man in his seventies, regularly entices the female guests to join him for a dance. We'd have preferred to take her to Italy for a vacation, but since my money tree has yet to sprout (possibly because I consistently water it with long naps) Piazza Italia provided an affordable alternative. Mom loved it.

My mom's brother Pat, his wife Pam and my sister-in-law Laurie joined us for the celebration. We all crowded around a couple of small tables that the owner had pulled together to accommodate our party. The tablecloths were white, the gnocchi was superb and the small television above the bar glowed with an Italian league women's volleyball match, broadcast via satellite. Several times during the meal I looked up at the screen to gawk at the long-legged, athletic girls, and to admire the ingenuity of the advertisers who had emblazoned their logos on the backside of the players' skin-tight shorts. One player was particularly attractive, and I studied her advertisement with great interest.

"What is Peroni's?" I finally asked.

"I don't know," my mom answered. "Why do you ask?"

"Whatever the company does, it's a sponsor of one of the volleyball teams playing on TV, or at least a couple of the players." I motioned over to the television.

My brother, Kerry, had been ogling the same player. "I don't care how much Peroni's you buy, Chris—whatever Peroni's even is—there is no way a girl like that would ever talk to you."

"Actually, I think Peyronie's is a disease," my Aunt Pam said. Pam had worked as a part-time transcriber of medical records for several years and as a result she'd developed a solid knowledge base about a wide range of diseases.

"A disease?" I asked. "That player is advertising a disease? Well, I'm sold. I'll let her give it to me."

My aunt Pam blushed a bit. "I'm not sure you want it," she said.

"Why not?" I asked.

"I can't remember exactly how you get it—it might be genetic—but the disease is characterized by a growth on the penis. If I recall, it interferes with erections. I think it typically makes it hook to the right."

"It?" I asked.

"Christopher, that's enough," Mom insisted.

"I'm just trying to learn about Peroni's, Mom." I'd only recently started having uninhibited conversations with my mom and other adult relatives, and I enjoyed testing the limits, and setting new ones.

Toward the end of our Peroni's discussion the waiter approached to refill water glasses.

"If you want Peroni's, we have it here," he said.

"You mean the entire staff has it?" I laughed.

"Did you get it from that volleyball player?" Kerry asked excitedly.

"No, it's an Italian beer," the waiter said, a bit confused. "We sell it by the bottle."

"Really?" I asked.

"Yeah. It's the only beer we carry."

"Well I'd like three bottles of it," I said.

"You want three bottles of Peroni's?"

"Yeah." I paused to look at my Aunt Pam, then continued. "Cause mine hooks to the left and I want to see if I can straighten this sucker out."

Aunt Pam spit some red wine, spraying the white tablecloth. Mom's olive colored cheeks turned as red as the wine. The waiter raised his eyebrows, but then turned and walked toward the bar to get the beer. And somewhere in Italy my great-grandmother rolled over in her grave, puzzled as to why she was sent back and someone like me gets to stay.

Atomic Defense

Working from home doesn't work. There might be exceptions, I suppose. Somewhere in this world there could be a person with the enviable job of testing couch cushion comfort or television-tube longevity. It's also possible that someone is compensated to intermittently monitor the performance of their refrigerator light. I can't confirm the existence of such jobs, each perfectly suited for the stay-at-home professional, but I recently read about a lady in my native Oregon who gets paid to count salmon as they pass through a fish ladder, and who would've thought someone would pay a person to do that?

When I set up my home office I was a licensed attorney with the fleeting desire to start a topflight law practice. I'd been practicing law on and off for about four years at the time. During that span, my most notable professional achievement involved finding the perfect cherry-wood frame to display my law degree. Still, I maintained the blissful dream of becoming a legal legend. I was serious now, I told myself, truly ready to embrace the practice of law and apply the knowledge that I'd garnered from nine years of post-high school education.[1]

---

[1] I've always loved the acquisition of knowledge but have never really developed an interest in applying it.

Within minutes of opening my one-man, home-based law firm, my half-hearted plans fell apart. The superficial ambition I'd mustered was trounced by my lack of interest in the practice of law. Before I could turn on my computer, I reverted to my previous occupational pursuit: sitting comfortably in front of the television, watching soft-core pornography, praying that someone would offer me a lucrative contract to count exposed nipples as they passed by on the television screen.

My one room loft in downtown Portland was both office and living quarters during my short career as a full-time lawyer. Prior to opening my practice I spent an entire weekend creating the perfect work space, adorning my desk with all the necessary equipment—a humming fax machine, a printer, cable internet hookup, heavy duty stapler, a portable kegerator on wheels. Space limitations forced me to squeeze my new desk between a plush couch, a tiny table and a stack of letters from the landlord reminding me that I needed to pay rent. Despite the cramped quarters, the end result was a cathedral to productivity.

When the sun rose on the Monday after I'd organized my work space, I jumped out of bed upbeat, veins pounding with motivation. Determined to capitalize on this rare professional momentum I didn't waste time pulling on pants. I headed to work wearing only boxers, a violation of my self-imposed dress code, the one that required me to don pants, a shirt and a craftily constructed paper hat during working hours. I also ignored the policy that required me to actually perform legal work. Though I had every intention of making it to my desk, the twenty-eight foot commute from pillow to my work station required me to pass the couch. I tried not to stop, but the cushy cushions lured me in. I plopped down, planning to stay only for a minute, but proceeded to watch television for the next eleven hours, moving only to check the refrigerator light.

The History Channel spent the entire day asserting that Hitler was one dastardly son-of-a-bitch. The evidence was powerful and convincing, but I didn't leap to conclusions. I'm the type who needs to hear all the facts before forming a firm opinion, a personal trait I attribute to an eye-opening experience I had in third grade. The sour episode exposed how distasteful an unfounded accusation can be. It started when Mrs. Williams, my third grade teacher, asked one of my classmates, Troy Wriggle, to collect the spelling tests that we'd just completed. A ruckus broke out during the collection process and Troy, panicky about his exam performance, used the disruption as an opportunity to switch his test with mine. He grabbed my exam from the stack of papers and erased my name. In its place, he wrote his name. To complete the scam, Troy scribbled my name on his paper—a basic primary school cheating ploy. Troy didn't target my exam for the switch; it was strictly a matter of chance. Comically, Troy outperformed me on the test, so by switching our names he had effectively s-c-r-e-w-e-d himself.

Mrs. Williams easily spotted Troy's attempted deception. His hasty erasure left behind indisputable and damning evidence that there'd been a switch. Considering the relative test scores, Mrs. Williams initially fingered me as the culprit. She pulled me out of recess and delivered a sermon about honesty.

"Umm...okay Mrs. Williams, I'll be honest," I said, having no idea what she was talking about, yet lying through my teeth.

Handwriting comparisons and anonymous witnesses eventually placed blame, and the higher test score, on Troy, acquitting me of being a competent speller.[2] This experience taught me how imperative it is to hear all the facts before making an accusation. Unlike most valuable lessons I've learned, I retained this one for more than a passing moment.

The History Channel used all of Monday to outline Hitler's immorality, and then spent the rest of the week detailing the condemning evidence. I rested on my couch, in the shadow of a perfectly organized work station, ignoring my vocation, con-

---

[2] A blessed visionary, I foresaw the advent of computers and spellcheck software and decided not to waste energy on memorizing the spelling of words.

templating the slight possibility that Hitler was the victim of one hell of a frame job. I weighed the evidence, sitting in judgment for up to twelve hours at a stretch. By Friday afternoon I'd reached a verdict. Hitler was a complete, inhumane prick. Guilty as charged.

The following week the History Channel put Lee Harvey Oswald on trial. Again I sat in judgment, transfixed by the television, glued to the couch. I changed my voicemail and set up an automatic e-mail response to alert my clients that I'd be out for the entire week—jury duty called. On Friday I acquitted Oswald of all counts, small consolation for a defendant long dead.

After only two weeks at the helm of my fledgling law practice, I'd already resolved two highly publicized cases, finding one scoundrel guilty and a conspiracy puppet innocent. On the downside, my state-of-the-art work station looked like a feather duster's fantasy, and I'd billed less than two hours. My firm, I realized, was in dire need of competent, responsible management.

"God I wish I could fire me," I stated several times while picking Skittles out of the crevices between the couch cushions.

Each morning during those first two weeks I'd spend up to ten minutes lying in bed, firming my constitution, mentally preparing for the treacherous commute. Determined to forge past the couch and into productivity, I'd leap up and make a dash for my desk, but my mental fortitude was no match for my physical addiction to leisure. Like a recovering drug addict forced to walk past a crack house on the way to work, I scarcely stood a chance.

After completing work on the Oswald trial, I considered selling my couch, the opiate that had transformed me into a lethargic lump and threatened to kill my ailing legal career. Its green, velvety upholstery concealed much more than a feathery interior; deep inside the couch's comfortable goodness lurked superpowers worthy of tights and a cape. The cushions possessed a potent traction beam that worked in concert with the frame's sleep-inducing venom, and these combined to trap me like a fly in a web. As soon as I was in range—*THWACK!*—the couch locked on to my affinity for relaxation and reeled me in. Couched into submission—or as the intelligentsia say, *sofaed*—I was forced to spend the day in a prone position, expelling violent snores in an attempt to free myself from professional purgatory. A year earlier, when I'd purchased the couch at a deep discount, I'd felt magnificently thrifty. Now the couch was costing me lawyerly fame. In the end, you always get what you pay for.

I wanted to quit my couch habit, I really did. A few times I broke free from its grip long enough to go for a jog or a bike ride, but I was never able to get anywhere near my desk. After two weeks of trying to break my couch habit, and failing, I tried to incorporate it into my work day. If the couch wouldn't let me get to my desk, I figured I'd bring my work to the couch. Any office supplies I might need were easily accessible, a mere ten feet away at my work station. It seemed a reasonable compromise. *Oh yes,* I thought, *I can have my couch and do work, too!*

My hopes of becoming a functioning couch-a-holic faded with each passing, unproductive day. Another month of verdicts passed. Ghengis Kahn: *fearless.* Bubonic Plague: *merciless.* Columbus: *fortuitously lost.* J. Edgar Hoover: *size 14.*

After lazing through the Hoover trial I admitted that in order for me to get any work done I'd have to leave my loft. The following Monday, instead of trying to sidestep the couch and make it to my desk, I hopped out of bed, pulled on pants for the first time in weeks, and sprinted out the door, certain that if I dared to look back at the couch I'd turn into a pillar of food stamps. I walked briskly out of the building and headed to the city library, my briefcase packed with contracts and documents that needed attention. At the library I settled in and got to work. By 1:00 in the afternoon I'd accomplished more than I had in the previous month.

A little after 1:30, I packed up my things and walked the sixteen blocks back to my loft to fix lunch, a money-saving decision necessitated by a shriveling bank account. The cupboards in my loft were nearly as empty as Hitler's heart, but I managed to scrape together a sandwich, found a half-full bag of stale chips and grabbed a Diet Coke out of the fridge. I carried my blue-collar lunch over to the couch and set it down on the battered chest that was spending its fourth year standing in for the coffee table I'd been intending to buy. Before sitting, I removed my jeans and tossed them on my brown leisure chair. As I lowered down onto the velvety cushions, I shot a longing look over at my meticulously organized desk.

As soon as my bottom touched velvet, sluggishness began its seductive ritual. My eyes grew heavy, evidenced by long moments of complete darkness. I fought back, gulping down half the can of Diet Coke, the caffeine spending its fourth year standing in for the motivation I'd been hoping to find. After so many days lunching through work, I was intent on having a working lunch. I slapped my face three times in an attempt to impart lucidity, and then grabbed a legal pad from my briefcase. The first page on the pad listed all the work issues that required my attention, painstakingly arranged in descending order of importance. *Call Tony* was the first item on the list. *Burn couch* was at the bottom of the page. I picked up the phone and dialed Tony.

Tony is my cousin and, at the time, a client. Months earlier at a family gathering he'd told me about an ongoing dispute he was having with his employer. When you're a lawyer, regardless of your ability or specialty, family and friends bounce legal issues off you all the time. I don't discourage this practice because the idea of helping friends and family has always appealed to me. Tony told me that he'd been laid off after twenty years of working for the same company. He was trying to get reinstated and asked me if he had any legal recourse. I answered honestly—*professional suicide for a lawyer?*—and told him I had no idea. Schooled and experienced in corporate law, I have scant knowledge of employment issues and had spent nearly no time in the courtroom. Complicating the issue, Tony was a member of a labor union, a vexing establishment that adds layers of complexity to any employment matter.

Wanting to help, I agreed to research the issue. A whirlwind later, after reading up on the applicable law and court procedure, I filed a lawsuit against Tony's employer in federal court. The circumstances of his layoff heavily suggested that Tony's union representative, entrusted with the job of protecting workers' rights, had instead buried Tony's valid grievance in order to win some contractual concessions from company management. The union rep, after displaying initial enthusiasm for challenging Tony's layoff, stopped pursuing the claim immediately after he had a meeting with the employer to negotiate the details of a new collective bargaining agreement. Unfortunately, laws that forbid asshole employers from conspiring with self-serving, corrupt union representatives require pesky amounts of direct, supporting evidence. Such evidence is rare; most culprits being smart enough not to memorialize their nefarious deeds in a memo or e-mail. (*Dear Company: Glad discussions about the renewal of the collective bargaining agreement went well last week. Thanks for the hooker! That was cool! As agreed during the meeting, I will bury Tony's valid grievance because you want me to and, hell, I'm willing to sell him out to make my job easier. Best regards, Tony's union representative*). Despite the long odds, justice demanded that we try, so I poured myself in.

As I finished dialing Tony's number, I grabbed a pen and carefully drew a line through *Call Tony*. Tony answered after the third ring. We exchanged salutations and I updated him on the status of his case.

"There's a Rule 16 conference this Wednesday in the judge's chambers, so why don't we meet on Friday and I can update you on everything."

"Friday sounds fine. How about 4:00 at Marsee's Bakery?"

"Sure, that works." I penned it onto my calendar.

"What is a Rule 16 conference?" Tony asked.

"A preliminary meeting with the judge and opposing counsel to discuss the case."

"Oh."

The discussion turned to non-legal matters: Tony's college-aged daughter was going to Australia for a semester abroad, he was working on a kitchen remodel, the status of his ongoing job search. As he spoke, I opened his file to note the conversation. The case binder I'd put together was packed with several legal documents: the complaint, the defendant's answer, discovery papers and several court notices. Every time a party files a document in a federal case, or when a procedural meeting is scheduled, the court clerk sends out a notice to the attorneys. I'd received several of them.

As we continued chatting, I flipped through the court notices to see if there was anything germane that I'd forgotten to address. While perusing the file, I came across a notice letter that stopped me dead:

Rule 16 meeting, Monday, June 7th, 2:00 p.m.

The notice made no sense. I knew the meeting was scheduled for Wednesday. I pulled my calendar out of my briefcase for confirmation. There, in the square for Wednesday, June 9th, I saw the comforting note that I scribbled weeks ago: *Rule 16 conference, 2:00.* I looked over at the clock on the wall. 1:56 p.m.

I casually searched the file for the court notice denoting the June 9th meeting date. As I rifled through the file Tony continued to talk about the new cabinets he was installing. To maintain appearances, I muttered, "Uh-uh, sounds good," every few seconds. I thumbed through the file a second time but still couldn't find the court notice stating that the conference was scheduled for the 9th. I began to really worry. I was sure the meeting was on Wednesday. I looked at the clock. 1:58.

Panic began to seep in. As Tony continued to chat I pulled out my laptop and hastily plugged in the long cable-modem connector that extended from the modem on my desk. I quickly logged on to the federal court website to check the online case file.

"Uh-huh, I bet she's having a great time in Australia, Tony. Sounds great."

The court website indicated that the Rule 16 conference was scheduled for Monday, June 7th at 2:00. How, once again, could I be the only person who is right? Panic, absolute panic. I quickly told Tony I had another call.

"Sorry Tony, got to go." I hung up without waiting for a reply.

I was scrambling now. In the best conditions I could make it from my door to the courthouse in eight minutes. First, though, I needed to put on some clothes. Boxers, t-shirt and flip-flops seemed a tad casual for a meeting with a federal judge.

I'd recently taken both my suits to the dry cleaners, intending to pick them up on Tuesday, a full day in advance of the scheduled conference, or so I thought. Without a suit, I needed to improvise. I found some tan slacks and a white dress shirt in my closet, both slightly wrinkled, and I pulled them on as quickly as I could. Then I discovered an old, bluish blazer in the back of the closet, mildly ruffled, ignored for years. The jacket was not a traditional blue blazer, but rather an old suit jacket, the accompanying pants long since discarded. The dark blue fabric had a pattern of funky, unflattering flecks, mostly green but with hints of orange. Mold or by design? When I'd finished piecing together the ensemble, I took a moment to pose in front of my full-length mirror. At best, the outfit shouted: *This man thought his court meeting was on June 9th—oops!*

The wall clock read 2:02. *I set that clock ahead didn't I? I must have. Yes, I did. It is at least ten minutes fast.* I checked my cell phone. 2:03. Shit.

Needing to buy time, I called judge's chambers. No one answered. I left message. "Car trouble, waiting for cab, meteor, sniper fire, war in the Middle East, brain transplant, tough day, be there in ten minutes, mea culpa, mea culpa." I jammed several loose documents related to Tony's case into my briefcase and scrambled out the door.

While riding the elevator down to the parking garage, another worry hit: *Was I required to prepare any documents for a Rule 16 conference?* This was my first litigation. I'd never been to a conference like this before. I had a lunch scheduled with a litigator friend of mine the next day to discuss the particulars of a Rule 16 meeting, but that was no help to me now. I knew the relevant law and had command of the applicable facts, but I didn't know if I was required to prepare anything formal for the meeting. Should I bring some muffins? Maybe a side dish? Panic proliferated.

When I arrived at my car, I ripped open the door and jumped behind the wheel. As the engine came to life, so did the digital clock on the dash. 2:06. Seconds later my cell phone rang.

"I am trying to reach Mr. Kemper," a female voice said.

"This is Chris."

"I am calling from Judge Jenkins chambers. I'm his administrative assistant. Everyone has arrived for the Rule 16 meeting. Are you coming?"

"Absolutely. I'm on my way."

I repeated the excuse about car problems and informed her that I'd left a message just a few minutes earlier.

"Oh. Okay," she responded. "The judge's clerk is out today so no one got your message. Thanks for calling, sorry we didn't get that. We will wait, but hurry." Nice lady. I appreciated her calm.

Because I'm the world's best driver, I am comfortable swerving through traffic, ignoring signals and endangering the lives of pedestrians, certain that my brilliant reflexes will steer me clear of any real trouble. I raced through downtown and made great time. When the courthouse came into view, the clock on the dash read 2:11.

The only available street parking near the courthouse was a handicap spot—*Damn, why hadn't I fallen out of a tree as a kid!*—so I zoomed a couple blocks away to a Star Park. I pulled my car up to the small employee booth and threw the keys at the attendant as I jumped out of the car.

"In a hurry," I yelled as the keys flew over his head and under another parked car. "Got to go, sorry, park it in the river if you want. Sell it. I don't care." I threw a ten dollar bill over my shoulder as I ran off. Panic was new to me, and it showed.

I sprinted a block and a half to the courthouse steps tying my tie in stride, my briefcase strap choking me. As I ran up to the entrance, I caught sight of a Thomas Jefferson quote that is carved into the courthouse's marble facade:

The Boisterous Sea of Liberty is Never without a Wave

You ain't kidding, I thought. *And right now I could use a life jacket.*

I deftly navigated security and plunged into the elevator, continuously hitting the 5th floor button as if playing an old-style arcade game. *Faster! Faster!* When the elevator stopped, the doors opened and I stepped into a sizable, well-decorated waiting room. The two opposing attorneys were already there, smug looks and all, along with the judge's administrative assistant. I looked at my cell phone. 2:14. *I should be a NASCAR driver!* I apologized profusely for two minutes as the other attorneys smirked. Both were neatly dressed, but they appeared dumpy, bland and beaten down, like they'd surrendered to a middling life. They embodied everything I strive to avoid. I quietly prayed that life would always keep a comfortable couch between me and their existence.

After finishing my overzealous apology—*I spoke too much! They know I'm lying*—the judge entered the room and invited us into the inner office. He wore a traditional black robe, de facto immunity from poor fashion sense. Given my unflattering dress I half expected the judge to offer me one of his spares. *Here son, I really think you should put this on.*

Once everyone took a seat, I again apologized and reiterated my excuse, this time adding a twist.

"Car trouble made me late Your Honor, but I lost more time by stopping by the Lotus Bar when I first arrived. I thought that's where you held all your Rule 16 meetings. I waited there for nearly five minutes before I figured out you guys were over here."

The Lotus is a grubby drinking establishment near the courthouse. The judge chuckled mildly. Thank God.

"Well it doesn't surprise me that you'd head over there," the judge said. "Judge Hamilton has a clerk who went to law school with you and she told us some interesting stories."

I imagined the conversation. *"...and he was drunk all the time. Never once saw him in class either."* Fuck.

"Oh really," I said. "Well Your Honor, I've been out of law school for some time now, so there is no way this former classmate could've told you everything about me. For instance, did you know I've committed all my free time over the past few years to selfless charity work?"

"I'm sure you have," the judge smiled.

The meeting turned to business. The judge led a general discussion of the case and we all worked to finalize discovery schedules. The meeting went well, relatively. I managed to say some intelligent things. After forty minutes, it was over. Goodbyes were shared and we departed.

Back at the parking lot I apologized to the attendant for my hurried behavior and gave him an extra $10. When I arrived back at my loft I retrieved a beer from the fridge, removed my slacks and fell onto the couch. I felt like I'd dodged a bullet, but the experience exposed deeper wounds. I couldn't imagine going back into corporate law, an exercise in providing answers to questions I care nothing about, and now I knew that representing individuals wouldn't work either, because I'd always care too much, a drawback that would commonly cause me to worry and panic. I needed a profession that inspired rather than bored, but one where my shoulders, and mine alone, bore the brunt of any personal missteps or mistakes. To paraphrase Churchill, that afternoon wasn't the end of my legal career, nor was it the end of the beginning, but it was, quite assuredly, the beginning of the end.

The coming months were filled with Tony's case, losing

sleep and constantly spinning my mind. The judge ultimately dismissed the lawsuit because we couldn't produce any direct evidence that the union official had conspired with company management. According to the summary judgment ruling, the assertion that an illicit agreement had been struck between the union representative and Tony's employer was based on conjecture and speculation, and that wasn't enough to allow the case to proceed. For my legal career, the dismissal of Tony's case marked the end of the end.

The day after the summary judgment was issued I packed up my work station—after vacuuming off a thick layer of dust—and transitioned out of law and into indecision. Life would soon reveal its grand plan, of this I was confident. As far as I was concerned though, I'd never pursue a full-time legal career. A vocation in law had never been a dream of mine anyway. I attended law school for the same reason men flocked to the National Guard during the Vietnam War: enrollment bought three more years of avoiding the horrors of mundane employment, a personal war I was intent on dodging, a concept to which I conscientiously object.

My decision to abandon a legal career triumphed over a single, lingering regret. It didn't bother me that I hadn't made any significant money as a lawyer, nor that I had failed to pacify even a single wave separating the common man from the liberty he so richly deserves. I would've liked to accomplish these things, but, for me, a career in law didn't inspire—and I owned the wrong couch. What *did* trouble me was that by forsaking the legal profession, I was dooming the greatest legal concept ever conceived to a virtual death sentence. I call it the Atomic Defense, a criminal defense theory that I'd fashioned more than a decade earlier, born from countless episodes of Perry Mason and a few high school science classes. The theory is capable of turning the criminal justice system on its head. When properly applied, it renders the tired concepts of guilt and innocence meaningless. It bothered me that my only legal brainchild was at risk of suffering the same fate as my perfectly conceived home office; an eternity wallowing in dust. I knew in order for me to wholly dispense with the practice of law that I had to ensure that the Atomic Defense got its day in court. Put on your seatbelt lady justice, here we go.

* * *

I loved watching *Perry Mason*. Every day at noon, KPTV Channel 12 served up a black and white episode. I'd sit transfixed, glued to the couch as Perry sliced up District Attorney Hamilton Burger like a vegetable at Benihana. No matter how damning the evidence against Perry's client, D.A. Burger never won a conviction. Through brute charisma and calm brilliance, Perry yanked the cloak of guilt off his client and attached it to someone else. Perry was so outstanding that he once won a case even after his client confessed to the crime on the witness stand.

"So you admit you stabbed the victim over and over and over with this knife," Burger hounded. He waved around the murder weapon, a long, serrated knife, State's exhibit A. Perry's client slumped in the witness chair, resigned to spending the rest of his life in jail.

"Yes," Perry's client whispered.

The screen flashed to a shot of Perry's face. He sat calm, unaffected.

"You intended to kill the victim when you stabbed her, didn't you?" Burger hammered.

"Absolutely, I hated her!" Perry's client barked back, tears rolling down his face.

Again the camera turned to Perry. He looked over at his sexy assistant Della Street and gave a half grin.

"So you walked in, saw her sleeping on the couch, snuck up and stabbed her to death?"

"Yes, yes, I did it! I did it!"

"The prosecution rests!" Burger exclaimed, a sly smile painting his lips, certain that he'd finally beaten Perry.

He has finally won, I thought. *Perry Mason has actually lost a case.*

Despite the damning confession, Perry stood up confidently, his imposing frame filling the screen. Before he began to question his client, Paul Drake, a private investigator who often worked for Perry, rushed into the courtroom. Perry looked back at Paul as if he knew he'd be arriving with important news. Paul quickly whispered something in Perry's ear. Perry nodded, as if confirming a suspicion. Della Street looked on, pretty as a picture.

Perry turned to his client. "Are you sure you killed her?" Perry asked.

His client looked confused and took a moment to answer. "Yes. I stabbed her four times. I told you that. She was dead when I left," the man replied.

"But was she alive when you got there?"

The courtroom fell silent for an instant, and then a soft chatter filled the gallery. The defendant raised his eyebrows.

"What do you mean?" he asked.

"I don't think the victim was alive when you stabbed her!" announced Perry in his deep, powerful tone.

Accusatory glances darted around the courtroom, no one doubting for a moment that Perry was on to something. Suddenly, the defendant's gardener, seated in the back of the courtroom, leapt to his feet. Without any prompting, he confessed to the crime, unburdening his guilty soul and sending D.A. Burger to another defeat.

"Okay, okay! I did it!" he screamed. "I poisoned her in the morning, before he stabbed her. She was dead when *I* left. I would have gotten away with it too if I would have just sat here quietly rather than admitting the whole scheme in open court."

On the way out of the courtroom, Burger stopped to chat with Perry. Despite losing, Burger chuckled at the odd turn that the case had taken, happy to have lost again in the interest of justice. I sat mesmerized by Perry's brilliance, hopeful that after my Major League baseball career and two terms as the President of the United States that I too could be an unbeatable attorney—or at least have an assistant as hot as Della Street.

"So let me get this straight," I'd tell a new client. "Your fingerprints are all over the murder weapon, you confessed to the crime and the authorities found the body buried in a shallow grave right where you said it was?"

"That's right," the client would mutter.[3]

"Well, none of that should be a problem," I'd assure. "I can get you out of this, don't you worry."[4]

I knew I could never match Perry's virtuosity in the courtroom, or his amazing luck. To achieve his level of legal renown, I'd either need to move to Hollywood and find the right script or develop some kind of courtroom gimmick, some miracle defense theory capable of overcoming damning evidence. When my parents nixed the idea of moving to California to jumpstart my fledgling acting career, I spent the commercial breaks during each *Perry Mason* episode working on a surefire legal defense capable of removing the residue of guilt from my future clients, no matter their culpability.

My attempt to create a catchall criminal defense met with little success, but my enthusiasm for the project was invigorated any time I viewed a brilliant performance by Perry. Still, the general concept failed to coalesce into anything specific. By the time I started high school, with girls to chase and sports to play, I had little time for *Perry Mason* and the idea of an all-purpose defense theory was relegated to an afterthought.

---

[3] Do authorities ever discover a murder victim in an extraordinarily deep grave? There seems to be a direct correlation between the depth at which a body is buried and getting away with the crime, yet every year murderers by the hundreds plop their victims in miserably shallow graves. Inevitably the body is discovered and the guilty are convicted, betrayed by their aversion to manual labor. It's like there is a comfortable couch separating these criminals from their shovels.

[4] Of course after I won acquittals for guilty clients I'd dole out my own justice, billing my clients to death and disposing of the bodies in very, very deep graves.

The idea sat dormant until my junior year when I enrolled in Mr. Beeson's chemistry class. Mr. Beeson taught chemistry and biology at our high school with passion and flair, and his desk never collected dust. He wore the same pullover to school nearly every day, no matter the weather. It was an odd looking, oversized sweater speckled with flecks of green and orange. Mold or by design? The exams he gave always had a peculiar number of questions, like 19 or 23, because, he explained, "Calculating test score percentages when there is an odd number in the denominator keeps my mind sharp." Science folks are strange that way, which makes them interesting.

It was Mr. Beeson who introduced me to the scientific underpinnings of the Atomic Defense. Early in the semester he gave a lecture on the theory of mass conservation. The concept piqued my interest and I began scouring the detailed information in my science textbook rather than simply doodling warnings in the margins—*this experiment went awry in '84 and killed three students, but the school board did a full scale cover-up and claimed that the dead students had "moved" to another district. Be careful, and good luck!*

By semester's end, I'd distilled the mass conservation theory into the Atomic Defense, a fail-proof get out of jail free card. Two parts chemistry, one part biology, together a Perry Mason dream and district attorney's nightmare, the Defense is scientifically unassailable, like DNA testing and the perfection of Ben & Jerry's Chocolate Chip Cookie Dough Ice Cream. And it's powerful enough to excuse the guilty of any violation of manmade law.

* * *

Bunsen burners flaming, our chemistry class performed experiments that revealed an indisputable truth: Nature is an eccentric old coot. No matter what Mr. Beeson instructed us to burn, break, distill or evaporate, our calculations proved, time and again, that Nature refuses to create or destroy its precious atoms.[5] Chemical bonds break, solids phase into liquid, and then, as things heat up, the atoms become a gas. But regardless of the rigors that we put various compounds through, at the end of the experiment, my classmates and I ended up with the same amount of mass that we'd started with—it was just in a different form.

As a result of Nature's stinginess, the earth is operating with the same supply of atoms that the planet had when it exploded onto the scene about 4.5 billion years ago. During this time, Nature hasn't taken a single atom out of circulation, not even for a tune-up, and it hasn't cycled in any new ones. A few wayward meteors have crashed into earth, delivering a smidgen of new atoms, and we've lost some atoms by launching several satellites into space so we can spy on the Iranians. But other than that, Nature is working with the same building blocks that were originally used to construct the earth. And Nature uses these ancient atoms to construct everything on earth, including humans. That's not just oddly cheap, it's dangerous.[6]

To give perspective, the Boston Celtics won eight straight NBA championships in the late '50s and early '60s. The team was, without question, basketball's greatest professional dynasty. Now let's assume that Nature created our planet out of champion-caliber atoms, a selfless collection of molecules unsurpassed in quality, the envy of the entire universe. Like the champion Celtics, these earthly atoms work almost perfectly together, each one willing to sacrifice for the good of the team. Now fast forward 4.5 billion years. Nature hasn't taken a single atom out of the game, nor has it acquired any new players. By comparison, if Nature owned the Celtics, we'd still be watching Bill Russell and Bob Cousy limp around on the Boston Garden's parquet floor.

---

[5] Nature makes an exception to this rule for nuclear reactions, where mass is converted to energy, but other than that, Nature holds onto its mass like a miser.

[6] I will say this for Nature—it's a hell of a bean counter. Billions of years and it's barely lost a single atom. I can't go a day without losing a pen.

And a billion years from now, with Nature in charge, Boston fans would still be watching the same players, their decayed skeletons wired together and attached to the rafters of the Boston Garden like marionettes, manipulated up and down the court by cheap labor from the planet Zork. I'm a believer in recycling, but everything has its limits. Nature's original collection of earthly atoms may have been of the highest quality, but we need some fresh blood because, quite literally, these atoms form our blood. To make matters worse, Nature has booby-trapped every single atom, making it impossible for humans to intervene with any sort of atom renovation program. If we break an atom open to see what's under the hood, all we get is one hell of an explosion and barrels of nasty waste.[7]

Now everyone knows you can't make cake from crap, except my younger brother who I once tricked into thinking I could do just that. And it follows that Nature can't consistently produce quality goods from ancient parts. Use building blocks that are older than the Big Bang and you get winged birds that can't fly (ostriches and penguins), animals that need 15 pairs of legs to walk (centipedes) and dishonest, violent, petulant people by the tens of thousands (Oakland Raider fans). Garbage in, garbage out. To better understand how this works, let's trace the life of a hypothetical carbon atom. I'll call our atom Ted. Like almost every other atom on earth, Ted has been working here for 4.5 billion years.

For the first couple billon years, Ted sat relatively idle, trapped deep in the bowels of the planet, buried several miles under what is now Siberia. Then one day a volcano spit Ted to the surface. After years of toiling around in the atmosphere,

---

[7] If I could take over for Nature I would not only replace every worn out atom, I'd fashion every new atom after a popcorn seed. That way when you break an atom apart, instead of death and destruction (or waste-making energy) you'd get a tasty little treat. This would make atomic power a viable option AND, more importantly, would reduce the cost of movie theatre popcorn, which is really yummy but prohibitively expensive.

looking for something to do, Carbon Ted got hired on as part of a growing eucalyptus tree that was located in what is now modern day China. Soon after joining the eucalyptus tree, a dinosaur walked by and ate some of the tree's leaves. In the process, the dinosaur ate and digested Ted. As a result, Ted went to work in the dinosaur's intestines, an unpleasant job by any measure, and he traveled with the large beast across a frozen strip of land that once connected Russia and Alaska. Ted wasn't overly thrilled with his work, but he was making friends with some of the other atoms inside the dinosaur, and he actually seemed to have a knack for digestion. But as the dinosaur wandered into Alaska, a violent earthquake struck and triggered a massive mudslide that buried the large reptile, killing it instantly and trapping Ted, once again, underground. For hundreds of million years, the dinosaur and the other animals killed in the mudslide decayed until they eventually formed a trapped pocket of dark, thick liquid that people call oil—or if you're in the Bush Administration, you call Master. The oil remained trapped for another billion years or so until it was pumped to the surface by humans. Once on the surface, Ted was loaded into the Exxon Valdez and got to play a supporting role in an environmental disaster. Spilled from the ship's hull, Ted latched on to a young seal. The seal was later rescued by a fast-responding group of volunteers who ferried the struggling animal ashore to be scrubbed and cleaned. Ted was so frightened that someone would blame him for grounding the ship that he burrowed deep into the seal's skin to hide. Nearly all his atomic friends were eventually washed off the seal, but Ted remained, snugly tucked into the animal's glistening coat. A local villager assisting in the cleanup took the seal home, explaining to the other volunteers that he would nurse the critter back to health.

"I'll call him Smiley," he told everyone, "and I'll take good care of him."

The next day the man killed the seal, skinned it and threw the various seal parts, along with Ted, into a stewpot. A couple days later, the villager brought his seal stew to a potluck party. An Inuit man at the gathering ate a bowl of the stew and swallowed Ted. The very next morning, the Inuit man flew to Seattle to visit his aunt. Soon after he arrived at his aunt's house, he used the toilet, depositing Ted into the Seattle sewer system. After the sewage was treated, it was sold to a local farmer as fertilizer. The farmer sprayed the sewage, and Ted, onto his freshly planted cornfield. A few months later, Ted was part of a golden kernel of sweet corn. The farmer harvested the corn and brought it to the local farmer's market in Redmond, Washington. The corncob that contained Carbon Ted was sold to a Microsoft executive. After buying the corn, the executive stopped by his office to make sure that all of Microsoft's products were littered with the annoying bugs that make software monopolies enjoyable to run. Then he drove home, boiled the corn, and gobbled Ted up. Ted circulated through the executive's digestive system, was absorbed into the bloodstream and ended up getting a temporary job working in the executive's brain. *Bingo!* As a result of Ted's work history, the executive literally had shit for brains, just as many of his subordinates at Microsoft had speculated.

Nature constantly shuffles inventory around in this manner to cover up its dangerous practice of reusing the same old materials over and over. This sleight of hand worked for billions of years until scientists, armed with electron microscopes, discovered that, in reality, every atom in every living organism, including people, is working on short-term assignment. A hydrogen atom that is part of your liver today could be shipped off tomorrow to work for a water molecule in the Adriatic. At about the same time that you lose a hydrogen atom, Nature sends a replacement, possibly a hydrogen atom that had been working in the lungs of a wild stallion roaming the Wyoming wilderness. This ongoing atomic exchange makes it possible for men to technically assert that they do, in fact, have a horse dick. It follows that nearly everyone can claim to be cat quick, rock solid, pretty as a picture and as strong as an ox. Yes, your boss actually *is* a jackass, at least in part. If you could trace the history of all the atoms that make up your body at any moment in time, you'd find some exciting, and disturbing, news. Your atomic history is filled with glory and humiliation. None of this, however, disguises the fact that we're all made from parts that are older than dirt.

It's this scientific reality that removes blame from human shoulders and places it, quite properly, on Nature's lap. The tragic truth is that we're all a conglomeration of old atomic junk, through no fault of our own. Sure, people commit crimes, but the Atomic Defense makes it clear that humans are the real victims. We are constructed out of old, shoddy materials that cause us to fall apart physically and short-circuit mentally. The less fortunate, the people who get a particularly bad atomic draw at any given point, can also break down ethically and morally. And who can blame them?

In the event a jury wrongly decides that they *can* blame a person for breaking the law, overlooking or ignoring the grizzled nature of the defendant's atomic makeup, a secondary prong of the Atomic Defense provides a safety net. Even if a person is convicted, Nature's atomic policy makes it unethical, immoral and, quite likely, unconstitutional to imprison a human being. Scientific studies reveal that it takes, on average, seven years for a person's atomic composition to completely change. Seven years from now, you will be a completely different person, made up of almost entirely different—but still old—atomic parts.[8] Therefore, by the time a criminal is convicted and hauled off to jail, many of the atoms that participated in the crime will have already fled, likely to some exotic South American country that doesn't have an extradition treaty with the United States, leaving innocent replacement atoms to do the time. This scientific

---

[8] Conversely, your current atomic makeup will be scattered to the winds and your formal physical self will be traveling the world, crossing oceans, climbing mountains, doing all the things you can't afford to do. So feel free to say, "Yeah, I've been to Algiers. Not recently, mind you, but I've been—and I'm planning a trip to Italy, Croatia and Argentina too." Toss out destinations at will, because, eventually, part of you will travel to every country in the world.

truth makes every incarcerated person innocent, at least partially, and, in time—about seven years—completely.

I will never have the opportunity to present the Atomic Defense in a courtroom for several reasons—primarily because of my continued ownership of a green, velvety couch. The concept still fidgets in my head, though, eager to be freed to pursue legal fame. Therefore I hereby abandon my exclusive rights to the Atomic Defense and offer it, free of charge, to any aspiring Perry Mason.[9] The general implementation guide below can be applied to any criminal proceeding. Used properly, the Defense will make it possible for lawbreakers to walk from the courthouse free of shackles, liberated to pursue a law-abiding life amongst the boisterous waves of criminality perpetually propagated by Nature's ancient atoms.

ATOMIC DEFENSE: Guide to Implementation

The Atomic Defense is the defense of last resort. It should only be used when a traditional legal defense, like innocence, is unavailable. Only use the Defense in cases where your client is undeniably guilty, such as when they're captured on security videotape leaving a Target store with a toaster hidden under their jacket. Once in court, put your client on the stand and begin the following line of questioning:

Attorney: So you took the toaster from the store without paying for it, is that correct?

Client: Yes.

Attorney: And the toaster was concealed under your jacket?

Client: Yes.

Attorney: Did you intend to steal the toaster?

Client: When I left the store, yes, I intended to steal the toaster.

---

[9] Free of charge after all royalties, fees, service charges, administrative charges and other, unspecified charges are paid...and then paid again.

Attorney: But are you sure the toaster wasn't concealed in your jacket when you entered the store?

At this point, pause for a moment in hopes that some idiot in the courtroom gallery will stand up and publicly confess to the crime. *"Yes, I did it! I hid the toaster under his jacket in the parking lot before he went in. I'm to blame...and I would have gotten away with it if I wasn't so stupid. I mean, look at me. I wasn't even a suspect in this case but here I am, in open court, admitting to the crime. If for nothing else, I need to go to jail for being criminally stupid!"*

If a surprise confession fails to bail your client out, continue the questioning.

Attorney: So, if you admit you stole the toaster, why are we here in court today?

Client: Well, you see, I did steal the toaster, but I'm not legally responsible for the theft!

Attorney: What in good heavens do you mean? (Act surprised when you say this, and make sure you use a high-pitched voice to assure the jurors are awake and engaged.)

(The following answer will take considerable pre-trial coaching. It's vital that your client has a firm grasp of the script.)

Client: You see, I'm an atomic wasteland. For some reason, Nature keeps sending me the worst of its atomic inventory. It's the luck of the draw, I suppose, and I've never been lucky. Even though the atoms in my body are continuously recycled—meaning that some of the atoms I have today will be gone tomorrow, replaced by some of their atomic brethren—I always seem to get replacement atoms that are worse than the ones that I had before, and you can't reasonably expect a piece of junk to refrain from stealing toasters. This fact, by itself, creates reasonable doubt, my favorite little companion.

Attorney: Fascinating. Please continue.

Client: So Your Honor, and members of the jury, I took that toaster when I thought store security wasn't looking. I didn't do it because I had a burning desire to toast something. I did it because an oxygen atom in my head went haywire. You see, this oxygen atom, sent by Nature to work in my brain for a few weeks, used to be part of a goat's ass, which is awfully distressing. And prior to that, the oxygen was located on the bottom of a rhinoceros' foot, and those rhinos are extremely heavy so the physical strain on this oxygen atom was enormous. And before that it was part of a tree, one of those uncomfortable looking, wind-blown trees rooted to the side of a cliff that's always exposed to violent weather conditions. And before that, the oxygen was part of a piano that Beethoven almost bought, but instead the piano was sold to a snotty kid named Sid who couldn't play a lick, and once you come that close to greatness and end up with tone-deaf Sid, you'd be depressed for a few millennia too. Then, right before I entered the Target store, Nature informed this oxygen atom that its next assignment would involve a long stint at sea as part of a water molecule. Well, you see, this oxygen atom hates hydrogen atoms—it had a bad relationship with one back during the Middle Ages—and it couldn't bear the thought of floating aimlessly in the ocean for hundreds of years sandwiched between two hydrogens. Additionally, this oxygen atom was an extra in the movie *Jaws*—you may have seen it lying in the sand in one of the beach scenes—and it's been deathly afraid of sharks ever since. So instead of concentrating on its job in my brain, this oxygen atom was fretting about its future and struggling to cope with its past. Apparently the strain was just too much. Right before I entered Target, the oxygen atom flipped out and attacked my brain's moral compass. Hoping to somehow alter its fate, it forced me to steal that toaster. After I was arrested, sure enough, that oxygen atom went AWOL. It jumped bail, boarded the jet stream and headed off to Belize. If you want the true culprit, Belize is the where that atom is, or at least was. Those little guys move fast! Like everyone in this courtroom, I want justice, but justice requires that we place blame where blame belongs. In this case, that's squarely on the valence shell of that dastardly oxygen atom or, if you prefer, its mob boss, Nature. And I can say without hesitation, ladies and gentlemen of the jury, that I've changed. I'm not the man I was back on that fateful shoplifting day, at least not physically."

Attorney: The defense rests, Your Honor, and quite comfortably.

* * *

Going public with the Atomic Defense has allowed me to empathize with scientists who worked on the Manhattan Project. Creating something powerful enough to change the world—and possibly destroy it—is at once a source of pride and the cause of anxiety. And although I believe that revealing the Atomic Defense is required to balance Justice's scale, I fret over the potential consequences. In the hands of any decent attorney, the Defense can secure acquittals for even the most nefarious criminals, like the Nazis who were tried in Nuremberg after World War II.

I once saw a History Channel special on the Nuremberg trials. Despite the program's concerted attempt to create drama, the outcome was as predictable as a beauty pageant with a single entrant. Several high ranking Nazis were on trial—the ones brave enough not to commit suicide—and they'd all played a major role in ravaging an entire continent. There was no way any of them were going free, at least not without a legal tool, like the Atomic Defense, capable of overriding their unspeakable evil deeds. If the Defense would have been around back then, I can imagine Perry Mason in the Nuremberg Palace of Justice, his imposing figure casting a shadow on his Nazi clients, with Della Street taking notes at the defense table. Just before resting his case, Paul Drake rushes into the room and scurries up to Perry's side.

Perry stops the proceeding. "A moment please, Your Honor."

Paul lays some documents on the defense table for Perry to review. Before looking at the documents, Perry shoots a bawdy look toward Della, just because he can. As Perry starts his review of the documents, the camera zooms in. One of the papers shows a diagram of a nitrogen atom and a map of Afghanistan. The camera flashes back to Perry. He breaks into a broad smile. Over the next fifteen minutes, Perry proceeds to explain to the court that the entire blame for World War II lies with a nitrogen atom that developed an opium addiction while working in Afghanistan's poppy fields. Perry describes how in 1901, or maybe it was 1902, this drug-crazed nitrogen atom staggered out of the poppy fields in a stupor and hitchhiked to Austria. In the small Austria town of Linz the nitrogen atom encountered a young boy named Adolf. The nitrogen asked the boy for some money so it could buy another opium fix. When young Adolf refused, the nitrogen atom infiltrated his brain and disconnected his conscience, which caused all sorts of unfortunate side effects. Thereafter, Adolf lusted for power at any cost—and the sad result needed no further explanation. To support the theory, Perry would certainly point out the lyrical similarities between the words nitrogen and Nazi. He'd go on to explain that the crystalline structure of a nitrogen atom is hexagonal, and how this is similar to the six distinct interlinked line segments in a swastika. With the entire responsibility for World War II placed on a single nitrogen atom—which surely escaped Hitler's head long before his body was doused with gasoline and burned—the Nazi defendants would beat the rap and go free. The Allies would, of course, initiate a worldwide hunt to track down Herr Nitrogen. Despite their best efforts the little rascal would manage to stay one step ahead, hop-scotching the globe and causing widespread havoc before swinging through the Middle East to share a hookah with Saddam and…

I'm not sure if shifting criminal responsibility from man to atoms, and ultimately Nature, is a good thing or not, and I certainly harbor a bit of apprehension. Still, I'll rest easy because I came up with the concept of the Atomic Defense over seven years ago, and all my atoms from that time period have long since departed. As a result, the present day me had nothing to do with it.

End Note:
I don't care how you cook your primordial soup or what god or brand of atheism you subscribe to; living organisms are a miracle. The science in *Atomic Defense* is accurate—give or take. Atoms aren't alive—they have no minds or feelings. They don't care if they're part of a car or a building, a pine tree or a rhododendron. These little bits of matter just go where Nature sends them, every job temporary, but steady employment assured. What is so awe-inspiring is that atoms can spend millions of years as inanimate objects and then, when put together in just the right way—a process often triggered by a married couple sharing a bottle of wine or high school sweethearts abusing a bottle of Jack Daniels—the result exceeds the sum of its parts. Like magic these lifeless pieces of matter come together and somehow create thoughts and feelings. And then, just as quickly, when a person dies, these atomic parts contentedly go back to being part of a rock or a urinal, or a hot air balloon.

To put this ancient, unsolvable mystery into contemporary perspective, consider this scenario: a little kid sits in a giant room with millions of Lego pieces. He has about 106 different types of Lego pieces—more of some, fewer of others, similar to how there are 106 different types of atoms on earth, in varying proportions to one another. This industrious boy takes the pieces and builds a ship, a fort, and a tank. He sits in his room for billions of years—*now that's what I call getting grounded*—and builds all types of things. Then one day, using the same lifeless pieces that he's been playing with all along, the boy builds a structure that suddenly starts to move and make noise. Soon, without the boy's help, the structure begins to eat and talk. It grows larger and more complex. When the Lego Creature surpasses the boy in size it starts rampaging around the room, destroying things and gobbling up resources. This goes on for several years, and each day the Lego Creature grows bigger and stronger. Then, as suddenly as the Lego Creature sprang to life, it begins to falter. It slows down, becomes increasingly less active, and spends most of its time playing Bingo and reminiscing about the good old days. Then one day the

Lego Creature drops to the floor, lifeless.

After the Lego Creature dies, the boy runs into the kitchen to tell his mom what has happened. The boy recounts the rise and fall of the Lego Creature in great detail. His mom listens intently. When the boy finishes his tale, she makes a quick phone call and then tells the boy to pack up some of his clothes and toiletries. A couple hours later a Lincoln Town Car pulls up in their driveway and the mom tells the boy to get in the backseat. She explains to him that he is being sent to an inpatient drug rehab facility, and that he can't come home until he recants his impossibly ridiculous and crazy story. And who could blame her?

clinging to anonymity

28 Minutes

People are to time as dogs are to people. Time leashes us to our employers during the day. It kicks anyone with a deadline and occasionally forgets to feed us, closing restaurants and grocery stores before we have a chance to purchase nourishment. And time has no qualms about passing us by, as if unconcerned about our needs and desires. No matter how unfairly time treats us though, we loyally check in on it several times a day. And, come nightfall, sitting at home, scratching the ear of an enduringly faithful dog, we reflect on our lives, thankful for the time that we have.

Like a wicked dog owner, time exploits our unwavering worship, loafing when we request hustle and accelerating when we beg it to slow down. Some people fight back, wielding their day-planners and Palm Pilots, believing they can tame time. But as death descends we are reminded that time perceives all of us as expendable lapdogs.

In mid-morning, when my alarm clock goes off, I often feel like hunting time down, locking it in a pillory and pelting it with rotten fruit. But time has proven impossibly elusive, a truth made all the more frustrating in light of the incredible array of tools we've developed to track it. Hours, minutes, seconds; each helps us to pinpoint time's exact whereabouts, yet we can't seem to find time when we need it. This creates a frustrating paradox: as we continually ponder where time went, the clock on the wall discloses its exact location.

During a recent family gathering, my mom exclaimed, "It's not 8:00 already, is it?" She owns a watch, but like the rest of us she refuses to consult it with such questions; questions watches are specifically designed to answer. This is, admittedly, unfair to the watch, a device that rarely lies, but somehow, with a wave of its wand, time makes us question the truthfulness of even our most reliable timepiece.

A vacation may last two weeks, but when the fun is done and we arrive back home, it feels like only a day or two has passed. Vicki Burns kicked me in the crotch in 8th grade, the result of a disagreement over whether she dreamed of kissing me every night, and the pain seemed to throb for hours. In reality, within five minutes of the assault, my eyes had rolled back into place and my testicles had returned to their respective sacks, dazed but pain-free. A New York minute and a Siberian minute are worlds apart, literally and figuratively. Amazingly, time craftily creates these illusions without the aid of smoke, mirrors, psychedelic mushrooms or powerful lobbyists. It is, without question, an incomparable magician that day in and day out enjoys performing its paramount trick: disrupting our ability to accurately perceive its passage.

*　*　*

I remember the day I was born; least imaginative waterslide ever invented. For nine months I waited, impatiently fidgeting in the womb, excited to glide into life. When the time finally came, my highly anticipated trip from womb to world turned out to be laboriously slow, the track unimaginatively simple. No hairpin turns. No loopty-loops. Just a straight, narrow path without anywhere to stop for refreshments.[1] All in all, a poorly planned throughway. Disneyland should install a similar ride at each of its theme parks to assure that there's always at least one attraction without a long line.

"Hey Dad, we've been waiting to ride Thunder Mountain for two hours. I give up. Let's go over to The Birth. There's never a line over there."

My memory of my birth isn't crystal, but I vividly remember wondering, *What's the holdup?*—a thought made all the more annoying by the complete lack of traffic. Based on the short distance and the simplicity of the route, the voyage should've been a snap. When the slow, incremental progress finally brought me to the end of the channel, I crowned into the world, consumed with anticipation, fully expecting a gregarious greeting. The long gestation had provided my parents ample time to organize an elaborate celebration. Surely the room would be adorned with balloons and streamers. There'd be a clown juggling balls of pink cotton candy. A live band would rock the room into an appropriate frenzy. But when I poked my head out I was greeted instead by crushing disappointment. No decorations. No candy. No clown. No band; not even a simple three piece ensemble. Adding to the insult, my dashing good looks were concealed by a nasty slathering of guck that smelled of vegemite.

"Time of birth, 10:34 a.m.," announced the doctor. The man, dressed all in white, looked far too young and inexperienced to be delivering a child of my importance.

"10:34!" yelped a blonde nurse, one of two female nurses in the room. "I won, I won! I won the pool!" she exclaimed while wildly waving her poorly manicured hands.

The brunette nurse—whose nails were exquisite, done in a splendid soft pink—congratulated the blonde. Then, in unison, the doctor and the two nurses gazed at a bland clock hang-

---

[1] This was before Starbucks, so now...?

ing on the wall.

"You definitely won," the doctor confirmed, "you called the time of birth almost to the minute."

Money exchanged hands, congratulations were offered...to the blonde nurse, not my parents. Worst of all, after scrubbing me clean, the blonde nurse wrapped me in a *pink* blanket.

"All the blue ones are in the wash," she chuckled as she gently rocked me in her arms. She looked at the clock again. "I can't believe I won!"

I struggled to get free. I wanted to rip the clock off the wall and yank off its arms. This was my day and I wasn't going to share the limelight. After destroying the clock, I'd head directly to the laundry room. I'd take hostages and make dire threats until a clean blue blanket was provided. I fought to get loose from my pink straight-jacket, determined to set things right. When my physical prowess proved insufficient to power an escape, I pondered my options, like a superhero with an array of talents to select from. Instead of employing my nostril-burning flatulence or ear-piercing screams, I opted to talk my way to freedom by employing my exceptional oratory skills. I cleared my throat in preparation, ready to announce my general dissatisfaction with the proceedings. A tirade of eloquent condemnation perched on my tongue, ready to scold.

As I prepared to decree that my parents were the luckiest people on the planet—and in the same breath demand a blue blanket—I noticed a strange looking man standing in the corner. His presence gave me pause. The man had a disturbing aura and a pock-marked face. Before I could regain my composure and launch into an impassioned denouncement of my treatment, the mystery man rushed toward me, knife drawn. The blonde nurse, seemingly startled, handed me over without a fight. Barely born and I already had to deal with the humiliation of being forsaken by a woman.

I figured the mystery man was a mugger looking for an easy payday, willing to steal from a baby despite the fact that I had no candy. Because my only material possessions were a tattered pink blanket and to-die-for dimples, I had trouble understanding the man's incentive. I looked to my parents for aide, or at least an explanation, but they seemed disinterested.

"Honey, I am going to check on the other kids," my father said casually as he cowered for the exit.

"Tell them I'm doing fine," Mom replied as Dad slipped out the door.

Who were these people, these parents of mine? First, they failed to provide an elaborate reception to honor my arrival. Next, they refused to lift a finger to protect me from a knife-wielding psycho. As the knife-man set me down on a small table near my mom's hospital bed, I began to question my parents' financial wherewithal. Had I been born into poverty? Had my parents sold me to the mysterious knife-man for a few bucks, a few tabs of acid and a jug of moonshine?

"Nice pink blanket!" the knife-man roared as he pinned me down.

The room erupted into laughter. No one seemed concerned that a man with a knife and a wicked grin was attacking me. Once he removed the blanket, he grappled to get control of my umbilical cord, fumbling to grip the slimy lifeline. I wiggled ferociously, intent on escape. My mom, prone in her hospital bed, diverted her eyes from the chaos—or was she refusing to watch the desecration of the child she'd just sold to make rent?

If I survived, I'd have revenge on my parents. There would be retribution. For years to come I'd wake them in the middle of the night with false cries for help. I'd crap my pants, spit out my food and, later in life, steal their liquor and crash their cars. Their dishonorable actions would come full circle; I'd personally see to it.

But retribution would have to wait. I had more pressing concerns. Knife-man was mumbling deliriously, growing increasingly upset with my fidgety attempts to protect my umbilical cord from the chopping block. Blessed with extraordinary quickness,

I continued to frustrate his efforts. Finally, however, I relented, fearful that the knife-man might give up on the umbilical chord and turn his blade on my penis; not improbable given that it would yield about the same length of flesh.

I went limp, willing to sacrifice my umbilical to save my manhood. The man cackled and swung his knife. The blade struck true, slicing through the cord as the two nurses howled demonic approval. I began to cry. Knife-man quickly disappeared with his fleshy souvenir. The brunette nurse stepped up to the table and wrestled with the umbilical stub, violently seizing it in her hands. With lightening quickness she spun the stub into an overhand knot and pressed the lump of flesh into the small indentation in the center of my tummy.

I was appalled. The overhand knot is boringly simple. A ribbon bow on a begrudging birthday gift rates a more decorative knot. I wailed for a Windsor; would have settled for a half-Windsor. Any bozo can tie a Shelby or Nicky knot. So many elaborate options and the brunette nurse branded me with a simple overhand knot, a permanent reminder of my humble beginnings.

I unleashed a scowl, my first, directing it squarely at the brunette nurse. She hid her dread well, smiling back, and swabbed my stomach with a warm, wet cloth. When she finished cleaning me, she leaned down to rewrap me in the pink blanket. As she came close, I brushed my hand across her left breast and tightly closed my hand on her nipple. I squeezed it for several seconds. Tie a cheap knot, wrap me in a pink blanket, expect me to cop a feel. I felt no shame.

"When can visitors come in?" my mom asked the blonde nurse.

"In about two hours, 1:30 or so," replied the blonde. She walked over to the bed and gently set me in my mother's arms.

"Christopher," my mom whispered, "when the big hand on the clock gets to the six and the little hand gets between the one and the two, you can see your brother Karl and sister Katrina! Aren't you excited?"

In a word, no. I was upset. Bringing my brother and sister into the room meant further parceling of *my* attention. I was also infuriated that Mom was showing such reverence for the clock, just like the doctor and nurses had earlier. Where was my reverence? My juggling clown? In the real world, it seemed, time ruled supreme, governing with an unfeeling iron fist. I preferred the womb, a place where meals marked time; cereal meant morning, fish and salad denoted night. Cigarettes and alcohol meant my mom already had two healthy kids and she was in a gambling mood.

The world was going to hear my discontent. The only thing that would shut my mouth was a silver spoon, and there weren't any lying around. I once again cleared my throat, preparing to lodge a formal complaint, primed to state my case and display my prodigious speaking skills. Before I could launch my oratory assault, the brunette nurse thwarted me.

She grabbed me by the ankles and twirled me upside down, stopping my speech before I could start. I feared that she wanted a souvenir too, a piece of fleshy greatness to remember the momentous moment of my birth. With only one remaining cord dangling from my midsection, adrenaline kicked in. I fought valiantly, swinging and flailing with every fiber of my being. Frustrated by my fierce counterattack, the nurse slapped my ass over and over again until I cried like a baby.[2]

"Isn't that precious?" the blonde nurse cackled.

This had gone too far. I gathered up some phlegm for a retaliatory loogie. Someone was going to pay for these transgressions against my physical privacy. Despite my best effort, the intended retaliation slipped out of my mouth and drooled onto my chin. For nearly a minute the spit sat on my face, unattended, driving me to the breaking point. To punish my parents, and the world, I decided to conceal my miraculous speaking abilities. I would not be Super Baby. I would not parade around the country on

---

[2] At that moment I hated her. I now look back on the episode fondly.

the talk show circuit. I'd selfishly hide my extraordinary gifts. Right then, I took a vow, not of silence, but of babbling loudness, something I swore to maintain for at least a year.[3]

After that first day, I never saw the delivery doctor again. I haven't seen the knife-man or the two nurses either. Other than my family members, the only character from the day of my birth that I have seen is the clock. It plays a commanding role in my life, telling me when to wake, when to work, when to eat. It dictates entrance into R-rated movies and the legal purchase of alcohol. It terminates the acceptability of picking your nose in public and pissing the bed. There are only two times each year that I get to turn the tables, springing time forward the first Sunday in April, forcing it to fall back the last Sunday in October. Other than that I take instructions from time like a blindly loyal dog.

Time wields its power like a perpetual pack rat, extracting my perception, replacing it with confusion. Even while predictably marching along, time can make an hour feel like a month, or a blink. It can make twenty-eight minutes feel like anything. The only thing time can't do is turn back the clock, something that would allow my parents another chance at affording me a proper welcome, juggling clown included.

* * *

On a Saturday afternoon in the fall of '78 my father gave me an official Pittsburgh Steelers watch. It didn't have any "official" markings, but my father told me it was official and that was better than any authenticating stamp or certificate. No particular occasion explained the gift, just a perk for "a well-behaved boy." I never learned the identity of this do-gooder, but I suspected it was Alex, a kid who lived next door, so for a whole week I stopped

---

[3] Family and friends contend that I'm still holding true to this vow.

throwing rocks at him. At the same time that I received my watch, each of my siblings were given a gift of equal value. It was great living in a house where parents doled out goodies like government subsidies, rarely distinguishing between the deserving and the devious. Unlike the government, my parents did this out of benevolence, not incompetence (or corruption).

The Steelers were the best team in the National Football League that year and I loved them for it. I lived in Oregon, a state with no NFL franchise, a situation that easily allowed me to change favorite teams at a moment's notice. Each year I watched the Super Bowl with great intrigue, eager to learn which team I'd be supporting at the start of the next season. I loved my teams, but never blindly; my loyalty always sat in plain view, shining on the scoreboard for all to see.

The moment my dad handed me the Steelers watch I strapped it tightly to my left wrist. When bedtime came, the watch went with me, firmly attached to assure its safety. My old watch, a similar timepiece decorated with a Dallas Cowboys logo, had been collecting dust on my dresser for months. The Cowboys were languishing in second place, an intolerable disappointment that banished the Dallas watch to the sidelines. With a new Steelers watch shining on my arm, the Cowboys timepiece became expendable. I tossed it in the garbage can, right on top of a Jimmy Carter poster I'd discarded a couple days earlier. Carter's chances of reelection were dwindling. Interest rates had climbed another ¾ of a point and I sensed Reagan had a surprise up his sleeve for October. I felt sorry for Jimmy, a sincerely kindhearted man, but compassion aside, I had no qualms burying the living if they were residing anywhere other than the mountain top.

I slipped my left hand under my favorite pillow as I drifted off, sure the football fairy would deliver a Pittsburgh victory in the morning. I awoke at the first hint of sunlight peeking through my window, admired my new watch for a moment, then ran upstairs to secure a bowl of Captain Crunch, necessary energy for a fan who might need to jump ship at any time. Sugar cereal was a rarity in our house and I hoarded as much as my belly could hold. After placing my cereal bowl in the dishwasher, I slid my tongue across the roof of my mouth, examining the damage. The skin was severely tattered, Captain Crunch's calling card. It would pester me for a day or two, but with a Steelers victory planned for later in the afternoon and a stomach bloated with sugary goodness, happiness was all I knew.

* * *

This Time is Too Slow

Growing up Catholic, Sunday morning meant a trip to church. After eating breakfast I'd shower and pull on my church attire. Clean brown cords, a blue short-sleeved collared shirt and penny loafers, each shoe decorated with a single shiny penny. Attendance was mandatory in our family; an excusatory note from Jesus himself wouldn't have mattered.

Dear Mr. and Mrs. Kemper: Howdy! Just wanted to shoot you a note and let you know that Chris has my permission to skip church today. He is such a good boy and he has an important football game to watch on television. Please let him stay home so he can watch the game, and in return I'll overlook that jug of strawberry wine you heisted from the neighbors during your first year of marriage. Love, Jesus.

I'd hand the authentic note to my parents, hopeful.

"Let's go to church and have a little talk with the Son of God," my mom would respond. We'd pile in the car and head to mass, Mom fully prepared to debate Jesus on the propriety of missing church service to watch a sporting event.

A typical Sunday mass lasts an hour by the clock, an eternity by perception, especially for a kid. With my cool Steelers watch attached to my wrist, I held out hope that things would be different. The watch was new *and* official, a combination that might give it the power to run through mass the way Pittsburgh ran over opponents. My previous watches had all succumbed to the bore of church, each contracting an aggressive form of leprosy as soon as I entered the cathedral; an affliction that wretchedly crippled their arms and seemed to thwart time's progress.

Despite initial optimism, my Steelers watch got off to a shaky start and never recovered. The choir opened the service with a long, somber hymn, lulling the watch into a slumber. From that point on, the watch performed like a frightened rookie, hesitant in its movements, unsure of its role. If its lackluster performance was any indication of how the Steelers would perform later in the day, there was a distinct possibility I'd have a new favorite team by nightfall.

In the following weeks the Steelers continued their dominance on the gridiron, but the watch performed miserably in church. Still, when my mom suggested that I leave the watch at home one Sunday to assure that God received at least a little of my attention, I declined. The Steelers were in first place and the playoffs were about to start, so I needed to wear the watch everywhere so people would associate me with a winner. And I couldn't bear the thought of attending church without a timepiece wrapped around my wrist. While others tested their faith, I sat in the church pew testing my willpower, battling the constant urge to look at the time. I once refrained from looking at my watch for a whole seven minutes during a church service, my record to this day.

Every time I consulted my Steelers watch during mass I ended up disappointed. Feverishly optimistic, I constantly overestimated how much time had passed since my last peek. To protest time's lollygagging, after checking my watch, I'd let out a loud sigh or gasp. Hoping for a miracle, I'd then contort my neck to check my father's watch, seeking a second opinion, a weakness reserved for people who are unhappy with the first. My dad's watch never offered relief and a second wave of disappointment would hit. I'd sigh again, loudly.

Many of the older parishioners in the surrounding pews interpreted my frequent moans as a sign of piety.

"Listen to that boy," I heard them whisper. "He is so emotional about the power of the Holy Trinity that he can barely contain himself. He's going to be a priest, bet you dollars to doughnuts."

They would smile, looking at me with a distinct sparkle. I represented all that was good in my generation, or so they thought. My mom knew differently. After each of my outbursts, she'd flash me an un-Christian look. My father knew differently, too; he checked his watch almost as much as I did.

When I wasn't checking my watch or misleading older parishioners about my piety, I'd bow my head and pray. *Dear God, organized religion is doing you a horrible disservice,* I'd start. *They claim they're committed to doing your work—and they do accomplish many good things—but in the process they have somehow managed to make you excruciatingly boring. You are the Supreme Being, creator of everything, seer of all and the origin of all the energy in the universe. That's some pretty good material to work with, yet religion makes you seem downright pedestrian. For the love of you, do something! Send me a sign, change the rules... speed up my watch!*

At the end of my prayer, I'd check my watch. Frustrated, I'd sigh and gasp. The elderly parishioners nearby would beam, delighted. Mom would reach over and yank some of the short hairs on the back of my neck.

"She must want him to go into business instead of the priesthood," I'd hear an aged parishioner in the row behind us whisper. "I think she ought to be more supportive of her son's divine path."

Amen! I'd think. Then I'd look at my watch and moan, and the cycle would start over.

During the NFL season, Sunday mass lasted just under fifty minutes, the small time reduction a direct result of Father Murphy's love of football. Instructed by the Church to keep his hands off of women, Father Murphy, our longtime parish priest, channeled his earthly desires toward the football field. Without the support of Papal edict, each fall he would shorten our Sunday commitment in order to maximize his television time. After the church service he'd rush home and kneel in front of the tube to watch NFL games, praying that his teams would find salvation and cover the spread. To shorten mass, Father Murphy would fast-forward through the rituals and shortchange the sermon, sending everyone home early as if Jesus had commanded him not to miss kickoff. I appreciated his effort, but mass still seemed to take forever.

Starting in the fall of 1978, Father Murphy began furtively including NFL point spreads in the weekly church bulletin. He didn't insert the entire range of scheduled games, limiting the list, I suspect, to the games that he had bet on. Father disguised the information as suggested Bible readings.

Dear Congregants. Please read the following Bible passages this week:

LUKE: plus 13.5
John: plus 9
PSALMS: over 54.5
CORINTHIANS: plus 12.5
Genesis: Pick 'em

I easily deciphered the code. Luke denoted the Lions, John meant the Jets, Psalms the Patriots, Corinthians the Cowboys and Genesis the Giants. All caps denoted the team was playing at home. I'm sure that several of the older folks in our small congregation lost sleep searching the Bible for *Luke plus 12.5 parlayed with Corinthians over 44.5,* fearing these bogus readings held the secret to salvation.

Father Murphy probably placed the betting information in the bulletin in an attempt to infiltrate God's subconscious. The subliminal messages just might lead God to cause a missed field goal here, a fluke touchdown there, all in order to assure that Father's bets paid off. Throughout the fall that I received my Steelers watch, Father found new ways to carve additional minutes off the church service. And with the Steelers slashing through opponents with ease, my devotion to the franchise spiked.

On the final weekend of the NFL regular season that fall Father Murphy failed to show up for work. Because our starting priest was faking an injury so he could sit on his couch and cheer on modern gladiators, the local diocese sent in a substitute. All the second-string priests who had previously filled in at our parish had struggled, stuttering and stammering, fumbling the chalice and performing the service out of order. Granted they had good attitudes and tried hard, but they were all backups for a reason. But on this magical Sunday, things were different. I am not claiming Jesus appeared at our small rural church and presided over mass, but the substitute sent by the diocese was nothing short of a living saint.

The man was cadaverous; an ancient relic who probably could've offered an eyewitness account of the Crusades. Despite his wrinkles he possessed a youthful briskness. At the beginning of mass he moved up the center aisle with a sense of urgency. The lightning entrance set the tone for the delight to come. This renegade priest meant business, a bibleslinger with an attitude. When he reached the altar, he spun around and commenced firing the word of God with immaculate efficiency. What followed is something members of our congregation still recount while sipping lemonade on their covered porches as the Oregon rain falls harmlessly around them. When the substitute entered the church to start the service, I checked my Steelers watch. It was 10:01 a.m.

Father Unintelligible spoke rapidly. His words were difficult to understand; sometimes impossible. For the first time in years I listened intently, intrigued by a robed man doing a brilliant impression of the Tower of Babel. He mumbled, yelped, possibly even yodeled for a brief moment, but he never spoke clearly. His feverish pace turned mass into a full-body aerobics class. Heart rates accelerated to dangerous levels as congregants hurriedly stood, sat, kneeled and prayed, frantically trying to keep up. I checked my watch frequently, clocking the unfolding miracle.

"Good God in heaven," I thought, *"fourteen minutes into mass and he's already starting the sermon."*

More commotion than communal, the proceedings confused rather than enlightened, completely confounding several crotchety farmers in attendance. Their quizzical looks revealed their disorientation. They glanced around the church at one another, uncertain whether they'd arrived safely at mass or had mistakenly stumbled into a cattle auction. Many of them raised their hands every time the priest paused to catch his breath, placing bids on burly cows the pastor seemed to be auctioning. Old rivalries surfaced. The crusty farmers glared at each other in very un-churchlike ways, attempting to intimidate their rivals, part of a strategy to stem the bidding on nonexistent livestock.

When communion started, I checked my watch again. Barring all hell breaking loose, a record was certain. Father Unintelligible kept up the blazing pace, tossing out communal hosts like Frisbees. After communion, he immediately began babbling again, cutting the choir off before they could complete the first verse of *Amazing Grace*. Members of the choir quickly conceded defeat and fell silent. An elderly member of the congregation named Jack, known for his loud, off-key singing, was the only person who continued. He wasn't going to let some substitute priest stop him from hazing *Grace*. Jack belched forth his fury but Father Unintelligible didn't even pause, racing to the finish over Jack's penetrating screech.

As Jack plowed into the third verse of *Amazing Grace*, the substitute cued the choir to begin their closing hymn, *Joy to the World*. The competing songs rattled the old church and the priest sprang from behind the altar like a gazelle worried about the roof collapsing. The exit processional took the form of a foot race between Father Unintelligible and the two winded alter boys. Caught up in the emotion, I stood and applauded, certain I'd never again see such a divine feat during my earthly stay. At the point of tears, I watched my new hero race out of sight. My Steelers watch read 10:29. Twenty-eight minutes to complete an entire mass. I'd witnessed a miracle.

Father Unintelligible's performance marked the first and only time that any watch I owned showed signs of life inside a chapel. Still, not even a miracle can overcome the time vortex that haunts Catholic mass. The twenty-eight minutes seemed to take about forty-five. Time just passes slower in some environments, and faster in others, an anomaly in time's regularity that I've come to accept.

* * *

This Time is Too Fast

There was a troubling message on the chalkboard.
Pop algebra exam today. Sit down and put your books and notes away.
"This isn't going to be a major part of your grade," Mr. Schoboethe promised as we took our seats. "The test is primarily for *me* to evaluate *my* teaching, what I'm conveying clearly, and what I'm not. The results of this exam will only impact your grade for the semester if your final letter grade is on the borderline between two possible results. In those cases, I'll use this test to break the tie."

It was fall semester of my sophomore year. I'd taken a math class from Mr. Schoboethe as a freshman. He was an outstanding teacher, a favorite of mine. It bothered me that when he graded my exam he'd have no other option but to evaluate himself a failure. I'm an excellent test-taker for scheduled exams, the pressure of an imminent deadline stimulating me into action, but short of this, my mind lies dormant, resting up for the next time it's called upon to meet expectations. Since it's impossible to cram for a surprise test, such ambushes tend to expose my procrastinating nature.[4]

I looked at my Steelers watch, its face battered from years of use. The year my father gave me the watch the Steelers had won the Super Bowl. The following year they'd repeated as champions. The back-to-back Super Bowl wins culminated a run of four championships in a six year span, an accomplishment that convinced me to pledge allegiance to the franchise. When my father died during the summer before my freshman year, the watch was upgraded from a fond possession to cherished memory. I vowed never to discard it, no matter how poorly the Steelers played.

The face of the watch was worn and faded but it still kept good time. When Mr. Schoboethe dropped the pop quiz on my desk, it was five seconds shy of 10:15 a.m.

"There is only one question," Mr. Schoboethe told the class. "You have 30 minutes to complete the exam. Good luck."

With that, my Steelers watch took off, its hands displaying the championship-caliber determination long absent in Pittsburgh.[5] It was as if a pack of rabid dingoes were chasing the watch hands, their pursuit gallantly led by the headless horseman, a villain with surprisingly keen predatory skills despite missing four vital senses. I asked the watch hands—old friends by now—to slow the pace, but they continued to gallop. I dove into the question, sorting through the information as fast as I could, intent on keeping up. But by the time I finished *reading* the question my Steelers watch had raced ahead six minutes. It was 10:21.

The six minutes I spent reading the question hadn't paid dividends. I understood the concept of the problem but had no idea how to go about answering it. The situation was dire.

---

[4] I even cram for dental exams, staying up late the night before an appointment, dusting off my toothbrush, scrubbing and flossing until my gums bleed.

[5] That is until Super Bowl XL. Pittsburgh 21, Seattle 10. About time!

Perspiration launched an attack on my light blue t-shirt. The material lapped up the onslaught of sweat. Navy-blue blotches sprouted where the sweat soaked in, trumpeting my anguish. I scanned the problem a second time, hoping another look might magically ignite mathematical literacy. Nothing came to me. Absolutely nothing.

My perspiration factory fired up the boilers, upping output. Rumors swirled that my internal sweat factory was utilizing child labor, adding guilt to my panic. The sweat poured from my glands and my shirt readily absorbed the moisture. Several dark-blue blotches on my shirt expanded and began to resemble the five oceans of the world in relative size, shape and global positioning. If I was in Mr. Klein's world geography class, I'd have been elated, the proud pioneer of an ingenious cheat sheet. But the humiliating splotches of sweat offered no such salvation in this setting. With life's skewed sense of humor, I had little doubt that during my next geography pop quiz my perspiration would decorate my shirt with the algebra equations I needed now.

The test question involved two trains heading towards each other on the same railroad track. The facts specified the number of miles separating the two trains and explained that each train was moving at a constant rate of speed. Train #1 was scheduled to make three separate stops, each lasting four minutes, and after each stop, it would shift to a slower, but still constant rate of speed. The new rate of speed would be 20% slower than the rate of speed prior to the stop. The question contained a bunch of other information, some relevant, some not. My job was to sort through the data, create the proper algebraic equations and determine when the horrific wreck would occur. "Show all work!" the question demanded.

After going through the question a second time, I again looked at my watch. 10:26. Eleven minutes gone, or was it thirteen? I was so frazzled, my ability to add and subtract was failing, a mental breakdown that didn't bode well for salvaging partial credit. Seconds were evaporating, minutes disappearing. The oceans on my shirt expanded, as if global warming had stepped on the accelerator. The next few minutes blurred by. My panic-stricken pencil alternated between displaying its incompetence and erasing the evidence. Fifteen minutes into the exam, I'd made no progress and my perspiration had submerged the entire world.

I drifted into submission, yielding to a superior adversary. As my mind lost consciousness, my life didn't flash before my eyes, a slew of excuses did: *The test was biased against white, country kids. Algebra had no real world application and my mind rightfully refused to use up valuable storage space for such nonsense. It is so unfair for Lisa to wear such a revealing shirt during a test.* I also thought of my mom, the years she spent prepping me to attend a private Catholic high school. For a brief moment, I wished I would have followed her advice. A Catholic school might, just might, administer algebra pop quizzes in the on-campus cathedral, a situation that could possibly allow a church's stagnating time vortex to work to my advantage, buying time to concoct an intellectual cover up.

As the excuses and dreams waned, an odd numbness started to invade my body. A sense of calm followed; acceptance is a wonderful, healing tonic. Once I abandoned hope, failing the exam didn't bother me at all. It's the act of concession that taxes and punishes. The math portion of my brain soon took its last gasp and, reflexively, my salivating imagination stepped in to take up the battle. Instead of trying to solve the problem, it tried to derail it. When faced with the question, *"When do the trains collide?"* my imagination didn't hesitate. *"That's easy. Never!"*

One of the trains suddenly ran out of steam and rolled to a stop. A problem with the tracks stalled the progress of the other locomotive. Mechanical failure. A fair maiden tied to the tracks. Snow drifts. A union strike. Hookers.[6] Staring at my blank exam paper, absent applicable knowledge, I decided to answer with a diatribe.

---

[6] When my imagination takes over, for some reason hookers always become part of the delusional shrapnel.

You sick, despicable man, Mr. Schoebothe! Two trains colliding? You're willing to risk untold number of imaginary lives to make a mathematical point? Well I refuse to join in on your soulless game. I happen to be a person who places unlimited value on a human life. Yes, that's right, you can value something without assigning it a specific number. You should try it! The important things in life are priceless and invaluable. Friendship, health, the love of a woman; things you probably know nothing about because you are too consumed with dreaming up innocent folks to kill in horrific, hypothetical accidents. What if I had a cousin on one of the trains? Or a friend? Or my mom? What then? You want to know when these trains collide? Too soon for my liking, that's when!

Building on momentum, I scribbled ever faster.

Further, the golden spike was hammered home in Utah in 1869, thus completing the transcontinental railroad, and ever since then railroad companies have been sued by drooling trial lawyers. As a result of costly lawsuits, railroad executives decided to invest in equipment to improve railroad safety. Additionally, federal regulations have been passed that require frequent track inspections. And still today, lawyers sit perched like...like that big scavenger bird that feeds on carcasses. What is the name of that thing? Circling around and around, waiting to pick clean a dead animal. What is the name of that damn bird?! Anyway, the lawyers are just waiting to sue, so the railroad folks aren't able to let their guard down on any of that safety stuff.

Damn! Why can't I think of the name of that stupid bird? It's jammed in my gray matter right next to all the algebra knowledge I worked so hard to learn over the last three weeks. My brain is full of bottlenecks!

Anyway, aside from the safety improvements that serve to prevent such an accident, you want me to assume that both these trains are on schedule, that neither has been delayed? Do you know how absurd that is? We don't live in Japan. Have you ever known a train to be on time? Come on! Amtrak is subsidized by the government precisely because it is a rusting relic incapable of meeting schedules or budgets. And trains are operated by unionized labor and you can't fire those guys for anything short of a shooting spree. You know what happens when you can't lose your job? You don't give a crap about schedules, that's what! There's an outside chance that one train could buck the odds and be on time, but both? Please! And, on top of all this, both trains are traveling at a constant rate of speed? Give me a break!

Here's a questions for you: Imagine two students are walking to the principal's office, both anxious to report on the behavior of a particular algebra teacher. One student received a "B" on this pop quiz and is smiling and happy, ready to hail the instructor as a great educator. The other student failed this exam. Which of the two students gets to the principal's office first? For extra credit, which of these students will convincingly make false accusations that a certain algebra teacher is trading grades for drugs? And for bonus points, after the accusations are made, how long until the teacher collides with unemployment (or do you want to bank on your union to protect your job)? Answer that, smart guy.

To sum up without doing any addition (or algebra), with all the death and destruction in the world, you shouldn't be adding more. Next time you give an exam, I suggest you make the collision between two people running toward each other with the intent of embracing in a loving hug.

Can I get a hall pass so I can go talk to the principal?
VULTURE!!! They're called vultures!

As I finished scrawling my answer, I consulted my Steelers watch. 10:43. Twenty-eight minutes had passed since the start of the exam. I used my two minutes of free time to bask in the glow of ineptitude. These two minutes seemed to last longer than the preceding twenty-eight. As the oceans on my shirt began to recede, I looked again at my trusty watch, its arms seemingly tired from the exertion. It had run its heart out for 28 minutes and now seemed to be bent over, hands on its knees, trying to catch its breath. Even if my watch had been using a supercharged battery or illicit steroids, I still couldn't comprehend how it was able to cram twenty-eight minutes into such a short span of time. That's a question no algebraic equation will ever be able to answer.

* * *

This Time is Just Right

I can count the number of random trysts I've had on one hand. If I had the misfortune of losing nine fingers in a wacky turkey-carving accident, my remaining digit would still suffice to tabulate my one-night stands. What a night it was.

For a single evening, life worked the way I'd dreamed. Go to a bar. Meet an attractive girl. Dance with her. After dancing for a while, grab her hand and lead her to the parking lot to kiss for half an hour. The girl then asks if I want to go back to her place, and I accept. We sit on her couch for a long time, talking freely, sharing our minds before moving on to carnal pleasures. Simple. Elegant. Perfect.

Nothing seemed out of the ordinary when I left home on the evening of July 23, 1993. I wore unfashionable clothes and applied the same deodorant I always used. Before leaving I strapped on my trusty Steelers watch. The watch face was marked with fifteen years of adventure and abuse, a ticking reminder of a once great Super Bowl franchise and a treasured memory of the man I try to model.

I'd worked late that day at my temporary farm job, so when I arrived at my favorite watering hole, Wanker's Corner, several of my friends were already there. They were all seated at a picnic table on the back patio, engaged in excited conversation. Several full pitchers of beer, and a few empty ones, decorated the table. I quickly filled an empty pint glass and joined in. For the next hour I drank beer. After that I started to abuse it.

A little past 10:30, with a healthy dose of confidence warming my stomach, I decided to seek out female companionship.

"I'm going to walk around and meet some girls," I announced to my friends. "I'm feeling pretty generous tonight, so maybe I'll bring a couple back to the table for you clowns." I left the table under a hail of taunts and catcalls.

For several minutes I circled the bar like a shark—to the extent sharks circle with their eyes glued to the floor. My attempts to attract the attention of females were as conspicuous as a Budweiser bottle cap discarded on the bar floor and covered up by peanut shells. I soon shuffled back to the table, dejected and alone. As I sat, Karl and my friend, John, howled their delight.

"Very impressive!" Karl mocked.

"You are the master!" John snickered. "You should probably let us show you how it's done."

Both Karl and John are highly-skilled social icebreakers, each armed with the inability to feel embarrassment, as if the area of their brains that detects inappropriate behavior blew a fuse after years of excessive use. The two of them stood in unison and set out to strike up a conversation with any girl too slow to get out of their way. Like me, their approach rarely worked, but I envied them for always leaving their mark—better to fail and be heard than to slink away quietly. As the two scurried into the crowd, hurrying off to crash into rejection, I took a long swig of beer, refueling for another foray into the rugged terrain of single-hood.

I took the precaution of detecting the exit signs; social lifeboats that my friends often forced me to utilize on a moment's notice. If Karl and John returned to the table followed by a large, riled-up stranger ready to defend his girlfriend's honor, I had no intention of going down with the ship.

A few minutes after departing, the two returned with four girls in tow, highly suggestive that they'd signed some kind of long-term pact with the Devil. Karl grabbed an unoccupied picnic table and pulled it flush with ours. Everyone at the table spread out and the girls sat down in the open spots.

The girl next to me joined the ongoing conversation with appealing confidence. She wore khaki shorts, a casual blue blouse and white canvas shoes. Her dark brown skin advertised the terrific summer weather. Blonde hair. Tall, around 5'7". While waiting for the perfect opportunity to dazzle her with an outlandishly funny comment, I tried to make eye contact by staring at her feet.

"You like my shoes?" she asked during a lull in the conversation.

"What?" I replied.

"You're staring at my shoes, so I was wondering if you like 'em." She was feisty.

"Well, if I were barefoot and lived in a world filled with shards of glass, yeah, I'd like them."

She looked down at my shoes. "Well I wouldn't wear yours even if I lived in a world covered in tacks and nails."

"You want to dance?" I asked.

"Sure!" she replied without hesitation.

I was suspicious. She seemed too eager, too willing, like an alien intruder looking for a host body to maintain its evil offspring until the day designated for attack. She grabbed my arm and dragged me toward the dance floor. As we neared the dance area, a zone where conversation succumbs to the drum of music, she screamed, "My name is Caroline." She spun in a circle and started to dance. I looked at my watch. It was 11:22 p.m.

We danced for nearly an hour. After fifty-seven minutes of semi-coordinated gyration, I began sobering up and slowing down. Growing sobriety caused me to question my unique dancing style. I started thinking instead of flowing, a death knell for any dancer. As self-consciousness proliferated, I looked down at my watch and then peeked over at Caroline. She'd caught me checking the time and stopped dancing. Her hands were on her hips, a pout on her face.

"Am I boring you?" she mouthed.

"No!" I screamed back. I wanted to say more, make an attempt to remedy the perceived slight, but the blasting music made a detailed explanation impossible.

She started to dance again, quickly returning to her smooth, unencumbered style. I tried to restart my groove but sobriety had repossessed the silky-suave moves that alcohol had afforded. Steadily I regressed, becoming increasingly stiff, until I resembled Cinderella hobbling around on one glass slipper. The fairy tale was ending. With no other option, I called on my go-to move, the club and drag.™

Tangent:

The club and drag (C&D™) is my gateway to a first kiss. Despite its barbaric title, the technique is harmless, implemented with great care and consideration whenever I need to bridge the kiss chasm; that daunting gulf between the desire to kiss a girl and actually locking lips. The C&D™ effectively bridges the kiss chasm, allowing me to bypass all the nasty stuff lurking in the chasm's ravine; awkward silences, sweaty brow, dry mouth, gummy palms, stuttering speech.

There are alternative methods to overcome the kiss chasm. For example, a lot of men are confident enough to ask a girl to go on a walk, or they employ a quick quip to break the ice. Other men might motion suggestively with their eyes. These approaches casually communicate a desire to kiss. Every time I had tried one of these modern techniques I ended up freefalling into the kiss chasm, visions of a girl running for the door flashing through my head. After several years of slamming into the kiss chasm's humbling floor, I realized I needed a new angle, something that could overcome the shell of shyness that enveloped me every time I met a girl I liked.

Technically I didn't discover the C&D™, I rediscovered it, something I'm obliged to point out in deference to the pioneering baboons that formulated the basic method. I came across it one night at a party, the result of instinctual panic instead of cunning calculation. I have, however, tinkered with the original recipe, fine-tuning the approach so as not to run afoul of base social etiquette—or the law.

I was hanging out at a party during my sophomore year in college when I happened upon the C&D™. I was trying my best to impress a girl named Nicole, a girl I'd met my freshman year. From the day we met I had desperately wanted to kiss her, and I sensed a mutual attraction. But I could never find a subtle way to get her alone to share me feelings—and, hopefully, a smooch. Several of my friends made traversing the kiss chasm look so effortless; their molehill was my Everest, and the challenge always caused my confidence to retract like a frightened potato bug. The oddity is that I can talk until the cows come home—the one thing I refuse to bring to a party is silence—but place me in front of a girl who I want to kiss and I struggle to spit out an intelligible word.

That night, standing in a small circle of people across from Nicole, I quietly took in her words and gazed longingly at her lips. Several times she made suggestive eye contact with me, and my yearning flared to a fever pitch. Paralyzed by desire, I failed to act for reasons Freud couldn't explain. While I searched for the confidence to ask her out, a group of friends approached and asked if anyone would like to go with them to a local bar. I knew one of the guys in the group was interested in Nicole and, suddenly, something inside me broke free. Without approval from my brain, my right arm reached out and gently grasped Nicole's left hand. I pedaled the two of us toward the backyard deck without saying a word. When we got outside, I pulled her close and kissed her. She kissed back. That is the essence of the C&D™. No cheesy lines. No need to have a fish tank or a cool poster in your bedroom. No name dropping or stalking. Just pure, unfettered passion, like baboons, but less baboonish. Since that evening, every first kiss I've had has been a product of the C&D™. **End Tangent**

After the next song ended, Caroline gave me a sultry look, the kind that implicitly authorizes the *C&D*™. My right hand latched onto her left wrist and I whisked her out the door and into the parking lot. After briefly locking eyes, we kissed. She was an amazing kisser, each peck a mini-massage.

After kissing for a few minutes, leaning against the hood of my car, she eased away and sized me up.

"You want to go back to my place?" she asked.

I pretended to consider the offer, looking back at the bar, then at my Steelers watch.

"I suppose," I replied. Caroline smiled broadly and then turned and walked off. I fell in step, close behind.

"My name is Chris, by the way."

"I know," she said. "One of your friends told me before we started dancing."

After stopping to get some ice cream at a 24-hour café we drove to her apartment. The main room was filled with boxes. Caroline explained that she was moving to Chicago in a few days to start a new job, a fact that might have scared away lesser men, the kind afraid of being exploited by the opposite sex. She moved some things off the couch to give us a place to sit down. We kissed and talked for nearly two hours—a first kiss entirely cures my conversational malady.

Caroline was smart and sincere. As we talked I became increasingly disappointed that she was moving away. At 3:34 she grabbed my arm and led me to her bedroom.

When we entered the bedroom Caroline turned off the main light. A lamp on her nightstand with a dark purple shade dispensed a meek glow. I filled with nervous excitement. We slowly disrobed. There was just enough light to appreciate Caroline's form. She was terrifically beautiful. Thank God for functioning pupils.

The last thing I took off was my Steelers watch. I set it on the nightstand, right under the lamp. While setting it down, I took a moment to check the time. 3:43.

"Am I boring you again?" Caroline asked.

"Definitely not!" I answered anxiously. "I was just wondering why it took life so long to introduce me to someone so incredible."

She raised her eyebrows, disbelievingly.

"It has a lot of sentimental value?" I offered.

"That's better." Her eyebrows relaxed.

She turned off the lamp, wrapping the room in darkness. We

rolled around as if we had known each other for years. After several minutes of exploration, I pulled myself up on my knees, hopefully placing my hands on Caroline's underwear. She lifted her hips in consent. A more exhilarating feeling does not exist.

As a fluke happenchance, I had a condom. A realist, I rarely carried one. To me, carrying a condom seemed as rational as walking around with a garage door opener in my pocket hoping to meet someone willing to give me their house. For the first time in my life, I had adult sex. Different positions. Slow. Fast. She climaxed. When I finished, I collapsed on the bed, beyond satisfied, surprised by my own performance.

Caroline turned on the lamp and began to walk out of the room.

"Is that what no-strings attached sex is like?" I joked, half-hoping there were a few strings.[7]

She stopped at the door and turned back. "What's your name again?"

"Jorge?" I responded.

She laughed. "That's what I thought."

Caroline continued out of the room. I got up and removed the condom. With no better place to put it, I shoved it into one of my shoes. Then, curious as to how the clock measured my performance, I grabbed my Steelers watch off the nightstand. 4:01 a.m. Exactly twenty-eight minutes from the moment we had lain down. That's about what I had figured. I set the watch back down before Caroline returned. We slept late.

The morning greeted me with a completely new social chasm to tackle, one I'd heard of but never thought I'd actually encounter. Yet here I was, facing the morning-after chasm; the ancient gulf that separates a person who awakes in a strange bed from a graceful exit. I wasn't in a hurry to leave, but I felt uncomfortable lying awake while Caroline continued to slumber. I

---

[7] Truth be told—sex itself is a string, if not a rope, that can easily get tangled into a knotty mess.

never have developed a technique to conquer the morning-after chasm; necessity truly is the mother of invention.

When Caroline finally woke she drove me back to Wanker's Corner. My car was the only one in the parking lot. I asked her for her phone number and she reeled it off, adding the caveat that she was leaving in a few days. Before I got out of her car she leaned over and gave me a quick kiss that felt like our last. Not wanting to tarnish the memory, I never did call her. I still remember the last four digits of her number: 2518.

As I sat in my car, it dawned on me that my wrist was naked. I'd left my Steelers watch sitting on Caroline's nightstand. I looked over to catch sight of her white four-door pulling away. She glanced over and waved enthusiastically. I thought about stopping her, but it seemed best to let her go. A sense of acceptance swept over me. I knew I'd never see her or my watch again.

Driving home I determined that the loss of the Steelers watch was a sign sent by my father. The whole evening had been a gift from him to me, to tell me he was watching over me and that he thought it was time for me to move on to another stage in life. After nearly fifteen years of service, it was time to retire my Steelers timepiece, the one that had told me when to come and go during my entire adolescence. I was thankful that its final resting place wasn't a church or a classroom, places where watches are forced to limp and sprint respectively. Instead, my Steelers watch now could rest in peace, lounging in watch nirvana; that rare, miraculous place where time and perception march in cadence, hand in hand.

clinging to anonymity

C Eye A

During the summer months Oregon baseball fans head to PGE Park to watch the Portland Beavers, a triple-A team affiliated with the San Diego Padres. The Beavers generally attract a few thousand fans, but on Thursday nights the attendance swells. It's not that the Beavers play better on Thursdays, or that the club gives away bobble-head dolls at the gate. The increase is attributable to Thirsty Thursday, a promotion in which 16 oz. cups of domestic beer are sold in sexy, see through plastic cups for only two bucks. Fans and non-fans alike show up in large numbers to enjoy the cheap beer, temporarily transforming the stadium into the largest watering hole in town. While the ballplayers strive to get the attention of big league management, thousands of fans just strive to get noticed. The guys look like they've spent an hour in front of a mirror trying to appear as if they just rolled off the couch, and the girls wear clothes that show off their dedication to the gym, or to pizza. As much as I enjoy cold beer and baseball, I derive just as much pleasure from the people-watching.

A couple years ago I began dating Jill, a girl who enjoys going to the ballpark, particularly when it's sunny. Soon after we began dating she started joining me and my group of friends for Thirsty Thursday outings. Her attendance didn't influence the amount of beer I drank or my enjoyment of the quality baseball, but it did impact my uninhibited gawking. Even the most relaxed and open-minded couples have to moderate their people-watching tactics out of respect for their mate. The female shouldn't let eyes linger too long on a tanned, muscular guy, and the male has to avoid looking at a voluptuous girl with an expression that says, "Good Lord, those can't be real."

During one of the first Thirsty Thursdays that Jill attended she ran up to the concourse to buy a few beers just after the third inning ended. I gave her twenty bucks—it was my turn to buy—and she fought her way up the busy aisle toward the concession stand. While she was gone my friend Mike and I struck up a conversation about the various ploys that guys use to gaze at another girl without drawing the ire of their significant other. Mike had recently gotten married, an event that formalizes the need for discretion when eyeballing females, so he was eager to discuss the subject.

Jill was gone for about fifteen minutes—the concession stand lines on Thirsty Thursday make the game of baseball seem fast-paced by comparison—so Mike and I had a chance to really examine the issue. We both acknowledged that, with our twenties behind us, the catalyst for looking at girls had changed from lust to appreciation. There's no better artist than nature. We also figured that once our youth gave way to our sixties that lust would probably reenter the equation. Because great art deserves close examination, Mike and I determined that a stealthy glance at a girl was counterproductive—you never really get a good look, and if you get caught the calculated attempt to conceal amplifies the guilt. Instead, we decided that the best course of action was to openly stare at the person of interest, and to use a cover statement to explain your actions.

Cover statements like, "I think I went to school with that

girl," and, "She goes to my gym," allow you to look at another girl in the presence of a girlfriend or wife without ruffling feathers. Mike's favorite was, "I think that girl works at the Starbucks by my office." I settled on, "That girl looks just like my cousin." I like the excuse because the taboo of incest provides some extra cover. If she looks like my cousin, the natural assumption is that I can't be attracted to her. Mike and I came up with several other cover statements, some ridiculous, others intricate. We felt like pioneers in a movement that would let guys gawk while keeping our naïve female counterparts in the dark.

When Jill returned, she tiptoed her way down the aisle past other fans, doing her best to balance a cardboard tray holding three full beers. I ogled her every step of the way, no cover statement necessary.

Mike nudged me. "Jill reminds me of this anchorwoman who used to work on Channel 4 in L.A."

"That's great," I said. "Can I use that sometime?"

"Sure."

Jill sat down in the empty seat between us and gave us each a beer. We all sipped our drinks and chatted as the Thirsty Thursday fans partied around us, eclipsing any view of the game.

I was in the middle of a story when Jill interrupted.

"I think that guy over there went to Oregon State." She motioned toward a tanned, fit guy wearing shorts and a tight t-shirt.

Mike started laughing so hard beer came out his nose.

"What's so funny?" she asked.

"You're telling me that guy went to Oregon State?" I chuckled.

"Yeah, I think so," Jill said earnestly.

For the next inning or so the three of us chatted about how shelled peanuts perfectly compliment beer, discussed the percentage of people at the game who knew the score (16%, we determined), and debated which drug we would legalize if we were starting a society, alcohol or weed (weed, hands down). Then Jill struck again.

"See that guy over there?" she said. "I think he used to work at the coffee shop over on 23rd."

Mike burst into laugher, then added, "And I think that girl over there used to work at a Starbucks by my office." He motioned to a beautiful girl a few rows below us.

I joined in. "And the girl sitting next to her kinda looks like my cousin." I leaned over and kissed Jill on the cheek, proud of her in some odd way. She looked at me, a bit perplexed.

"What?" she asked.

"Nothing," I said.

I finished my beer and I set the empty cup under my seat. "I'm going to head up and get another round."

"My turn to pay," Mike offered. He handed me a ten dollar bill.

Before I could stand to leave, Jill grabbed the sleeve of my shirt. "See that guy down there in the green? We know him from somewhere, don't we?"

Mike again exploded with laughter. I erupted with pride. Her comment was a terrific cover statement, incorporating the disarming suggestion that we both knew the guy.

"What is so funny," Jill demanded.

"I don't know him," I said. "But see that girl next to him in the tank top?"

"Yeah."

"Now those *can't* be real." I kissed Jill's cheek again and stood to leave.

Challenge Quest

"No one can pee on that electric fence and live." My cousin Tom crossed his arms and swung his head toward the fence that corralled his family's small herd of cattle.

"Johnny Bench probably could," my brother Karl argued, referring to the gifted Cincinnati Reds catcher.

"Nope, not even Johnny Bench," Tom said.

"Are you kidding?" I bragged. I tugged open my zipper. "Watch this!" I walked over to the fence and released a stream onto the middle wire. The barbed metal snapped and hissed. Electrons, eager to explore a new path, charged up the stream and slammed into my groin. I fell to the ground and twisted in the dirt. For several seconds I remained prone, motionless, frozen in a fetal position, my blue jeans cuffing my ankles. Karl and Tom were hushed, silenced by fear, aware that their weekly allowances would die with me.

The punch of electricity was fierce and immediate, arriving in one brisk, powerful jolt. But the pain dissipated almost immediately, fleeing the scene as if it had pressing work to do in some Third World country. I soon regained sensation in my extremities, followed shortly by a return of my motor skills.

To allow drama to build I stayed down longer than necessary, my face pressed into the dirt, clumps of grass pricking my ears. I enjoyed Karl and Tom's palpable fear. Their discomfort brought me joy, like an early Christmas present. When I felt that I'd maximized their anxiety levels, I stood up slowly, wobbling for effect. I reached down to my ankles, pulled up my pants and then dabbed at the scattered dribbles of urine that spotted the denim.

"I told you I could do it," I said matter-of-factly, brushing blades of grass off my shirt. "Wasn't even a challenge."

* * *

I've struggled with genius all my life. It's a troubling affliction that creates all kinds of danger, from atomic bombs to electric fences. In order to prevent my genius from inventing any destructive or dangerous items that the world just doesn't need, I've battled to reign it in. After years of struggle I eventually learned to live in tenuous harmony with my prolific mind. Still, I dream of a simpler life, an uncomplicated existence filled with comics and Disney animations, a world where everyone speaks like George W. Bush but nobody has any power.

My mom alerted me to my plight early in life, and she reminded me often. "Chris, you're so special," she crowed continuously, "promise you'll never forget that." I always nodded in agreement, and I've fulfilled the promise admirably. She assured my siblings that they too were special, but always with a wink or a nod in my direction to indicate that such comments were born from motherhood diplomacy. I understood perfectly. My siblings were special for the simple fact that they were hers. I was special based on merit.

Lamenting genius is tricky under a bombardment of envy, but as a testament to my ingenuity, I've formulated a long list of complaints. One big problem with being absurdly bright is that genius comes equipped with a dangerous inquisitiveness. For instance, Karl and my sister Katrina were able to fire up the family lawnmower without significant risk to their physical well-being. Before yanking the mower's engine cord, they'd survey our half-acre of lawn, searching for toys, large rocks and similar items. After removing any debris, they'd spend the next hour and a half safely pushing the mower around our expansive yard.

But where they saw yard debris, I saw opportunity. When I mowed the lawn, gripping curiosity required me to leave the lawn cluttered with rubbish, even convinced me to haphazardly scatter additional articles about, all so I could find out if G.I. Joe and the garden hose could withstand the assault of a whirling metal blade. Several of these objects shot out from under the mower as I passed over them, striking my legs at high speed and inflicting sizable welts. Star Wars action figures were particularly ruthless, blasting from the mower's undercarriage as if Jabba the Hut had placed a bounty on my shins. But the excruciating pain couldn't dampen my intrigue with propulsion, and I continued to run the mower over all sorts of clutter. As with most of my experiments, the results left me in tears.

"Damn you brain!" I'd cry. "Why is your capacity to store information infinite, and your desire to acquire knowledge so persistent?"

The countless hours that I spent in hospital waiting rooms gave me plenty of time to reflect on the downside of genius. After several visits to the E.R. I determined that my insatiable curiosity was a minor annoyance compared to the primary negative consequence associated with genius: the affliction makes it nearly impossible to find a worthy challenge. Personally speaking, any time an undertaking threatens to test my mettle, a flurry of wizardry erupts in my mind. No matter the complexity of the problem, I instantly arrive at a simple solution, one that distills the excitement from the ordeal and effectively robs obstacles of their treachery.

This might sound desirable, but true challenges are like vegetables; they may be a bit troublesome to digest, but an occasional dose is required for healthy development. This truth creates a troubling catch-22.34193.[1] A lack of challenge in a person's life impedes proper development, leaving the mind malnourished, yet it's almost impossible to challenge the truly brilliant. This paradox has clogged my mind with intense frustration.

My youth was a string of easy victories, hollow triumphs that were unable to provide the worthwhile lessons that come from valiant struggle. A true challenge tests the parameters of human ability, pumps adrenaline, builds character and provides the bliss of accomplishment. These are life's tasty condiments, and the absurdly smart rarely get to taste them. Fearful that I'd been condemned to a life of bland success, I prayed early for a real challenge worthy of my glorious abilities, but every night I went to bed disappointed.

After years of waiting, I realized I would have to go on the offensive and seek my grail. This revelation occurred to me on a bright day shortly after my sixth birthday. I was sitting at the kitchen table on Saturday morning, the sun beaming through the window. In the course of fifteen minutes, as I nibbled on a cinnamon roll, I beat my father at tic-tac-toe seven times in a row. Dad spent the entire episode with his head in the newspaper, a sorry attempt to conceal his mounting embarrassment. At that moment, as my disgraced father hid behind the sports section, my frustration came to a head. Humiliating my family with feats of greatness left me empty; each of them blanketed in shame. I owed it to them to ferret out obstacles to test my mind, so I made the decision to put down my shield, unsheathe my determination and embark on a journey to locate a formidable challenge to nourish my intellect. I would launch a Challenge Quest, a quixotic search for a true challenge. In addition to the benefits for my family, my personal development required a Quest. The desire burned deep in me to detect my limits, and

---

[1] Laymen brazenly round this off to "catch-22."

to confirm or debunk my pestering suspicion that I had none.

"Dad, I'm sorry you can't beat me at tic-tac-toe," I said.

"What were we playing?" he asked sheepishly, looking out from behind the paper.

"Don't play stupid, Dad. The results speak for themselves. I just want you to know that, first and foremost, I love you. Secondly, I am going to start a Challenge Quest. I will hunt down a challenge if it kills me. I will find something to busy my genius so your self-esteem can heal and prosper."

"You could start by trying not to pee your bed for a whole week. That seems to give you some trouble."

"That's no trouble at all," I shot back. "Mom washes the sheets and remakes my bed. And anyway, what I am looking for is a *real* challenge, something with the courage to test my ability while I'm awake. The search will be like finding a needle in a haystack, but I'm going to do my best."

"Or like finding shrimp in the ocean," he suggested.

I nodded solemn agreement. He was horrible at tic-tac-toe, but he had his moments. His analogy capably expanded upon my example, adeptly capturing the enormity of the task ahead.

I stood from my unsteady kitchen chair, paused dramatically, then strode out of the room, respectful of the magnanimity of the moment. The initiation of a quest is a monumental thing. It demands reverence. What follows is an account of my heroic Quest, constructed using truncated excerpts of a daily journal that I kept in my head.

March 16, 1975

"Here Challenge...Here Challenge...come out, come out wherever you are." Thus I begin the first day of my Challenge Quest. My taunt shall alert any and all challenges that I am on the hunt, a glorious quest filling my sail.

The goal of my Quest is to find and free the fair maiden imprisoned in the Tower of Difficulty. Her name is Iknow. Every challenge on earth has its unique Tower of Difficulty, proportional in size and strength to the challenge it represents. Imprisoned within each Tower is the maiden Iknow, waiting patiently for her champion. To anyone who attempts to free her, Iknow grants the treasure of insight. She reveals information about personal weaknesses and strengths, granting a would-be emancipator a glimpse at the peaks and troughs of their abilities, potential, character and soul. Iknow shares this information regardless of whether or not a person is successful in toppling the Tower of Difficulty. When determining how much information to reveal, Iknow weighs only the sincerity of the effort, not the outcome. The more formidable the Tower, the more energy and effort a person commits to the task, the more information Iknow is willing to divulge.

Iknow doesn't rely on a rigid manual to determine the volume and value of information she shares. Instead, she recognizes that every challenge is unique, each individual and effort distinctive. As a result, a similar obstacle can reap a wide range of rewards for differently situated people. For example, the physical achievement of getting out of bed in the morning isn't a strenuous chore for most people. Accordingly, Iknow doesn't provide significant informational riches for tackling this trivial task. When a healthy person crawls out of bed in the morning, overcoming their desire to sleep in, Iknow might whisper, "You're alive. You're alive." But if a person recovering from hip surgery fights their way out of bed, Iknow has more to say. "You're driven, perseverant, a fighter." When a paraplegic rolls from bed in the morning, claws their way over to their wheelchair and struggles into a seated position, Iknow is bound to swing up to their ear, a single hair her vine, and get downright gabby, applauding their inner strength, giving clarity to their flaws. In this way, the same Tower of Difficulty can result in a variety of informational rewards, each prize dependent on the particular circumstances. That's how the maiden Iknow works.[2]

---

[2] This analysis is entirely inapplicable if Iknow is on one of her heroin binges.

Unfortunately, my genius makes finding a Tower of Difficulty seemingly impossible. While commoners encounter Tower after Tower in life, often to the point that they're overwhelmed, I've gone years without finding anything more difficult than rolling out of bed in the morning. This is the reason I quest after a formidable challenge. I need a really tall Tower, one that will convince Iknow to tell me who I am and what I can be. I must find a formidable Tower of Difficulty. **END ENTRY**

March 24, 1975
It's been over a week and my taunts have failed to bait a true challenge. No Towers of Difficulty in sight. Maybe I will attempt to manufacture a challenge, design and construct my own Tower, much like a mad scientist who tinkers in a dark, secret laboratory in hopes of creating a living creature out of various rodent parts; with the slight variation in that I am a six-year old kid who is deathly afraid of rodents, alive or dead, and lives in a well-maintained home on River Road. For the good of the Quest, I shall henceforth disguise myself as a mischievous child in order to lull a true challenge into a sense of calm, thus making it easier for me to discover and seize my yearned-for grail. **END ENTRY**

April 19, 1975
Manufacturing a Challenge, take 209. Today I thought it might be challenging to throw a rock over the tree in our front yard. It wasn't. I threw a rock over the tree with ease. It sailed up and over the evergreen and right through the neighbor's window. Didn't get caught. No problem. No challenge. **END ENTRY**

May 12, 1975
Manufacturing a Challenge, take 896. I saw a man on television tear a phonebook in half using his bare hands. It looked like great fun. I thought it might be a challenge to see if I could resist

tearing our phone book in half with my bare hands. The phone book in our home sits in the kitchen next to the telephone. I walked past it three times today, stopping only once to look up the listing for Baskin-Robbins in order to make a prank phone call. Despite the heavy temptation to tear the book in two, I easily resisted. I thought resisting the urge would be much more difficult. Another challenge mirage. **END ENTRY**

June 18, 1975

Manufacturing a Challenge, take 1064. Mom and Dad went to a movie tonight and left us with a babysitter named Susan. She is a 16-year old girl who lives down the road. She's never babysat for us before. I thought it would be hard to convince her that I was a diabetic who needed to eat three scoops of ice cream before I went to bed. I told her if I didn't get the ice cream that I'd have a seizure. At first she didn't buy it. Then I started to quiver a bit and forced some drool out the corners of my mouth. Her resolve snapped like a twig. She gave me four scoops of ice cream. Will I ever find a challenge? Should I abandon this seemingly futile Quest? **END ENTRY**

October 31, Halloween, 1975

Manufacturing a Challenge, take 1439. Success is maddening! Tonight I grew even bolder in my search for a true challenge. While lounging at home in our warm living room after a successful trick-or-treat campaign, I asked Mom for all the extra Halloween candy that she hadn't given away. She said no, claiming, incorrectly, that I already had enough candy. Convincing her to give me some of the excess candy seemed a nearly impossible task, a true Tower.

I excused myself and went to my room. I dug out my costume from the previous year, a tattered bunny outfit, and quickly put it on. I then snuck out the back door and circled around the house to the front. I rang the door bell. A moment later my mom answered.

"Trick or treat," I mumbled through the mask, disguising my voice.

"Here you go!" Mom voluntarily dropped two small Snickers bars into my plastic pumpkin pail. These were two of the same chocolates that she had refused to give me minutes earlier.

"May I have a Butterfinger bar, too?" I politely asked.

Mom happily complied. After dropping the Butterfinger into my pail, she gave a look around, searching for my guardian.

"Little late to be out alone," she stated in a worried voice, "especially without your parents."

"My parents aren't very attentive," I sighed. "I look after them more than they look after me."

I turned and walked away. As soon as she closed the door, I circled around to the back and slipped in the patio entrance. I scurried to my bedroom, removed the bunny outfit and rejoined my family in the living room. Nobody was the wiser, I was the richer. During the entire operation, not one of my pores produced a single drip of perspiration. There was no up-tick in my heartbeat. Manufacturing a challenge is proving difficult. Will Iknow ever talk to me? **END ENTRY**

January 1, New Year's Day, 1976

I will henceforth employ two squires to assist me with my Quest. Effective immediately, Karl and Tom will assist in my search for a Tower of Difficulty capable of challenging my genius. Who better to assist with a challenge quest than a couple guys who find every aspect of life challenging? These eager squires will rejuvenate my lagging search. I trust they will pour themselves into the Quest with zeal, searching for uncommon feats to challenge my uncommon gifts. **END ENTRY**

February 7, 1976

I peed on an electric fence today and lived. Tom said no one could do it, but I did it with ease. Still, Iknow didn't talk to me afterwards. Apparently surviving a jolt of electricity doesn't equate to toppling a Tower for someone packing a brilliant mind.

This is the fourth time I've proven to Karl and Tom that I'm capable of surviving a punch of electricity from that fence. At their urging I've touched the same fence three other times—with the blade of a broken shovel, a wire coat hanger and an old Shasta pop can. These items all conducted electricity, but none of them delivered a challenging shock. Each time, after tolerating the short sting of electrocution, I suffered a mild bout of dizziness, but nothing worthy of Iknow's attention. Worse, when I touched the fence with the shovel blade, I was thrown back seven feet. Peeing on the fence only knocked me back four feet. If anything my Challenge Quest is moving in the wrong direction.
END ENTRY

February 18, 1976

Despite their inspired service and earnest desire, Karl and Tom lack imagination. Intentions glazed with goodness can't offset the disadvantage of imbecility. Eat a booger. Hang from a second story gutter. Swallow a cup full of jalapeño peppers without chewing. I've skated through each of their alleged challenges with ease. The urination stunt was the final straw. It was no Tower of Difficulty. It felt more like a spark of regression, not progress. I have no choice but to terminate their services.
END ENTRY

February 19, 1976

I gave Tom and Karl official notice of their termination today by showing them both my middle fingers at the same time. That makes it official. They didn't take the news well. They swore that they'd continue to offer their services, by force if necessary. I will do my best to avoid them. For my Challenge Quest to succeed, I need to follow a solitary path, one unencumbered by well-intentioned fools.

I am now past the halfway point of my first grade year and I still haven't found a single difficult thing in life. I've destroyed every obstacle that's dared confront me, overcoming each potential Tower as easily as a tornado robs a dandelion of its white, fluffy seeds. I feel like a scavenger hunt participant searching for a sunset high in the sky and a politician who speaks from the heart. **END ENTRY**

March 18, 1976

Today is my last day at David Hill Elementary, the public school I have attended for the past year and a half in the ritzy suburb of Hillsboro, Oregon.[3] I waltzed through kindergarten, napping without equal, and first grade here hasn't been the fertile ground for Towering challenges that I'd hoped for. I rummaged through every corner of this school for obstacles, assailed the teachers, searched with passion, but all I found were easily resolved math equations and words that seemed to spell themselves. With each passing day, my hopes are diminished, my talents lying fallow, bored by the tedium of gluing construction paper to the wall when no one is looking.

Everything is about to change, though. Yesterday, Dad told the family that we're uprooting, moving west to a town called Banks. I've visited there before—Dad's been working on constructing our new house out there for almost a year—and I look forward to the opportunity to comb the small, tousled town for a Tower of Difficulty. The possibility that Banks might hold a true challenge for me is helping balance the sadness of leaving behind friends. Banks seems like a quaint, special place, virgin territory for my search. **END ENTRY**

* * *

Located thirty miles due west of Portland, nestled into the

---

[3] Ritzy, like most things, is relative. After five years on Clark Air Force Base in the Philippines, which had a twelve-foot high fence separating the entire enclave from the locals, "ritzy" came to mean that there was a better than even chance that our television wouldn't be stolen out of the living room while we slept.

base of the Coastal Range, Banks epitomizes rural living. The town is populated with farmers who wake roosters and several burly, hard-working loggers, the only endangered species that garners support in the region. For the price of a bullet, several townsfolk are willing to euthanize a sickly pet. Throw in another fifty cents and they'll 'see to' the carcass, probably by 'burying' it in their family stewpot.

When we moved to Banks in the early part of 1976, many townsfolk believed that Dwight Eisenhower was the current president and, for practical purposes, I suppose they were right, the ripples of federal policy leisurely arriving in town decades after legislative action. National news was just as slow to arrive, as if it were being delivered by Pony Express.

A rattling U-Haul truck lugged our mishmash of material possessions to the home my father had built. U-Haul trucks are to change as a pterodactyl is to ancient, and Banks treats change like a pterodactyl sighting. As we rumbled down Main Street, scrutiny attached itself. People glared and whispered, pointed and exercised eyebrows. My father ignored the attention. He looked forward and drove with purpose. Karl and I sat silently next to him, doing our best to disregard the imagined danger. Stoically we pressed on, the Kemper men bravely pioneering the family West, searching for a better life, a mere dustbowl short of an epic novel.[4]

At the north end of town, my father hung a left at the Brown Derby Restaurant and we headed out of Banks and toward home. A mile later we turned again, this time to the right, up Canyon Creek Road, a pot-holed, gravel lane named for its canyon-sized tire ruts that resembled a pair of dry creek beds. A little over a mile farther, and after a 600-foot elevation climb, we were home.[5]

---

[4] Total trek: 17 miles west of previous residence.

[5] My dad, in a hurry to get the family out of a small, temporary apartment, ignored the traditional construction mantra of "measure twice, cut once." Instead, he employed his own maxim of "eye it, cut it, cuss, adjust," an approach that gave our new home an abundance of character.

Mom, Katrina and Kerry followed closely behind us in our old red station wagon. We all gathered in the driveway, the only cement in a mile's radius, and quietly admired our new home. Nearly an acre of upturned dirt skirted the five-bedroom structure. The lack of lawn, a temporary landscaping imperfection, allowed me to gaze past the agonizing mowing responsibilities that would burden my youth and focus on the beautiful, panoramic vista.

Banks sat below, standing sentinel at the edge of the valley, a tiny town under siege from swaths of meticulously maintained farmland. Perfect, asymmetric hills carpeted with majestic evergreens fenced the western horizon. To the east was snow-capped Mt. Hood. Plush greens in every direction. Refreshing, nature-scented air. This was the type of wholesomeness you'd expect to find in Norman Rockwell's thoughts.[6]

The Monday after we completed the move to Banks, Mom drove us to school for our baptism in rural education. During the drive, she pointed out the location of our bus stop, a small nook situated where our gravel road intersected the paved street to town. It was more than a mile from our front door. For the next four years I walked to and from that nook every school day, until finally the road leading up to our house was paved, allowing the school bus safe passage to our home and a few others that had sprouted nearby.

As we drove into town, I noticed a standard green and white population sign. The sign notified the world that Banks had five hundred inhabitants. Exactly five hundred. For twelve years, from our arrival in Banks until the afternoon I left for college, the sign never noted a change. My family referred to the inhabitants as the Banks 500, a term suggesting a NASCAR event but that was, in fact, a loving tribute to five hundred people who refused to die, procreate, adopt or move.

---

[6] You can't judge a book by its cover—you're probably nodding, thinking, "Yeah, I liked the cover of this book."—so it's quite possible that Rockwell's thoughts, in actuality, were plagued by darkness and gore.

It was here, in this small, stagnant town, that my search for a challenge bore fruit. On my very first day of school, I encountered a Tower of Difficulty capable of challenging my brilliance: I was forced to play dumb.

March 28, 1976
When we pulled into the school parking lot today, everyone stared at our old, ordinary station wagon as if we were arriving on a swooping pterodactyl. Karl sat in the front passenger seat next to Mom. I was buckled in the backseat next to Katrina, riled by nervous energy. I fought the urge to shrink down and hide by hitting my sister in the arm as hard as I could.

"Mom, Chris hit me!" Katrina yelped.

"Chris, why did you do that?"

"Because she's smaller than me and looked vulnerable."

"That is no reason to hit someone!" Mom yelled.

"Actually, that's the only reason to hit someone," I answered.

Mom stopped the car abruptly. She maneuvered around in the driver's seat to face me and fired a glare far fiercer than anything the locals had been able to summon.

"You know Chris, you're probably right." As she spoke she reached back and smacked my arm, hard, with a quick jab. "I probably won't hit you like that when you get bigger and stronger." She laughed at her own childishness. "Now out of the car, all of you."

"Mom, I'm scared," I whined as I opened the car door.

"You'll be fine," she assured. "Now hurry up! There are a lot of cars behind us!" As I began to close the door, she warned, "You all be good! And Chris, your mouth, you…be…careful!" I closed the door before her comment registered. Mom drove off.

After she had pulled onto the main road, driving out of sight, Karl walked over next to me. "I think you're right about that hitting stuff, too," he said. He smacked the left side of my head and then strolled toward the school building. In most circumstances, I'd have chased after him and spit on his shirt, but Mom's warning distracted me.

Careful? Her odd counsel reverberated in my head. Careful was an instructional tip she reserved for dangerous activities; riding my bike, cooking French toast, using my little brother as a Wiffle ball tee. Why had she singled me out? What did she mean by "careful?" Is this rural school dangerous? Are the Banks denizens haters of education, repulsed by the enlightened? Is the ability to count to ten considered blasphemy in this backwoods place? If these yokels catch me in the act of reading will they lash my body to a gasoline-soaked wooden post, surround me with ample kindling, and dance around the ensuing blaze, screaming, "Kill the Reader, the Reader!" as the flames censor me and my books from the earth? I've heard stories of atrocities in rural areas. Salem, Massachusetts isn't a myth. To the people of Banks, my genius might very well be mistaken for witchcraft. The rare sense of real fear ignited my mind. Prodigious brainstorming followed.

The last time my brain erupted in this manner was last December. It happened during an episode of Perry Mason. Perry was backed into an inescapable legal corner. There seemed to be irrefutable evidence that his client was guilty, but Perry never lost a case. Every time he entered the courtroom, Perry proved to the world that people who appear guilty are almost certainly innocent.[7] Before the episode concluded, Mom called me upstairs to unload the dishwasher.

"Christopher, for the last time come unload the dishwasher. Right now!"

I didn't see the end of the show and was never able to figure out how Perry orchestrated an acquittal. After unloading the dishwasher and reminding my mom that some day she'd have to hire someone to do her petty chores, I racked my mind trying to figure out a scenario, any string of events or momentous revela-

---

[7] As a person plagued with a constant appearance of guilt, I ardently believe Perry Mason to be correct on this matter.

tions, that Perry could have used to pave the road to innocence. I thought so hard and long that my head throbbed, pulsating with each beat of my heart. Later that night, a completely unexpected winter storm zoomed through the region, dropping five inches of snow. It was apparent to me that the surprise storm and my brainstorm were connected. When operating at full capacity, it seemed, my brain must emit massive electrical tremors powerful enough to disrupt local weather patterns.

With my mom's warning wringing fear from my brave bones, I needed a plan. Standing in the school parking lot, watching my new schoolmates enter the red brick building, I closed my eyes and urged my mind to rampage. I needed a snowstorm or some other weather-related reprieve to allow me time to investigate why Mom had warned me to be careful. I squeezed my eyes tighter, fixated on my predicament. Storm, mind, storm! Storm like you have never stormed before! After several seconds of deep mental focus, I looked to the sky, searching for signs of extreme weather change. Nothing. Not even a cloud.

The school bell rang and the students still milling around outside scrambled toward the blue double doors guarding the main entrance. After a moment of hesitation, I followed after them, doused in trepidation. The risk was palatable. Geniuses were not welcome here, I could sense it. I suspected that the water fountains inside would be segregated, most marked "Common Folk," one, maybe two, labeled "Genius." The water fountains for geniuses would, of course, be grungy and poorly kept, covered with graffiti, spouting dingy water, maybe even sludge. There'd be signs on most of the doors that would bar my entrance. "Brilliance Not Welcome Here" or "Illiterate Only." I could fight the good fight, try to change the system, sue for equal protection, equal treatment. Kemper the Genius v. Banks Board of Education had a nice ring. But I lacked the inner strength. I couldn't bear the thought of enduring years of strife and struggle. Some people are so strong, brave and full of fortitude. As a genius, I've never needed to be.

Upon entering the building, a silver lining emerged, engulfing my fright. This, I realized, was exactly the challenge I'd been hoping for, the turning point of my Quest, the ultimate Tower to test my genius. It's so simple, yet so intricate. I have stumbled into the only challenge capable of introducing struggle to my life. I will have to play dumb. Not just dumb, more than that, I'll have to act normal. Blending in with these rural folks is the only hope I have to avoid prejudice. They salivate at the scent of brilliance, undoubtedly anxious to unleash their fury on anyone with the gall to know all 26 letters of the alphabet. Careful indeed! **END ENTRY**

April 21, 1976

Playing dumb is difficult, like the sun playing dim. As with any skill, I will get better with practice. Every passing day brings improvement. I am growing adept at convincing classmates and townsfolk that I'm one of them. Maybe I'll be a spy one day, go undercover to help my country, possibly as a black Norwegian woman—that might be a challenge. I quickly and magnificently have adopted a common persona, but I remain guarded and wary. As with any creature that reverts to crawling after years of bipedal mobility, I am constantly at risk of giving myself away. Habits are hard to break. **END ENTRY**

May 19, 1976

I live in constant fear that my new classmates will kill me if they learn of my special gifts. I must work harder to suppress my talents. At the same time, I must unearth my flaws in order to further my ruse—but this is a daunting chore given that my flaws, if they exist, are so well camouflaged I can't even see them. Still, I need to find some, or manufacture a few, in order to create a dimwitted aura. My life depends on it.

Today I disabled my photographic memory. Though I've never used it—primarily because I've never had enough money to get the film developed—it is too dangerous to leave in my intellectual arsenal. Going forward, I will subtly shake my head during class, employing a slow, constant wobbling motion, swaying my neck back and forth so my mental lens can't focus.

I will also initiate strategic drooling. Drool is universally recognized as secreted stupidity, so I will allow saliva to escape the corners of my mouth on occasion, a fabulous prop to further my ploy. I shall emit drool frequently enough to attract attention, but measure my use so as not to be removed from mainstream classes. **END ENTRY**

June 2, 1976

Today the threat of attack against my genius seemed imminent. I saw some of my classmates gathering leaves, twigs and other flammables during recess—a surefire sign that they were preparing to burn something, or someone. I will fake an illness tomorrow morning so Mom will let me skip school and I can avoid the skewer.

Fabricating illness has become second nature. To make the act more convincing, I like to envision my classmates dancing around my scorching flesh as I burn at the stake. "Burn, Genius, burn!" they shout in my dreams. "If your math is so powerful, why won't it save you now?" These thoughts induce a fierce sweat that soaks and chills my body, all the evidence needed to fool a skilled physician. I've become so adept at faking illness that Mom never doubts.

"Chris, you feel so clammy," she frets, her hand against my forehead. "You are not going to school!" Her pronouncement is like pardon from the governor, canceling my fiery death at the hands of hillbilly classmates. **END ENTRY**

November 5, 1976

I'm in second grade now...and still alive, a testament to my skill. During afternoon recess I detected increased twig gathering activity. I also learned that Chuck Martin had brought a lighter to school, a key ingredient for the common man to start a bonfire of sufficient size and intensity to incinerate human flesh. When I saw Chuck and some of his friends piling up the twigs, I feared my cover had been blown, that my hidden genius had been compromised. I quickly retreated to the principal's office, seeking safety.

Upon entering the head office I saw Mrs. Rowe sitting behind her large, industrial size desk, shuffling paper. She is the school secretary by title. In truth, though, she runs the joint, something no one disputes. Despite no formal medical training, she doubles as the school nurse. The maladies that typically befall my schoolmates—the sniffles, bellyaches, urine-soaked pants, hurt feelings—require nurturing more than medical attention, and Mrs. Rowe fulfills the role capably.

I prepped my best sickly voice and then interrupted her work. "Mrs. Rowe, can you please call my mom and have her come pick me up." I quietly continued the sentence in my mind, "...because I don't want to burn to death at the hands of those who despise my intellectual prowess."

Mrs. Rowe stood up and came out from behind her desk, a comforting smile neutralizing her imposing figure. "Wait in the nurse's room," she said in a soothing voice. "I'll be with you in just a bit."

I entered the room, closed the door and went directly to a heating vent in the back corner. Such vents are perfect for fabricating fevers. As I'd done a few times in the past, I placed my forehead directly in the path of the warm air spewing from the vent. Minutes later Mrs. Rowe knocked on the door. I quickly and quietly moved across the room to a plain wooden chair. Once settled, I answered her knock.

"Come in," I sniffled.

The ruse played out as one would expect. Mrs. Rowe placed the back of her hand on my cheek and winced. "Chris, you're boiling up."

"I feel awful...and so hot," I said.

"I'll call your mom right now."

I felt no shame. Faking illness is far simpler than trying to convince the office staff that there is town-wide conspiracy to torture the absurdly bright. Mrs. Rowe phoned my mom. Ten minutes later our station wagon appeared in the parking lot, assuring my safety for yet another day.

"You're that sick are you?" Mom asked as I crawled into the passenger seat.

"More careful than sick, actually," I answered.

She gave me an odd look, but didn't probe.

"Better safe than singed," I added.

"You're going right to bed when we get home."

We drove home slowly. On the way, I decided to feign illness for at least two more days, skip a bit more school to let the heat pass. I bet if I would have faked a seizure today I could've gotten Mrs. Rowe to give me some ice cream. **END ENTRY**

November 6-7, 1976

I've spent the last two days watching Perry Mason episodes. During the commercials, I analyzed the evidence that condemns this town as a genius-hating haven. The two activities mesh well: as Perry searches for evidence to free his client, I review the clues that suggest my classmates and the Banks 500 are rabid hicks.

The entire town seems to be engaged in a coordinated effort to trick me into revealing my core genius. The inhabitants of this small place continuously try to win my trust so they can, I suspect, turn around and betray it. I must prevail. I must convince them I'm normal or, better yet, slightly skewed. But they are good, so good, at acting the part, at faking kindness. I fear I may slip up and impulsively begin to juggle while reciting multiplication tables. Or maybe one day I'll get caught performing long division without aid of paper and pencil. If this happens, if I make such a mistake and expose my true identity, I'll certainly be tarred and feathered, or worse.

As Perry has taught me, appearances and evidence are poor barometers of guilt. Since the seemingly innocent are invariably the guilty, this entire town must be denounced. From the moment we arrived, the people of Banks have welcomed me with unmatched hospitality and unprecedented kindness, displaying the wonderfully unique values of small town America. Little Peggy has diabetes? The town holds a pancake breakfast fundraiser. A third grader needs a new pair of shoes? They take up a collection. There was a fire at the Vandehey Farm? Everyone pitches in to help rebuild. The passionate willingness of each individual to lend a hand exceeds heartwarming. It is, on the surface, life distilled to its purest, precious essence. If you pee on life's electric fence, you'd be lucky to land in Banks, a place where the entire town is always ready to reach out to help you up. I've got them figured, though. If they discover how brilliant I am, I will be in such a pickle not even Perry will be able to save me. I wonder if this is how Clark Kent felt? **END ENTRY**

May 28, 1978

My fear of persecution grows in step with my genius, which is to say, exponentially. Third grade is proving just as easy as grades one and two, so I've started to supplement my trademark drool with sporadic but spectacular feats of public humiliation, all in order to douse any scent of brilliance I might accidentally emit. My latest foray into dramatic deception occurred today during the Third Grade Spelling Bee Competition. My exit from the competition was almost too perfect, caused by a gaffe so stunningly dense that I feared I might be inviting unwanted attention and stoking suspicion.

Every student in our class participated in the Spelling Bee, along with some second graders who'd qualified. Out of all the contestants, I was the only person eliminated in the first round. I misspelled the word "quack."

Mrs. William, my third grade teacher, moderated the competition.

"Chris, your first word is quack. Please spell quack."

"Can I use it in a sentence?" I asked.

"Do you mean would you like *meeeeeee* to use the word in a sentence?" Mrs. Williams responded.

"No. I meant exactly what I said. I'd like to use it in a sentence. For example: It's bothersome that you're asking me to spell a word as simple as quack."

"Just spell the word," Mrs. Williams grumbled.

"Sure, no problem. Q-a-c-k. Qack."

All the competitors broke into wild laughter. When the laughing subsided, Mrs. Williams, a rare smirk on her face, decided to make a point.

"Chris, what always comes after the letter q? Always!"

"I have no idea."

The class laughed again, in unison, this time louder.

"Chris, the letter u always comes after q. You know that."

"Always?" I asked.

"Yes, always."

I returned to my seat. Along the way I walked passed a giggling Ike Davis, a kid at risk of being knocked out of the Spelling Bee if asked to spell his own name.

"Duh Chris, u always follows q," he mocked, wagging his finger in my face.

His words didn't bother me. I ignored him, just as I'd ignored Mrs. Williams a couple weeks earlier when, during a spelling lesson, she'd perpetuated the myth that *q* and *u* have an inseparable relationship. My fellow competitors deemed me a failure, but I sat down a success. I'd fooled them all, yet again! They think I'm an idiot! After sitting down, I scanned the room, examining their faces, fools who will never discover I'm a walking, talking, drooling mastermind. Sure I was out of the competition, but I was safe from their discrimination, the percolating hate they seem ready to unleash at the first sign of brilliance. And I took solace from the fact that my numbskull classmates and Mrs. Williams would never visit Qatar, let alone acknowledge its existence. **END ENTRY**

November 23, 1980

Despite employing drool and general quackery, no charade is perfect. Mrs. Schnieder, my fifth grade teacher—wow she's hot, she makes me feel weird—has seen through my act. Today she tapped me for the role of Smarty the Elf in our holiday play. When she announced the acting assignments, I thought I was finished, even wrote out a short will, leaving my various possessions to my brothers and sister, and my first kiss, the one I'd never get to give, to Samantha Christianson. I was certain I'd been outed, pulled from the MENSA closet for all to see. This was what my mom had warned about years ago. I had tried so hard to be careful. Somehow, though, Mrs. Schnieder has detected that I've been brilliantly portraying an idiot. To save my hide, I need to concoct a massive stupidity counterattack. **END ENTRY**

December 18, 1980

Tonight I pulled it off again! During the holiday play, Smarty the Elf played the fool. The role of Smarty didn't include a large speaking part, but I did have a lengthy singing solo. When it came time for me to sing, I clammed up. The lyrics raced from my mind, leaving me speechless. All I could do was hum. I cleverly covered the mistake by improvising with a funky—I'd go so far as to say seductive—dance number. I gyrated on stage, the tassels on my elf hat bouncing and bounding in time with my body. I continued entertaining the crowd with my vibrant moves until it was time for Silly Elf to take over the song.

After the show, several classmates approached and consoled. Their sheepish sympathy assured it would be a long time before I was accused of being Smarty again. Though everyone acted as if I should feel bad or embarrassed, I felt great. The evening solidified my magnificence. Prior to the show, I wasn't aware of my natural gift for dance, or that I possessed the improvisational skills typically reserved for polished professionals. They expect me to feel bad? I am on top of the world! And not a single classmate or adult in attendance, not one, possessed a mind advanced enough, like mine, to appreciate the irony of Smarty the Elf forgetting his lines. Do I have an equal? I am becoming masterful at concealing my brilliance. I am, as they say, rising to the challenge. I can do this! Iknow should start talking to me any day now! **END ENTRY**

January 23, 1981
The phone rang today and nobody answered it. It was probably NASA calling to see if I wanted to join their astronaut program. **END ENTRY**

June 2, 1982
Mrs. Fischer told me that I can't follow rules. She's a teacher at my school. I don't like to correct teachers, it's risky, but I felt obligated to point out that she was wrong. I pulled her aside between classes and informed her that I was quite capable of following any rule that I had authored or amended. She didn't seem to understand. **END ENTRY**

June 4, 1983
On the front page of the newspaper today it was reported that scientists in Europe had achieved cold fusion in a laboratory. The report is false—after reading the article it is clear to me that they've done it wrong. **END ENTRY**

September 4, 1983
Time flies! I am in high school already. With so many years of harboring genius under my belt, acting the fool has become habit. Still, despite my fabulous depiction of a common kid, Iknow hasn't delivered the goods. I continue to overcome the overwhelming, daily challenge of concealing my genius, yet she remains silent. Why? **END ENTRY**

October 13, 1983

Today I printed out fliers offering amnesty to every girl who has refused to talk to me over the years. I posted the information throughout the school. The offer grants each girl a two week window to come forward and apologize—preferably with a kiss. I will unconditionally forgive any girl who accepts the offer. I hope my fair maiden Iknow, silent all these years, gets the message. **END ENTRY**

November 8, 1985

I can't believe I'm already a junior. Only a year and a half to go and I'll be out of this genius-hating town. Maybe Iknow is waiting until I complete this massive challenge, this complex cover-up, before she shares with me all that she knows.

Last week, Mr. Ball, my history instructor, assigned a three-to-five page typed report on Abraham Lincoln. He instructed the class to focus on the political, ethical and financial reasons for the Civil War and the principles that sustained Lincoln's commitment to the cause. How damn stupid is that? It's absurd to think an iconic figure like Abe can be summarized in so few pages. The assignment borders on disrespectful.

The paper was due today. My lack of interest in the assignment led to procrastination, and procrastination guided me to the encyclopedia. Encyclopedias are specifically crafted to boil down a rich, exciting life into a short, stale encapsulation, precisely what this report required. Sitting at a table last night with the family typewriter primed with paper, ready to go, I flipped to the entry for Abraham Lincoln and copied verbatim.

I was introduced to typing only a few months ago, so striking the proper keys consumed my attention. Each word, each sentence, meant nothing to me. I didn't absorb the meaning of the text. My primary focus was minimizing the use of whiteout, that vile liquid that whispers, "Failure. You're a failure."

Because the encyclopedia has presumably undergone a rigorous proofreading, I stayed true to the script and oblivious to

the context. I'm not really sure what I wrote. The layout of the typewriter keys, the elusive shift button and the seemingly random positioning of the letters required the entirety of my focus. Still, after finishing my report I didn't read it for errors, assuming the folks who put together the encyclopedia had gotten it right. I turned the report in during 5th period today. If I don't get an "A" I'll sue the people who published the encyclopedia.
END ENTRY

November 10, 1985

Mr. Ball blew up on me today. Not literally. His fat butt didn't burst. His flesh didn't fly. He blew up in a figurative sense. It turns out that when I pecked my five page report on Abe Lincoln that I inadvertently copied across the page columns, accidentally conjoining the lives of Abraham and his namesake, Benjamin Lincoln. Benjamin Lincoln is the entry that follows Abe in the old set of Encyclopedia Britannica that my parents bought years ago in Taiwan.[8] The result was a conglomeration of plagiarism—some information from Abe's life, some from Ben's—intertwined so thoroughly that the report made absolutely no sense.

Though the inclusion of Benjamin was an error, I remember him from an earlier chapter in our history book. He was a fine, patriotic fellow who fought in the American Revolution for the good guys (that's us!). He was captured by the British in a battle in New Orleans but, according to various accounts, either escaped or was part of a prisoner swap. After his escape or release, Ben climbed through the American ranks to become a senior commander, and he fought against the Tories in Yorktown. The Yorktown battle ended with the surrender of the

---

[8] The encyclopedia set was a knockoff, evidenced by the fact that every reference to Taiwan's rival, China, was blocked out. In the section where the entry for China should have appeared there were eight blank pages. Ironically, in the original Encyclopedia Britannica set, these pages detailed how Chinese merchants commonly infringed on intellectual property rights.

famed British General Cornwallis. After the battle, as a reward for his valor, the U.S. army gave Benjamin one of Cornwallis's swords as a keepsake.

Because Ben spent part of his soldiering life fighting in areas of the United States where several Civil War battles later took place, he had a tenuous historical connection to Abe. When grading my report, Mr. Ball chose to ignore this historical link and instead accused me of being a complete idiot. This assessment aided my cover as a dumb kid, but in reality he's the dumb one. Anyone with even limited powers of extrapolation could've identified the clear, almost cosmic connection that I'd unearthed in my report. The heroic Benjamin and the committed Abe both performed admirably in their respective wars, and both were certified American heroes who shared the same last name. Yet Mr. Ball saw fit to trash the report, ignoring my poignant, if accidental, juxtaposition of two true American patriots.

"I will give you one day to replace this garbage with an original report," Mr. Ball yelled. "One day, one chance. It appears you attempted to copy this from an encyclopedia or something. I'd love to hold you accountable for plagiarism but I don't know if I could make the case against you because, quite frankly, you are blessed with a keen inability to copy. Saved by your own folly! A new report on my desk by 3:00 tomorrow or you will flunk my class!"

I was miffed. I stared at Mr. Ball in disbelief, upset that he couldn't see the brilliance in my report. The copying mistake—probably attributable to the genius lounging in my subconscious—presented an erudite abstract of two patriotic legends, separated by nearly a century but linked by their devotion to America. Further, the identical last names gave the report a scintillating, suggestive undertone that the two men might be blood relatives, an intriguing angle that provided fodder for a discussion on the relationship between genetics and strong leadership characteristics. And he wanted me to rewrite it?

"Did you just roll your eyes?" Mr. Ball barked.

"No. I was winding them. I need to do that twice a day or they stop working."

I retyped a report on Abe tonight. I stopped my fingers only to graffiti typos with whiteout. Each time I used the whiteout it taunted, "Failure. You're a failure." This time, however, the whiteout is undoubtedly referring to Mr. Ball and his failure to comprehend the layered complexity of my original report. I can't wait for the end of high school so I can end this charade and escape into the learned world, free to exhibit my genius. I hope someday to find an intellectual utopia where pioneering reports on historical American figures named Lincoln are embraced, not trashed. **END ENTRY**

June 16, 1987

I have spent the majority of my senior year basking in the bosom of success, my Challenge Quest nearly complete. Not a single person suspects me of being brilliant, not even the folks who administer the SAT. But Iknow hasn't opened up to me yet, saving her insight, I figure, for a graduation gift. The prospect of merging her knowledge with my brain is titillating. I feel primed to explode onto the world stage, me and my mind, free at last to consume our slice of prestige. **END ENTRY**

June 17, 1987

Einstein and I are quite similar. He too kept his genius quiet for years, waiting patiently for a safe environment to expose his gifts to the world. He didn't speak until he was three years old. Later in life, he took the disguise of a low-level patent clerk in a small government office in Switzerland. Me, I took the disguise of a common kid in a small Oregon town. I look forward to following in his footsteps. He quantified E, proving to the world that it equals mc^2; I wonder what letter I'll become famous for defining? I hope it's S, or maybe D. I like those letters. First, though, I have to meet Iknow. Graduation day is only two days away! **END ENTRY**

June 19, 1987—Morning

Graduation Day! The crowning end to my Quest. For the first time in my life I used Q-tips, meticulously cleaning my ears, readying them for Iknow's sweet voice. I've grappled for nearly twelve years to keep my intellect in check. Tonight, finally, the payoff. Iknow will reward me! She will unload her powerful wisdom this evening, likely chiming in right after the band closes the ceremony with a mangled version of Pomp and Circumstance. I'm bubbling with anticipation. It's shooting through me like electricity. I look suave in my navy blue graduation robe and my mortarboard cap. Maybe I'll start wearing the robe all the time.

Post-Ceremony. The ceremony brought one close call. Principal Schlegal took the podium to announce the class valedictorian. As he read the name, I stood up and started walking toward the stage. Who knew that the award favored grade point average over natural intelligence? People shrieked when I stood, and shrieked louder when Mr. Schlegal announced Mary Jo VanDyke as the valedictorian. I quickly returned to my seat, head down, hoping no one in the audience could connect the obvious dots between me and genius. The moment was a bold exclamation point to my Quest, one last moment of charade to celebrate years of feigning a silly, oblivious demeanor.

The band played Pomp and Circumstance with surprising volume. Their instruments blared so loudly that the racket drowned out Iknow's voice. I could only hear the tooting horns and thundering percussions. The racket muted the insight I'd longed for, toiled for. I feel cheated, as if I've arrived at the end of the rainbow and the pot of gold I deserve has been replaced with soggy Lucky Charms.

Some claim that a quest is an inherently selfish act. Well, those morons never spent twelve years acting stupid. I am thankful that I avoided the savagery of my classmates and the townsfolk, but after rising to meet my true challenge, after conquering the formidable task of fooling an entire town into believing I'm a feebleminded dimwit, I want my reward. Oh Iknow, where are you? **END ENTRY**

September 17, 1987

I am leaving for college tomorrow and Iknow has yet to speak to me. I don't know what else I could have done to get her attention. Did Iknow refuse to speak with Sir Edmund Hillary as he stood atop of Everest? Was she silent when Neil Armstrong took a giant leap for mankind? Maybe I was so good at playing dumb that Iknow fell for it, too. Twelve years of meticulously chipping away at the tallest Tower of Difficulty in the world and I'm denied my just reward because I made it look too easy. Talent is a double-edged sword. I will move forward despite this setback, the world's smartest man, still seeking elusive, essential wisdom. **END ENTRY**

September 18, 1987

Before backing my 1969 VW Bug out of the driveway to depart for Stanford, I pulled out my acceptance letter to make sure that it was real. How I'd been accepted to such a prestigious enclave of higher learning is a testament to my unmatched ability to fool people. I read the letter again, as I had so many times before, examining each typed letter to assure I hadn't misunderstood the content. When I came to the last sentence, I froze. There, as clear as my brilliance, was the message I'd been waiting for all these years, a typo I'd somehow missed until now.

"My colleagues will be very pleased to answer any questions you may have about academics at Stanford, just as Iknow they look forward to meeting you in the classroom."

How appropriate! I'd earned Iknow's attention by playing dumb, and she had used a typo to tell me exactly where to find her! Oh, how clever! I threw my Bug into reverse and stepped on the gas, anxious to meet the girl who I'd dreamt of for so long. As I zipped backwards, I waved goodbye to Mom. She waved back. I grinned and accelerated. The Bug, caught up in the excitement, flew across the road and rammed into our mailbox, knocking it over. The engine stalled, then died. After a half hour of trying to get the Bug restarted, I gave up. Oh well, what's one more day? I'll drive down to meet Iknow tomorrow. **END ENTRY**

Post Script: Marilyn vos Savant, born August 11, 1946, was said to have the highest IQ ever recorded. On one IQ test she scored a 228. Not bad! (Her surname is the source for term "savant," a word synonymous with genius). Recently, however, Marilyn lost the title of world's smartest person to Sho Yano, a kid born in 1991 in…Portland, Oregon, a lovely city just 30 miles from my hometown of Banks. Sho's IQ is so high it has been deemed immeasurable. He reportedly played Chopin on the piano at age 3 and scored a 1500 on the SAT at age 8. He graduated from college at the top of his class at age 12 and now attends medical school. What's truly strange is that I clearly remember frequenting Portland during spring and summer break in 1990, but I have no recollection of sleeping with his mother.

End Note:
In the personal essay I penned for my Stanford application—its working title, *Wool, Meet Eyes*—I didn't harp about my numerous achievements; I begged. "Please, please, please. For once in my life would someone *please* challenge me intellectually? Can you do it Stanford University? I doubt it."

After this opening challenge I dismissed my mediocre SAT scores as the result of rampant computer error at the grading center. Then I took advantage of Stanford's preference for legacy applicants—those people with family members who've previously attended the university. In essence, this is affirmative action for the well-heeled or, in my case, for the unscrupulous. I fabricated an uncle, an aunt and two cousins and claimed they'd matriculated at Stanford, and ended the essay by gushing about my lifelong dream of carrying on our family's (falsified) Stanford tradition.

"My Uncle Bob, Class of '61 (or '62, or '54. I'm sure it's in your files), is responsible for initiating my love affair with Stanford. During my childhood I listened with wide eyes as he spoke passionately about the institution and the wonderful experiences he enjoyed there. It's not just his keen intellect and breadth of knowledge that impresses me, but also his ability to overcome life's obstacles with grace and confidence. Every time I have asked him about his intellectual and personal development, he always speaks about his four years studying in the shadow of the Stanford foothills. What a gift Stanford gives! Speaking of gifts, and by way of example, Uncle Bob is currently pondering a multi-million dollar donation to a yet-to-be-determined private university. The challenge of deciphering the tax implications associated with a charitable dispersal of such magnitude is difficult, but he seems up to the task! I actually spoke with him yesterday and he asked if I had an opinion as to a deserving recipient. I told him I'd have to get back to him because I'm currently consumed with worry over my Stanford application."

Since Stanford failed to detect the factual inaccuracies in my application, I got to spend five enjoyable years—yes, five (I'm a methodical student)—in sunny Palo Alto. The Farm was fantastically fun, populated with a terrific faculty and a diverse student body. I adore the place and wouldn't trade the experience for less than $135,000 plus 8.25% interest accruing from the date of my graduation. (If you are interested in purchasing the experience, please send me a check for $135,000.00 plus accrued interest. Experience, along with your bonus copy of my Stanford degree, will be shipped within 7-10 business days after the check clears).

Undermining Authority

"And if you don't start keeping your room clean I'm going to take away your rollerblades," the lady warned.

On the other end of this threat was a boy of about nine or ten. He sat across the table from the lady, head down. When he peeked up at her, she started in again, calm but firm. "And your chores, you have to start doing your chores on time."

I was with my brother, Karl, and a couple of our buddies, Joe and Darrell. We all sat down in a booth adjacent to the lady and the boy. The four of us were working as counselors at boy's camp just outside of town. The camp catered to wealthy kids from New York. We'd all worked there for at least three summers and we sympathized with the lady, aware of just how wonderful and difficult kids that age can be.

It was our day off and the four of us had spent the morning running errands—laundry, buying toiletries, getting haircuts and shopping at the Champion outlet in town. We'd come to Friendly's to buy ice cream and start a much-needed afternoon of relaxation away from camp and the kids we adored. I assumed the lady giving the lecture was the boy's mother, and she gave no indication of letting up.

"And another thing..." she kept saying, using a sweet tone that belied the content of her message.

Karl and Darrell were sitting with their backs to her. Joe and I sat across from them and we both had a clear view of the boy's face. He had a sincere, sad frown and seemed truly bothered that he'd disappointed his mom. An ice cream sundae sat in front of him, untouched, a testament to the tricky balance a good parent tries to strike between tough love and the strong desire to keep a child happy. We listened to a whole laundry list of minor transgressions. After each offense the lady described the behavioral change needed for the boy to make his amends.

"Should we be taking notes?" Joe whispered.

"Or maybe give her some advice," Darrell grinned.

The waitress arrived to take our order. We all asked for elaborate ice cream concoctions, sundaes heaped with fruit, chocolate syrup and assorted sprinkles. When the waitress returned several minutes later with our desserts, the lady was still at it, telling the boy that he had to stop tying parachutes to his sister's dolls and throwing them from the second story window. She never raised her voice once. The four of us were impressed.

"She's doing a great job—but she should give the kid credit for at least tying parachutes to the dolls," Karl said.

"And she's a bit long-winded," Darrell added. He twisted around in his seat so that his head was perched right behind the lady's bouffant hair. He made eye contact with the boy and wagged his finger as if lecturing him. The boy started to laugh.

The lady snapped at the boy. "This is not funny," she said. "You need to take what I'm saying seriously."

The grin on the kid's face was so innocent and refreshing I couldn't help myself. I swiped some whipped cream off my sundae and put it on my chin and cheeks. I looked over at the boy and made a silly face while sticking out my tongue. The boy erupted into laughter.

"You are going to make me mad," the lady said, still impressively calm. "This is absolutely not funny. Your dad and I love you very much, but you are becoming a young man and you need to start acting like it."

Darrell grabbed the cherry from his ice cream and softly pinched it in his lips, then turned and again wagged his finger at the boy. Karl smeared some ice cream on his forehead and crossed his eyes. Joe, who's 6'11", sat up straight and began flapping his arms like a bird. I wiped more ice cream on my face and hung my ice cream spoon from my nose. The kid was laughing so hard tears were running down his face.

"What is going on!" the lady demanded, completely oblivious to the circus going on behind her.

The boy looked up, over his mom's head, toward Joe, who was still flapping his arms and was now bobbing his head like a chicken. The lady turned slowly. We froze. Karl, ice cream dripping into his eyes. Darrell, his long index finger in mid-waggle. Joe's arms outstretched as if he were a gliding condor.

The lady shook her head. "Are you gentlemen trying to undermine my authority?"

The spoon fell from my nose, banged off the table and bounced to the floor. "No," I said as I watched the spoon rattle to a stop. I looked up at her. "We're just letting you know that you could have it much worse. Much, much worse. Look at us."

"Yeah," Karl quickly added. "He seems like a good kid. You're doing a great job."

Joe, hands now in his lap, continued our collective backpedal. "Yeah! We've been listening and we agree with everything you were saying, and how you were saying it."

The boy was still laughing, his face red.

"You should listen to your mom," Darrell said. "She's very smart." Darrell started to wag his finger again. "And do not, I repeat, do not take our example."

When the boy settled down we explained to the lady that we all worked at a local boy's camp and spent most of the day with kids her son's age. We lauded her parenting style, and her son's attitude and demeanor. The lady in turn told us that she lived nearby. "I just brought him here for some ice cream, and to set some clear rules now that he's becoming older and more adventurous." She paused several times to give her son a loving look. "He really is a good boy," she said.

"I'm sure he is," Karl agreed.

The boy was glowing.

"You gentlemen sure made a mess of your desserts," the lady said. "Why don't you let me pay for those?"

"We appreciate it, but no thanks," Joe said firmly.

"I insist," she said.

She persisted and we continued to fight the offer, but when she asked the waitress to deliver our bill to her, we relented. The total cost was about fifteen bucks.

After she paid, she and the boy said goodbye and departed. The four of us dug into our mutilated desserts.

"That was too easy," I said. "Do you see the potential here? We could hit nice restaurants, amusement parks...maybe even a bank. This is a goldmine. There really is a sucker born every minute."

"You're underestimating it," Joe said. "If only one sucker is born each minute, then the government must be secretly manufacturing them somewhere in order to supplement the supply."

We all laughed and dug into our free ice cream, which tasted a whole lot better than the kind you have to pay for.

Story Time

I picked strawberries as a kid. For six long years, from the time I was seven until I got a job at a local farm moving irrigation pipe, stacking hay bales and shoveling manure, I toiled in the berry fields, plucking ripe red berries off the vine from early morning through mid-afternoon. Picking berries didn't interest me, and the pay was lousy—because it was tied directly to performance—so I spent most of my time working on my throwing accuracy. Most of the berries I picked became projectiles. I'd sling them through the air like a leather-wrapped Wilson baseball, usually toward one of my older siblings. I loved disrupting their diligent work.

On the baseball field, when I pitched, I wasn't allowed to throw the ball until the catcher was ready. Things were different in the berry fields. I never consulted with anyone before hurling a berry, and I purposefully aimed for people who had no idea they were about to be clocked in the back of the head.

"That was my fastball," I'd tell my sister, Katrina, after bouncing a berry off her back.

"Take your base, Karl," I'd yell over to my brother after my curve ball splattered against his shoulder.

Mom picked us up from the berry fields at 3:00 sharp. Before our seatbelts were on, she'd ask us how many flats we'd picked. Katrina always piped up first, happy to gloat.

"Seventeen," she'd say. She'd hold up her dark, berry-stained hands as proof.

"I picked fourteen and a half flats," Karl would boast, his hands moderately stained.

"Nine," I'd lie, overstating my accomplishment by two. As the lie left my mouth, I'd wave my right hand—the hand I throw with—for Mom to see, its grotesquely stained fingers implying hard work. I kept my left hand, soft as cream and barely scuffed, buried behind me.

On days that I had a baseball game, upon arriving home from the berry field I'd hustle to the shower, soap up, rinse off and towel dry as quickly as possible. Then I'd put on my baseball uniform and adjust every garment, each sock and stirrup, until I looked like a pro. Dressed for glory, I'd run to our back deck, facing west, and scan the sky for rain clouds that might interfere with my two favorite words: Play ball!

* * *

The night we were scheduled to play Reedville, our Little League rival, the sky burned bright blue. With the chance of a rain-out eliminated, I confidently left my watch post on the back deck and wandered into the house to relieve some nervous energy on my father.

Days earlier I had actually *relieved* myself on Dad. I was watching a baseball game on television in our living room. Vin Scully was announcing, my Cincinnati Reds were playing and I wasn't willing to miss a single pitch. When the pressure on my bladder became too much to take, I walked over to the sliding glass door that led out to our deck. I slipped the door open, positioned myself in a way that allowed me to keep my eyes glued to the television, and opened the spigot. The urine bounced off the wooden deck planks, rolled through the gaps between the two-by-fours and cascaded onto the patio below. My dad was working on the patio and his head bore the brunt of the downpour.

"Oh, shit! Sorry, Dad!"

"Don't you mean 'oh, piss?'" he yelled up.

After Dad showered away my spray, he summoned me from my bedroom, where I'd gone to hide. He brought me into the living room and blindfolded me, then spun me around several times. I wobbled a bit and almost fell. Before I fully recovered, Dad instructed me to find my way to the bathroom.

"It's a little game I like to call *Pin Your Pee to the Toilet,*" he said.

Unable to see anything, and disoriented from the spinning, I bounced into walls, banged my shins into furniture and nearly knocked my mom's collection of small spoons off its mount on the wall. After five minutes of exploring the house while blindfolded, and finding both bathrooms, I felt capable of navigating our home blind drunk if necessary, a skill that came in handy during my high school years.

When I came in from the deck on the night of the Reedville game, I found my father sitting at the dining room table.

"No chance of a rain-out today, Dad," I said happily.

"You're not going to pee on me again are you?"

"Don't much feel like it today. Maybe tomorrow. I'll let you know...or maybe I won't." I smiled with perverse pride.

Dad was working on some tax forms, part of his job as a certified public accountant. Home computers still had not hit IBM's bottom-line, so Dad was filling in the forms by hand.

"Can I do anything to help you?" I asked.

"Get these flies out of here," he said, motioning to the three or four insects buzzing around the room.

The dutiful son, I sprinted into the kitchen. We kept our fly-swatter in a tall cabinet, hanging on a nail, hovering over a nest of various cleaning products. When I got close to the cabinet

I dropped into a clumsy baseball slide and streaked across the kitchen's linoleum floor. As my feet neared one of our kitchen chairs—that for my purposes was a second baseman trying to apply the tag—I hooked my legs to avoid contact. My feet slammed into the cabinet and I used the impact as leverage to pop my body up. Once standing, I confidently signaled "safe" and slapped a few imaginary high fives before dusting off my spotless baseball uniform. After grabbing the flyswatter I headed back to the dining room, intent on hitting a few home runs.

My strategy against the flies was simple and formulated: swing to kill. As I flailed around the dining room, Dad ducked and bobbed to avoid my arrant swats. When only one fly remained, I stepped back to prepare for my big moment. The bases were loaded. Game on the line. Kemper at bat. The fly, seconds away from becoming a towering home run, charged into the window seeking escape.

"Dad! Hey Dad," I hollered.

He looked up from his tax forms.

"Give me a sign," I urged.

Dad was coaching Karl's team that summer, not mine. To be fair, each summer he alternated the team he coached, and the previous year he had coached my team. Current coach or not, the hand signals he used to send instructions to players were seared into my mind.

As usual, Dad played along. He ran through a series of signs, moving both hands around his body in a manner that's considered sane only on a baseball diamond or in Italy. He touched his ear, nose, and chin, and swiped his hands along his arms and chest, all in a flurry of motion. Only the movement of his right hand mattered—his left hand was a decoy in the process. I zeroed in with game-ready seriousness, ready to swing. Frustrating my eagerness, Dad gave me the "take" sign.

"How the hell am I going to kill this fly if you won't let me swing away," I moaned. "I can hit this fly, just give me a chance. Let me swing away."

He started in with another sequence of signs, but he failed to give me a signal I recognized.

"What the hell was that? You didn't even give a sign."

"It's a new one I just started using," he replied. "It means 'piss on it.'"

He laughed at his own little joke.

"Fine," I said. I went for my zipper. Before I could get my fly down, he started in with a new series of signals, and finally gave me what I wanted. *Hit away.*

Apparently the deceptively intelligent fly had somehow decoded my dad's signals. As soon as I stepped up to the window with my swatter, it took off, buzzing for its life.[1] The fly sought safety in the faux chandelier above our dining room table. I waited patiently. The fly bounced around in the elaborate light fixture for several seconds, and then suddenly dive-bombed the table. As it descended, I took an unorthodox, downward hack. The frenzied insect quickened its descent, but the head of the swatter gained ground. Just above the surface of the table, I made sweet, perfect contact.

The result was a long home run over the left field wall. I broke into a celebratory home run trot, swaggering around the table the same way that I planned to circle the bases in the event I hit a real home run. When I'd completed my self-choreographed celebration—I was way ahead of the sports curve on self-aggrandizing dances—I turned to my father to accept his praise.

Dad wasn't exactly glowing with pride. He was looking at one of his tax forms with a frown. I walked over to see what the problem was. When I reached his side, I glanced down at the table. Smashed into the middle of one of his meticulously filled-out forms was the fly carcass. I stood silent, a bit frightened. Dad slowly swiped his right thumb across the paper to remove the mess. Anxious to help, I ran to the kitchen and grabbed a paper

---

[1] The moment marked the only time in my baseball career that my presence in the batter's box, even an imaginary one, instilled fear in any living creature.

towel, put a dab of water on it, and then returned to the table. Dad took the paper towel and softly rubbed at the tax form. Despite his care, a distinct, noticeable smear remained.

I'd never before seen my father upset. He shot me a glare. *Was this what my dad looked like when he was angry?* I wasn't scared of what he might do, only that I had disappointed him.

The intensity of his gaze soon faded and he returned his attention to the defaced tax form. He studied it closely, pondering options. After a short wait, he seized the pen resting next to his right hand and spun it around on his fingers, all the while keeping his eyes fixed on the smudge. He positioned the tip of the pen next to the stain. After hesitating just a moment, he scribbled the words, *Dead Fly*. He added a small arrow leading from the words to the smear.

"That should do it," he said. As he spoke, he looked over at me. I looked backed with the glow of a child in the presence of his idol.

Unsatisfied with the extent of my reaction, Dad raised his pen again. After a short contemplation, he carefully inserted the word *Dragon* next to the word *Fly*. *Dead DragonFly*. I smiled wide, as if I'd just hit a towering home run.

In his own way my father was a magician. A wave of his imagination turned dull things into captivating ones. Mistakes became opportunities, if for nothing more than as fodder for a joke to put a klutz at ease. He could make a drive through an ordinary tunnel seem like an amusement park ride, and he commonly created enthralling tales from events as mundane as a trip to the grocery store.

When Dad told a story, people listened. I learned several incredible things from his stories, things my schoolteachers couldn't wrap their minds around.

During a show-and-tell in second grade, I told my classmates that while growing up my father knew a kid who had a wooden leg with a real foot attached. The boy's family was so destitute that the wooden leg was made from the limb of an old pine tree.

At that point, I held up a pine branch, about two feet in length, for the class to see. Then I held the piece of wood next to my leg to give an example of what a wooden leg with a real foot would look like. My classmates locked on my every word, captivated and wide-eyed. I continued to explain that because the boy's father fashioned the wooden leg from a live tree limb, the fake leg occasionally sprouted small branches. For trimming purposes, the school granted the poor boy the special privilege of bringing a hacksaw to school, wildly ironic since he had lost the leg in a bizarre hacksaw accident.

"Chris, that is simply not true," our teacher Ms. Adams said.

"Oh really?" I shot back. "And I suppose my dad's great-grandfather wasn't able to juggle live birds." I returned to my seat in a huff.

After a summer baseball practice, as we were picking up equipment, one of my teammates asked my father if he'd been a good baseball player as a kid. By all accounts, he was a tremendous athlete, but humility didn't allow him an honest answer. He gathered the team in the dugout.

"I think I had some great potential," he started. "But my Little League coach was Father O'Hare, the head priest at Verboort Elementary, the small Catholic school I attended as a child. Father O'Hare was really religious, even for a priest, and he coached our baseball team."

"A priest coached your baseball team," asked one of my teammates.

"Yep. And he always insisted that we 'keep our eye off the ball.' Father O'Hare claimed that if God wanted us to catch or hit the baseball, then God would steer the ball to our glove or our bat." My dad waited for this to sink in, then continued.

"I started playing baseball when I was five years old, but because I was told never to look at the ball, I didn't actually see a baseball until I was twelve. That's the year Father O'Hare moved away and we got a new Little League coach. I don't like to make excuses," Dad insisted, "but never looking at the ball made playing baseball pretty difficult."

He went on to chronicle the ineptness of his Little League team and the follies that naturally flow from kids trying to play baseball while averting their eyes.

"The most valuable player on my Little League team was the first aid kit," he sighed. "You guys are so advanced with your baseball skills that we don't even need one of those."

The story left us astonished, laughing and feeling like the best Little League team in the world.

Three weeks after learning of Father O'Hare's baseball stratagem, my dad and I were driving home from an away baseball game, a win against Aloha. Between licks of my Dairy Queen ice cream cone, I informed him that Chad, a player on our team, was the dumbest person in the world.

"He can't even add or subtract. It's like the number eight is a pair of handcuffs that locks up his brain."

"Be nice to Chad," my father replied. "He has his gifts, math just may not be one of them. Anyway, it's not his fault that his family makes him use a vertacus to do math. Using a vertacus to do math is like playing baseball without looking at the ball."

"What's a vertacus?" I asked.

"You know that abacus we have it home in the den?"

"Yeah."

"Well, it's like that, but different."

He went on to describe the unflattering cloud of mathematical bewilderment dangling over Chad's family as a result of the vertacus. "Generations ago," he explained, "Chad's uncle invented the vertacus, which is just like an abacus, but the beads slide up and down instead of side to side."

"Really?" I asked.

"Yep," he assured. "Well, you see, the problem with the vertacus is that Chad's uncle never incorporated a method to keep the counting pegs from immediately falling back down. So when you let go of the beads they drop to the bottom and you never really get anywhere. Makes it tough to do math, but

Chad's family still swears by the device and makes him use it."

"Is that why Chad is so dumb?" I asked.

"Chad is not dumb. He just has the wrong tools. It's like trying to hit a baseball with a hockey stick. So don't make fun of Chad. And never mention the vertacus to anyone. It will embarrass him."

I'd recently turned fourteen and, having shed a bit of my gullibility, I suspected Dad was lying. Well, not actually lying, because lies involve a self-serving, ulterior motive. My dad didn't always adhere to the truth, but he never lied.

Six days after telling me about the vertacus, he died.[2]

* * *

The gift of storytelling travels in my family, but no one in our clan was better at it than my father. His facial expressions, the pacing, pauses, accelerations, tone, creativity; everything was impeccable. Karl received the gift but unfortunately he uses it on the same ten stories, telling them over and over again as if practicing for some mythical international storytelling championship. The storytelling gene didn't entirely skip me, but it didn't set up camp in my bones, choosing, instead, to stop by occasionally for a cup of tea, only to disappear back to the Old World for months on end.

My paternal grandfather was an excellent storyteller as well, blessed with a wonderful imagination. After my dad passed away, my grandfather, a quiet man who required prodding, spoke more freely during family gatherings to fill the storytelling void. And Grandpa gave me my first beer, storytelling's bosom friend.

After my father's funeral, back at my grandparents' house,

---

[2] The fact that my dad lived to be forty-eight years old proves that there is no proportionality incorporated into the concept that only the good die young. If there were a direct correlation between how kind a person was and how early they died, my father would never have been born.

Grandpa appeared from the kitchen with three beers in his hands. He gave one to Karl and one to me, then sat in his chair and popped his open. My mom looked on without saying a word. I opened my beer and took a gulp, my first, and promptly realized beer is an acquired taste. I forged on though, feeling as if I was partaking in an important rite of passage. Each swallow was a struggle, made easier only by the joy I derived from carrying out a strictly forbidden activity with full immunity. I soon had a small buzz. But it wasn't the beer that made that awful afternoon bearable. It was the stories my grandfather told; simple tales about simple experiences that far exceeded the sum of their parts.

"I wanted to be a racist growing up," Grandpa explained, "but there weren't many black people here in rural Oregon. I worked with a black guy once at the lumber mill. I meant to hate him, I really did, but all us workers got dirty so fast, covered with dust and wood chips, that I never was able to distinguish him from the others. Before I knew it he was one of my best friends. Damn conspiracy I tell ya. Dr. King shoulda dreamed that everyone worked in sawmills."

As he sunk further into his rocking chair, readying himself to tell more stories, mostly about my father, he paused for a long moment, and then asked Grandma to get me and Karl a second beer.

Rules of Engagement

When I hear someone telling a story, whether I'm hanging out in a coffee shop or in a bar, or waiting in line at the grocery store, I can't help but to listen and judge, review and analyze. I mentally grade each effort, determine whether it's rehearsed or spontaneous, and unfairly measure the storyteller against the skills of my father and granddad.

My informal storytelling studies have taught me that a lot of people have difficulty with even the most basic elements of delivering an interesting, entertaining tale. In addition to my dream that one day everyone works in sawmills, I hope that I'll see a day when no storyteller has to confront the uncomfortable silence that follows a wayward story attempt. To this end, I've created eight rules to assist anyone with a story perched on their tongue. These rules are based on years of listening to stories both good and bad, and from committing storytelling gaffes of every kind, many of which you can find in these pages.[1] Adherence to these rules isn't a guaranteed prophylactic against the occasional ora-

---

[1] Find all 43,567 and I will refund the cost of this book!

tory rain-out, but following these guidelines will increase the likelihood that ominous storytelling clouds will stay away, resting harmlessly in the distance.

The Rules:

ONE: Always Provide Context

Failing to insert necessary contextual information into a tale is a grave storytelling crime. When telling a story, it is critical to start at the beginning, or at least incorporate the contextual information required for someone to easily follow along. Stories without context are like cigarettes without a lighter; they're nothing but frustrated potential.[2]

An ancient example of proper context in a story is found in the Book of Genesis.[3] At the outset of the story, we learn that God made the heavens and Earth. After performing a few other nifty tricks, God then made Adam. It is important to the story that the information is offered in this order to avoid confusion. If the author had told us that God made Adam and then placed him on Earth without first explaining that God made Earth, well, that's how you pave the road to storytelling hell.[4]

I am occasionally open to a relationship with the opposite sex that begins in the middle, or even starts at the end, but when it comes to stories without a sensible beginning, no thanks. If you

---

[2] Cigarette smokers never seem to have matches. "Have a light?" is their common cry, as if they were once again caught off guard by the need for fire to enjoy their chosen vice. I carry a can of refried beans in my backpack sometimes just in case a smoker asks me for a light. After apologizing to the smoker for not having matches or a lighter, I pull out the can of beans and ask, "Have an opener?"

[3] A potential employer asked me to send their H.R. department a resume. I faxed them a piece of paper with my name, address and phone number, and a statement that said: "Experience: See Genesis, 1-12." I didn't get the job. I suspect they determined I was overqualified.

[4] A story about God creating Adam before creating Earth could be quite intriguing if properly prefaced: "In the beginning, God DIDN'T create the heavens and Earth, He just created Adam and dropped him into vast nothingness." Let the wacky, drifting-through-space excitement begin!

can't provide the listener with a meaningful story map, or if you are incapable of giving necessary foundational information that allows the listener to connect the narrative dots, then you aren't telling a story, you're spreading gossip.

TWO: Character Development

Character development is a direct descendant of foundational context. For a listener to appreciate your story it's imperative that you explain who the people in the story are and why they're important. If you don't develop the characters, you aren't going to succeed.

An acquaintance of mine—I'll call her Jill[5]—is a serial violator of the character development protocol. She's under the misimpression that a character's name, by itself, provides enough informational background to avoid narrative confusion. Though I never have met the people Jill talks about in her stories, she refers to them by name, as if I've been friends with them for years.

I met Jill for lunch one day and she told me a story about a big event that had occurred at her work the previous week. "Big" is the exact word she used to describe the event, and she used it on multiple occasions. She informed me that her office had "officially" shut down at 3:30 on Friday to give Joe a good-bye party.[6] Joe was moving on to greener pastures, partially because he was tired of working with Julie and Leslie, who are both total bitches. Joe apparently was taking a job offered to him by Dave, Marci's husband. As an aside, Jill disclosed that Marci was cheating on Dave and that in the last month alone she had slept with Mike and Mark, a couple of guys who know Fred. Fred is friends with Jill's friend Sam, but Jill doesn't know Fred directly.

---

[5] Jill Anne Smith, 543 NW McCoy St., Portland, Oregon 08998, Born 6/29/80, SS# 554-34-9919, parents Nad and Lois, interests include: skiing, long walks, indie films and bands, yo-yos and wine.

[6] For all you managers out there, you're kidding yourself if you think your staff doesn't shut down long before 3:30 on Friday, regardless of any official proclamation.

Although I didn't know any of the people Jill was talking about, the morsel about Mark and Mike having sex with Marci sparked my interest. But Jill went on to explain that Marci's foray into infidelity with Mike and Mark had occurred on separate nights, thereby robbing that prong of the story of any real potential. Now, if Mike, Mark and Marci had rendezvoused on the same night, well that's one of a rare genre of stories that's interesting despite a complete failure to follow any storytelling rules.

Jill continued with her story, lamenting how Joe would be missed because he was such a joker. His humor kept Stan and Lisa laughing, and life in the office was always better when Lisa and Stan were happy. The farewell food was quite good: Joan brought a pasta salad, Jose made his famous bean dip, Marge pitched in with mounds of chicken wings and a guy named Krecow brought the drinks.

I didn't know anything about the people Jill mentioned in her story, which made her dull tale nearly unbearable. The only thing I derived from her rambling was that Jill and I have vastly different opinions as to what constitutes a "big" event.[7] As a storyteller, this is not the mild reaction you're hoping to evoke, unless you are a mute, in which instance the mere ability to verbalize anything is deemed a victory.

To sum, characters without context are mere pretext, so please sufficiently introduce your characters to avoid confusion.

THREE: Pick a starting point

How did the world get its start? Humans have asked this question ever since we have had brains capable of contemplation. To select a beginning point for your story you have to ask some basic questions: *What do I really know about this subject? Do I know enough to try and tell this story? How far back should I go in providing background? How much guessing should I do? Is there any way I can convince someone*

---

[7] We had a similar disagreement regarding the parameters of "big" after sleeping together in 1994.

to pay me for this?

To avoid the snags inherent in these thorny queries, countless storytellers have employed a variety of lazy phrases to avoid the arduous task of navigating to a reasonable starting point.

Once upon a time...

In the beginning...

Yesterday, or maybe it was last week, or last month, I really can't remember because I was drinking...

Granted, no story has a true, definitive beginning, but the storytelling art demands that you make an effort to identify a reasonable launch point. Some leeway is allowed if you're talking about the Big Bang and the origin of the universe, but if you're story concerns something that happened last week and you find yourself slouching toward *Once upon a time,* remember that stories are like mathematical equations: an early mistake taints the entire process, and in the world of storytelling, listeners rarely wait around to grant partial credit.

FOUR: Balance the level of detail

Ivan Doig's writing is a fabulous example of masterful, measured detail—particularly his book *This House of Sky*.[8] At the other extreme there's a passage in Genesis heaped with an excruciating scoop of boring facts that dilutes the majesty of heaven and earth into annoying drivel.

The passage reads: "Irad became the father of Mehujael; Mehujael became the father of Methushael, and Methushael became the father of Lamech, and Lamech took to himself two wives..." It continues on like this for almost two pages. If any of the people mentioned in the passage were key players in the Bible, this level of detail *might* be acceptable *if* the characters are properly developed and the information about who married whom is presented with literary flair. But the clumsy inclusion of these people reads like the author just wanted to give a liter-

---

[8] Ivan, please send me $400.00 as agreed.

ary shout-out to his posse, something that is no less annoying in holy print than when done by a hip-hop star on MTV.

Mention of Irad and Mehujael might be cool in a book of baby names, but in Genesis their presence only serves to hinder the greater tale. A tight story uses only anecdotal embellishment and analytical tangents that entertain and provide relevant context, or that help the story progress toward climax and closure. Stories should only include a polygamist named Lamech if he has something to do with the plot, or if you plan to examine the question of whether he is lucky for having multiple sex partners, or crazy for having multiple wives.

FIVE: TV Movies Suck

Following the first four rules is relatively simple; hobos have mastered them. Unfortunately, even if you follow rules 1 through 4 to the letter, you still can't deliver a good story without quality content. There is a common misconception that *content* is the same as subject matter, but any event or person can form the basis of a good story. Instead, quality content is dependent on the inclusion of some level of complexity, no matter how simple. If the tale isn't going to activate a listener's brain with some smidgen of uncertainty, intrigue or doubt, don't tell it. The ability to discern gratifying content from mind-numbing garbage eludes millions of storytellers, even some who tell stories for a living, such as people who write TV movies.

People who write television movies seem to start with the premise that it's their job to extract every ounce of creativity, intelligence and drama from a story. Logical leaps are avoided in favor of grating clichés. The result is a disastrously trite, predictable tale, a story where the poor, abused little girl is—*Ohmygod!*—adopted by the rich, loving family and—*Ohmygod, I can't believe it!*—the devious drug dealer ends up dead or in jail. As a storyteller, never start a tale if the listener can discern the outcome before you finish introducing the characters.

Developing a good feel for quality content requires a fair

amount of trial and listener misery, but if you want a surefire approach to testing the worth of a story's content before sharing it with others, submit the idea to a TV movie producer. If the studio offers to purchase the story or encourages you in any way to hone the script, abandon the idea forever and never mention it to another person again. (Of course, agree to sell the idea to the movie studio, promise the producer you'll deliver the final manuscript in a few months, then cash the check, fake your death, go on an around-the-world traveling adventure using the studio's money, and write a story about that).

SIX: No Stealth Stories

A stealth story is a tale that starts out with a positive, even hopeful promise about where the story is going, but then, for no discernable reason, the storyteller abruptly reverses course. The beginning of the story is merely a hook, inserted to fool you into thinking that it won't hurt you to give a listen. But as soon as your defenses are down, the storyteller reroutes the tale to an annoying destination. Hearing a stealth story is like boarding a flight to Hawaii and having it diverted to North Korea due to foul weather.

I have a friend named Dane who is a serial stealth storyteller. He often starts a story by promising, "This is the funniest thing ever..." or, "You're going to love this..." After an intriguing start, Dane proceeds to tell a story wrought with boring details and no point. I can only assume that immediately after stating that a great story is imminent, Dane decides he'd be better off unloading a crappy story that he's had in stock for a long time. The only enjoyment I reap from Dane's stories is the intellectual stimulation I derive from wondering what he does with all the wonderful stories he professes to own.

But at least Dane's stealth stories are relatively harmless. There's a troubling strain of stealth stories that begin with a heartwarming sentiment, such as, *I'm not prejudiced...* or *I'm not a racist...*, and then, right after this comforting assurance, the storyteller inserts the crown jewel of stealth words: but.

During a search for a new apartment a few years back, I had a property manager show me a few vacant spots in his building. As he showed me around, the manager promised me that the surrounding neighborhood was extremely safe.

"I'm not prejudiced or racist," he started.

I nodded approvingly. The manager hesitated for a moment and shifted his eyes around to make sure we were alone, and then continued.

"...but...there aren't many of them blacks or Hispanics around here, so you don't have to worry about getting ripped off or hassled. We do our best to keep those people out."

I decided to make a point.

"That's really good to know," I said. "By the way, I'm not gay..." I paused as he nodded approvingly. I looked around to make sure we were alone, and then added, "...buuuuutttttt...I'd really like to plant my erect penis firmly in your ass."

The manager dispensed with any stealthy introduction and proceeded directly to the meat of his response.

"You fucking fag."

"I'd like to stay," I replied. "...but I want to leave." And I left.

SEVEN: No Double Stealth Stories

The Double Stealth Story is a nasty sub-genre of stealth stories and it mustn't be confused with the double stuff Oreo, which is twice as good as the original. Double Stealth stories are at least twice as devious as their stealth brethren and, despite appearances, these stories are always told for the exclusive benefit of the storyteller. Like stealth stories, Double Stealth tales start out with a promising, upbeat opening. But then, instead of changing course, the storyteller continues down the same path, one that turns out to be full of lies and deceit. Double Stealth stories are told for the sole purpose of manipulation, and are a favorite technique of carnival game workers and disreputable salespeople.

Epilogue

About two years ago I was in the market for a new vehicle, the result of my misguided belief that the awful car I drove was to blame for my lack of dates. On a cloudy, humid Sunday afternoon, I went to a Ford used car lot near my home, wanting to upgrade my ride.[9] Within seconds of stepping onto the lot, a salesman came rushing up.

"Hi, I'm John Goody," the man said. He handed me his card.

Mr. Goody looked to be in his mid-twenties but he had already acquired a middle-aged paunch. Sweat poured from his body and a strong garlic odor seeped through his cheap suit.

"You seem like a man looking to buy a car," he said.

"That's almost mystical the way you figured that out," I mocked. "I *am* in the market for a car."

Without inquiring as to the type of car I might be interested in, Mr. Goody unleashed a double stealth barrage.

"This over here is a truly great car," he assured, motioning to a tan-colored four-door Ford Taurus.

"Really?" I asked.

"Oh yes," John assured. "Its gas mileage efficiency is unmatched. This thing is as reliable as the sun rising in the west. You want roomy? You could hold your wedding reception in the backseat. There was only one previous owner, a little old lady, and she only used it to go to the grocery store and to visit her grandchildren. It's in great condition, but even if something did go wrong, we offer a really nice limited warranty. But I am hesitant to let you take it on a test drive because I fear you'll be ready to kill for this car once you feel how well it handles. It's that good at this price."

Fluent in Double Stealth speak, I translated his words in my head.

"This is a great car. Its gas mileage efficiency is unmatched if

---

[9] You know that if you're upgrading your ride at a used Ford dealer that you are driving a truly pathetic car.

every inch of road you drive is a 45% downgrade. Call this car *Mr. Reliable*. In no time, you can dispense with formality and call it by its first name, *Un*, or its middle name, *Fucking*. You want roomy, just last night me and my girl came down here and practiced for our wedding night in the backseat and we still had enough room for her friend to sit in there with us and film the whole thing. The previous owner was this sweet little old lady who couldn't see a lick, but that didn't stop her from driving it every week to visit her grandchildren who live two states away. And of course we've covered up a multitude of dents and extensive damage with some low quality body work, and we turned the odometer back 80,000 miles. The limited warranty lasts 24 hours and extends only to air freshener replacement. I am hesitant to let you take it on a test drive because I am not sure it will start and I want you to sign a contract before you wise up to this scam. See, I made some poor decisions in my life and I really need to earn the commission on this sale so I can pay off my drug dealer, who is growing more erratic and dangerous by the day. And the reason I want you to buy this particular piece of crap is that the owner of the lot promised to give a $1,000 bonus to anyone who sells this junk heap. I think he's offering the incentive because he bought the car for a tenth of its blue-book value from some guys we're pretty sure stole the car from the old lady."

Despicable.[10]

EIGHT: Stop the Presses

There are several reasons to abandon a story before *The End*. A proficient storyteller must have the triage skills to determine whether a story can be saved, or whether it's best to cover it with a sheet and move on. Some listeners are too kind, hindering your learning curve by politely nodding every so often as if they're interested. Others are refreshingly blunt, rolling their eyes or

---

[10] By the way, if you are interested in buying a used Ford Taurus, give me a call!

simply walking away in the middle of a bad story.[11] Accurately monitoring listener interest is an intricate skill, one that takes significant practice to master. There are, however, some universal signs that plainly indicate that it's time to abort your tale, such as:

- A listener grabs your throat and chokes you. Unless you are nude and are involved in a long-term sexual relationship with the person choking you, this is not an attempt to involve you in some erotic sexcapade.
- A listener interrupts your story and plays a solitary round of the childish game, *Would You Rather*, a game that requires a participant to choose between two horrible fates. If, for example, you are telling a story and a listener interrupts, asking no one in particular, "Would you rather screw a cow while it is giving birth, or listen to the rest of this story"—and then he barely pauses before saying, "Screw the cow...twice"—it's time to stop.
- If someone listening to your story hails a police officer and readily admits to the officer that he has an outstanding drug warrant, and then demands to be arrested, you should provide bail, but don't finish the story.
- If a person interrupts to say that he can't listen to the rest of your story because he has tickets to a band of midgets playing full size instruments, stop the story and go with him, 'cause that concert sounds like the possible makings of a good tale.
- If mid-story the listener asks, "Can you mime the rest?"
- The story appears in *Clinging to Anonymity*.

In these and similar scenarios, avoid throwing good words after bad, or horrible words after horrific ones.
Good things.
Cue Porky Pig.

---

[11] It's good to be honest with a storyteller—it is the only way people learn—but it's the height of bad taste to return an unsatisfying book for a refund. So don't even think about it.

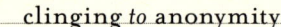

About the Author

Christopher J. Kemper, 5'10", 185 lbs., untraditional good looks, muscular/athletic build, good quickness, to-die-for dimples, tends to procrastinate. Was heavily recruited out of high school by various crime syndicates but turned down the lucrative life for college at Stanford. ~~Earned~~ Finagled law degree from University of Oregon. Has held various jobs, none for more than 11 days, and now spends most of his time saving kittens trapped high in trees (after putting them on a high limb and calling local media outlets to witness the "rescue"), as well as helping little old ladies cross the street whether they want to or not. He pays the bills by tap dancing in the gray areas of the law and is a famed provider of unsolicited advice. Wrote *Clinging to Anonymity* in four cumulative days (over a three year span) and has threatened to write another book unless 1,000,000 copies of *Clinging* are sold. To help achieve this 1,000,000 book goal, and to prevent Mr. Kemper from inflicting another scar on the literary landscape, please instruct everyone you know to visit www.christopherjkemper.com.

clinging to anonymity